T0303402

ROBERT LOUIS STEVENSON
THE STRANGE CASE
OF DR JEKYLL
AND MR HYDE
& OTHER TALES

FLAME TREE PUBLISHING
6 Melbray Mews, Fulham,
London SW6 3NS, United Kingdom
www.flametreepublishing.com

First published and copyright © 2021
Flame Tree Publishing Ltd

This edition of *The Strange Case of Dr Jekyll and Mr Hyde* is based on the original publication by Longmans, Green & Co., 1886. Short stories originally published as follows: 'The Body Snatcher' in the *Pall Mall Christmas Extra* in 1884; 'The Story of a Lie' in *New Quarterly Magazine* in 1879; 'Markheim' in *The Broken Shaft: Tales of Mid-Ocean* (T. Fisher Unwin, 1885); 'The Bottle Imp' in the *New York Herald* (February 1891); 'The Pavilion on the Links' in *Cornhill Magazine* (Sept-Oct 1880).

21 23 25 24 22
1 3 5 7 9 10 8 6 4 2

ISBN: 978-1-83964-476-4

Cover and pattern art is created by Flame Tree Studio, inspired by the posters and advertisements for early black and white movie adaptations of classic gothic novels. Some artwork elements courtesy of Svekloid/Shutterstock.

Judith John (Glossary) is a writer and editor specializing in literature and history. A former secondary school English Language and Literature teacher, she has subsequently worked as an editor on major educational projects, including *English A: Literature* for the Pearson International Baccalaureate series. Judith's major research interests include Romantic and Gothic literature, and Renaissance drama.

A copy of the CIP data for this book is available
from the British Library.

Designed and created in the UK | Printed and bound in China

ROBERT LOUIS STEVENSON
THE STRANGE CASE
of DR JEKYLL
and MR HYDE
& OTHER TALES

Reading List and Glossary of Terms
With a New Introduction by
CAROLINE McCRACKEN-FLESHER

FLAME TREE PUBLISHING

ROBERT LOUIS STEVENSON

CONTENTS

Publisher's Note for this Edition

When it was first published in 1886, the main story in this volume was titled *Strange Case of Dr Jekyll and Mr Hyde*. Since then, Robert Louis Stevenson's tale has been reprinted many times, with numerous variations on its original title, from *The Strange Case of Dr Jekyll and Mr Hyde* (as we have called this edition), *Dr Jekyll and Mr Hyde* to, simply, *Jekyll and Hyde*. It is referred to in our Introduction, written by Dr Caroline McCracken-Flesher, by its original name, *Strange Case of Dr Jekyll and Mr Hyde*.

INTRODUCTION
& FURTHER READING

INTRODUCTION

'WE MUST NEVER MEET': DR JEKYLL, MR HYDE – AND US

Passing through Southampton by train in April 1886, Robert Louis Stevenson's family heard 'what we thought at first was the news boy crying the papers' – but the call was 'DOCtor Jekyll! DOCtor Jekyll!' Since its publication in January *Strange Case of Dr Jekyll and Mr Hyde* (as it was originally called) had achieved national recognition. By June it had sold 40,000 copies in Britain and 70,000 in America. (By way of comparison, H. Rider Haggard's recent sensation, *King Solomon's Mines*, took 15 months to sell 31,000 copies in Britain.) Moreover, its critique of human duality was providing fodder for preachers across the country. Stevenson's mother found it 'very overpowering to hear one's own son talked of from the pulpit as "one of the greatest masters of the English language now living."' Jekyll and Hyde were entering the popular consciousness as a byword for the split self. The novel was lending a language, even as Freud began to develop his, to a contemporary society at once proper and suffering under intense social and psychological pressure.

The book Stevenson wrote as 'a penny (12 penny) dreadful; it is dam dreadful' quickly captured the imagination. The queen herself, Stevenson's mother learned, 'has been reading *Jekyll*'; an American playwright dramatized the novel for Richard Mansfield, the transatlantic star of Gilbert and Sullivan operettas. But as the story settled into popular discourse, its compelling representation of human duplicity confused the bounds of fiction and actuality. The Scottish Stevenson was living in Bournemouth when he wrote and published the book. In the local bookshop a customer asked for 'that book about *a medical man who lives here in Bournemouth*, who took something, and came to a bad end.' Mansfield, who brought the roles of Jekyll/Hyde to London in 1888, found himself under suspicion for the Ripper murders – for who could possibly be to blame except the doubling actor who played the duplicitous doctor?

Jekyll and Hyde continues to resonate in our culture and our lives. We begin to suspect our neighbours; we recognize in the doctor's dilemma a challenge to our own sense of self. We know of this powerful story, this strange duality, whether we have read the novel or not. And movies, now counting around one hundred, keep Jekyll and his nefarious counterpart Hyde fresh and ferocious in our minds. Generation after generation, we read our individual challenges into Stevenson's slim and elegant tale. Stevenson barely touches on Mr Hyde's dastardly deeds – but we know our own, and we see them in him.

'A LIKELY PLACE': THE WORLD OF ROBERT LOUIS STEVENSON – AND HENRY JEKYLL

Robert Louis Stevenson was a well-brought-up young man who by 35 – the age at which he wrote *Strange Case of Dr Jekyll and Mr Hyde* – had seen something of the world. And Stevenson engaged with the cultures and people around him, whether at home in Edinburgh, in France, where he met his wife-to-be (American, and married), on board the emigrant ship headed for California in pursuit of her or in Switzerland for his health. *Jekyll and Hyde* echoes to those experiences.

In 1885 Stevenson was reading French psychology. Theories exploring the doubleness of the brain – its mirrored but differently operating halves – were advancing rapidly. Charcot emphasized hysteria (which he believed was present in both men and women) and hypnotism; Janet reported on somnambulism and suggestibility. It is not surprising that Stevenson recognized and exercised such theories in his own mind and art. If Jekyll is a professional man, proud of his presence in the world, Stevenson came from a well-to-do and professional family. He was a grandson of the manse on his mother's side while his father's family were noted engineers, responsible for lighthouses around Scotland. If Jekyll willed Mr Hyde into being to address 'a certain impatient gaiety of disposition ... such as I found it hard to reconcile with my imperious desire to carry my head high', Stevenson also knew what it was to kick against the pricks. Reared by a Calvinist nurse and a family committed to respectable religious and social practice, the writer repeatedly found himself embroiled in arguments with parents who were proud of their Edinburgh boy, yet shocked by his bohemian tendencies.

The Doctors and the Dreamer

How this life and these theories combine toward *Jekyll and Hyde* is made clear in Stevenson's later 'A Chapter on Dreams' (1888). Here, an Edinburgh student starts 'to dream in sequence and thus to lead a double life – one of the day, one of the night – one that he had every reason to believe was the true one, another that he had no means of proving to be false.' Stevenson admits that he himself is the dreamer. Moreover, a key dream represents him as a doctor.

Scotland was famous for its medical men. Eighteenth-century surgeons such as John Hunter gave way to Robert Knox the anatomist, then to James Young Simpson the anaesthesiologist and Joseph Lister, trialling antiseptics in Glasgow and Edinburgh. Yet the doctor could also be a devil: Knox collaborated with the murderers Burke and Hare to supply his overflowing classes; Simpson, father of young Stevenson's close friend, experimented in narcotics as part of his after-dinner entertainments. Jekyll, in a house reminiscent of Hunter's London home – with its separate entrances for society and for specimens – and his interest in experimental pharmaceutics, brings together the history and vagaries of nineteenth-century medicine.

The Doctor, the Deviant and Mr Darwin

Hyde, it is not hard to see, evolves from the discoveries of sister sciences. Charles Darwin published *The Origin of Species* in 1859. Readers have seen in Jekyll's avatar a clear reference to man's precursors. Hyde is 'younger, lighter, happier in body', with a hand 'lean, corded, knuckly, of a dusky pallor and thickly shaded with a swart growth of hair'. He has an 'odd, light footstep.' Theories of phrenology, which claimed to read inward psychology from outward signs, seem at play in Hyde's 'deformity' – particularly the theories of Cesar Lombroso that quantified criminality by craniology.

Still it is what Hyde does *not* do, and what he does not show, that prove most provocative. Stevenson does not detail Hyde's crimes. He tramples a child, and attacks an old man, both crimes largely symbolic in nature. As such, they are in keeping with a story for which Stevenson's wife told him his first draft 'missed the moral.' Stevenson now gives a moral: Hyde attacks society. Yet, Lombroso notwithstanding, Hyde bears few marks of his atavism on his body. Here another context brings society itself into question. Stevenson's drafts hint that what Jekyll wished to hide includes homosexuality. In 1885 the 'Labouchere Amendment' made 'gross indecency' (among men) prosecutable, expanding and introducing uncertainty into precisely what behaviour fell subject to the law.

Hyde's disproportionate acts, together with the 'subjective disturbance' that others experience in his vicinity regardless of those acts, invoke both Labouchere and Darwin's second book, *The Descent of Man* (1871). For Darwin, man advances through a developed social and moral sense. In *Jekyll and Hyde* this sense polices a behaviour that is oddly hidden, rather than revealed, by Hyde's violence. And Hyde's indeterminacies – we never really learn what he looks like, for example – produce a public response that is at once visceral yet perplexed. This is a response that implicates its hosts. That upright citizen Mr Utterson, with his circle of male friends, all focused on their professional practice, and his late-night 'terror of the law and the law's officers', falls within, not outside, the area he would police. It is not surprising, then, that when Jekyll concludes his strange case Mr Utterson has nothing left to say.

STEVENSON'S STORY OF THE STRANGE CASE

Stevenson first referenced *Jekyll and Hyde* as a pot-boiler: 'I drive on with *Jekyll*, bankruptcy at my heels,' he griped, later insisting that the novel was written to pay 'Byles the Butcher.' Still, while he was writing Stevenson was enjoying an extended conversation with Henry James about literary art – about the relation between the romance and the real. If *Jekyll and Hyde* was a pot-boiler, it was nonetheless aesthetically conscious and informed.

The author, in fact, spun a web of myths around the book's origins and development. Having decided to write a story for the Christmas market, inspiration lagged, the story goes, until one night he started yelling in his sleep. Upon being woken, he complained: 'Why did you wake me? ... I was dreaming a fine bogey tale.' Stevenson had conceived the image of a man 'pursued for some crime' who ingests a powder and transforms 'in the presence of his pursuers.' Then, we are told, he wrote for three days, subjected his work to family critique and responded to his wife's concern that he'd 'missed the moral' by burning his draft and starting all over again. Such 'facts' are debatable. But does *Jekyll and Hyde* itself yield to an easy moralistic reading?

Stevenson called the book his 'gnome'. Dark and transformative, it was also, he claimed, a profoundly Scottish work: 'the Scotch side came out plain in *Dr Jekyll*.' What exactly does he mean by 'the Scotch side'? Anxiety about and policing of the socio-religious self bears Calvinist roots. Yet 'Ethics,' he continued, 'are my veiled mistress; I love them, but I know not what they are.' Scotland provides the context, but neither the intent nor the meaning. Stevenson later clarified: 'There is no harm in a voluptuary; and none ... in what prurient fools call "immorality." The harm was in Jekyll, because he was a hypocrite.' *Jekyll and Hyde*'s core duality invites moralistic thinking: the issue should be good versus evil, propriety versus sexuality. But Stevenson's explanation undoes boundaries, questions the social basis of moralities, throws us back into uncertainty. Generations of readers have thus struggled to codify Stevenson's intentions and the novel's assumptions. *Jekyll and Hyde*'s binary structure sustains a lot of possibility.

'ODD, SUBJECTIVE DISTURBANCES': READERS AND REACTIONS

Few non-biblical stories of assault and battery make it into the pulpit. But such was the lot of *Strange Case of Dr Jekyll and Mr Hyde*. Victorian preachers embraced it for its depiction of how minor sins lead to major, and so to retribution. Part of the story's appeal lay in that tempting binary opposition; but part lay in the story's darkness, its manifestation of the other closer than a brother, bound in the body – the alternate that we cannot elude. Thus Andrew Lang, Stevenson's friend and a folklorist in the making, categorized it as 'Poe with the addition of a moral sense.' Yet the problem remained: what moral?

To *The Academy*, the book looked like shilling trash. Still, it was considered 'weirdly imaginative in conception and ... faultlessly ingenious in construction', proving 'a marvellous exploration into the recesses of human nature.' 'Though it is more than possible that Mr Stevenson wrote with no ethical intent', this reviewer observed, 'its impressiveness as a parable is equal to its fascination as a work of art.' That is, *Jekyll and Hyde* communicated the challenge and the feeling of the moral tale, but eluded specificity in expression or interpretation of its core dynamic. The role of meaning making thus fell to the reader. Under this responsibility, the critics piled up indications of the disturbing feeling that comes from reading *Jekyll and Hyde*. The book 'thrilled and possessed' its readers; the words 'terrific' and 'terrible', occurring repeatedly but imprecisely, expressed the awe-ful burden that *Jekyll and Hyde* imposed on them: the terrifying obligation to investigate 'the meaning of the word *self*.'

As *The Times* perceived, *Jekyll and Hyde*'s medical mystery reminds us that 'we are still groping by doubtful lights on the dim limits of boundless investigation.' In addition, it reminds us that we do not really know ourselves. That is an uncomfortable moment to occupy; it is one that we cannot outlive. And yet, as over a century of criticism and adaptation suggests, it is a problem we will not – cannot – leave alone.

'CLOSER THAN A WIFE, CLOSER THAN AN EYE': JEKYLL AND HYDE TODAY

In an era when politicians carry their religion before them like a shield against criticism rather than as a lamp to guide them, and when 'reality' television showcases behaviour that is suspect even behind closed doors, *Jekyll and Hyde*'s critique of public reputation versus private hypocrisy may seem at last outmoded. However, that is precisely what makes it a novel very much for our time.

Open to the Eye

Movies adapted Stevenson's tale for the screen early on. From the first, silent version in 1908 to whatever today's most recent manifestation may be, the Jekyll/Hyde transformation has allured with the opportunity for special effects. The medium has always favoured Stevenson's message through cuts and lap-dissolves. The advances of stop-motion photography and prosthetic make-up can be measured forward in increments from (in 1920) John Barrymore's detachable fingertips, flying off as he transforms. Now CGI advances enable film-makers to show what Stevenson himself could only suggest: the transformation from Jekyll to Hyde.

Behind these visual representations, themselves a cover for a more complex tale, directors have engaged with the Jekyll/Hyde duality in terms appropriate to their successive periods. Barrymore's Prohibition-era Jekyll (1920) transforms through a potion and hangs out in gin joints and opium dens. In 1941, on the eve of America's entry into the Second World War, Spenser Tracy's doctor is concerned to discover the origins of evil, as his policing society is pushed to determine what evil necessarily requires a response. Jekyll has ingested sparkling powders and Hyde has turned female.

The story's binary structure invites: it shows our anxiety to externalize, fix in place and deal with the challenges that perplex us, the vague evils that haunt us. Even today, however, as the succession of movies shows, we can only deal with our problems for a moment. The relevance of *Jekyll and Hyde* to this and every time perhaps lies in what it leaves unresolved, and what it can only leave unresolved.

Closed to the Mind

If Utterson finds nothing to say as the story apparently ends, it is because no easy resolution is possible. Jekyll cannot quite accept himself as Hyde: that is where the story begins, and that is where the story leaves us. We gain information, but not understanding – neither scientific nor human. Like Jekyll, and like Utterson, we do not know what to do.

A key example connects past and present. When behaviour exceeds all usual social bounds, what can we do? 'Not much' seems to be the answer. But something is essential, even if it is oblique, and even if it can never be enough. What Stevenson offers is discredit. The word 'credit' appears repeatedly in the text. When Hyde is first caught in an atrocity, he is forced into a pay-out. Notably, however, those who come to his victim's rescue threaten to ruin his reputation, his social credit. These rescuers are Mr Enfield, who is no saint, and an attending Scottish doctor who, according to the terms of the times, would stand as a professional man, but not necessarily as a hero of good works. For Mr Hyde in his ill deeds, no response can be proportionate. Indeed, the society finds itself consistently confused in the face of his unreasoning violence. It has to fall back on the perplex bound up in credit, the balance of money and respectability that haunts us today. There is no perfect solution. Still, even the most imperfect society must do something.

Available for Occupation

Although some human problems are always with us, *Jekyll and Hyde* seems prescient in others. The novel stands as a precursor not just for science fiction but also for science fact, and for the dilemmas of our present day. Medicine was changing rapidly even as Stevenson wrote. The early nineteenth century was an age of dissection, as doctors sought to understand the human body through anatomy. During the Victorian era the apothecary gave way to the pharmacist. Doctors increasingly sought to understand the invisible complexities of the mind. Jekyll, as the layout of his house makes clear, stands heir to the anatomist and chemist who preceded him. He is at the cutting edge of his discipline, pondering the double brain and, in advance of Freud, its unconscious drives. Retellings of the story typically situate it within their contemporary science. For us, in the era of Prozac, the tale raises concerns about mind-altering drugs, however attractive – about their use and side-effects. In the midst of the opioid crisis Jekyll stands revealed as a recreational user who falls into habit and then into addiction. His notebook, with its escalating hysteria as he fails to replicate his high, to sustain his transformation, signals the loss of self when science is not fully understood and yet is thoughtlessly embraced.

The Doctor's Dilemma

Jekyll, Stevenson said, was a hypocrite. But before he was a hypocrite, he had undue pride. He aimed to carry his head high in public, indeed to 'wear a more than commonly grave countenance before the public.' And he sought to do so while indulging vices (whatever they may be) that he self-servingly describes as 'such as [have] made the happiness of many.' Careless reading positions Jekyll as a hero of science and Hyde as his nemesis – a belief that motivates many a Hollywood rendition of the tale. But Jekyll has a 'sly cast.' That 'smooth face' signifies some unpleasant characteristics.

As Stevenson wrote, Louis Pasteur was working to understand rabies, developing 'pasteurization', refining vaccination. In contemporary newspapers a doubting public, much like the anti-vaxxers of our day, ridiculed his studies. But Pasteur kept right on going. Jekyll, however, wants to look good in public while being up to no good in private. His research is almost incidental to a prideful purpose. Like Frankenstein before him, he pushes science beyond the known but for his own ends; like Frankenstein, he takes no responsibility until it is too late. With scientific advances came challenges to ethics.

Here it is worth noting that for doctors, professional ethics began as a commitment in the craft not to protect patients so much as to preserve medical reputations. Jekyll shows that the real challenge is to the doctor himself, and to the society that supports him.

Mental Contagion

Jekyll's challenge is infectious. He finds that Hyde grows quietly upon him. He welcomes him, becomes repulsed by him and then finds himself ambushed and usurped by him. Like a virus, Hyde exploits his host. And, like a carrier, Jekyll infects those around him. Mr Enfield says at the beginning of the story that he never speaks ill or tells stories of anyone – because you never know the ramifications. Instantly those ramifications start to accumulate: Mr Utterson recognizes the house and Enfield's account resonates with a story he is already uncomfortably 'within', that of his friend Dr Jekyll's odd last will and testament. Before long Hyde has called Utterson into being as 'Seek.' The lawyer finds himself skulking outside Jekyll's door, waiting for Hyde and then lying to him. Soon he is in a cab with the police, travelling through a London that is 'like some city in a nightmare.' In his disquiet Utterson finds himself 'conscious of some touch of that terror of the law and the law's officers, which may at times assail the most honest.'

Hyde, Women and Other Others

Two communities seem excluded from Stevenson's story and must not be overlooked today. Even the earliest critics noted the relative absence of women in *Jekyll and Hyde*. Stevenson's *Kidnapped* (1886), with its intense relationship between young David Balfour and Alan Breck Stewart, might stand subject to the same critique, but similarity does not make for an explanation or a justification. Nor do people outside the professional class of doctors and lawyers figure largely. Yet in an author who set off across the Atlantic in pursuit of a married, older and forceful woman – a woman considered rather lower-class by his literary friends – and who then co-wrote with her, these omissions invite analysis.

A contemporary women reviewer gives a perspective that still may apply today. For Frances Julia Wedgewood, it was worthy of note that 'no woman's name occurs in the book. No romance is even suggested in it.' The book, she observed, 'depends on the interest of an idea.' The idea itself was not necessarily gendered – nor, we might add, classed or racialized. Indeed the core binary can be occupied from any position. Thus moments of racial and gender sensitivity have produced movies by the titles *Dr Black, Mr Hyde* (1976), *Dr Jekyll and Sister Hyde* (1971) and *Dr Jekyll and Ms Hyde* (1995). Although he resisted reductive interpretations of his tale, Stevenson did ultimately call it 'my allegory.' But with its core binarism and indeterminate Mr Hyde, that allegory stands open for occupation and interpretation. Who knows how Hyde will appear tomorrow?

Others and Readers

What we do know is that we had better watch out. Stevenson wrote before Michel Foucault studied the cultural archaeology of punishment – how it moves from bodily torture in the public square to incarceration, and to social policing. Society, like Mr Enfield and Mr Utterson, is always watching. It can also enlist the force of the law. Jekyll, of course, knows enough to police himself. But before the era of surveillance cameras and online tracking, he neglects to govern his inner Hyde. Moreover the watcher, too, is watched. What secrets do we share, unawares? Today the inner self looks outward from Facebook; it storms in tweets. When the private sphere is a public marketplace, who sees what we do?

CLOSING THE 'STRANGE CASE'?

Everyone knows, or thinks they know, the story of Dr Jekyll and his alter ego. In this volume *Strange Case of Dr Jekyll and Mr Hyde* (1886) stands alongside some of Stevenson's best short fiction, including its ghostly precursor, 'The Body Snatcher'(1884), which draws directly on the Edinburgh scandal of Dr Knox the anatomist and the murderers Burke and Hare. Two lesser-known and earlier fictions also deserve particular notice in the context of *Jekyll and Hyde*: 'The Story of a Lie' (1879) and 'The Pavilion on the Links' (1880). What brings these somewhat precious tales by a younger Stevenson into alignment with the darkness that is Mr Hyde? These, too, were stories that Stevenson wrote with money on his mind. On the emigrant ship to America he had taken a berth one level above steerage so that he would have a desk to write 'The Story of a Lie'. 'I think the story good', he declared – but he conceived of it as an illustrated, popular work, designed to put ready money in his pocket. Of 'The Pavilion', he elaborated: '... 'tis a mere story, and has no higher pretension: Dibbs [money] is its name.'

Stevenson was consequently taken aback when both stories did well. Had his agent actually read 'The Pavilion', he believed that it would never have been sent to Leslie Stephen at *The Cornhill*, a magazine with strong aspirations to art and reputation. Stephen accepted it, however, and published the tale. The critics actually embraced the work. *The Examiner* found it 'breathless and powerful' – if, strangely, not unlike *Wuthering Heights*. This double triumph changed the story in the author's own estimation. What was it about these two tales by a Stevenson not yet established in reputation as a novelist that caught critical attention and a popular audience?

Like *Jekyll and Hyde*, both tales exercise an art that, for those opposed to genre tales (such as adventure romance), might surprise. Jekyll's story emerges through looping narratives that repeat time, reproducing the tale, again and again, as different than we thought. First Mr Enfield gives a clue, then Mr Utterson ponders; Dr Lanyon explains a transformation we cannot understand, and finally Dr Jekyll explains – or does he? Similarly, the narrator of 'The Story of a Lie' revisits an encounter and re-describes the disreputable person he has met according to the predilections of his listener. The subject shifts according to how, and to whom, it is described. In 'The Pavilion', an urgent tale is suddenly thrust into the past when the female lead in a courtship in process is assertively and repeatedly described as 'my wife.' The focus shifts from plot and collapses time according to the relations of people.

Behind these alternately claustrophobic and jarring recursions of time, lies ... the liar. As with Jekyll, however, the liar may not be who we think. This in turn means that the hero may not be unproblematic. In 'The Story of a Lie', a conventional white lie designed to impress a girl entraps all concerned in a tawdry, exploitative relation – until the tables turn. For 'The Pavilion', our misanthropic narrator gradually shows forth as both a hero of romance and a stalker who claims 'my wife' from two men – a father and a competitor in love. Neither of them are quite as he says.

Liars all? Stevenson gets us thinking about it. More importantly, in tales pushing the high melodrama of science fiction and the low romance of domesticity, he gets us thinking more deeply about ourselves.

Caroline McCracken-Flesher, University of Wyoming

Caroline McCracken-Flesher is Professor of English at the University of Wyoming. She is an honorary fellow of the Association for the Study of Scottish Literature. Her books include *Possible Scotlands: Walter Scott and the Story of Tomorrow*, *The Doctor Dissected: A Cultural Autopsy of the Burke and Hare Novels*, and *Approaches to Teaching the Works of Robert Louis Stevenson*.

FURTHER READING

Arata, Stephen, 'The Sedulous Ape: Atavism, Professionalism, and Stevenson's "Jekyll and Hyde"', *Criticism*: 37.2, pages 233–59 (Spring 1995)

Denisoff, Dennis, 'Consumerism and Stevenson's Misfit Masculinities', in *Robert Louis Stevenson: Writer of Boundaries*, eds. Ambrosini, Richard and Dury, Richard, pages 286–98 (University of Wisconsin Press, 2006)

Fielding, Penny, *The Edinburgh Companion to Robert Louis Stevenson* (Edinburgh University Press, 2010)

Guest, Kristin, 'Jekyll and Hyde, Inc.: Limited Liability, Companification, and Gothic Subjectivity', *Victorian Literature and Culture*: 44.2, pages 315–29 (June 2016)

Halberstam, Jack, *Skin Shows: Gothic Horror and the Technology of Monstrosity* (Duke University Press, 1995)

Harman, Claire, *Myself and the Other Fellow: A Life of Robert Louis Stevenson* (Harper, 2006)

Lacey, Nicola. 'Psychologizing Jekyll, Demonising Hyde: The Strange Case of Criminal Responsibility', *Law Society Economy Working Papers*: 18 (2009)

Maixner, Paul, ed., *Robert Louis Stevenson: The Critical Heritage* (Routledge, 1981)

Reid, Julia, *Robert Louis Stevenson, Science, and the Fin de Siècle* (Palgrave, 2009)

Sedgewick, Eve Kosofsky, *Epistemology of the Closet* (University of California Press, 2008)

Stevenson, Robert Louis. *The Letters of Robert Louis Stevenson*, eds. Booth, Bradford A. and Mehew, Ernest (8 vols.) (Yale University Press, 1994)

Stiles, Anne, 'Robert Louis Stevenson's *Jekyll and Hyde* and the Double Brain', *SEL Studies in English Literature 1500–1900*: 46.4, pages 879–900 (2006)

Veeder, William and Hirsch, Gordon, *Dr Jekyll and Mr Hyde after One Hundred Years* (University of Chicago Press, 1988)

Walkowitz, Judith R., *City of Dreadful Delight: Narratives of Sexual Danger in Late-Victorian London* (University of Chicago, 1992)

OTHER MEDIA

Caroline McCracken-Flesher's talk 'Jekyll and Hyde, Science and Scandal' (University of Wyoming Saturday University) is available on YouTube (search www.youtube.com).

Information on film versions of *Dr Jekyll and Mr Hyde* is available in the 'Derivative Works' section of The Robert Louis Stevenson Archive (www.robert-louis-stevenson.org).

ROBERT LOUIS STEVENSON
THE STRANGE CASE
OF DR JEKYLL
AND MR HYDE

CHAPTER 1

The Story of the Door

Mr Utterson the lawyer was a man of a rugged countenance, that was never lighted by a smile; cold, scanty and embarrassed in discourse; backward in sentiment; lean, long, dusty, dreary, and yet somehow lovable. At friendly meetings, and when the wine was to his taste, something eminently human beaconed from his eye; something indeed which never found its way into his talk, but which spoke not only in these silent symbols of the after-dinner face, but more often and loudly in the acts of his life. He was austere with himself; drank gin when he was alone, to mortify a taste for vintages; and though he enjoyed the theatre, had not crossed the doors of one for twenty years. But he had an approved tolerance for others; sometimes wondering, almost with envy, at the high pressure of spirits involved in their misdeeds; and in any extremity inclined to help rather than to reprove.

"I incline to Cain's heresy," he used to say quaintly: "I let my brother go to the devil in his own way." In this character, it was frequently his fortune to be the last reputable acquaintance and the last good influence in the lives of down-going men. And to such as these, so long as they came about his chambers, he never marked a shade of change in his demeanour.

No doubt the feat was easy to Mr Utterson; for he was undemonstrative at the best, and even his friendship seemed to be founded in a similar catholicity of good-nature. It is the mark of a modest man to accept his friendly circle ready-made from the hands of opportunity; and that was the lawyer's way. His friends were those of his own blood or those whom he had known the longest; his affections, like ivy, were the growth of time, they implied no aptness in the object. Hence, no doubt, the bond that united him to Mr Richard Enfield, his distant kinsman, the well-known man about town. It was a nut to crack for many, what these two could see in each other, or what subject they could find in common. It was reported by those who encountered them in their Sunday walks, that they said nothing, looked singularly dull, and would hail with obvious relief the appearance of a friend. For all that, the two men put the greatest store by these excursions, counted them the chief jewel of each week, and not only set aside occasions of pleasure, but even resisted the calls of business, that they might enjoy them uninterrupted.

It chanced on one of these rambles that their way led them down a by-street in a busy quarter of London. The street was small and what is called quiet, but it drove a thriving trade on the week-days. The inhabitants were all doing well, it seemed, and all emulously hoping to do better still, and laying out the surplus of their gains in coquetry; so that the shop fronts stood along that thoroughfare with an air of invitation, like rows of smiling saleswomen. Even on Sunday, when it veiled its more florid charms and lay comparatively empty of passage, the street shone out in contrast to its dingy neighbourhood, like a fire in a forest; and with its freshly painted shutters, well-polished brasses, and general cleanliness and gaiety of note, instantly caught and pleased the eye of the passenger.

Two doors from one corner, on the left hand going east, the line was broken by the entry of a court; and just at that point, a certain sinister block of building thrust forward its gable on the street. It was two stories high; showed no window, nothing but a door on the lower story and a blind forehead of discoloured wall on the upper; and bore in every feature, the marks of prolonged and sordid negligence. The door, which was equipped with neither bell nor knocker, was blistered and distained. Tramps slouched into the recess and struck matches on the panels; children kept shop upon the steps; the schoolboy had tried his knife on the mouldings; and for close on a generation, no one had appeared to drive away these random visitors or to repair their ravages.

Mr Enfield and the lawyer were on the other side of the by-street; but when they came abreast of the entry, the former lifted up his cane and pointed.

"Did you ever remark that door?" he asked; and when his companion had replied in the affirmative, "It is connected in my mind," added he, "with a very odd story."

"Indeed?" said Mr Utterson, with a slight change of voice, "and what was that?"

"Well, it was this way," returned Mr Enfield: "I was coming home from some place at the end of the world, about three o'clock of a black winter morning, and my way lay through a part of town where there was literally nothing to be seen but lamps. Street after street, and all the folks asleep – street after street, all lighted up as if for a procession and all as empty as a church – till at last I got into that state of mind when a man listens and listens and begins to long for the sight of a policeman. All at once, I saw two figures: one a little man who was stumping along eastward at a good walk, and the other a girl of maybe eight or ten who was running as hard as she was able down a cross street. Well, sir, the two ran into one another naturally enough at the corner; and then came the horrible part of the thing; for the man trampled calmly over the child's body and left her screaming on the ground. It sounds nothing to hear, but it was hellish to see. It wasn't like a man; it was like some damned Juggernaut. I gave a view-halloa, took to my heels, collared my gentleman, and brought him back to where there was already quite a group about the screaming child. He was perfectly cool and made no resistance, but gave me one look, so ugly that it brought out the sweat on me like running. The people who had turned out were the girl's own family; and pretty soon, the doctor, for whom she had been sent, put in his appearance. Well, the child was not much the worse, more frightened, according to the Sawbones; and there you might have supposed would be an end to it. But there was one curious circumstance. I had taken a loathing to my gentleman at first sight. So had the child's family, which was only natural. But the doctor's case was what struck me. He was the usual cut-and-dry apothecary, of no particular age and colour, with a strong Edinburgh accent, and about as emotional as a bagpipe. Well, sir, he was like the rest of us; every time he looked at my prisoner, I saw that Sawbones turn sick and white with the desire to kill him. I knew what was in his mind, just as he knew what was in mine; and killing being out of the question, we did the next best. We told the man we could and would make such a scandal out of this, as should make his name stink from one end of London to the other. If he had any friends or any credit, we undertook that he should lose them. And all the time, as we were pitching it in red hot, we were keeping the women off him as best we could, for they were as wild as harpies. I never saw a circle of such hateful faces; and there was the man in the middle, with a kind of black, sneering coolness – frightened too, I could see that – but carrying it off, sir, really like Satan. 'If you choose to make capital out of this accident,' said he, 'I am naturally helpless. No gentleman but wishes to avoid a scene,' says he. 'Name your figure.' Well, we screwed him up to a hundred pounds for the child's family; he would have clearly liked to stick out; but there was something about the lot of us that meant mischief, and at last he struck. The next thing was to get the money; and where do you think he carried us but to that place with the door? – whipped out a key, went in, and presently came back with the matter of ten pounds in gold and a cheque for the balance on Coutts's, drawn payable to bearer and signed with a name that I can't mention, though it's one of the points of my story, but it was a name at least very well known and often printed. The figure was stiff; but the signature was good for more than that, if it was only genuine. I took the liberty of pointing out to my gentleman that the whole business looked apocryphal, and that a man does not, in real life, walk into a cellar door at four in the morning and come out of it with another man's cheque for close upon a hundred pounds. But he was quite easy and sneering. 'Set your mind at rest,' says he, 'I will stay with you till the banks open and cash the cheque myself.' So we all set off, the doctor, and the child's father, and our friend and myself, and passed the rest of the night in my chambers; and next day, when we had breakfasted, went in a body to the bank. I gave in the check myself, and said I had every reason to believe it was a forgery. Not a bit of it. The cheque was genuine."

"Tut-tut," said Mr Utterson.

"I see you feel as I do," said Mr Enfield. "Yes, it's a bad story. For my man was a fellow that nobody could have to do with, a really damnable man; and the person that drew the cheque is the very pink of the proprieties, celebrated too, and (what makes it worse) one of your fellows who do what they call good. Blackmail, I suppose; an honest man paying through the nose for some of the capers of his youth. Black Mail House is what I call that place with the door, in consequence. Though even that, you know, is far from explaining all," he added, and with the words fell into a vein of musing.

From this he was recalled by Mr Utterson asking rather suddenly: "And you don't know if the drawer of the cheque lives there?"

"A likely place, isn't it?" returned Mr Enfield. "But I happen to have noticed his address; he lives in some square or other."

"And you never asked about the place with the door?" said Mr Utterson.

"No, sir: I had a delicacy," was the reply. "I feel very strongly about putting questions; it partakes too much of the style of the day of judgment. You start a question, and it's like starting a stone. You sit quietly on the top of a hill; and away the stone goes, starting others; and presently some bland old bird (the last you would have thought of) is knocked on the head in his own back-garden and the family have to change their name. No, sir, I make it a rule of mine: the more it looks like Queer Street, the less I ask."

"A very good rule, too," said the lawyer.

"But I have studied the place for myself," continued Mr Enfield. "It seems scarcely a house. There is no other door, and nobody goes in or out of that one but, once in a great while, the gentleman of my adventure. There are three windows looking on the court on the first floor; none below; the windows are always shut but they're clean. And then there is a chimney which is generally smoking; so somebody must live there. And yet it's not so sure; for the buildings are so packed together about that court, that it's hard to say where one ends and another begins."

The pair walked on again for a while in silence; and then, "Enfield," said Mr Utterson, "that's a good rule of yours."

"Yes, I think it is," returned Enfield.

"But for all that," continued the lawyer, "there's one point I want to ask: I want to ask the name of that man who walked over the child."

"Well," said Mr Enfield, "I can't see what harm it would do. It was a man of the name of Hyde."

"Hm," said Mr Utterson. "What sort of a man is he to see?"

"He is not easy to describe. There is something wrong with his appearance; something displeasing, something downright detestable. I never saw a man I so disliked, and yet I scarce know why. He must be deformed somewhere; he gives a strong feeling of deformity, although I couldn't specify the point. He's an extraordinary looking man, and yet I really can name nothing out of the way. No, sir; I can make no hand of it; I can't describe him. And it's not want of memory; for I declare I can see him this moment."

Mr Utterson again walked some way in silence and obviously under a weight of consideration.

"You are sure he used a key?" he inquired at last.

"My dear sir..." began Enfield, surprised out of himself.

"Yes, I know," said Utterson; "I know it must seem strange. The fact is, if I do not ask you the name of the other party, it is because I know it already. You see, Richard, your tale has gone home. If you have been inexact in any point, you had better correct it."

"I think you might have warned me," returned the other, with a touch of sullenness. "But I have been pedantically exact, as you call it. The fellow had a key; and what's more, he has it still. I saw him use it, not a week ago."

Mr Utterson sighed deeply but said never a word; and the young man presently resumed. "Here is another lesson to say nothing," said he. "I am ashamed of my long tongue. Let us make a bargain never to refer to this again."

"With all my heart," said the lawyer. "I shake hands on that, Richard."

CHAPTER 2

The Search for Mr Hyde

That evening Mr Utterson came home to his bachelor house in sombre spirits and sat down to dinner without relish. It was his custom of a Sunday, when this meal was over, to sit close by the fire, a volume of some dry divinity on his reading-desk, until the clock of the neighbouring church rang out the hour of twelve, when he would go soberly and gratefully to bed. On this night, however, as soon as the cloth was taken away, he took up a candle and went into his business-room. There he opened his safe, took from the most private part of it a document endorsed on the envelope as Dr Jekyll's Will, and sat down with a clouded brow to study its contents. The will was holograph, for Mr Utterson, though he took charge of it now that it was made, had refused to lend the least assistance in the making of it; it provided not only that, in case of the decease of Henry Jekyll, M.D., D.C.L., L.L.D., F.R.S., etc., all his possessions were to pass into the hands of his "friend and benefactor Edward Hyde," but that in case of Dr Jekyll's "disappearance or unexplained absence for any period exceeding three calendar months," the said Edward Hyde should step into the said Henry Jekyll's shoes without further delay and free from any burden or obligation, beyond the payment of a few small sums to the members of the doctor's household. This document had long been the lawyer's eyesore. It offended him both as a lawyer and as a lover of the sane and customary sides of life, to whom the fanciful was the immodest. And hitherto it was his ignorance of Mr Hyde that had swelled his indignation; now, by a sudden turn, it was his knowledge. It was already bad enough when the name was but a name of which he could learn no more. It was worse when it began to be clothed upon with detestable attributes; and out of the shifting, insubstantial mists that had so long baffled his eye, there leaped up the sudden, definite presentment of a fiend.

"I thought it was madness," he said, as he replaced the obnoxious paper in the safe, "and now I begin to fear it is disgrace."

With that he blew out his candle, put on a great-coat, and set forth in the direction of Cavendish Square, that citadel of medicine, where his friend, the great Dr Lanyon, had his house and received his crowding patients. "If any one knows, it will be Lanyon," he had thought.

The solemn butler knew and welcomed him; he was subjected to no stage of delay, but ushered direct from the door to the dining-room where Dr Lanyon sat alone over his wine. This was a hearty, healthy, dapper, red-faced gentleman, with a shock of hair prematurely white, and a boisterous and decided manner. At sight of Mr Utterson, he sprang up from his chair and welcomed him with both hands. The geniality, as was the way of the man, was somewhat theatrical to the eye; but it reposed on genuine feeling. For these two were old friends, old mates both at school and college, both thorough respecters of themselves and of each other, and, what does not always follow, men who thoroughly enjoyed each other's company.

After a little rambling talk, the lawyer led up to the subject which so disagreeably preoccupied his mind.

"I suppose, Lanyon," said he "you and I must be the two oldest friends that Henry Jekyll has?"

"I wish the friends were younger," chuckled Dr Lanyon. "But I suppose we are. And what of that? I see little of him now."

"Indeed?" said Utterson. "I thought you had a bond of common interest."

"We had," was the reply. "But it is more than ten years since Henry Jekyll became too fanciful for me. He began to go wrong, wrong in mind; and though of course I continue to take an interest in him for old sake's sake, as they say, I see and I have seen devilish little of the man. Such unscientific balderdash," added the doctor, flushing suddenly purple, "would have estranged Damon and Pythias."

This little spirit of temper was somewhat of a relief to Mr Utterson. "They have only differed on some point of science," he thought; and being a man of no scientific passions (except in the matter of conveyancing), he even added: "It is nothing worse than that!" He gave his friend a few seconds to recover his composure, and then approached the question he had come to put. "Did you ever come across a protégé of his – one Hyde?" he asked.

"Hyde?" repeated Lanyon. "No. Never heard of him. Since my time."

That was the amount of information that the lawyer carried back with him to the great, dark bed on which he tossed to and fro, until the small hours of the morning began to grow large. It was a night of little ease to his toiling mind, toiling in mere darkness and besieged by questions.

Six o'clock struck on the bells of the church that was so conveniently near to Mr Utterson's dwelling, and still he was digging at the problem. Hitherto it had touched him on the intellectual side alone; but now his imagination also was engaged, or rather enslaved; and as he lay and tossed in the gross darkness of the night and the curtained room, Mr Enfield's tale went by before his mind in a scroll of lighted pictures. He would be aware of the great field of lamps of a nocturnal city; then of the figure of a man walking swiftly; then of a child running from the doctor's; and then these met, and that human Juggernaut trod the child down and passed on regardless of her screams. Or else he would see a room in a rich house, where his friend lay asleep, dreaming and smiling at his dreams; and then the door of that room would be opened, the curtains of the bed plucked apart, the sleeper recalled, and lo! there would stand by his side a figure to whom power was given, and even at that dead hour, he must rise and do its bidding. The figure in these two phases haunted the lawyer all night; and if at any time he dozed over, it was but to see it glide more stealthily through sleeping houses, or move the more swiftly and still the more swiftly, even to dizziness, through wider labyrinths of lamplighted city, and at every street corner crush a child and leave her screaming. And still the figure had no face by which he might know it; even in his dreams, it had no face, or one that baffled him and melted before his eyes; and thus it was that there sprang up and grew apace in the lawyer's mind a singularly strong, almost an inordinate, curiosity to behold the features of the real Mr Hyde. If he could but once set eyes on him, he thought the mystery would lighten and perhaps roll altogether away, as was the habit of mysterious things when well examined. He might see a reason for his friend's strange preference or bondage (call it which you please) and even for the startling clause of the will. At least it would be a face worth seeing: the face of a man who was without bowels of mercy: a face which had but to show itself to raise up, in the mind of the unimpressionable Enfield, a spirit of enduring hatred.

From that time forward, Mr Utterson began to haunt the door in the by-street of shops. In the morning before office hours, at noon when business was plenty, and time scarce, at night under the face of the fogged city moon, by all lights and at all hours of solitude or concourse, the lawyer was to be found on his chosen post.

"If he be Mr Hyde," he had thought, "I shall be Mr Seek."

And at last his patience was rewarded. It was a fine dry night; frost in the air; the streets as clean as a ballroom floor; the lamps, unshaken, by any wind, drawing a regular pattern of light and shadow. By ten o'clock, when the shops were closed, the by-street was very solitary and, in spite of the low growl of London from all round, very silent. Small sounds carried far; domestic sounds out of the houses were clearly audible on either side of the roadway; and the rumour of the approach of any passenger preceded him by a long time. Mr Utterson had been some minutes at his post, when he was aware of an odd, light footstep drawing near. In the course of his nightly patrols, he had long grown accustomed to the quaint effect with which the footfalls of a single person, while he is still a great way off, suddenly spring out distinct from the vast hum and clatter of the city. Yet his attention had never before been so sharply and decisively arrested; and it was with a strong, superstitious prevision of success that he withdrew into the entry of the court.

The steps drew swiftly nearer, and swelled out suddenly louder as they turned the end of the street. The lawyer, looking forth from the entry, could soon see what manner of man he had to deal with. He was small and very plainly dressed, and the look of him, even at that distance, went somehow strongly against the watcher's inclination. But he made straight for the door, crossing the roadway to save time; and as he came, he drew a key from his pocket like one approaching home.

Mr Utterson stepped out and touched him on the shoulder as he passed. "Mr Hyde, I think?"

Mr Hyde shrank back with a hissing intake of the breath. But his fear was only momentary; and though he did not look the lawyer in the face, he answered coolly enough: "That is my name. What do you want?"

"I see you are going in," returned the lawyer. "I am an old friend of Dr Jekyll's - Mr Utterson of Gaunt Street - you must have heard my name; and meeting you so conveniently, I thought you might admit me."

"You will not find Dr Jekyll; he is from home," replied Mr Hyde, blowing in the key. And then suddenly, but still without looking up, "How did you know me?" he asked.

"On your side," said Mr Utterson, "will you do me a favour?"

"With pleasure," replied the other. "What shall it be?"

"Will you let me see your face?" asked the lawyer.

Mr Hyde appeared to hesitate, and then, as if upon some sudden reflection, fronted about with an air of defiance; and the pair stared at each other pretty fixedly for a few seconds. "Now I shall know you again," said Mr Utterson. "It may be useful."

"Yes," returned Mr Hyde, "it is as well we have met; and *à propos*, you should have my address." And he gave a number of a street in Soho.

"Good God!" thought Mr Utterson, "can he, too, have been thinking of the will?" But he kept his feelings to himself and only grunted in acknowledgment of the address.

"And now," said the other, "how did you know me?"

"By description," was the reply.

"Whose description?"

"We have common friends," said Mr Utterson.

"Common friends?" echoed Mr Hyde, a little hoarsely. "Who are they?"

"Jekyll, for instance," said the lawyer.

"He never told you," cried Mr Hyde, with a flush of anger. "I did not think you would have lied."

"Come," said Mr Utterson, "that is not fitting language."

The other snarled aloud into a savage laugh; and the next moment, with extraordinary quickness, he had unlocked the door and disappeared into the house.

The lawyer stood awhile when Mr Hyde had left him, the picture of disquietude. Then he began slowly to mount the street, pausing every step or two and putting his hand to his brow like a man in mental perplexity. The problem he was thus debating as he walked, was one of a class that is rarely solved. Mr Hyde was pale and dwarfish, he gave an impression of deformity without any nameable malformation, he had a displeasing smile, he had borne himself to the lawyer with a sort of murderous mixture of timidity and boldness, and he spoke with a husky, whispering and somewhat broken voice; all these were points against him, but not all of these together could explain the hitherto unknown disgust, loathing, and fear with which Mr Utterson regarded him. "There must be something else," said the perplexed gentleman. "There *is* something more, if I could find a name for it. God bless me, the man seems hardly human! Something troglodytic, shall we say? or can it be the old story of Dr Fell? or is it the mere radiance of a foul soul that thus transpires through, and transfigures, its clay continent? The last, I think; for, O my poor old Harry Jekyll, if ever I read Satan's signature upon a face, it is on that of your new friend."

Round the corner from the by-street, there was a square of ancient, handsome houses, now for the most part decayed from their high estate and let in flats and chambers to all sorts and conditions of men: map-engravers, architects, shady lawyers and the agents of obscure enterprises. One house, however, second from the corner, was still occupied entire; and at the door of this, which wore a great air of wealth and comfort, though it was now plunged in darkness except for the fan-light, Mr Utterson stopped and knocked. A well-dressed, elderly servant opened the door.

"Is Dr Jekyll at home, Poole?" asked the lawyer.

"I will see, Mr Utterson," said Poole, admitting the visitor, as he spoke, into a large, low-roofed, comfortable hall, paved with flags, warmed (after the fashion of a country house) by a bright, open fire, and furnished with costly cabinets of oak. "Will you wait here by the fire, sir? or shall I give you a light in the dining room?"

"Here, thank you," said the lawyer, and he drew near and leaned on the tall fender. This hall, in which he was now left alone, was a pet fancy of his friend the doctor's; and Utterson himself was wont to speak of it as the pleasantest room in London. But tonight there was a shudder in his blood; the face of Hyde sat heavy on his memory; he felt (what was rare with him) a nausea and distaste of life; and in the gloom of his spirits, he seemed to read a menace in the flickering of the firelight on the polished cabinets and the uneasy starting of the shadow on the roof. He was ashamed of his relief, when Poole presently returned to announce that Dr Jekyll was gone out.

"I saw Mr Hyde go in by the old dissecting room door, Poole," he said. "Is that right, when Dr Jekyll is from home?"

"Quite right, Mr Utterson, sir," replied the servant. "Mr Hyde has a key."

"Your master seems to repose a great deal of trust in that young man, Poole," resumed the other musingly.

"Yes, sir, he do indeed," said Poole. "We have all orders to obey him."

"I do not think I ever met Mr Hyde?" asked Utterson.

"O, dear no, sir. He never dines here," replied the butler. "Indeed we see very little of him on this side of the house; he mostly comes and goes by the laboratory."

"Well, good-night, Poole."

"Good-night, Mr Utterson."

And the lawyer set out homeward with a very heavy heart. "Poor Harry Jekyll," he thought, "my mind misgives me he is in deep waters! He was wild when he was young; a long while ago to be sure; but in the law of God, there is no statute of limitations. Ay, it must be that; the ghost of some old sin, the cancer of some concealed disgrace: punishment coming, *pede claudo*, years after memory has forgotten and self-love condoned the fault." And the lawyer, scared by the thought, brooded a while on his own past, groping in all the corners of memory, lest by chance some Jack-in-the-Box of an old iniquity should leap to light there. His past was fairly blameless; few men could read the rolls of their life with less apprehension; yet he was humbled to the dust by the many ill things he had done, and raised up again into a sober and fearful gratitude by the many that he had come so near to doing, yet avoided. And then by a return on his former subject, he conceived a spark of hope. "This Master Hyde, if he were studied," thought he, "must have secrets of his own; black secrets, by the look of him; secrets compared to which poor Jekyll's worst would be like sunshine. Things cannot continue as they are. It turns me cold to think of this creature stealing like a thief to Harry's bedside; poor Harry, what a wakening! And the danger of it; for if this Hyde suspects the existence of the will, he may grow impatient to inherit. Ay, I must put my shoulder to the wheel if Jekyll will but let me," he added, "if Jekyll will only let me." For once more he saw before his mind's eye, as clear as a transparency, the strange clauses of the will.

CHAPTER 3

Dr Jekyll was Quite at Ease

A fortnight later, by excellent good fortune, the doctor gave one of his pleasant dinners to some five or six old cronies, all intelligent, reputable men and all judges of good wine; and Mr Utterson so contrived that he remained behind after the others had departed. This was no new arrangement, but a thing that had befallen many scores of times. Where Utterson was liked, he was liked well. Hosts loved to detain the dry lawyer, when the light-hearted and the loose-tongued had already their foot on the threshold; they liked to sit a while in his unobtrusive company, practising for solitude, sobering their minds in the man's rich silence after the expense and strain of gaiety. To this rule, Dr Jekyll was no exception; and as he now sat on the opposite side of the fire – a large, well-made, smooth-faced man of fifty, with something of a slyish cast perhaps, but every mark of capacity and kindness – you could see by his looks that he cherished for Mr Utterson a sincere and warm affection.

"I have been wanting to speak to you, Jekyll," began the latter. "You know that will of yours?"

A close observer might have gathered that the topic was distasteful; but the doctor carried it off gaily. "My poor Utterson," said he, "you are unfortunate in such a client. I never saw a man so distressed as you were by my will; unless it were that hide-bound pedant, Lanyon, at what he called my scientific heresies. Oh, I know he's a good fellow – you needn't frown – an excellent fellow, and I always mean to see more of him; but a hide-bound pedant for all that; an ignorant, blatant pedant. I was never more disappointed in any man than Lanyon."

"You know I never approved of it," pursued Utterson, ruthlessly disregarding the fresh topic.

"My will? Yes, certainly, I know that," said the doctor, a trifle sharply. "You have told me so."

"Well, I tell you so again," continued the lawyer. "I have been learning something of young Hyde."

The large handsome face of Dr Jekyll grew pale to the very lips, and there came a blackness about his eyes. "I do not care to hear more," said he. "This is a matter I thought we had agreed to drop."

"What I heard was abominable," said Utterson.

"It can make no change. You do not understand my position," returned the doctor, with a certain incoherency of manner. "I am painfully situated, Utterson; my position is a very strange – a very strange one. It is one of those affairs that cannot be mended by talking."

"Jekyll," said Utterson, "you know me: I am a man to be trusted. Make a clean breast of this in confidence; and I make no doubt I can get you out of it."

"My good Utterson," said the doctor, "this is very good of you, this is downright good of you, and I cannot find words to thank you in. I believe you fully; I would trust you before any man alive, ay, before myself, if I could make the choice; but indeed it isn't what you fancy; it is not so bad as that; and just to put your good heart at rest, I will tell you one thing: the moment I choose, I can be rid of Mr Hyde. I give you my hand upon that; and I thank you again and again; and I will just add one little word, Utterson, that I'm sure you'll take in good part: this is a private matter, and I beg of you to let it sleep."

Utterson reflected a little, looking in the fire.

"I have no doubt you are perfectly right," he said at last, getting to his feet.

"Well, but since we have touched upon this business, and for the last time I hope," continued the doctor, "there is one point I should like you to understand. I have really a very great interest in poor Hyde. I know you have seen him; he told me so; and I fear he was rude. But, I do sincerely take a great, a very great interest in that young man; and if I am taken away, Utterson, I wish you to promise me that you will bear with him and get his rights for him. I think you would, if you knew all; and it would be a weight off my mind if you would promise."

"I can't pretend that I shall ever like him," said the lawyer.

"I don't ask that," pleaded Jekyll, laying his hand upon the other's arm; "I only ask for justice; I only ask you to help him for my sake, when I am no longer here."

Utterson heaved an irrepressible sigh. "Well," said he, "I promise."

CHAPTER 4

The Carew Murder Case

Nearly a year later, in the month of October, 18—, London was
startled by a crime of singular ferocity and rendered all the more
notable by the high position of the victim. The details were few and
startling. A maid servant living alone in a house not far from the river,
had gone upstairs to bed about eleven. Although a fog rolled over the
city in the small hours, the early part of the night was cloudless, and
the lane, which the maid's window overlooked, was brilliantly lit by
the full moon. It seems she was romantically given, for she sat down
upon her box, which stood immediately under the window, and fell
into a dream of musing. Never (she used to say, with streaming tears,
when she narrated that experience), never had she felt more at peace
with all men or thought more kindly of the world. And as she so sat
she became aware of an aged and beautiful gentleman with white hair,
drawing near along the lane; and advancing to meet him, another and
very small gentleman, to whom at first she paid less attention. When
they had come within speech (which was just under the maid's eyes)
the older man bowed and accosted the other with a very pretty manner
of politeness. It did not seem as if the subject of his address were of
great importance; indeed, from his pointing, it sometimes appeared as
if he were only inquiring his way; but the moon shone on his face as he
spoke, and the girl was pleased to watch it, it seemed to breathe such an

47

innocent and old-world kindness of disposition, yet with something high too, as of a well-founded self-content. Presently her eye wandered to the other, and she was surprised to recognize in him a certain Mr Hyde, who had once visited her master and for whom she had conceived a dislike. He had in his hand a heavy cane, with which he was trifling; but he answered never a word, and seemed to listen with an ill-contained impatience. And then all of a sudden he broke out in a great flame of anger, stamping with his foot, brandishing the cane, and carrying on (as the maid described it) like a madman. The old gentleman took a step back, with the air of one very much surprised and a trifle hurt; and at that Mr Hyde broke out of all bounds and clubbed him to the earth. And next moment, with ape-like fury, he was trampling his victim under foot and hailing down a storm of blows, under which the bones were audibly shattered and the body jumped upon the roadway. At the horror of these sights and sounds, the maid fainted.

It was two o'clock when she came to herself and called for the police. The murderer was gone long ago; but there lay his victim in the middle of the lane, incredibly mangled. The stick with which the deed had been done, although it was of some rare and very tough and heavy wood, had broken in the middle under the stress of this insensate cruelty; and one splintered half had rolled in the neighbouring gutter – the other, without doubt, had been carried away by the murderer. A purse and a gold watch were found upon the victim: but no cards or papers, except a sealed and stamped envelope, which he had been probably carrying to the post, and which bore the name and address of Mr Utterson.

This was brought to the lawyer the next morning, before he was out of bed; and he had no sooner seen it, and been told the circumstances, than he shot out a solemn lip. "I shall say nothing till I have seen the body," said he; "this may be very serious. Have the kindness to wait while I dress." And with the same grave countenance he hurried through his breakfast and drove to the police station, whither the body had been carried. As soon as he came into the cell, he nodded.

"Yes," said he, "I recognize him. I am sorry to say that this is Sir Danvers Carew."

"Good God, sir," exclaimed the officer, "is it possible?" And the next moment his eye lighted up with professional ambition. "This will make a deal of noise," he said. "And perhaps you can help us to the man." And he briefly narrated what the maid had seen, and showed the broken stick.

Mr Utterson had already quailed at the name of Hyde; but when the stick was laid before him, he could doubt no longer; broken and battered as it was, he recognized it for one that he had himself presented many years before to Henry Jekyll.

"Is this Mr Hyde a person of small stature?" he inquired.

"Particularly small and particularly wicked-looking, is what the maid calls him," said the officer.

Mr Utterson reflected; and then, raising his head, "If you will come with me in my cab," he said, "I think I can take you to his house."

It was by this time about nine in the morning, and the first fog of the season. A great chocolate-coloured pall lowered over heaven, but the wind was continually charging and routing these embattled vapours; so that as the cab crawled from street to street, Mr Utterson beheld a marvellous number of degrees and hues of twilight; for here it would be dark like the back-end of evening; and there would be a glow of a rich, lurid brown, like the light of some strange conflagration; and here, for a moment, the fog would be quite broken up, and a haggard shaft of daylight would glance in between the swirling wreaths. The dismal quarter of Soho seen under these changing glimpses, with its muddy ways, and slatternly passengers, and its lamps, which had never been extinguished or had been kindled afresh to combat this mournful reinvasion of darkness, seemed, in the lawyer's eyes, like a district of some city in a nightmare. The thoughts of his mind, besides, were of the gloomiest dye; and when he glanced at the companion of his drive, he was conscious of some touch of that terror of the law and the law's officers, which may at times assail the most honest.

As the cab drew up before the address indicated, the fog lifted a little and showed him a dingy street, a gin palace, a low French eating-house, a shop for the retail of penny numbers and twopenny salads, many ragged children huddled in the doorways, and many women of different nationalities passing out, key in hand, to have a morning glass; and the next moment the fog settled down again upon that part, as brown as umber, and cut him off from his blackguardly surroundings. This was the home of Henry Jekyll's favourite; of a man who was heir to a quarter of a million sterling.

An ivory-faced and silvery-haired old woman opened the door. She had an evil face, smoothed by hypocrisy; but her manners were excellent. Yes, she said, this was Mr Hyde's, but he was not at home; he had been in that night very late, but had gone away again in less than an hour; there was nothing strange in that; his habits were very irregular, and he was often absent; for instance, it was nearly two months since she had seen him till yesterday.

"Very well, then, we wish to see his rooms," said the lawyer; and when the woman began to declare it was impossible, "I had better tell you who this person is," he added. "This is Inspector Newcomen of Scotland Yard."

A flash of odious joy appeared upon the woman's face. "Ah!" said she, "he is in trouble! What has he done?"

Mr Utterson and the inspector exchanged glances. "He don't seem a very popular character," observed the latter. "And now, my good woman, just let me and this gentleman have a look about us."

In the whole extent of the house, which but for the old woman remained otherwise empty, Mr Hyde had only used a couple of rooms; but these were furnished with luxury and good taste. A closet was filled with wine; the plate was of silver, the napery elegant; a good picture hung upon the walls, a gift (as Utterson supposed) from Henry Jekyll, who was much of a connoisseur; and the carpets were of many plies and agreeable in colour. At this moment, however, the rooms bore every mark of having been recently and hurriedly ransacked; clothes lay about the floor, with their pockets inside out; lock-fast drawers stood open; and on the hearth there lay a pile of gray ashes, as though many papers had been burned. From these embers the inspector disinterred the butt-end of a green cheque book, which had resisted the action of the fire; the other half of the stick was found behind the door; and as this clinched his suspicions, the officer declared himself delighted. A visit to the bank, where several thousand pounds were found to be lying to the murderer's credit, completed his gratification.

"You may depend upon it, sir," he told Mr Utterson: "I have him in my hand. He must have lost his head, or he never would have left the stick or, above all, burned the cheque book. Why, money's life to the man. We have nothing to do but wait for him at the bank, and get out the handbills."

This last, however, was not so easy of accomplishment; for Mr Hyde had numbered few familiars – even the master of the servant-maid had only seen him twice; his family could nowhere be traced; he had never been photographed; and the few who could describe him differed widely, as common observers will. Only on one point, were they agreed; and that was the haunting sense of unexpressed deformity with which the fugitive impressed his beholders.

CHAPTER 5

Incident of the Letter

It was late in the afternoon, when Mr Utterson found his way to Dr Jekyll's door, where he was at once admitted by Poole, and carried down by the kitchen offices and across a yard which had once been a garden, to the building which was indifferently known as the laboratory or the dissecting rooms. The doctor had bought the house from the heirs of a celebrated surgeon; and his own tastes being rather chemical than anatomical, had changed the destination of the block at the bottom of the garden. It was the first time that the lawyer had been received in that part of his friend's quarters; and he eyed the dingy, windowless structure with curiosity, and gazed round with a distasteful sense of strangeness as he crossed the theatre, once crowded with eager students and now lying gaunt and silent, the tables laden with chemical apparatus, the floor strewn with crates and littered with packing straw, and the light falling dimly through the foggy cupola. At the further end, a flight of stairs mounted to a door covered with red baize; and through this, Mr Utterson was at last received into the doctor's cabinet. It was a large room, fitted round with glass presses, furnished, among other things, with a cheval-glass and a business table, and looking out upon the court by three dusty windows barred with iron. A fire burned in the grate; a lamp was set lighted on the chimney shelf, for even in the houses the fog began to lie thickly; and there, close up to the warmth, sat Dr Jekyll, looking deadly sick. He did not rise to meet his visitor, but held out a cold hand and bade him welcome in a changed voice.

"And now," said Mr Utterson, as soon as Poole had left them, "you have heard the news?"

The doctor shuddered. "They were crying it in the square," he said. "I heard them in my dining-room."

"One word," said the lawyer. "Carew was my client, but so are you, and I want to know what I am doing. You have not been mad enough to hide this fellow?"

"Utterson, I swear to God," cried the doctor, "I swear to God I will never set eyes on him again. I bind my honour to you that I am done with him in this world. It is all at an end. And indeed he does not want my help; you do not know him as I do; he is safe, he is quite safe; mark my words, he will never more be heard of."

The lawyer listened gloomily; he did not like his friend's feverish manner. "You seem pretty sure of him," said he; "and for your sake, I hope you may be right. If it came to a trial, your name might appear."

"I am quite sure of him," replied Jekyll; "I have grounds for certainty that I cannot share with any one. But there is one thing on which you may advise me. I have – I have received a letter; and I am at a loss whether I should show it to the police. I should like to leave it in your hands, Utterson; you would judge wisely, I am sure; I have so great a trust in you."

"You fear, I suppose, that it might lead to his detection?" asked the lawyer.

"No," said the other. "I cannot say that I care what becomes of Hyde; I am quite done with him. I was thinking of my own character, which this hateful business has rather exposed."

Utterson ruminated a while; he was surprised at his friend's selfishness, and yet relieved by it. "Well," said he, at last, "let me see the letter."

The letter was written in an odd, upright hand and signed "Edward Hyde": and it signified, briefly enough, that the writer's benefactor, Dr Jekyll, whom he had long so unworthily repaid for a thousand generosities, need labour under no alarm for his safety, as he had means of escape on which he placed a sure dependence. The lawyer liked this letter well enough; it put a better colour on the intimacy than he had looked for; and he blamed himself for some of his past suspicions.

"Have you the envelope?" he asked.

"I burned it," replied Jekyll, "before I thought what I was about. But it bore no postmark. The note was handed in."

"Shall I keep this and sleep upon it?" asked Utterson.

"I wish you to judge for me entirely," was the reply. "I have lost confidence in myself."

"Well, I shall consider," returned the lawyer. "And now one word more: it was Hyde who dictated the terms in your will about that disappearance?"

The doctor seemed seized with a qualm of faintness: he shut his mouth tight and nodded.

"I knew it," said Utterson. "He meant to murder you. You have had a fine escape."

"I have had what is far more to the purpose," returned the doctor solemnly: "I have had a lesson – O God, Utterson, what a lesson I have had!" And he covered his face for a moment with his hands.

On his way out, the lawyer stopped and had a word or two with Poole. "By the by," said he, "there was a letter handed in today:

what was the messenger like?" But Poole was positive nothing had come except by post; "and only circulars by that," he added.

This news sent off the visitor with his fears renewed. Plainly the letter had come by the laboratory door; possibly, indeed, it had been written in the cabinet; and if that were so, it must be differently judged, and handled with the more caution. The newsboys, as he went, were crying themselves hoarse along the footways: "Special edition. Shocking murder of an M.P." That was the funeral oration of one friend and client; and he could not help a certain apprehension lest the good name of another should be sucked down in the eddy of the scandal. It was, at least, a ticklish decision that he had to make; and self-reliant as he was by habit, he began to cherish a longing for advice. It was not to be had directly; but perhaps, he thought, it might be fished for.

Presently after, he sat on one side of his own hearth, with Mr Guest, his head clerk, upon the other, and midway between, at a nicely calculated distance from the fire, a bottle of a particular old wine that had long dwelt unsunned in the foundations of his house. The fog still slept on the wing above the drowned city, where the lamps glimmered like carbuncles; and through the muffle and smother of these fallen clouds, the procession of the town's life was still rolling in through the great arteries with a sound as of a mighty wind. But the room was gay with firelight. In the bottle the acids were long ago resolved; the imperial dye had softened with time, As the colour grows richer in stained windows; and the glow of hot autumn afternoons on hillside vineyards was ready to be set free and to disperse the fogs of London. Insensibly the lawyer melted. There was no man from whom he kept fewer secrets than Mr Guest; and he was not always sure that he kept as many as he meant. Guest had often been on business to the doctor's; he knew Poole; he could scarce have failed to hear of Mr Hyde's familiarity about the house; he might draw conclusions: was it not as well, then, that he should see a letter which put that mystery to rights? and above all since Guest, being a great student and critic of handwriting, would consider the step natural and obliging? The clerk, besides, was a man of counsel; he would scarce read so strange a document without dropping a remark; and by that remark Mr Utterson might shape his future course.

"This is a sad business about Sir Danvers," he said.

"Yes, sir, indeed. It has elicited a great deal of public feeling," returned Guest. "The man, of course, was mad."

"I should like to hear your views on that," replied Utterson. "I have a document here in his handwriting; it is between ourselves, for I scarce know what to do about it; it is an ugly business at the best. But there it is; quite in your way a murderer's autograph."

Guest's eyes brightened, and he sat down at once and studied it with passion. "No, sir," he said: "not mad; but it is an odd hand."

"And by all accounts a very odd writer," added the lawyer.

Just then the servant entered with a note.

"Is that from Dr Jekyll, sir?" inquired the clerk. "I thought I knew the writing. Anything private, Mr Utterson?"

"Only an invitation to dinner. Why? Do you want to see it?"

"One moment. I thank you, sir"; and the clerk laid the two sheets of paper alongside and sedulously compared their contents. "Thank you, sir," he said at last, returning both; "it's a very interesting autograph."

There was a pause, during which Mr Utterson struggled with himself. "Why did you compare them, Guest?" he inquired suddenly.

"Well, sir," returned the clerk, "there's a rather singular resemblance; the two hands are in many points identical: only differently sloped."

"Rather quaint," said Utterson.

"It is, as you say, rather quaint," returned Guest.

"I wouldn't speak of this note, you know," said the master.

"No, sir," said the clerk. "I understand."

But no sooner was Mr Utterson alone that night than he locked the note into his safe, where it reposed from that time forward. "What!" he thought. "Henry Jekyll forge for a murderer!" And his blood ran cold in his veins.

CHAPTER 6

Remarkable Incident of Dr Lanyon

Time ran on; thousands of pounds were offered in reward, for the death of Sir Danvers was resented as a public injury; but Mr Hyde had disappeared out of the ken of the police as though he had never existed. Much of his past was unearthed, indeed, and all disreputable: tales came out of the man's cruelty, at once so callous and violent; of his vile life, of his strange associates, of the hatred that seemed to have surrounded his career; but of his present whereabouts, not a whisper. From the time he had left the house in Soho on the morning of the murder, he was simply blotted out; and gradually, as time drew on, Mr Utterson began to recover from the hotness of his alarm, and to grow more at quiet with himself. The death of Sir Danvers was, to his way of thinking, more than paid for by the disappearance of Mr Hyde. Now that that evil influence had been withdrawn, a new life began for Dr Jekyll. He came out of his seclusion, renewed relations with his friends, became once more their familiar guest and entertainer; and whilst he had always been known for charities, he was now no less distinguished for religion. He was busy, he was much in the open air, he did good; his face seemed to open and brighten, as if with an inward consciousness of service; and for more than two months, the doctor was at peace.

On the 8th of January Utterson had dined at the doctor's with a small party; Lanyon had been there; and the face of the host had looked from one to the other as in the old days when the trio were inseparable friends. On the 12th, and again on the 14th, the door was shut against the lawyer. "The doctor was confined to the house," Poole said, "and saw no one." On the 15th, he tried again, and was again refused; and having now been used for the last two months to see his friend almost daily, he found this return of solitude to weigh upon his spirits. The fifth night he had in Guest to dine with him; and the sixth he betook himself to Dr Lanyon's.

There at least he was not denied admittance; but when he came in, he was shocked at the change which had taken place in the doctor's appearance. He had his death-warrant written legibly upon his face. The rosy man had grown pale; his flesh had fallen away; he was visibly balder and older; and yet it was not so much, these tokens of a swift physical decay that arrested the lawyer's notice, as a look in the eye and quality of manner that seemed to testify to some deep-seated terror of the mind. It was unlikely that the doctor should fear death; and yet that was what Utterson was tempted to suspect. "Yes," he thought; "he is a doctor, he must know his own state and that his days are counted; and the knowledge is more than he can bear." And yet when Utterson remarked on his ill-looks, it was with an air of greatness that Lanyon declared himself a doomed man.

"I have had a shock," he said, "and I shall never recover. It is a question of weeks. Well, life has been pleasant; I liked it; yes, sir, I used to like it. I sometimes think if we knew all, we should be more glad to get away."

"Jekyll is ill, too," observed Utterson. "Have you seen him?"

But Lanyon's face changed, and he held up a trembling hand. "I wish to see or hear no more of Dr Jekyll," he said in a loud, unsteady voice. "I am quite done with that person; and I beg that you will spare me any allusion to one whom I regard as dead."

"Tut-tut," said Mr Utterson; and then after a considerable pause, "Can't I do anything?" he inquired. "We are three very old friends, Lanyon; we shall not live to make others."

"Nothing can be done," returned Lanyon; "ask himself."

"He will not see me," said the lawyer.

"I am not surprised at that," was the reply. "Some day, Utterson, after I am dead, you may perhaps come to learn the right and wrong of this. I cannot tell you. And in the meantime, if you can sit and talk with me of other things, for God's sake, stay and do so; but if you cannot keep clear of this accursed topic, then, in God's name, go, for I cannot bear it."

As soon as he got home, Utterson sat down and wrote to Jekyll, complaining of his exclusion from the house, and asking the cause of this unhappy break with Lanyon; and the next day brought him a long answer, often very pathetically worded, and sometimes darkly mysterious in drift. The quarrel with Lanyon was incurable. "I do not blame our old friend," Jekyll wrote, "but I share his view that we must never meet. I mean from henceforth to lead a life of extreme seclusion; you must not be surprised, nor must you doubt my friendship, if my door is often shut even to you. You must suffer me to go my own dark way. I have brought on myself a punishment and a danger that I cannot name. If I am the chief of sinners, I am the chief of sufferers also. I could not think that this earth contained a place for sufferings and terrors so unmanning; and you can do but one thing, Utterson, to lighten this destiny, and that is to respect my silence." Utterson was amazed; the dark influence of Hyde had been withdrawn, the doctor had returned to his old tasks and amities; a week ago, the prospect had smiled with every promise of a cheerful and an honoured age; and now in a moment, friendship, and peace of mind, and the whole tenor of his life were wrecked. So great and unprepared a change pointed to madness; but in view of Lanyon's manner and words, there must lie for it some deeper ground.

A week afterwards Dr Lanyon took to his bed, and in something less than a fortnight he was dead. The night after the funeral, at which he had been sadly affected, Utterson locked the door of his business room, and sitting there by the light of a melancholy candle, drew out and set before him an envelope addressed by the hand and sealed with the seal of his dead friend. "*Private*: for the hands of G. J. Utterson *alone* and in case of his predecease *to be destroyed unread*," so it was emphatically superscribed; and the lawyer dreaded to behold the contents. "I have buried one friend today," he thought: "what if this should cost me another?" And then he condemned the fear as a disloyalty, and broke the seal. Within there was another enclosure, likewise sealed, and marked upon the cover as "not to be opened till the death or disappearance of Dr Henry Jekyll." Utterson could not trust his eyes. Yes, it was disappearance; here again, as in the mad will which he had long ago restored to its author, here again were the idea of a disappearance and the name of Henry Jekyll bracketed. But in the will, that idea had sprung from the sinister suggestion of the man Hyde; it was set there with a purpose all too plain and horrible. Written by the hand of Lanyon, what should it mean? A great curiosity came on the trustee, to disregard the prohibition and dive at once to the bottom of these mysteries; but professional honour and faith to his dead friend were stringent obligations; and the packet slept in the inmost corner of his private safe.

It is one thing to mortify curiosity, another to conquer it; and it may be doubted if, from that day forth, Utterson desired the society of his surviving friend with the same eagerness. He thought of him kindly; but his thoughts were disquieted and fearful. He went to call indeed; but he was perhaps relieved to be denied admittance; perhaps, in his heart, he preferred to speak with Poole upon the doorstep and surrounded by the air and sounds of the open city, rather than to be admitted into that house of voluntary bondage, and to sit and speak with its inscrutable recluse. Poole had, indeed, no very pleasant news to communicate. The doctor, it appeared, now more than ever confined himself to the cabinet over the laboratory, where he would sometimes even sleep; he was out of spirits, he had grown very silent, he did not read; it seemed as if he had something on his mind. Utterson became so used to the unvarying character of these reports, that he fell off little by little in the frequency of his visits.

CHAPTER 7

Incident at the Window

It chanced on Sunday, when Mr Utterson was on his usual walk with Mr Enfield, that their way lay once again through the by-street; and that when they came in front of the door, both stopped to gaze on it.

"Well," said Enfield, "that story's at an end at least. We shall never see more of Mr Hyde."

"I hope not," said Utterson. "Did I ever tell you that I once saw him, and shared your feeling of repulsion?"

"It was impossible to do the one without the other," returned Enfield. "And by the way, what an ass you must have thought me, not to know that this was a back way to Dr Jekyll's! It was partly your own fault that I found it out, even when I did."

"So you found it out, did you?" said Utterson. "But if that be so, we may step into the court and take a look at the windows. To tell you the truth, I am uneasy about poor Jekyll; and even outside, I feel as if the presence of a friend might do him good."

The court was very cool and a little damp, and full of premature twilight, although the sky, high up overhead, was still bright with sunset. The middle one of the three windows was half-way open; and sitting close beside it, taking the air with an infinite sadness of mien, like some disconsolate prisoner, Utterson saw Dr Jekyll.

"What! Jekyll!" he cried. "I trust you are better."

"I am very low, Utterson," replied the doctor, drearily, "very low. It will not last long, thank God."

"You stay too much indoors," said the lawyer. "You should be out, whipping up the circulation like Mr Enfield and me. (This is my cousin – Mr Enfield – Dr Jekyll.) Come, now; get your hat and take a quick turn with us."

"You are very good," sighed the other. "I should like to very much; but no, no, no, it is quite impossible; I dare not. But indeed, Utterson, I am very glad to see you; this is really a great pleasure; I would ask you and Mr Enfield up, but the place is really not fit."

"Why then," said the lawyer, good-naturedly, "the best thing we can do is to stay down here and speak with you from where we are."

"That is just what I was about to venture to propose," returned the doctor with a smile. But the words were hardly uttered, before the smile was struck out of his face and succeeded by an expression of such abject terror and despair, as froze the very blood of the two gentlemen below. They saw it but for a glimpse, for the window was instantly thrust down; but that glimpse had been sufficient, and they turned and left the court without a word. In silence, too, they traversed the by-street; and it was not until they had come into a neighbouring thoroughfare, where even upon a Sunday there were still some stirrings of life, that Mr Utterson at last turned and looked at his companion. They were both pale; and there was an answering horror in their eyes.

"God forgive us, God forgive us," said Mr Utterson.

But Mr Enfield only nodded his head very seriously and walked on once more in silence.

CHAPTER 8

The Last Night

Mr Utterson was sitting by his fireside one evening after dinner, when he was surprised to receive a visit from Poole.

"Bless me, Poole, what brings you here?" he cried; and then taking a second look at him, "What ails you?" he added; "is the doctor ill?"

"Mr Utterson," said the man, "there is something wrong."

"Take a seat, and here is a glass of wine for you," said the lawyer. "Now, take your time, and tell me plainly what you want."

"You know the doctor's ways, sir," replied Poole, "and how he shuts himself up. Well, he's shut up again in the cabinet; and I don't like it, sir – I wish I may die if I like it. Mr Utterson, sir, I'm afraid."

"Now, my good man," said the lawyer, "be explicit. What are you afraid of?"

"I've been afraid for about a week," returned Poole, doggedly disregarding the question, "and I can bear it no more."

The man's appearance amply bore out his words; his manner was altered for the worse; and except for the moment when he had first announced his terror, he had not once looked the lawyer in the face. Even now, he sat with the glass of wine untasted on his knee, and his eyes directed to a corner of the floor. "I can bear it no more," he repeated.

"Come," said the lawyer, "I see you have some good reason, Poole; I see there is something seriously amiss. Try to tell me what it is."

"I think there's been foul play," said Poole, hoarsely.

"Foul play!" cried the lawyer, a good deal frightened and rather inclined to be irritated in consequence. "What foul play? What does the man mean?"

"I daren't say, sir," was the answer; "but will you come along with me and see for yourself?"

Mr Utterson's only answer was to rise and get his hat and great-coat; but he observed with wonder the greatness of the relief that appeared upon the butler's face, and perhaps with no less, that the wine was still untasted when he set it down to follow.

It was a wild, cold, seasonable night of March, with a pale moon, lying on her back as though the wind had tilted her, and a flying wrack of the most diaphanous and lawny texture. The wind made talking difficult, and flecked the blood into the face. It seemed to have swept the streets unusually bare of passengers, besides; for Mr Utterson thought he had never seen that part of London so deserted. He could have wished it otherwise; never in his life had he been conscious of so sharp a wish to see and touch his fellow-creatures; for struggle as he might, there was borne in upon his mind a crushing anticipation of calamity. The square, when they got there, was all full of wind and dust, and the thin trees in the garden were lashing themselves along the railing. Poole, who had kept all the way a pace or two ahead, now pulled up in the middle of the pavement, and in spite of the biting weather, took off his hat and mopped his brow with a red pocket-handkerchief. But for all the hurry of his coming, these were not the dews of exertion that he wiped away, but the moisture of some strangling anguish; for his face was white and his voice, when he spoke, harsh and broken.

"Well, sir," he said, "here we are, and God grant there be nothing wrong."

"Amen, Poole," said the lawyer.

Thereupon the servant knocked in a very guarded manner; the door was opened on the chain; and a voice asked from within, "Is that you, Poole?"

"It's all right," said Poole. "Open the door." The hall, when they entered it, was brightly lighted up; the fire was built high; and about the hearth the whole of the servants, men and women, stood huddled together like a flock of sheep. At the sight of Mr Utterson, the housemaid broke into hysterical whimpering; and the cook, crying out, "Bless God! it's Mr Utterson," ran forward as if to take him in her arms.

"What, what? Are you all here?" said the lawyer peevishly. "Very irregular, very unseemly; your master would be far from pleased."

"They're all afraid," said Poole.

Blank silence followed, no one protesting; only the maid lifted up her voice and now wept loudly.

"Hold your tongue!" Poole said to her, with a ferocity of accent that testified to his own jangled nerves; and indeed, when the girl had so suddenly raised the note of her lamentation, they had all started and turned toward the inner door with faces of dreadful expectation. "And now," continued the butler, addressing the knife-boy, "reach me a candle, and we'll get this through hands at once." And then he begged Mr Utterson to follow him, and led the way to the back garden.

"Now, sir," said he, "you come as gently as you can. I want you to hear, and I don't want you to be heard. And see here, sir, if by any chance he was to ask you in, don't go."

Mr Utterson's nerves, at this unlooked-for termination, gave a jerk that nearly threw him from his balance; but he re-collected his courage and followed the butler into the laboratory building and through the surgical theatre, with its lumber of crates and bottles, to the foot of the stair. Here Poole motioned him to stand on one side and listen; while he himself, setting down the candle and making a great and obvious call on his resolution, mounted the steps and knocked with a somewhat uncertain hand on the red baize of the cabinet door.

"Mr Utterson, sir, asking to see you," he called; and even as he did so, once more violently signed to the lawyer to give ear.

A voice answered from within: "Tell him I cannot see any one," it said complainingly.

"Thank you, sir," said Poole, with a note of something like triumph in his voice; and taking up his candle, he led Mr Utterson back across the yard and into the great kitchen, where the fire was out and the beetles were leaping on the floor.

"Sir," he said, looking Mr Utterson in the eyes, "was that my master's voice?"

"It seems much changed," replied the lawyer, very pale, but giving look for look.

"Changed? Well, yes, I think so," said the butler. "Have I been twenty years in this man's house, to be deceived about his voice? No, sir; master's made away with; he was made, away with eight days ago, when we heard him cry out upon the name of God; and *who's* in there instead of him, and *why* it stays there, is a thing that cries to Heaven, Mr Utterson!"

"This is a very strange tale, Poole; this is rather a wild tale, my man," said Mr Utterson, biting his finger. "Suppose it were as you suppose, supposing Dr Jekyll to have been – well, murdered, what could induce the murderer to stay? That won't hold water; it doesn't commend itself to reason."

"Well, Mr Utterson, you are a hard man to satisfy, but I'll do it yet," said Poole. "All this last week (you must know) him, or it, or whatever it is that lives in that cabinet, has been crying night and day for some sort of medicine and cannot get it to his mind. It was sometimes his way – the master's, that is – to write his orders on a sheet of paper and throw it on the stair. We've had nothing else this week back; nothing but papers, and a closed door, and the very meals left there to be smuggled in when nobody was looking. Well, sir, every day, ay, and twice and thrice in the same day, there have been orders and complaints, and I have been sent flying to all the wholesale chemists in town. Every time I brought the stuff back, there would be another paper telling me to return it, because it was not pure, and another order to a different firm. This drug is wanted bitter bad, sir, whatever for."

"Have you any of these papers?" asked Mr Utterson.

Poole felt in his pocket and handed out a crumpled note, which the lawyer, bending nearer to the candle, carefully examined. Its contents ran thus: "Dr Jekyll presents his compliments to Messrs. Maw. He assures them that their last sample is impure and quite useless for his present purpose. In the year 18–, Dr J. purchased a somewhat large quantity from Messrs. M. He now begs them to search with the most sedulous care, and should any of the same quality be left, to forward it to him at once. Expense is no consideration. The importance of this to Dr J. can hardly be exaggerated." So far the letter had run composedly enough, but here with a sudden splutter of the pen, the writer's emotion had broken loose. "For God's sake," he had added, "find me some of the old."

"This is a strange note," said Mr Utterson; and then sharply, "How do you come to have it open?"

"The man at Maw's was main angry, sir, and he threw it back to me like so much dirt," returned Poole.

"This is unquestionably the doctor's hand, do you know?" resumed the lawyer.

"I thought it looked like it," said the servant rather sulkily; and then, with another voice, "But what matters hand-of-write?" he said. "I've seen him!"

"Seen him?" repeated Mr Utterson. "Well?"

"That's it!" said Poole. "It was this way. I came suddenly into the theatre from the garden. It seems he had slipped out to look for this drug or whatever it is; for the cabinet door was open, and there he was at the far end of the room digging among the crates. He looked up when I came in, gave a kind of cry, and whipped upstairs into the cabinet. It was but for one minute that I saw him, but the hair stood upon my head like quills. Sir, if that was my master, why had he a mask upon his face? If it was my master, why did he cry out like a rat, and run from me? I have served him long enough. And then..." The man paused and passed his hand over his face.

"These are all very strange circumstances," said Mr Utterson, "but I think I begin to see daylight. Your master, Poole, is plainly seized with one of those maladies that both torture and deform the sufferer; hence, for aught I know, the alteration of his voice; hence the mask and the avoidance of his friends; hence his eagerness to find this drug, by means of which the poor soul retains some hope of ultimate recovery – God grant that he be not deceived! There is my explanation; it is sad enough, Poole, ay, and appalling to consider; but it is plain and natural, hangs well together, and delivers us from all exorbitant alarms."

"Sir," said the butler, turning to a sort of mottled pallor, "that thing was not my master, and there's the truth. My master" here he looked round him and began to whisper – "is a tall, fine build of a man, and this was more of a dwarf." Utterson attempted to protest. "O, sir," cried Poole, "do you think I do not know my master after twenty years? Do you think I do not know where his head comes to in the cabinet door, where I saw him every morning of my life? No, sir, that thing in the mask was never Dr Jekyll – God knows what it was, but it was never Dr Jekyll; and it is the belief of my heart that there was murder done."

"Poole," replied the lawyer, "if you say that, it will become my duty to make certain. Much as I desire to spare your master's feelings, much as I am puzzled by this note which seems to prove him to be still alive, I shall consider it my duty to break in that door."

"Ah Mr Utterson, that's talking!" cried the butler.

"And now comes the second question," resumed Utterson: "Who is going to do it?"

"Why, you and me," was the undaunted reply.

"That's very well said," returned the lawyer; "and whatever comes of it, I shall make it my business to see you are no loser."

"There is an axe in the theatre," continued Poole; "and you might take the kitchen poker for yourself."

The lawyer took that rude but weighty instrument into his hand, and balanced it. "Do you know, Poole," he said, looking up, "that you and I are about to place ourselves in a position of some peril?"

"You may say so, sir, indeed," returned the butler.

"It is well, then, that we should be frank," said the other. "We both think more than we have said; let us make a clean breast. This masked figure that you saw, did you recognize it?"

"Well, sir, it went so quick, and the creature was so doubled up, that I could hardly swear to that," was the answer. "But if you mean, was it Mr Hyde? – why, yes, I think it was! You see, it was much of the same bigness; and it had the same quick, light way with it; and then who else could have got in by the laboratory door? You have not forgot, sir that at the time of the murder he had still the key with him? But that's not all. I don't know, Mr Utterson, if ever you met this Mr Hyde?"

"Yes," said the lawyer, "I once spoke with him."

"Then you must know as well as the rest of us that there was something queer about that gentleman – something that gave a man a turn – I don't know rightly how to say it, sir, beyond this: that you felt it in your marrow kind of cold and thin."

"I own I felt something of what you describe," said Mr Utterson.

"Quite so, sir," returned Poole. "Well, when that masked thing like a monkey jumped from among the chemicals and whipped into the cabinet, it went down my spine like ice. Oh, I know it's not evidence, Mr Utterson. I'm book-learned enough for that; but a man has his feelings, and I give you my Bible-word it was Mr Hyde!"

"Ay, ay," said the lawyer. "My fears incline to the same point. Evil, I fear, founded – evil was sure to come – of that connection. Ay, truly, I believe you; I believe poor Harry is killed; and I believe his murderer (for what purpose, God alone can tell) is still lurking in his victim's room. Well, let our name be vengeance. Call Bradshaw."

The footman came at the summons, very white and nervous.

"Pull yourself together, Bradshaw," said the lawyer. "This suspense, I know, is telling upon all of you; but it is now our intention to make an end of it. Poole, here, and I are going to force our way into the cabinet. If all is well, my shoulders are broad enough to bear the blame. Meanwhile, lest anything should really be amiss, or any malefactor seek to escape by the back, you and the boy must go round the corner with a pair of good sticks and take your post at the laboratory door. We give you ten minutes to get to your stations."

As Bradshaw left, the lawyer looked at his watch. "And now, Poole, let us get to ours," he said; and taking the poker under his arm, led the way into the yard. The scud had banked over the moon, and it was now quite dark. The wind, which only broke in puffs and draughts into that deep well of building, tossed the light of the candle to and fro about their steps, until they came into the shelter of the theatre, where they sat down silently to wait. London hummed solemnly all around; but nearer at hand, the stillness was only broken by the sounds of a footfall moving to and fro along the cabinet floor.

"So it will walk all day, sir," whispered Poole; "ay, and the better part of the night. Only when a new sample comes from the chemist, there's a bit of a break. Ah, it's an ill conscience that's such an enemy to rest! Ah, sir, there's blood foully shed in every step of it! But hark again, a little closer – put your heart in your ears, Mr Utterson, and tell me, is that the doctor's foot?"

The steps fell lightly and oddly, with a certain swing, for all they went so slowly; it was different indeed from the heavy creaking tread of Henry Jekyll. Utterson sighed. "Is there never anything else?" he asked.

Poole nodded. "Once," he said. "Once I heard it weeping!"

"Weeping? how that?" said the lawyer, conscious of a sudden chill of horror.

"Weeping like a woman or a lost soul," said the butler. "I came away with that upon my heart, that I could have wept too."

But now the ten minutes drew to an end. Poole disinterred the axe from under a stack of packing straw; the candle was set upon the nearest table to light them to the attack; and they drew near with bated breath to where that patient foot was still going up and down, up and down, in the quiet of the night.

"Jekyll," cried Utterson, with a loud voice, "I demand to see you." He paused a moment, but there came no reply. "I give you fair warning, our suspicions are aroused, and I must and shall see you," he resumed; "if not by fair means, then by foul! if not of your consent, then by brute force!"

"Utterson," said the voice, "for God's sake, have mercy!"

"Ah, that's not Jekyll's voice – it's Hyde's!" cried Utterson. "Down with the door, Poole!"

Poole swung the axe over his shoulder; the blow shook the building, and the red baize door leaped against the lock and hinges. A dismal screech, as of mere animal terror, rang from the cabinet. Up went the axe again, and again the panels crashed and the frame bounded; four times the blow fell; but the wood was tough and the fittings were of excellent workmanship; and it was not until the fifth, that the lock burst in sunder and the wreck of the door fell inwards on the carpet.

The besiegers, appalled by their own riot and the stillness that had succeeded, stood back a little and peered in. There lay the cabinet before their eyes in the quiet lamplight, a good fire glowing and chattering on the hearth, the kettle singing its thin strain, a drawer or two open, papers neatly set forth on the business-table, and nearer the fire, the things laid out for tea: the quietest room, you would have said, and, but for the glazed presses full of chemicals, the most commonplace that night in London.

Right in the midst there lay the body of a man sorely contorted and still twitching. They drew near on tiptoe, turned it on its back and beheld the face of Edward Hyde. He was dressed in clothes far too large for him, clothes of the doctor's bigness; the cords of his face still moved with a semblance of life, but life was quite gone; and by the crushed phial in the hand and the strong smell of kernels that hung upon the air, Utterson knew that he was looking on the body of a self-destroyer.

"We have come too late," he said sternly, "whether to save or punish. Hyde is gone to his account; and it only remains for us to find the body of your master."

The far greater proportion of the building was occupied by the theatre, which filled almost the whole ground story and was lighted from above, and by the cabinet, which formed an upper story at one end and looked upon the court. A corridor joined the theatre to the door on the by-street; and with this the cabinet communicated separately by a second flight of stairs. There were besides a few dark closets and a spacious cellar. All these they now thoroughly examined. Each closet needed but a glance, for all were empty, and all, by the dust that fell from their doors, had stood long unopened. The cellar, indeed, was filled with crazy lumber, mostly dating from the times of the surgeon who was Jekyll's predecessor; but even as they opened the door they were advertised of the uselessness of further search, by the fall of a perfect mat of cobweb which had for years sealed up the entrance. Nowhere was there any trace of Henry Jekyll, dead or alive.

Poole stamped on the flags of the corridor. "He must be buried here," he said, hearkening to the sound.

"Or he may have fled," said Utterson, and he turned to examine the door in the by-street. It was locked; and lying near by on the flags, they found the key, already stained with rust.

"This does not look like use," observed the lawyer.

"Use!" echoed Poole. "Do you not see, sir, it is broken? much as if a man had stamped on it."

"Ay," continued Utterson, "and the fractures, too, are rusty." The two men looked at each other with a scare. "This is beyond me, Poole," said the lawyer. "Let us go back to the cabinet."

They mounted the stair in silence, and still with an occasional awe-struck glance at the dead body, proceeded more thoroughly to examine the contents of the cabinet. At one table, there were traces of chemical work, various measured heaps of some white salt being laid on glass saucers, as though for an experiment in which the unhappy man had been prevented.

"That is the same drug that I was always bringing him," said Poole; and even as he spoke, the kettle with a startling noise boiled over.

This brought them to the fireside, where the easy-chair was drawn cosily up, and the tea-things stood ready to the sitter's elbow, the very sugar in the cup. There were several books on a shelf; one lay beside the tea-things open, and Utterson was amazed to find it a copy of a pious work, for which Jekyll had several times expressed a great esteem, annotated, in his own hand, with startling blasphemies.

Next, in the course of their review of the chamber, the searchers came to the cheval glass, into whose depths they looked with an involuntary horror. But it was so turned as to show them nothing but the rosy glow playing on the roof, the fire sparkling in a hundred repetitions along the glazed front of the presses, and their own pale and fearful countenances stooping to look in.

"This glass have seen some strange things, sir," whispered Poole.

"And surely none stranger than itself," echoed the lawyer in the same tones. "For what did Jekyll" – he caught himself up at the word with a start, and then conquering the weakness – "what could Jekyll want with it?" he said.

"You may say that!" said Poole. Next they turned to the business-table. On the desk among the neat array of papers, a large envelope was uppermost, and bore, in the doctor's hand, the name of Mr Utterson. The lawyer unsealed it, and several enclosures fell to the floor. The first was a will, drawn in the same eccentric terms as the one which he had returned six months before, to serve as a testament in case of death and as a deed of gift in case of disappearance; but, in place of the name of Edward Hyde, the lawyer, with indescribable amazement, read the name of Gabriel John Utterson. He looked at Poole, and then back at the paper, and last of all at the dead malefactor stretched upon the carpet.

"My head goes round," he said. "He has been all these days in possession; he had no cause to like me; he must have raged to see himself displaced; and he has not destroyed this document."

He caught up the next paper; it was a brief note in the doctor's hand and dated at the top.

"O Poole!" the lawyer cried, "he was alive and here this day. He cannot have been disposed of in so short a space, he must be still alive, he must have fled! And then, why fled? and how? and in that case, can we venture to declare this suicide? Oh, we must be careful. I foresee that we may yet involve your master in some dire catastrophe."

"Why don't you read it, sir?" asked Poole.

"Because I fear," replied the lawyer solemnly. "God grant I have no cause for it!" And with that he brought the paper to his eyes and read as follows:

MY DEAR UTTERSON – When this shall fall into your hands, I shall have disappeared, under what circumstances I have not the penetration to foresee, but my instinct and all the circumstances of my

nameless situation tell me that the end is sure and must be early. Go then,
and first read the narrative which Lanyon warned me he was to place in
your hands; and if you care to hear more, turn to the confession of

Your unworthy and unhappy friend,
HENRY JEKYLL.

"There was a third enclosure?" asked Utterson.

"Here, sir," said Poole, and gave into his hands a considerable
packet sealed in several places.

The lawyer put it in his pocket. "I would say nothing of this
paper. If your master has fled or is dead, we may at least save his
credit. It is now ten; I must go home and read these documents
in quiet; but I shall be back before midnight, when we shall send
for the police."

They went out, locking the door of the theatre behind them;
and Utterson, once more leaving the servants gathered about the
fire in the hall, trudged back to his office to read the two narratives
in which this mystery was now to be explained.

CHAPTER 9

Dr Lanyon's Narrative

On the ninth of January, now four days ago, I received by the evening delivery a registered envelope, addressed in the hand of my colleague and old school-companion, Henry Jekyll. I was a good deal surprised by this; for we were by no means in the habit of correspondence; I had seen the man, dined with him, indeed, the night before; and I could imagine nothing in our intercourse that should justify formality of registration. The contents increased my wonder; for this is how the letter ran:

10th December, 18–
DEAR LANYON – You are one of my oldest friends; and although we may have differed at times on scientific questions, I cannot remember, at least on my side, any break in our affection. There was never a day when, if you had said to me, 'Jekyll, my life, my honour, my reason, depend upon you,' I would not have sacrificed my left hand to help you. Lanyon, my life, my honour my reason, are all at your mercy; if you fail me tonight I am lost. You might suppose, after this preface, that I am going to ask you for something dishonourable to grant. Judge for yourself.

I want you to postpone all other engagements for tonight – ay, even if you were summoned to the bedside of an emperor; to take a cab, unless your carriage should be actually at the door; and with this letter in your hand for consultation, to drive straight to my house. Poole, my butler, has his orders; you will find, him waiting your arrival with a locksmith. The door of my cabinet is then to be forced: and you are to go in alone; to open the glazed press (letter E) on the left hand, breaking the lock if it be shut; and to draw out, with all its contents as they stand, the fourth drawer from the top or (which is the same thing) the third from the bottom. In my extreme distress of wind, I have a morbid fear of misdirecting you; but even if I am in error, you may know the right drawer by its contents: some powders, a phial and a paper book. This drawer I beg of you to carry back with you to Cavendish Square exactly as it stands.

That is the first part of the service: now for the second. You should be back, if you set out at once on the receipt of this, long before midnight; but I will leave you that amount of margin, not only in the fear of one of those obstacles that can neither be prevented nor foreseen, but because an hour when your servants are in bed is to be preferred for what will then remain to do. At midnight, then, I have to ask you to be alone in your consulting-room, to admit with your own hand into the house a man who will present himself in my name, and to place in his hands the drawer that you will have brought with you from my cabinet. Then you will have played your part and earned my gratitude completely. Five minutes afterwards, if you insist upon an explanation, you will have understood that these arrangements are of capital importance; and that by the neglect of one of them, fantastic as they must appear, you might have charged your conscience with my death or the shipwreck of my reason.

Confident as I am that you will not trifle with this appeal, my heart sinks and my hand trembles at the bare thought of such a possibility. Think of me at this hour, in a strange place, labouring under a blackness of distress that no fancy can exaggerate, and yet well aware that, if you will but punctually serve me, my troubles will roll away like a story that is told. Serve me, my dear Lanyon, and save

Your friend,

H.J.

P.S. – I had already sealed this up when a fresh terror struck upon my soul. It is possible that the post office may fail me, and this letter not come into your hands until tomorrow morning. In that case, dear Lanyon, do my errand when it shall be most convenient for you in the course of the day; and once more expect my messenger at midnight. It may then already be too late; and if that night passes without event, you will know that you have seen the last of Henry Jekyll.

Upon the reading of this letter, I made sure my colleague was insane; but till that was proved beyond the possibility of doubt, I felt bound to do as he requested. The less I understood of this farrago, the less I was in a position to judge of its importance; and an appeal so worded could not be set aside without a grave responsibility. I rose accordingly from table, got into a hansom, and drove straight to Jekyll's house. The butler was awaiting my arrival; he had received by the same post as mine a registered letter of instruction, and had sent at once for a locksmith and a carpenter. The tradesmen came while we were yet speaking; and we moved in a body to old Dr Denman's surgical theatre, from which (as you are doubtless aware) Jekyll's private cabinet is most conveniently entered. The door was very strong, the lock excellent; the carpenter avowed he would have great trouble and have to do much damage, if force were to be used; and the locksmith was near despair. But this last was a handy fellow, and after two hours' work, the door stood open. The press marked E was unlocked; and I took out the drawer, had it filled up with straw and tied in a sheet, and returned with it to Cavendish Square.

Here I proceeded to examine its contents. The powders were neatly enough made up, but not with the nicety of the dispensing chemist; so that it was plain they were of Jekyll's private manufacture; and when I opened one of the wrappers I found what seemed to me a simple crystalline salt of a white colour. The phial, to which I next turned my attention, might have been about half full of a blood-red liquor, which was highly pungent to the sense of smell and seemed to me to contain phosphorus and some volatile ether. At the other ingredients I could make no guess. The book was an ordinary version book and contained little but a series of dates. These covered a period of many years, but I observed that the entries ceased nearly a year ago and quite abruptly. Here and there a brief remark was appended to a date, usually no more than a single word: "double" occurring perhaps six times in a total of several hundred entries; and once very early in the list and followed by several marks of exclamation, "total failure!!!" All this, though it whetted my curiosity, told me little that was definite. Here were a phial of some tincture, a paper of some salt, and the record of a series of experiments that had led (like too many of Jekyll's investigations) to no end of practical usefulness. How could the presence of these articles in my house affect either the honour, the sanity, or the life of my flighty colleague? If his messenger could go to one place, why could he not go to another? And even granting some impediment, why was this gentleman to be received by me in secret? The more I reflected the more convinced I grew that I was dealing with a case of cerebral disease: and though I dismissed my servants to bed, I loaded an old revolver, that I might be found in some posture of self-defence.

Twelve o'clock had scarce rung out over London, ere the knocker sounded very gently on the door. I went myself at the summons, and found a small man crouching against the pillars of the portico.

"Are you come from Dr Jekyll?" I asked.

He told me "yes" by a constrained gesture; and when I had bidden him enter, he did not obey me without a searching backward glance into the darkness of the square. There was a policeman not far off, advancing with his bull's eye open; and at the sight, I thought my visitor started and made greater haste.

These particulars struck me, I confess, disagreeably; and as I followed him into the bright light of the consulting-room, I kept my hand ready on my weapon. Here, at last, I had a chance of clearly seeing him. I had never set eyes on him before, so much was certain. He was small, as I have said; I was struck besides with the shocking expression of his face, with his remarkable combination of great muscular activity and great apparent debility of constitution, and – last but not least – with the odd, subjective disturbance caused by his neighbourhood. This bore some resemblance to incipient rigour, and was accompanied by a marked sinking of the pulse. At the time, I set it down to some idiosyncratic, personal distaste, and merely wondered at the acuteness of the symptoms; but I have since had reason to believe the cause to lie much deeper in the nature of man, and to turn on some nobler hinge than the principle of hatred.

This person (who had thus, from the first moment of his entrance, struck in me what I can only describe as a disgustful curiosity) was dressed in a fashion that would have made an ordinary person laughable; his clothes, that is to say, although they were of rich and sober fabric, were enormously too large for him in every measurement – the trousers hanging on his legs and rolled up to keep them from the ground, the waist of the coat below his haunches, and the collar sprawling wide upon his shoulders. Strange to relate, this ludicrous accoutrement was far from moving me to laughter. Rather, as there was something abnormal and misbegotten in the very essence of the creature that now faced me – something seizing, surprising, and revolting – this fresh disparity seemed but to fit in with and to reinforce it; so that to my interest in the man's nature and character, there was added a curiosity as to his origin, his life, his fortune and status in the world.

These observations, though they have taken so great a space to be set down in, were yet the work of a few seconds. My visitor was, indeed, on fire with sombre excitement.

"Have you got it?" he cried. "Have you got it?" And so lively was his impatience that he even laid his hand upon my arm and sought to shake me.

I put him back, conscious at his touch of a certain icy pang along my blood. "Come, sir," said I. "You forget that I have not yet the pleasure of your acquaintance. Be seated, if you please." And I showed him an example, and sat down myself in my customary seat and with as fair an imitation of my ordinary manner to a patient, as the lateness of the hour, the nature of my pre-occupations, and the horror I had of my visitor, would suffer me to muster.

"I beg your pardon, Dr Lanyon," he replied civilly enough. "What you say is very well founded; and my impatience has shown its heels to my politeness. I come here at the instance of your colleague, Dr Henry Jekyll, on a piece of business of some moment; and I understood..." He paused and put his hand to his throat, and I could see, in spite of his collected manner, that he was wrestling against the approaches of the hysteria – "I understood, a drawer..."

But here I took pity on my visitor's suspense, and some perhaps on my own growing curiosity.

"There it is, sir," said I, pointing to the drawer, where it lay on the floor behind a table and still covered with the sheet.

He sprang to it, and then paused, and laid his hand upon his heart: I could hear his teeth grate with the convulsive action of his jaws; and his face was so ghastly to see that I grew alarmed both for his life and reason.

"Compose yourself," said I.

He turned a dreadful smile to me, and as if with the decision of despair, plucked away the sheet. At sight of the contents, he uttered one loud sob of such immense relief that I sat petrified. And the next moment, in a voice that was already fairly well under control, "Have you a graduated glass?" he asked.

I rose from my place with something of an effort and gave him what he asked.

He thanked me with a smiling nod, measured out a few minims of the red tincture and added one of the powders. The mixture, which was at first of a reddish hue, began, in proportion as the crystals melted, to brighten in colour, to effervesce audibly, and to throw off small fumes of vapour. Suddenly and at the same moment, the ebullition ceased and the compound changed to a dark purple, which faded again more slowly to a watery green. My visitor, who had watched these metamorphoses with a keen eye, smiled, set down the glass upon the table, and then turned and looked upon me with an air of scrutiny.

"And now," said he, "to settle what remains. Will you be wise? will you be guided? will you suffer me to take this glass in my hand and to go forth from your house without further parley? or has the greed of curiosity too much command of you? Think before you answer, for it shall be done as you decide. As you decide, you shall be left as you were before, and neither richer nor wiser, unless the sense of service rendered to a man in mortal distress may be counted as a kind of riches of the soul. Or, if you shall so prefer to choose, a new province of knowledge and new avenues to fame and power shall be laid open to you, here, in this room, upon the instant; and your sight shall be blasted by a prodigy to stagger the unbelief of Satan."

"Sir," said I, affecting a coolness that I was far from truly possessing, "you speak enigmas, and you will perhaps not wonder that I hear you with no very strong impression of belief. But I have gone too far in the way of inexplicable services to pause before I see the end."

"It is well," replied my visitor. "Lanyon, you remember your vows: what follows is under the seal of our profession. And now, you who have so long been bound to the most narrow and material views, you who have denied the virtue of transcendental medicine, you who have derided your superiors – behold!"

He put the glass to his lips and drank at one gulp. A cry followed; he reeled, staggered, clutched at the table and held on, staring with injected eyes, gasping with open mouth; and as I looked there came, I thought, a change – he seemed to swell – his face became suddenly black and the features seemed to melt and alter – and the next moment, I had sprung to my feet and leaped back against the wall, my arm raised to shield me from that prodigy, my mind submerged in terror.

"O God!" I screamed, and "O God!" again and again; for there before my eyes – pale and shaken, and half-fainting, and groping before him with his hands, like a man restored from death – there stood Henry Jekyll!

What he told me in the next hour, I cannot bring my mind to set on paper. I saw what I saw, I heard what I heard, and my soul sickened at it; and yet now when that sight has faded from my eyes, I ask myself if I believe it, and I cannot answer. My life is shaken to its roots; sleep has left me; the deadliest terror sits by me at all hours of the day and night; I feel that my days are numbered, and that I must die; and yet I shall die incredulous. As for the moral turpitude that man unveiled to me, even with tears of penitence, I cannot, even in memory, dwell on it without a start of horror. I will say but one thing, Utterson, and that (if you can bring your mind to credit it) will be more than enough. The creature who crept into my house that night was, on Jekyll's own confession, known by the name of Hyde and hunted for in every corner of the land as the murderer of Carew.

HASTIE LANYON

CHAPTER 10

Henry Jekyll's Full Statement of the Case

I was born in the year 18— to a large fortune, endowed besides with excellent parts, inclined by nature to industry, fond of the respect of the wise and good among my fellow-men, and thus, as might have been supposed, with every guarantee of an honourable and distinguished future. And indeed the worst of my faults was a certain impatient gaiety of disposition, such as has made the happiness of many, but such as I found it hard to reconcile with my imperious desire to carry my head high, and wear a more than commonly grave countenance before the public. Hence it came about that I concealed my pleasures; and that when I reached years of reflection, and began to look round me and take stock of my progress and position in the world, I stood already committed to a profound duplicity of life. Many a man would have even blazoned such irregularities as I was guilty of; but from the high views that I had set before me, I regarded and hid them with an almost morbid sense of shame. It was thus rather the exacting nature of my aspirations than any particular degradation in my faults, that made me what I was, and, with even a deeper trench than in the majority of men, severed in me those provinces of good and ill which divide and compound man's dual nature. In this case, I was driven to reflect deeply and inveterately on that hard law of life, which lies at the root of religion and is one of the most plentiful springs of distress. Though so profound a double-dealer,

I was in no sense a hypocrite; both sides of me were in dead earnest; I was no more myself when I laid aside restraint and plunged in shame, than when I laboured, in the eye of day, at the furtherance of knowledge or the relief of sorrow and suffering. And it chanced that the direction of my scientific studies, which led wholly toward the mystic and the transcendental, reacted and shed a strong light on this consciousness of the perennial war among my members. With every day, and from both sides of my intelligence, the moral and the intellectual, I thus drew steadily nearer to that truth, by whose partial discovery I have been doomed to such a dreadful shipwreck: that man is not truly one, but truly two. I say two, because the state of my own knowledge does not pass beyond that point. Others will follow, others will outstrip me on the same lines; and I hazard the guess that man will be ultimately known for a mere polity of multifarious, incongruous, and independent denizens. I, for my part, from the nature of my life, advanced infallibly in one direction and in one direction only. It was on the moral side, and in my own person, that I learned to recognize the thorough and primitive duality of man; I saw that, of the two natures that contended in the field of my consciousness, even if I could rightly be said to be either, it was only because I was radically both; and from an early date, even before the course of my scientific discoveries had begun to suggest the most naked possibility of such a miracle, I had learned to dwell with pleasure, as a beloved daydream, on the thought of the separation of these elements. If each, I told myself, could but be housed in separate identities, life would be relieved of all that was unbearable; the unjust delivered from the aspirations might go his way, and remorse of his more upright twin; and the just could walk steadfastly and securely on his upward path, doing the good things in which he found his pleasure, and no longer exposed to disgrace and penitence by the hands of this extraneous evil. It was the curse of mankind that these incongruous fagots were thus bound together – that in the agonized womb of consciousness, these polar twins should be continuously struggling. How, then, were they dissociated?

I was so far in my reflections when, as I have said, a side-light began to shine upon the subject from the laboratory table. I began to perceive more deeply than it has ever yet been stated, the trembling immateriality, the mist-like transience of this seemingly so solid body in which we walk attired. Certain agents I found to have the power to shake and to pluck back that fleshly vestment, even as a wind might toss the curtains of a pavilion. For two good reasons, I will not enter deeply into this scientific branch of my confession. First, because I have been made to learn that the doom and burthen of our life is bound for ever on man's shoulders, and when the attempt is made to cast it off, it but returns upon us with more unfamiliar and more awful pressure. Second, because, as my narrative will make, alas! too evident, my discoveries were incomplete. Enough, then, that I not only recognized my natural body for the mere aura and effulgence of certain of the powers that made up my spirit, but managed to compound a drug by which these powers should be dethroned from their supremacy, and a second form and countenance substituted, none the less natural to me because they were the expression, and bore the stamp, of lower elements in my soul.

I hesitated long before I put this theory to the test of practice. I knew well that I risked death; for any drug that so potently controlled and shook the very fortress of identity, might by the least scruple of an overdose or at the least inopportunity in the moment of exhibition, utterly blot out that immaterial tabernacle which I looked to it to change. But the temptation of a discovery so singular and profound, at last overcame the suggestions of alarm. I had long since prepared my tincture; I purchased at once, from a firm of wholesale chemists, a large quantity of a particular salt which I knew, from my experiments, to be the last ingredient required; and late one accursed night, I compounded the elements, watched them boil and smoke together in the glass, and when the ebullition had subsided, with a strong glow of courage, drank off the potion.

The most racking pangs succeeded: a grinding in the bones, deadly nausea, and a horror of the spirit that cannot be exceeded at the hour of birth or death. Then these agonies began swiftly to subside, and I came to myself as if out of a great sickness. There was something strange in my sensations, something indescribably new and, from its very novelty, incredibly sweet. I felt younger, lighter, happier in body; within I was conscious of a heady recklessness, a current of disordered sensual images running like a millrace in my fancy, a solution of the bonds of obligation, an unknown but not an innocent freedom of the soul. I knew myself, at the first breath of this new life, to be more wicked, tenfold more wicked, sold a slave to my original evil; and the thought, in that moment, braced and delighted me like wine. I stretched out my hands, exulting in the freshness of these sensations; and in the act, I was suddenly aware that I had lost in stature.

There was no mirror, at that date, in my room; that which stands beside me as I write, was brought there later on and for the very purpose of these transformations. The night, however, was far gone into the morning – the morning, black as it was, was nearly ripe for the conception of the day – the inmates of my house were locked in the most rigorous hours of slumber; and I determined, flushed as I was with hope and triumph, to venture in my new shape as far as to my bedroom. I crossed the yard, wherein the constellations looked down upon me, I could have thought, with wonder, the first creature of that sort that their unsleeping vigilance had yet disclosed to them; I stole through the corridors, a stranger in my own house; and coming to my room, I saw for the first time the appearance of Edward Hyde.

I must here speak by theory alone, saying not that which I know, but that which I suppose to be most probable. The evil side of my nature, to which I had now transferred the stamping efficacy, was less robust and less developed than the good which I had just deposed. Again, in the course of my life, which had been, after all, nine-tenths a life of effort, virtue and control, it had been much less exercised and much less exhausted. And hence, as I think, it came about that Edward Hyde was so much smaller, slighter and younger than Henry Jekyll. Even as good shone upon the countenance of the one, evil was written broadly and plainly on the face of the other. Evil besides (which I must still believe to be the lethal side of man) had left on that body an imprint of deformity and decay. And yet when I looked upon that ugly idol in the glass, I was conscious of no repugnance, rather of a leap of welcome. This, too, was myself. It seemed natural and human. In my eyes it bore a livelier image of the spirit, it seemed more express and single, than the imperfect and divided countenance I had been hitherto accustomed to call mine. And in so far I was doubtless right. I have observed that when I wore the semblance of Edward Hyde, none could come near to me at first without a visible misgiving of the flesh. This, as I take it, was because all human beings, as we meet them, are commingled out of good and evil: and Edward Hyde, alone in the ranks of mankind, was pure evil.

I lingered but a moment at the mirror: the second and conclusive experiment had yet to be attempted; it yet remained to be seen if I had lost my identity beyond redemption and must flee before daylight from a house that was no longer mine; and hurrying back to my cabinet, I once more prepared and drank the cup, once more suffered the pangs of dissolution, and came to myself once more with the character, the stature and the face of Henry Jekyll.

That night I had come to the fatal cross-roads. Had I approached my discovery in a more noble spirit, had I risked the experiment while under the empire of generous or pious aspirations, all must have been otherwise, and from these agonies of death and birth, I had come forth an angel instead of a fiend. The drug had no discriminating action; it was neither diabolical nor divine; it but shook the doors of the prison-house of my disposition; and like the captives of Philippi, that which stood within ran forth. At that time my virtue slumbered; my evil, kept awake by ambition, was alert and swift to seize the occasion; and the thing that was projected was Edward Hyde. Hence, although I had now two characters as well as two appearances, one was wholly evil, and the other was still the old Henry Jekyll, that incongruous compound of whose reformation and improvement I had already learned to despair. The movement was thus wholly toward the worse.

Even at that time, I had not yet conquered my aversion to the dryness of a life of study. I would still be merrily disposed at times; and as my pleasures were (to say the least) undignified, and I was not only well known and highly considered, but growing towards the elderly man, this incoherency of my life was daily growing more unwelcome. It was on this side that my new power tempted me until I fell in slavery. I had but to drink the cup, to doff at once the body of the noted professor, and to assume, like a thick cloak, that of Edward Hyde. I smiled at the notion; it seemed to me at the time to be humorous; and I made my preparations with the most studious care. I took and furnished that house in Soho, to which

Hyde was tracked by the police; and engaged as housekeeper a creature whom I well knew to be silent and unscrupulous. On the other side, I announced to my servants that a Mr Hyde (whom I described) was to have full liberty and power about my house in the square; and to parry mishaps, I even called and made myself a familiar object, in my second character. I next drew up that will to which you so much objected; so that if anything befell me in the person of Dr Jekyll, I could enter on that of Edward Hyde without pecuniary loss. And thus fortified, as I supposed, on every side, I began to profit by the strange immunities of my position.

Men have before hired bravos to transact their crimes, while their own person and reputation sat under shelter. I was the first that ever did so for his pleasures. I was the first that could thus plod in the public eye with a load of genial respectability, and in a moment, like a schoolboy, strip off these lendings and spring headlong into the sea of liberty. But for me, in my impenetrable mantle, the safety was complete. Think of it – I did not even exist! Let me but escape into my laboratory door, give me but a second or two to mix and swallow the draught that I had always standing ready; and whatever he had done, Edward Hyde would pass away like the stain of breath upon a mirror; and there in his stead, quietly at home, trimming the midnight lamp in his study, a man who could afford to laugh at suspicion, would be Henry Jekyll.

The pleasures which I made haste to seek in my disguise were, as I have said, undignified; I would scarce use a harder term. But in the hands of Edward Hyde, they soon began to turn toward the monstrous. When I would come back from these excursions, I was often plunged into a kind of wonder at my vicarious depravity. This familiar that I called out of my own soul, and sent forth alone to do his good pleasure, was a being inherently malign and villainous; his every act and thought centred on self; drinking pleasure with bestial avidity from any degree of torture to another; relentless like a man of stone. Henry Jekyll stood at times aghast before the acts of Edward Hyde; but the situation was apart from ordinary laws, and insidiously relaxed the grasp of conscience. It was Hyde, after all, and Hyde alone, that was guilty. Jekyll was no worse; he woke again to his good qualities seemingly unimpaired; he would even make haste, where it was possible, to undo the evil done by Hyde. And thus his conscience slumbered.

Into the details of the infamy at which I thus connived (for even now I can scarce grant that I committed it) I have no design of entering; I mean but to point out the warnings and the successive steps with which my chastisement approached. I met with one accident which, as it brought on no consequence, I shall no more than mention. An act of cruelty to a child aroused against me the anger of a passer-by, whom I recognized the other day in the person of your kinsman; the doctor and the child's family joined him; there were moments when I feared for my life; and at last, in order to pacify their too just resentment, Edward Hyde had to bring them to the door, and pay them in a cheque drawn in the name of Henry Jekyll. But this danger was easily eliminated from the future, by opening an account at another bank in the name of Edward Hyde himself; and when, by sloping my own hand backward, I had supplied my double with a signature, I thought I sat beyond the reach of fate.

Some two months before the murder of Sir Danvers, I had been out for one of my adventures, had returned at a late hour, and woke the next day in bed with somewhat odd sensations. It was in vain I looked about me; in vain I saw the decent furniture and tall proportions of my room in the square; in vain that I recognized the pattern of the bed curtains and the design of the mahogany frame; something still kept insisting that I was not where I was, that I had not wakened where I seemed to be, but in the little room in Soho where I was accustomed to sleep in the body of Edward Hyde. I smiled to myself, and, in my psychological way began lazily to inquire into the elements of this illusion, occasionally, even as I did so, dropping back into a comfortable morning doze. I was still so engaged when, in one of my more wakeful moments, my eyes fell upon my hand. Now the hand of Henry Jekyll (as you have often remarked) was professional in shape and size: it was large, firm, white and comely. But the hand which I now saw, clearly enough, in the yellow light of a mid-London morning, lying half shut on the bedclothes, was lean, corded, knuckly, of a dusky pallor and thickly shaded with a swart growth of hair. It was the hand of Edward Hyde.

I must have stared upon it for near half a minute, sunk as I was in the mere stupidity of wonder, before terror woke up in my breast as sudden and startling as the crash of cymbals; and bounding from my bed, I rushed to the mirror. At the sight that met my eyes, my blood was changed into something exquisitely thin and icy. Yes, I had gone to bed Henry Jekyll, I had awakened Edward Hyde. How was this to be explained? I asked myself, and then, with another bound of terror – how was it to be remedied? It was well on in the morning; the servants were up; all my drugs were in the cabinet – a long journey down two pairs of stairs, through the back passage, across the open court and through the anatomical theatre, from where I was then standing horror-struck. It might indeed be possible to cover my face; but of what use was that, when I was unable to conceal the alteration in my stature?

And then with an overpowering sweetness of relief, it came back upon my mind that the servants were already used to the coming and going of my second self. I had soon dressed, as well as I was able, in clothes of my own size: had soon passed through the house, where Bradshaw stared and drew back at seeing Mr Hyde at such an hour and in such a strange array; and ten minutes later, Dr Jekyll had returned to his own shape and was sitting down, with a darkened brow, to make a feint of breakfasting.

Small indeed was my appetite. This inexplicable incident, this reversal of my previous experience, seemed, like the Babylonian finger on the wall, to be spelling out the letters of my judgment; and I began to reflect more seriously than ever before on the issues and possibilities of my double existence. That part of me which I had the power of projecting, had lately been much exercised and nourished; it had seemed to me of late as though the body of Edward Hyde had grown in stature, as though (when I wore that form) I were conscious of a more generous tide of blood; and I began to spy a danger that, if this were much prolonged, the balance of my nature might be permanently overthrown, the power of voluntary change be forfeited, and the character of Edward Hyde become irrevocably mine. The power of the drug had not been always equally displayed. Once, very early in my career, it had totally failed me; since then I had been obliged on more than one occasion to double, and once, with infinite risk of death, to treble the amount; and these rare uncertainties had cast hitherto the sole shadow on my contentment. Now, however, and in the light of that morning's accident, I was led to remark that whereas, in the beginning, the difficulty had been to throw off the body of Jekyll, it had of late gradually but decidedly transferred itself to the other side. All things therefore seemed to point to this: that I was slowly losing hold of my original and better self, and becoming slowly incorporated with my second and worse.

Between these two, I now felt I had to choose. My two natures had memory in common, but all other faculties were most unequally shared between them. Jekyll (who was composite) now with the most sensitive apprehensions, now with a greedy gusto, projected and shared in the pleasures and adventures of Hyde; but Hyde was indifferent to Jekyll, or but remembered him as the mountain bandit remembers the cavern in which he conceals himself from pursuit. Jekyll had more than a father's interest; Hyde had more than a son's indifference. To cast in my lot with Jekyll was to die to those appetites which I had long secretly indulged and had of late begun to pamper. To cast it in with Hyde was to die to a thousand interests and aspirations, and to become, at a blow and for ever, despised and friendless. The bargain might appear unequal; but there was still another consideration in the scales; for while Jekyll would suffer smartingly in the fires of abstinence, Hyde would be not even conscious of all that he had lost. Strange as my circumstances were, the terms of this debate are as old and commonplace as man; much the same inducements and alarms cast the die for any tempted and trembling sinner; and it fell out with me, as it falls with so vast a majority of my fellows, that I chose the better part and was found wanting in the strength to keep to it.

Yes, I preferred the elderly and discontented doctor, surrounded by friends and cherishing honest hopes; and bade a resolute farewell to the liberty, the comparative youth, the light step, leaping impulses and secret pleasures, that I had enjoyed in the disguise of Hyde. I made this choice perhaps with some unconscious reservation, for I neither gave up the house in Soho, nor destroyed the clothes of Edward Hyde, which still lay ready in my cabinet. For two months, however, I was true to my determination; for two months I led a life of such severity as I had never before attained to, and enjoyed the compensations of an approving conscience. But time began at last to obliterate the freshness of my alarm; the praises of conscience began to grow into a thing of course; I began to be tortured with throes and longings, as of Hyde struggling after freedom; and at last, in an hour of moral weakness, I once again compounded and swallowed the transforming draught.

I do not suppose that, when a drunkard reasons with himself upon his vice, he is once out of five hundred times affected by the dangers that he runs through his brutish, physical insensibility; neither had I, long as I had considered my position, made enough allowance for the complete moral insensibility and insensate readiness to evil, which were the leading characters of Edward Hyde. Yet it was by these that I was punished. My devil had been long caged, he came out roaring. I was conscious, even when I took the draught, of a more unbridled, a more furious propensity to ill. It must have been this, I suppose, that stirred in my soul that tempest of impatience with which I listened to the civilities of my unhappy victim; I declare, at least, before God, no man morally sane could have been guilty of that crime upon so pitiful a provocation; and that I struck in no more reasonable spirit than that in which a sick child may break a plaything. But I had voluntarily stripped myself of all those balancing instincts by which even the worst of us continues to walk with some degree of steadiness among temptations; and in my case, to be tempted, however slightly, was to fall.

Instantly the spirit of hell awoke in me and raged. With a transport of glee, I mauled the unresisting body, tasting delight from every blow; and it was not till weariness had begun to succeed, that I was suddenly, in the top fit of my delirium, struck through the heart by a cold thrill of terror. A mist dispersed; I saw my life to be forfeit; and fled from the scene of these excesses, at once glorying and trembling, my lust of evil gratified and stimulated, my love of life screwed to the topmost peg. I ran to the house in Soho, and (to make assurance doubly sure) destroyed my papers; thence I set out through the lamplit streets, in the same divided ecstasy of mind, gloating on my crime, light-headedly devising others in the future, and yet still hastening and still hearkening in my wake for the steps of the avenger. Hyde had a song upon his lips as he compounded the draught, and as he drank it, pledged the dead man. The pangs of transformation had not done tearing him, before Henry Jekyll, with streaming tears of gratitude and remorse, had fallen upon his knees and lifted his clasped hands to God. The veil of self-indulgence was rent from head to foot, I saw my life as a whole: I followed it up from the days of childhood, when I had walked with my father's hand, and through the self-denying toils of my professional life, to arrive again and again, with the same sense of unreality, at the damned horrors of the evening. I could have screamed aloud; I sought with tears and prayers to smother down the crowd of hideous images and sounds with which my memory swarmed against me; and still, between the petitions, the ugly face of my iniquity stared into my soul. As the acuteness of this remorse began to die away, it was succeeded by a sense of joy. The problem of my conduct was solved. Hyde was thenceforth impossible; whether I would or not, I was now confined to the better part of my existence; and oh, how I rejoiced to think it! with what willing humility, I embraced anew the restrictions of natural life! with what sincere renunciation, I locked the door by which I had so often gone and come, and ground the key under my heel!

The next day, came the news that the murder had been overlooked, that the guilt of Hyde was patent to the world, and that the victim was a man high in public estimation. It was not only a crime, it had been a tragic folly. I think I was glad to know it; I think I was glad to have my better impulses thus buttressed and guarded by the terrors of the scaffold. Jekyll was now my city of refuge; let but Hyde peep out an instant, and the hands of all men would be raised to take and slay him.

I resolved in my future conduct to redeem the past; and I can say with honesty that my resolve was fruitful of some good. You know yourself how earnestly in the last months of last year, I laboured to relieve suffering; you know that much was done for others, and that the days passed quietly, almost happily for myself. Nor can I truly say that I wearied of this beneficent and innocent life; I think instead that I daily enjoyed it more completely; but I was still cursed with my duality of purpose; and as the first edge of my penitence wore off, the lower side of me, so long indulged, so recently chained down, began to growl for licence. Not that I dreamed of resuscitating Hyde; the bare idea of that would startle me to frenzy: no, it was in my own person, that I was once more tempted to trifle with my conscience; and it was as an ordinary secret sinner, that I at last fell before the assaults of temptation.

There comes an end to all things; the most capacious measure is filled at last; and this brief condescension to evil finally destroyed the balance of my soul. And yet I was not alarmed; the fall seemed natural, like a return to the old days before I had made discovery. It was a fine, clear, January day, wet under foot where the frost had melted, but cloudless overhead; and the Regent's Park was full of winter chirrupings and sweet with spring odours. I sat in the sun on a bench; the animal within me licking the chops of memory; the spiritual side a little drowsed, promising subsequent penitence, but not yet moved to begin. After all, I reflected, I was like my neighbours; and then I smiled, comparing myself with other men, comparing my active goodwill with the lazy cruelty of their neglect. And at the very moment of that vainglorious thought, a qualm came over me, a horrid nausea and the most deadly shuddering. These passed away, and left me faint; and then as in its turn the faintness subsided, I began to be aware of a change in the temper of my thoughts, a greater boldness, a contempt of danger, a solution of the bonds of obligation. I looked down; my clothes hung formlessly on my shrunken limbs; the hand that lay on my knee was corded and hairy. I was once more Edward Hyde. A moment before I had been safe of all men's respect, wealthy, beloved – the cloth laying for me in the dining-room at home; and now I was the common quarry of mankind, hunted, houseless, a known murderer, thrall to the gallows.

My reason wavered, but it did not fail me utterly. I have more than once observed that, in my second character, my faculties seemed sharpened to a point and my spirits more tensely elastic; thus it came about that, where Jekyll perhaps might have succumbed, Hyde rose to the importance of the moment. My drugs were in one of the presses of my cabinet; how was I to reach them? That was the problem that (crushing my temples in my hands) I set myself to solve. The laboratory door I had closed. If I sought to enter by the house, my own servants would consign me to the gallows. I saw I must employ another hand, and thought of Lanyon. How was he to be reached? how persuaded? Supposing that I escaped capture in the streets, how was I to make my way into his presence? and how should I, an unknown and displeasing visitor, prevail on the famous physician to rifle the study of his colleague, Dr Jekyll? Then I remembered that of my original character, one part remained to me: I could write my own hand; and once I had conceived that kindling spark, the way that I must follow became lighted up from end to end.

Thereupon, I arranged my clothes as best I could, and summoning a passing hansom, drove to an hotel in Portland Street, the name of which I chanced to remember. At my appearance (which was indeed comical enough, however tragic a fate these garments covered) the driver could not conceal his mirth. I gnashed my teeth upon him with a gust of devilish fury; and the smile withered from his face – happily for him – yet more happily for myself, for in another instant I had certainly dragged him from his perch. At the inn, as I entered, I looked about me with so black a countenance as made the attendants tremble; not a look did they exchange in my presence; but obsequiously took my orders, led me to a private room, and brought me wherewithal to write. Hyde in danger of his life was a creature new to me; shaken with inordinate anger, strung to the pitch of murder, lusting to inflict pain. Yet the creature was astute; mastered his fury with a great effort of the will; composed his two important letters, one to Lanyon and one to Poole; and that he might receive actual evidence of their being posted, sent them out with directions that they should be registered.

Thenceforward, he sat all day over the fire in the private room, gnawing his nails; there he dined, sitting alone with his fears, the waiter visibly quailing before his eye; and thence, when the night was fully come, he set forth in the corner of a closed cab, and was driven to and fro about the streets of the city. He, I say – I cannot say, I. That child of Hell had nothing human; nothing lived in him but fear and hatred. And when at last, thinking the driver had begun to grow suspicious, he discharged the cab and ventured on foot, attired in his misfitting clothes, an object marked out for observation, into the midst of the nocturnal passengers, these two base passions raged within him like a tempest. He walked fast, hunted by his fears, chattering to himself, skulking through the less-frequented thoroughfares, counting the minutes that still divided him from midnight. Once a woman spoke to him, offering, I think, a box of lights. He smote her in the face, and she fled.

When I came to myself at Lanyon's, the horror of my old friend perhaps affected me somewhat: I do not know; it was at least but a drop in the sea to the abhorrence with which I looked back upon these hours. A change had come over me. It was no longer the fear of the gallows, it was the horror of being Hyde that racked me. I received Lanyon's condemnation partly in a dream; it was partly in a dream that I came home to my own house and got into bed. I slept after the prostration of the day, with a stringent and profound slumber which not even the nightmares that wrung me could avail to break. I awoke in the morning shaken, weakened, but refreshed. I still hated and feared the thought of the brute that slept within me, and I had not of course forgotten the appalling dangers of the day before; but I was once more at home, in my own house and close to my drugs; and gratitude for my escape shone so strong in my soul that it almost rivalled the brightness of hope.

I was stepping leisurely across the court after breakfast, drinking the chill of the air with pleasure, when I was seized again with those indescribable sensations that heralded the change; and I had but the time to gain the shelter of my cabinet, before I was once again raging and freezing with the passions of Hyde. It took on this occasion a double dose to recall me to myself; and alas! Six hours after, as I sat looking sadly in the fire, the pangs returned, and the drug had to be re-administered. In short, from that day forth it seemed only by a great effort as of gymnastics, and only under the immediate stimulation of the drug, that I was able to wear the countenance of Jekyll. At all hours of the day and night, I would be taken with the premonitory shudder; above all, if I slept, or even dozed for a moment in my chair, it was always as Hyde that I awakened. Under the strain of this continually-impending doom and by the sleeplessness to which I now condemned myself, ay, even beyond what I had thought possible to man, I became, in my own person, a creature eaten up and emptied by fever, languidly weak both in body and mind, and solely occupied by one thought: the horror of my other self. But when I slept, or when the virtue of the medicine wore off, I would leap almost without transition (for the pangs of transformation grew daily less marked) into the possession of a fancy brimming with images of terror, a soul boiling with causeless hatreds, and a body that seemed not strong enough to contain the raging energies of life. The powers of Hyde seemed to have grown with the sickliness of Jekyll. And certainly the hate that now divided them was equal on each side. With Jekyll, it was a thing of vital instinct. He had now seen the full deformity of that creature that shared with him some of the phenomena of consciousness, and was co-heir with him to death: and beyond these links of community, which in themselves made the most poignant part of his distress, he thought of Hyde, for all his energy of life, as of something not only hellish but inorganic. This was the shocking thing; that the slime of the pit seemed to utter cries and voices; that the amorphous dust gesticulated and sinned; that what was dead, and had no shape, should usurp the offices of life. And this again, that that insurgent horror was knit to him closer than a wife, closer than an eye; lay caged in his flesh, where he heard it mutter and felt it struggle to be born; and at every hour of weakness, and in the confidence of slumber, prevailed against him and deposed him out of life. The hatred of Hyde for Jekyll, was of a different order. His terror of the gallows drove him continually to commit temporary suicide, and return to his subordinate station of a part instead of a person; but he loathed the necessity, he loathed the despondency into which Jekyll was now fallen, and he resented the dislike with which he was himself regarded. Hence the ape-like tricks that he would play me, scrawling in my own hand blasphemies on the pages of my books, burning the letters and destroying the portrait of my father; and indeed, had it not been for his fear of death, he would long ago have ruined himself in order to involve me in the ruin. But his love of life is wonderful; I go further: I, who sicken and freeze at the mere thought of him, when I recall the abjection and passion of this attachment, and when I know how he fears my power to cut him off by suicide, I find it in my heart to pity him.

It is useless, and the time awfully fails me, to prolong this description; no one has ever suffered such torments, let that suffice; and yet even to these, habit brought – no, not alleviation – but a certain callousness of soul, a certain acquiescence of despair; and my punishment might have gone on for years, but for the last calamity which has now fallen, and which has finally severed me from my own face and nature. My provision of the salt, which had never been renewed since the date of the first experiment, began to run low. I sent out for a fresh supply, and mixed the draught; the ebullition followed, and the first change of colour, not the second; I drank it and it was without efficiency. You will learn from Poole how I have had London ransacked; it was in vain; and I am now persuaded that my first supply was impure, and that it was that unknown impurity which lent efficacy to the draught.

About a week has passed, and I am now finishing this statement under the influence of the last of the old powders. This, then, is the last time, short of a miracle, that Henry Jekyll can think his own thoughts or see his own face (now how sadly altered!) in the glass. Nor must I delay too long to bring my writing to an end; for if my narrative has hitherto escaped destruction, it has been by a combination of great prudence and great good luck. Should the throes of change take me in the act of writing it, Hyde will tear it in pieces; but if some time shall have elapsed after I have laid it by, his wonderful selfishness and circumscription to the moment will probably save it once again from the action of his ape-like spite. And indeed the doom that is closing on us both, has already changed and crushed him. Half an hour from now, when I shall again and for ever re-indue that hated personality, I know how I shall sit shuddering and weeping in my chair, or continue, with the most strained and fear-struck ecstasy of listening, to pace up and down this room (my last earthly refuge) and give ear to every sound of menace. Will Hyde die upon the scaffold? or will he find courage to release himself at the last moment? God knows; I am careless; this is my true hour of death, and what is to follow concerns another than myself. Here then, as I lay down the pen and proceed to seal up my confession, I bring the life of that unhappy Henry Jekyll to an end.

ROBERT LOUIS STEVENSON
THE BODY SNATCHER

Every night in the year, four of us sat in the small parlour of the George at Debenham - the undertaker and the landlord, and Fettes and myself. Sometimes there would be more; but blow high, blow low, come rain or snow or frost, we four would be each planted in his own particular arm-chair. Fettes was an old drunken Scotchman, a man of education obviously, and a man of some property, since he lived in idleness. He had come to Debenham years ago, while still young, and by a mere continuance of living had grown to be an adopted townsman. His blue camlet cloak was a local antiquity, like the church-spire. His place in the parlour at the George, his absence from church, his old, crapulous, disreputable vices, were all things of course in Debenham. He had some vague Radical opinions and some fleeting infidelities, which he would now and again set forth and emphasize with tottering slaps upon the table. He drank rum - five glasses regularly every evening; and for the greater portion of his nightly visit to the George sat, with his glass in his right hand, in a state of melancholy alcoholic saturation. We called him the Doctor, for he was supposed to have some special knowledge of medicine, and had been known, upon a pinch, to set a fracture or reduce a dislocation; but beyond these slight particulars, we had no knowledge of his character and antecedents.

One dark winter night - it had struck nine some time before the landlord joined us - there was a sick man in the George, a great neighbouring proprietor suddenly struck down with apoplexy on his way to Parliament; and the great man's still greater London doctor had been telegraphed to his bedside. It was the first time that such a thing had happened in Debenham, for the railway was but newly open, and we were all proportionately moved by the occurrence.

"He's come," said the landlord, after he had filled and lighted his pipe.

"He?" said I. "Who? – not the doctor?"

"Himself," replied our host.

"What is his name?"

"Doctor Macfarlane," said the landlord.

Fettes was far through his third tumbler, stupidly fuddled, now nodding over, now staring mazily around him; but at the last word he seemed to awaken, and repeated the name "Macfarlane" twice, quietly enough the first time, but with sudden emotion at the second.

"Yes," said the landlord, "that's his name, Doctor Wolfe Macfarlane."

Fettes became instantly sober; his eyes awoke, his voice became clear, loud and steady, his language forcible and earnest. We were all startled by the transformation, as if a man had risen from the dead.

"I beg your pardon," he said, "I am afraid I have not been paying much attention to your talk. Who is this Wolfe Macfarlane?" And then, when he had heard the landlord out, "It cannot be, it cannot be," he added; "and yet I would like well to see him face to face."

"Do you know him, Doctor?" asked the undertaker, with a gasp.

"God forbid!" was the reply. "And yet the name is a strange one; it were too much to fancy two. Tell me, landlord, is he old?"

"Well," said the host, "he's not a young man, to be sure, and his hair is white; but he looks younger than you."

"He is older, though; years older. But," with a slap upon the table, "it's the rum you see in my face – rum and sin. This man, perhaps, may have an easy conscience and a good digestion. Conscience! Hear me speak. You would think I was some good, old, decent Christian, would you not? But no, not I; I never canted. Voltaire might have canted if he'd stood in my shoes; but the brains" – with a rattling fillip on his bald head – "the brains were clear and active, and I saw and made no deductions."

"If you know this doctor," I ventured to remark, after a somewhat awful pause, "I should gather that you do not share the landlord's good opinion."

Fettes paid no regard to me.

"Yes," he said, with sudden decision, "I must see him face to face."

There was another pause, and then a door was closed rather sharply on the first floor, and a step was heard upon the stair.

"That's the doctor," cried the landlord. "Look sharp, and you can catch him."

It was but two steps from the small parlour to the door of the old George Inn; the wide oak staircase landed almost in the street; there was room for a Turkey rug and nothing more between the threshold and the last round of the descent; but this little space was every evening brilliantly lit up, not only by the light upon the stair and the great signal-lamp below the sign, but by the warm radiance of the bar-room window. The George thus brightly advertised itself to passers-by in the cold street. Fettes walked steadily to the spot, and we, who were hanging behind, beheld the two men meet, as one of them had phrased it, face to face. Dr Macfarlane was alert and vigorous. His white hair set off his pale and placid, although energetic, countenance. He was richly dressed in the finest of broadcloth and the whitest of linen, with a great gold watch-chain, and studs and spectacles of the same precious material. He wore a broad-folded tie, white and speckled with lilac, and he carried on his arm a comfortable driving-coat of fur. There was no doubt but he became his years, breathing, as he did, of wealth and consideration; and it was a surprising contrast to see our parlour sot – bald, dirty, pimpled and robed in his old camlet cloak – confront him at the bottom of the stairs.

"Macfarlane!" he said somewhat loudly, more like a herald than a friend.

The great doctor pulled up short on the fourth step, as though the familiarity of the address surprised and somewhat shocked his dignity.

"Toddy Macfarlane!" repeated Fettes.

The London man almost staggered. He stared for the swiftest of seconds at the man before him, glanced behind him with a sort of scare, and then in a startled whisper, "Fettes!" he said, "You!"

"Ay," said the other, "me! Did you think I was dead too? We are not so easy shut of our acquaintance."

"Hush, hush!" exclaimed the doctor. "Hush, hush! this meeting is so unexpected – I can see you are unmanned. I hardly knew you, I confess, at first; but I am overjoyed – overjoyed to have this opportunity. For the present it must be how-d'ye-do and goodbye in one, for my fly is waiting, and I must not fail the train; but you shall – let me see – yes – you shall give me your address, and you can count on early news of me. We must do something for you, Fettes. I fear you are out at elbows; but we must see to that for auld lang syne, as once we sang at suppers."

"Money!" cried Fettes; "money from you! The money that I had from you is lying where I cast it in the rain."

Dr Macfarlane had talked himself into some measure of superiority and confidence, but the uncommon energy of this refusal cast him back into his first confusion.

A horrible, ugly look came and went across his almost venerable countenance. "My dear fellow," he said, "be it as you please; my last thought is to offend you. I would intrude on none. I will leave you my address, however—"

"I do not wish it – I do not wish to know the roof that shelters you," interrupted the other. "I heard your name; I feared it might be you; I wished to know if, after all, there were a God; I know now that there is none. Begone!"

He still stood in the middle of the rug, between the stair and doorway; and the great London physician, in order to escape, would be forced to step to one side. It was plain that he hesitated before the thought of this humiliation. White as he was, there was a dangerous glitter in his spectacles; but while he still paused uncertain, he became aware that the driver of his fly was peering in from the street at this unusual scene and caught a glimpse at the same time of our little body from the parlour, huddled by the corner of the bar. The presence of so many witnesses decided him at once to flee. He crouched together, brushing on the wainscot, and made a dart like a serpent, striking for the door. But his tribulation was not yet entirely at an end, for even as he was passing Fettes clutched him by the arm and these words came in a whisper, and yet painfully distinct, "Have you seen it again?"

The great rich London doctor cried out aloud with a sharp, throttling cry; he dashed his questioner across the open space, and, with his hands over his head, fled out of the door like a detected thief. Before it had occurred to one of us to make a movement the fly was already rattling toward the station. The scene was over like a dream, but the dream had left proofs and traces of its passage. Next day the servant found the fine gold spectacles broken on the threshold, and that very night we were all standing breathless by the bar-room window, and Fettes at our side, sober, pale, and resolute in look.

"God protect us, Mr Fettes!" said the landlord, coming first into possession of his customary senses. "What in the universe is all this? These are strange things you have been saying."

Fettes turned toward us; he looked us each in succession in the face. "See if you can hold your tongues," said he. "That man Macfarlane is not safe to cross; those that have done so already have repented it too late."

And then, without so much as finishing his third glass, far less waiting for the other two, he bade us goodbye and went forth, under the lamp of the hotel, into the black night.

We three turned to our places in the parlour, with the big red fire and four clear candles; and as we recapitulated what had passed, the first chill of our surprise soon changed into a glow of curiosity. We sat late; it was the latest session I have known in the old George. Each man, before we parted, had his theory that he was bound to prove; and none of us had any nearer business in this world than to track out the past of our condemned companion, and surprise the secret that he shared with the great London doctor. It is no great boast, but I believe I was a better hand at worming out a story than either of my fellows at the George; and perhaps there is now no other man alive who could narrate to you the following foul and unnatural events.

In his young days Fettes studied medicine in the schools of Edinburgh. He had talent of a kind, the talent that picks up swiftly what it hears and readily retails it for its own. He worked little at home; but he was civil, attentive, and intelligent in the presence of his masters. They soon picked him out as a lad who listened closely and remembered well; nay, strange as it seemed to me when I first heard it, he was in those days well favoured, and pleased by his exterior. There was, at that period, a certain extramural teacher of anatomy, whom I shall here designate by the letter K. His name was subsequently too well known. The man who bore it skulked through the streets of Edinburgh in disguise, while the mob that applauded at the execution of Burke called loudly for the blood of his employer. But Mr K— was then at the top of his vogue; he enjoyed a popularity due partly to his own talent and address, partly to the incapacity of his rival, the university professor. The students, at least, swore by his name, and Fettes believed himself, and was believed by others, to have laid the foundations of success when he had acquired the favour of this meteorically famous man. Mr K— was a *bon vivant* as well as an accomplished teacher; he liked a sly illusion no less than a careful preparation. In both capacities Fettes enjoyed and deserved his notice, and by the second year of his attendance he held the half-regular position of second demonstrator or sub-assistant in his class.

In this capacity the charge of the theatre and lecture-room devolved in particular upon his shoulders. He had to answer for the cleanliness of the premises and the conduct of the other students, and it was a part of his duty to supply, receive, and divide the various subjects. It was with a view to this last – at that time very delicate – affair that he was lodged by Mr K— in the same wynd, and at last in the same building, with the dissecting-rooms. Here, after a night of turbulent pleasures, his hand still tottering, his sight still misty and confused, he would be called out of bed in the black hours before the winter dawn by the unclean and desperate interlopers who supplied the table. He would open the door to these men, since infamous throughout the land. He would help them with their tragic burden, pay them their sordid price, and remain alone, when they were gone, with the unfriendly relics of humanity. From such a scene he would return to snatch another hour or two of slumber, to repair the abuses of the night, and refresh himself for the labours of the day.

Few lads could have been more insensible to the impressions of a life thus passed among the ensigns of mortality. His mind was closed against all general considerations. He was incapable of interest in the fate and fortunes of another, the slave of his own desires and low ambitions. Cold, light, and selfish in the last resort, he had that modicum of prudence, miscalled morality, which keeps a man from inconvenient drunkenness or punishable theft. He coveted, besides, a measure of consideration from his masters and his fellow-pupils, and he had no desire to fail conspicuously in the external parts of life. Thus he made it his pleasure to gain some distinction in his studies, and day after day rendered unimpeachable eye-service to his employer, Mr K—. For his day of work he indemnified himself by nights of roaring, blackguardly enjoyment; and when that balance had been struck, the organ that he called his conscience declared itself content.

The supply of subjects was a continual trouble to him as well as to his master. In that large and busy class, the raw material of the anatomists kept perpetually running out; and the business thus rendered necessary was not only unpleasant in itself, but threatened dangerous consequences to all who were concerned. It was the policy of Mr K— to ask no questions in his dealings with the trade. "They bring the body, and we pay the price," he used to say, dwelling on the alliteration – "*Quid pro quo.*" And, again, and somewhat profanely, "Ask no questions," he would tell his assistants, "for conscience sake." There was no understanding that the subjects were provided by the crime of murder. Had that idea been broached to him in words, he would have recoiled in horror; but the lightness of his speech upon so grave a matter was, in itself, an offence against good manners, and a temptation to the men with whom he dealt. Fettes, for instance, had often remarked to himself upon the singular freshness of the bodies. He had been struck again and again by the hang-dog, abominable looks of the ruffians who came to him before the dawn; and putting things together clearly in his private thoughts, he perhaps attributed a meaning too immoral and too categorical to the unguarded counsels of his master. He understood his duty, in short, to have three branches: to take what was brought, to pay the price, and to avert the eye from any evidence of crime.

One November morning this policy of silence was put sharply to the test. He had been awake all night with a racking toothache – pacing his room like a caged beast or throwing himself in fury on his bed – and had fallen at last into that profound, uneasy slumber that so often follows on a night of pain, when he was awakened by the third or fourth angry repetition of the concerted signal. There was a thin, bright moonshine; it was bitter cold, windy and frosty; the town had not yet awakened, but an indefinable stir already preluded the noise and business of the day. The ghouls had come later than usual, and they seemed more than usually eager to be gone. Fettes, sick with sleep, lighted them upstairs. He heard their grumbling Irish voices through a dream; and as they stripped the sack from their sad merchandise he leaned dozing, with his shoulder propped against the wall; he had to shake himself to find the men their money. As he did so his eyes lighted on the dead face. He started; he took two steps nearer, with the candle raised.

"God Almighty!" he cried. "That is Jane Galbraith!"

The men answered nothing, but they shuffled nearer the door.

"I know her, I tell you," he continued. "She was alive and hearty yesterday. It's impossible she can be dead; it's impossible you should have got this body fairly."

"Sure, sir, you're mistaken entirely," said one of the men.

But the other looked Fettes darkly in the eyes, and demanded the money on the spot.

It was impossible to misconceive the threat or to exaggerate the danger. The lad's heart failed him. He stammered some excuses, counted out the sum, and saw his hateful visitors depart. No sooner were they gone than he hastened to confirm his doubts. By a dozen unquestionable marks he identified the girl he had jested with the day before. He saw, with horror, marks upon her body that might well betoken violence. A panic seized him, and he took refuge in his room. There he reflected at length over the discovery that he had made; considered soberly the bearing of Mr K—'s instructions and the danger to himself of interference in so serious a business, and at last, in sore perplexity, determined to wait for the advice of his immediate superior, the class assistant.

This was a young doctor, Wolfe Macfarlane, a high favourite among all the reckless students, clever, dissipated and unscrupulous to the last degree. He had travelled and studied abroad. His manners were agreeable and a little forward. He was an authority on the stage, skilful on the ice or the links with skate or golf-club; he dressed with nice audacity, and, to put the finishing touch upon his glory, he kept a gig and a strong trotting-horse. With Fettes he was on terms of intimacy; indeed, their relative positions called for some community of life; and when subjects were scarce the pair would drive far into the country in Macfarlane's gig, visit and desecrate some lonely graveyard, and return before dawn with their booty to the door of the dissecting-room.

On that particular morning Macfarlane arrived somewhat earlier than his wont. Fettes heard him, and met him on the stairs, told him his story, and showed him the cause of his alarm. Macfarlane examined the marks on her body.

"Yes," he said with a nod, "it looks fishy."

"Well, what should I do?" asked Fettes.

"Do?" repeated the other. "Do you want to do anything? Least said soonest mended, I should say."

"Some one else might recognize her," objected Fettes. "She was as well known as the Castle Rock."

"We'll hope not," said Macfarlane, "and if anybody does – well, you didn't, don't you see, and there's an end. The fact is, this has been going on too long. Stir up the mud, and you'll get K— into the most unholy trouble; you'll be in a shocking box yourself. So will I, if you come to that. I should like to know how any one of us would look, or what the devil we should have to say for ourselves, in any Christian witness-box. For me, you know there's one thing certain – that, practically speaking, all our subjects have been murdered."

"Macfarlane!" cried Fettes.

"Come now!" sneered the other. "As if you hadn't suspected it yourself!"

"Suspecting is one thing—"

"And proof another. Yes, I know; and I'm as sorry as you are this should have come here," tapping the body with his cane. "The next best thing for me is not to recognize it; and," he added coolly, "I don't. You may, if you please. I don't dictate, but I think a man of the world would do as I do; and I may add, I fancy that is what K— would look for at our hands. The question is, Why did he choose us two for his assistants? And I answer, because he didn't want old wives."

This was the tone of all others to affect the mind of a lad like Fettes. He agreed to imitate Macfarlane. The body of the unfortunate girl was duly dissected, and no one remarked or appeared to recognize her.

One afternoon, when his day's work was over, Fettes dropped into a popular tavern and found Macfarlane sitting with a stranger. This was a small man, very pale and dark, with coal-black eyes. The cut of his features gave a promise of intellect and refinement which was but feebly realised in his manners, for he proved, upon a nearer acquaintance, coarse, vulgar and stupid. He exercised, however, a very remarkable control over Macfarlane; issued orders like the Great Bashaw; became inflamed at the least discussion or delay, and commented rudely on the servility with which he was obeyed. This most offensive person took a fancy to Fettes on the spot, plied him with drinks, and honoured him with unusual confidences on his past career. If a tenth part of what he confessed were true, he was a very loathsome rogue; and the lad's vanity was tickled by the attention of so experienced a man.

"I'm a pretty bad fellow myself," the stranger remarked, "but Macfarlane is the boy – Toddy Macfarlane I call him. Toddy, order your friend another glass." Or it might be, "Toddy, you jump up and shut the door." "Toddy hates me," he said again. "Oh yes, Toddy, you do!"

"Don't you call me that confounded name," growled Macfarlane.

"Hear him! Did you ever see the lads play knife? He would like to do that all over my body," remarked the stranger.

"We medicals have a better way than that," said Fettes. "When we dislike a dead friend of ours, we dissect him."

Macfarlane looked up sharply, as though this jest were scarcely to his mind.

The afternoon passed. Gray, for that was the stranger's name, invited Fettes to join them at dinner, ordered a feast so sumptuous that the tavern was thrown into commotion, and when all was done commanded Macfarlane to settle the bill. It was late before they separated; the man Gray was incapably drunk. Macfarlane, sobered by his fury, chewed the cud of the money he had been forced to squander and the slights he had been obliged to swallow. Fettes, with various liquors singing in his head, returned home with devious footsteps and a mind entirely in abeyance. Next day Macfarlane was absent from the class, and Fettes smiled to himself as he imagined him still squiring the intolerable Gray from tavern to tavern. As soon as the hour of liberty had struck he posted from place to place in quest of his last night's companions. He could find them, however, nowhere; so returned early to his rooms, went early to bed and slept the sleep of the just.

At four in the morning he was awakened by the well-known signal. Descending to the door, he was filled with astonishment to find Macfarlane with his gig, and in the gig one of those long and ghastly packages with which he was so well acquainted.

"What?" he cried. "Have you been out alone? How did you manage?"

But Macfarlane silenced him roughly, bidding him turn to business. When they had got the body upstairs and laid it on the table, Macfarlane made at first as if he were going away. Then he paused and seemed to hesitate; and then, "You had better look at the face," said he, in tones of some constraint. "You had better," he repeated, as Fettes only stared at him in wonder.

"But where, and how, and when did you come by it?" cried the other.

"Look at the face," was the only answer.

Fettes was staggered; strange doubts assailed him. He looked from the young doctor to the body, and then back again. At last, with a start, he did as he was bidden. He had almost expected the sight that met his eyes, and yet the shock was cruel. To see, fixed in the rigidity of death and naked on that coarse layer of sackcloth, the man whom he had left well clad and full of meat and sin upon the threshold of a tavern, awoke, even in the thoughtless Fettes, some of the terrors of the conscience. It was a *cras tibi* which re-echoed in his soul, that two whom he had known should have come to lie upon these icy tables. Yet these were only secondary thoughts. His first concern regarded Wolfe. Unprepared for a challenge so momentous, he knew not how to look his comrade in the face. He durst not meet his eye, and he had neither words nor voice at his command.

It was Macfarlane himself who made the first advance. He came up quietly behind and laid his hand gently but firmly on the other's shoulder.

"Richardson," said he, "may have the head."

Now Richardson was a student who had long been anxious for that portion of the human subject to dissect. There was no answer, and the murderer resumed: "Talking of business, you must pay me; your accounts, you see, must tally."

Fettes found a voice, the ghost of his own: "Pay you!" he cried. "Pay you for that?"

"Why, yes, of course you must. By all means and on every possible account, you must," returned the other. "I dare not give it for nothing, you dare not take it for nothing; it would compromise us both. This is another case like Jane Galbraith's. The more things are wrong the more we must act as if all were right. Where does old K— keep his money?"

"There," answered Fettes hoarsely, pointing to a cupboard in the corner.

"Give me the key, then," said the other, calmly, holding out his hand.

There was an instant's hesitation, and the die was cast. Macfarlane could not suppress a nervous twitch, the infinitesimal mark of an immense relief, as he felt the key between his fingers. He opened the cupboard, brought out pen and ink and a paper-book that stood in one compartment, and separated from the funds in a drawer a sum suitable to the occasion.

"Now, look here," he said, "there is the payment made – first proof of your good faith: first step to your security. You have now to clinch it by a second. Enter the payment in your book, and then you for your part may defy the devil."

The next few seconds were for Fettes an agony of thought; but in balancing his terrors it was the most immediate that triumphed. Any future difficulty seemed almost welcome if he could avoid a present quarrel with Macfarlane. He set down the candle which he had been carrying all this time, and with a steady hand entered the date, the nature, and the amount of the transaction.

"And now," said Macfarlane, "it's only fair that you should pocket the lucre. I've had my share already. By-the-by, when a man of the world falls into a bit of luck, has a few shillings extra in his pocket – I'm ashamed to speak of it, but there's a rule of conduct in the case. No treating, no purchase of expensive class-books, no squaring of old debts; borrow, don't lend."

"Macfarlane," began Fettes, still somewhat hoarsely, "I have put my neck in a halter to oblige you."

"To oblige me?" cried Wolfe. "Oh, come! You did, as near as I can see the matter, what you downright had to do in self-defence. Suppose I got into trouble, where would you be? This second little matter flows clearly from the first. Mr Gray is the continuation of

Miss Galbraith. You can't begin and then stop. If you begin, you must keep on beginning; that's the truth. No rest for the wicked."

A horrible sense of blackness and the treachery of fate seized hold upon the soul of the unhappy student.

"My God!" he cried, "but what have I done? and when did I begin? To be made a class assistant – in the name of reason, where's the harm in that? Service wanted the position; Service might have got it. Would *he* have been where I am now?"

"My dear fellow," said Macfarlane, "what a boy you are! What harm *has* come to you? What harm *can* come to you if you hold your tongue? Why, man, do you know what this life is? There are two squads of us – the lions and the lambs. If you're a lamb, you'll come to lie upon these tables like Gray or Jane Galbraith; if you're a lion, you'll live and drive a horse like me, like K–, like all the world with any wit or courage. You're staggered at the first. But look at K–! My dear fellow, you're clever, you have pluck. I like you, and K– likes you. You were born to lead the hunt; and I tell you, on my honour and my experience of life, three days from now you'll laugh at all these scarecrows like a High School boy at a farce."

And with that Macfarlane took his departure and drove off up the wynd in his gig to get under cover before daylight. Fettes was thus left alone with his regrets. He saw the miserable peril in which he stood involved. He saw, with inexpressible dismay, that there was no limit to his weakness, and that, from concession to concession, he had fallen from the arbiter of Macfarlane's destiny to his paid and helpless accomplice. He would have given the world to have been a little braver at the time, but it did not occur to him that he might still be brave. The secret of Jane Galbraith and the cursed entry in the day-book closed his mouth.

Hours passed; the class began to arrive; the members of the unhappy Gray were dealt out to one and to another, and received without remark. Richardson was made happy with the head; and before the hour of freedom rang Fettes trembled with exultation to perceive how far they had already gone toward safety.

For two days he continued to watch, with increasing joy, the dreadful process of disguise.

On the third day Macfarlane made his appearance. He had been ill, he said; but he made up for lost time by the energy with which he directed the students. To Richardson in particular he extended the most valuable assistance and advice, and that student, encouraged by the praise of the demonstrator, burned high with ambitious hopes, and saw the medal already in his grasp.

Before the week was out Macfarlane's prophecy had been fulfilled. Fettes had outlived his terrors and had forgotten his baseness. He began to plume himself upon his courage, and had so arranged the story in his mind that he could look back on these events with an unhealthy pride. Of his accomplice he saw but little. They met, of course, in the business of the class; they received their orders together from Mr K—. At times they had a word or two in private, and Macfarlane was from first to last particularly kind and jovial. But it was plain that he avoided any reference to their common secret; and even when Fettes whispered to him that he had cast in his lot with the lions and foresworn the lambs, he only signed to him smilingly to hold his peace.

At length an occasion arose which threw the pair once more into a closer union. Mr K— was again short of subjects; pupils were eager, and it was a part of this teacher's pretensions to be always well supplied. At the same time there came the news of a burial in the rustic graveyard of Glencorse. Time has little changed the place in question. It stood then, as now, upon a cross road, out of call of human habitations, and buried fathom deep in the foliage of six cedar trees. The cries of the sheep upon the neighbouring hills, the streamlets upon either hand, one loudly singing among pebbles, the other dripping furtively from pond to pond, the stir of the wind in mountainous old flowering chestnuts, and once in seven days the voice of the bell and the old tunes of the precentor, were the only sounds that disturbed the silence around the rural church. The Resurrection Man – to use a byname of the period – was not to be deterred by any of the sanctities of customary piety. It was part of his trade to despise and desecrate the scrolls and trumpets of old tombs, the paths worn by the feet of worshippers and mourners, and the offerings and the inscriptions of bereaved affection. To rustic neighbourhoods, where love is more than commonly tenacious, and where some bonds of blood or fellowship unite the entire society of a parish, the body-snatcher, far from being repelled by natural respect, was attracted by the ease and safety of the task. To bodies that had been laid in earth, in joyful expectation of a far different awakening, there came that hasty, lamp-lit, terror-haunted resurrection of the spade and mattock. The coffin was forced, the cerements torn, and the melancholy relics, clad in sackcloth, after being rattled for hours on moonless byways, were at length exposed to uttermost indignities before a class of gaping boys.

Somewhat as two vultures may swoop upon a dying lamb, Fettes and Macfarlane were to be let loose upon a grave in that green and quiet resting-place. The wife of a farmer, a woman who had lived for sixty years, and been known for nothing but good butter and a godly conversation, was to be rooted from her grave at midnight and carried, dead and naked, to that far-away city that she had always honoured with her Sunday best; the place beside her family was to be empty till the crack of doom; her innocent and almost venerable members to be exposed to that last curiosity of the anatomist.

Late one afternoon the pair set forth, well wrapped in cloaks and furnished with a formidable bottle. It rained without remission – a cold, dense, lashing rain. Now and again there blew a puff of wind, but these sheets of falling water kept it down. Bottle and all, it was a sad and silent drive as far as Penicuik, where they were to spend the evening. They stopped once, to hide their implements in a thick bush not far from the churchyard, and once again at the Fisher's Tryst, to have a toast before the kitchen fire and vary their nips of whisky with a glass of ale. When they reached their journey's end the gig was housed, the horse was fed and comforted, and the two young doctors in a private room sat down to the best dinner and the best wine the house afforded. The lights, the fire, the beating rain upon the window, the cold, incongruous work that lay before them, added zest to their enjoyment of the meal. With every glass their cordiality increased. Soon Macfarlane handed a little pile of gold to his companion.

"A compliment," he said. "Between friends these little d—d accommodations ought to fly like pipe-lights."

Fettes pocketed the money, and applauded the sentiment to the echo. "You are a philosopher," he cried. "I was an ass till I knew you. You and K— between you, by the Lord Harry! but you'll make a man of me."

"Of course we shall," applauded Macfarlane. "A man? I tell you, it required a man to back me up the other morning. There are some big, brawling, forty-year-old cowards who would have turned sick at the look of the d—d thing; but not you – you kept your head. I watched you."

"Well, and why not?" Fettes thus vaunted himself. "It was no affair of mine. There was nothing to gain on the one side but disturbance, and on the other I could count on your gratitude, don't you see?" And he slapped his pocket till the gold pieces rang.

Macfarlane somehow felt a certain touch of alarm at these unpleasant words. He may have regretted that he had taught his young companion so successfully, but he had no time to interfere, for the other noisily continued in this boastful strain:

"The great thing is not to be afraid. Now, between you and me, I don't want to hang – that's practical; but for all cant, Macfarlane, I was born with a contempt. Hell, God, Devil, right, wrong, sin, crime and all the old gallery of curiosities – they may frighten boys, but men of the world, like you and me, despise them. Here's to the memory of Gray!"

It was by this time growing somewhat late. The gig, according to order, was brought round to the door with both lamps brightly shining, and the young men had to pay their bill and take the road. They announced that they were bound for Peebles, and drove in that direction till they were clear of the last houses of the town; then, extinguishing the lamps, returned upon their course, and followed a by-road toward Glencorse. There was no sound but that of their own passage, and the incessant, strident pouring of the rain. It was pitch dark; here and there a white gate or a white stone in the wall guided them for a short space across the night; but for the most part it was at a foot pace, and almost groping, that they picked their way through that resonant blackness to their solemn and isolated destination. In the sunken woods that traverse the neighbourhood of the burying-ground the last glimmer failed them, and it became necessary to kindle a match and re-illumine one of the lanterns of the gig. Thus, under the dripping trees, and environed by huge and moving shadows, they reached the scene of their unhallowed labours.

They were both experienced in such affairs, and powerful with the spade; and they had scarce been twenty minutes at their task before they were rewarded by a dull rattle on the coffin lid. At the same moment Macfarlane, having hurt his hand upon a stone, flung it carelessly above his head. The grave, in which they now stood almost to the shoulders, was close to the edge of the plateau of the graveyard; and the gig lamp had been propped, the better to illuminate their labours, against a tree, and on the immediate verge of the steep bank descending to the stream. Chance had taken a sure aim with the stone. Then came a clang of broken glass; night fell upon them; sounds alternately dull and ringing announced the bounding of the lantern down the bank, and its occasional collision with the trees. A stone or two, which it had dislodged in its descent, rattled behind it into the profundities of the glen; and then silence, like night, resumed its sway; and they might bend their hearing to its utmost pitch, but naught was to be heard except the rain, now marching to the wind, now steadily falling over miles of open country.

They were so nearly at an end of their abhorred task that they judged it wisest to complete it in the dark. The coffin was exhumed and broken open; the body inserted in the dripping sack and carried between them to the gig; one mounted to keep it in its place, and the other, taking the horse by the mouth, groped along by wall and bush until they reached the wider road by the Fisher's Tryst. Here was a faint, diffused radiancy, which they hailed like daylight; by that they pushed the horse to a good pace and began to rattle along merrily in the direction of the town.

They had both been wetted to the skin during their operations, and now, as the gig jumped among the deep ruts, the thing that stood propped between them fell now upon one and now upon the other. At every repetition of the horrid contact each instinctively repelled it with the greater haste; and the process, natural although it was, began to tell upon the nerves of the companions. Macfarlane made some ill-favoured jest about the farmer's wife, but it came hollowly from his lips, and was allowed to drop in silence. Still their unnatural burden bumped from side to side; and now the head would be laid, as if in confidence, upon their shoulders, and now the drenching sack-cloth would flap icily about their faces. A creeping chill began to possess the soul of Fettes. He peered at the bundle, and it seemed somehow larger than at first. All over the country-side, and from every degree of distance, the farm dogs accompanied their passage with tragic ululations; and it grew and grew upon his mind that some unnatural miracle had been accomplished, that some nameless change had befallen the dead body, and that it was in fear of their unholy burden that the dogs were howling.

"For God's sake," said he, making a great effort to arrive at speech, "for God's sake, let's have a light!"

Seemingly Macfarlane was affected in the same direction; for, though he made no reply, he stopped the horse, passed the reins to his companion, got down and proceeded to kindle the remaining lamp. They had by that time got no farther than the cross-road down to Auchenclinny. The rain still poured as though the deluge were returning, and it was no easy matter to make a light in such a world of wet and darkness. When at last the flickering blue flame had been transferred to the wick and began to expand and clarify, and shed a wide circle of misty brightness round the gig, it became possible for the two young men to see each other and the thing they had along with them. The rain had moulded the rough sacking to the outlines of the body underneath; the head was distinct from the trunk, the shoulders plainly modelled; something at once spectral and human riveted their eyes upon the ghastly comrade of their drive.

For some time Macfarlane stood motionless, holding up the lamp. A nameless dread was swathed, like a wet sheet, about the body, and tightened the white skin upon the face of Fettes; a fear that was meaningless, a horror of what could not be, kept mounting to his brain. Another beat of the watch, and he had spoken. But his comrade forestalled him.

"That is not a woman," said Macfarlane, in a hushed voice.

"It was a woman when we put her in," whispered Fettes.

"Hold that lamp," said the other. "I must see her face."

And as Fettes took the lamp his companion untied the fastenings of the sack and drew down the cover from the head. The light fell very clear upon the dark, well-moulded features and smooth-shaven cheeks of a too familiar countenance, often beheld in dreams of both of these young men. A wild yell rang up into the night; each leaped from his own side into the roadway: the lamp fell, broke, and was extinguished; and the horse, terrified by this unusual commotion, bounded and went off toward Edinburgh at a gallop, bearing along with it, sole occupant of the gig, the body of the dead and long-dissected Gray.

ROBERT LOUIS STEVENSON
THE STORY OF A LIE

CHAPTER 1

Introduces the Admiral

When **Dick Naseby** was in Paris he made some odd acquaintances; for he was one of those who have ears to hear, and can use their eyes no less than their intelligence. He made as many thoughts as Stuart Mill; but his philosophy concerned flesh and blood, and was experimental as to its method. He was a type-hunter among mankind. He despised small game and insignificant personalities, whether in the shape of dukes or bagmen, letting them go by like sea-weed; but show him a refined or powerful face, let him hear a plangent or a penetrating voice, fish for him with a living look in some one's eye, a passionate gesture, a meaning and ambiguous smile, and his mind was instantaneously awakened. "There was a man, there was a woman," he seemed to say, and he stood up to the task of comprehension with the delight of an artist in his art.

And indeed, rightly considered, this interest of his was an artistic interest. There is no science in the personal study of human nature. All comprehension is creation; the woman I love is somewhat of my handiwork; and the great lover, like the great painter, is he that can so embellish his subject as to make her more than human, whilst yet by a cunning art he has so based his apotheosis on the nature of the case that the woman can go on being a true woman, and give her character free play, and show littleness, or cherish spite, or be greedy of common pleasures, and he continue to worship without

133

a thought of incongruity. To love a character is only the heroic way of understanding it. When we love, by some noble method of our own or some nobility of mien or nature in the other, we apprehend the loved one by what is noblest in ourselves. When we are merely studying an eccentricity, the method of our study is but a series of allowances. To begin to understand is to begin to sympathize; for comprehension comes only when we have stated another's faults and virtues in terms of our own. Hence the proverbial toleration of artists for their own evil creations. Hence, too, it came about that Dick Naseby, a high-minded creature, and as scrupulous and brave a gentleman as you would want to meet, held in a sort of affection the various human creeping things whom he had met and studied.

One of these was Mr Peter Van Tromp, an English-speaking, two-legged animal of the international genus, and by profession of general and more than equivocal utility. Years before he had been a painter of some standing in a colony, and portraits signed 'Van Tromp' had celebrated the greatness of colonial governors and judges. In those days he had been married, and driven his wife and infant daughter in a pony trap. What were the steps of his declension? No one exactly knew. Here he was at least, and had been any time these past ten years, a sort of dismal parasite upon the foreigner in Paris.

It would be hazardous to specify his exact industry. Coarsely followed, it would have merited a name grown somewhat unfamiliar to our ears. Followed as he followed it, with a skilful reticence, in a kind of social chiaroscuro, it was still possible for the polite to call him a professional painter. His lair was in the Grand Hotel and the gaudiest cafés. There he might be seen jotting off a sketch with an air of some inspiration; and he was always affable, and one of the easiest of men to fall in talk withal. A conversation usually ripened into a peculiar sort of intimacy, and it was extraordinary how many little services Van Tromp contrived to render in the course of six-and-thirty hours. He occupied a position between a friend and a courier, which made him worse than embarrassing to repay. But those whom he obliged could always buy one of his villainous little pictures, or, where the favours had been prolonged and more than usually delicate, might order and pay for a large canvas, with perfect certainty that they would hear no more of the transaction.

Among resident artists he enjoyed celebrity of a non-professional sort. He had spent more money – no less than three individual fortunes, it was whispered – than any of his associates could ever hope to gain. Apart from his colonial career, he had been to Greece in a brigantine with four brass carronades; he had travelled Europe in a chaise and four, drawing bridle at the palace-doors of German princes; queens of song and dance had followed him like sheep and paid his tailor's bills. And to behold him now, seeking small loans with plaintive condescension, sponging for breakfast on an art-student of nineteen, a fallen Don Juan who had neglected to die at the propitious hour, had a colour of romance for young imaginations. His name and his bright past, seen through the prism of whispered gossip, had gained him the nickname of *The Admiral*.

Dick found him one day at the receipt of custom, rapidly painting a pair of hens and a cock in a little water-colour sketching box, and now and then glancing at the ceiling like a man who should seek inspiration from the muse. Dick thought it remarkable that a painter should choose to work over an absinthe in a public café, and looked the man over. The aged rakishness of his appearance was set off by a youthful costume; he had disreputable gray hair and a disreputable sore, red nose; but the coat and the gesture, the outworks of the man, were still designed for show. Dick came up to his table and inquired if he might look at what the gentleman was doing. No one was so delighted as the Admiral.

"A bit of a thing," said he. "I just dash them off like that. I – I dash them off," he added with a gesture.

"Quite so," said Dick, who was appalled by the feebleness of the production.

"Understand me," continued Van Tromp; 'I am a man of the world. And yet – once an artist always an artist. All of a sudden a thought takes me in the street; I become its prey: it's like a pretty woman; no use to struggle; I must – dash it off.'

"I see," said Dick.

"Yes," pursued the painter; "it all comes easily, easily to me; it is not my business; it's a pleasure. Life is my business – life – this great city, Paris – Paris after dark – its lights, its gardens, its odd corners. Aha!" he cried, "to be young again! The heart is young, but the heels are leaden. A poor, mean business, to grow old! Nothing remains but the *coup d'œil*, the contemplative man's enjoyment, Mr—," and he paused for the name.

"Naseby," returned Dick.

The other treated him at once to an exciting beverage, and expatiated on the pleasure of meeting a compatriot in a foreign land; to hear him, you would have thought they had encountered in Central Africa. Dick had never found any one take a fancy to him so readily, nor show it in an easier or less offensive manner. He seemed tickled with him as an elderly fellow about town might be tickled by a pleasant and witty lad; he indicated that he was no precision, but in his wildest times had never been such a blade as he thought Dick. Dick protested, but in vain. This manner of carrying an intimacy at the bayonet's point was Van Tromp's stock-in-trade. With an older man he insinuated himself; with youth he imposed himself, and in the same breath imposed an ideal on his victim, who saw that he must work up to it or lose the esteem of this old and vicious patron. And what young man can bear to lose a character for vice?

At last, as it grew towards dinner-time, "Do you know Paris?" asked Van Tromp.

"Not so well as you, I am convinced," said Dick.

"And so am I," returned Van Tromp gaily. "Paris! My young friend – you will allow me? – when you know Paris as I do, you will have seen Strange Things. I say no more; all I say is, Strange Things. We are men of the world, you and I, and in Paris, in the heart of civilized existence. This is an opportunity, Mr Naseby. Let us dine. Let me show you where to dine."

Dick consented. On the way to dinner the Admiral showed him where to buy gloves, and made him buy them; where to buy cigars, and made him buy a vast store, some of which he obligingly accepted. At the restaurant he showed him what to order, with surprising consequences in the bill. What he made that night by his percentages it would be hard to estimate. And all the while Dick smilingly consented, understanding well that he was being done, but taking his losses in the pursuit of character as a hunter sacrifices his dogs. As for the Strange Things, the reader will be relieved to hear that they were no stranger than might have been expected, and he may find things quite as strange without the expense of a Van Tromp for guide. Yet he was a guide of no mean order, who made up for the poverty of what he had to show by a copious, imaginative commentary.

"And such," said he, with a hiccup, "such is Paris."

"Pooh!" said Dick, who was tired of the performance.

The Admiral hung an ear, and looked up sidelong with a glimmer of suspicion.

"Good night," said Dick; "I'm tired."

"So English!" cried Van Tromp, clutching him by the hand. "So English! So *blasé*! Such a charming companion! Let me see you home."

"Look here," returned Dick, "I have said good night, and now I'm going. You're an amusing old boy: I like you, in a sense; but here's an end of it for tonight. Not another cigar, not another grog, not another percentage out of me."

"I beg your pardon!" cried the Admiral with dignity.

"Tut, man!" said Dick; "you're not offended; you're a man of the world, I thought. I've been studying you, and it's over. Have I not paid for the lesson? *Au revoir*."

Van Tromp laughed gaily, shook hands up to the elbows, hoped cordially they would meet again and that often, but looked after Dick as he departed with a tremor of indignation. After that they two not unfrequently fell in each other's way, and Dick would often treat the old boy to breakfast on a moderate scale and in a restaurant of his own selection. Often, too, he would lend Van Tromp the matter of a pound, in view of that gentleman's contemplated departure for Australia; there would be a scene of farewell almost touching in character, and a week or a month later they would meet on the same boulevard without surprise or embarrassment. And in the meantime Dick learned more about his acquaintance on all sides: heard of his yacht, his chaise and four, his brief season of celebrity amid a more confiding population, his daughter, of whom he loved to whimper in his cups, his sponging, parasitical, nameless way of life; and with each new detail something that was not merely interest nor yet altogether affection grew up in his mind towards this disreputable stepson of the arts. Ere he left Paris Van Tromp was one of those whom he entertained to a farewell supper; and the old gentleman made the speech of the evening, and then fell below the table, weeping, smiling, paralysed.

CHAPTER 2

A Letter to the Papers

OLD **Mr Naseby** had the sturdy, untutored nature of the upper middle class. The universe seemed plain to him. "The thing's right," he would say, or "the thing's wrong"; and there was an end of it. There was a contained, prophetic energy in his utterances, even on the slightest affairs; he *saw* the damned thing; if you did not, it must be from perversity of will; and this sent the blood to his head. Apart from this, which made him an exacting companion, he was one of the most upright, hot-tempered, hot-headed old gentlemen in England. Florid, with white hair, the face of an old Jupiter, and the figure of an old fox-hunter, he enlivened the Vale of Thyme from end to end on his big, cantering chestnut.

He had a hearty respect for Dick as a lad of parts. Dick had a respect for his father as the best of men, tempered by the politic revolt of a youth who has to see to his own independence. Whenever the pair argued, they came to an open rupture; and arguments were frequent, for they were both positive, and both loved the work of the intelligence. It was a treat to hear Mr Naseby defending the Church of England in a volley of oaths, or supporting ascetic morals with an enthusiasm not entirely innocent of port wine. Dick used to wax indignant, and none the less so because, as his father was a skilful disputant, he found himself not seldom in the wrong. On these occasions, he would redouble in energy, and declare that black was white, and blue yellow, with much conviction and heat of manner; but in the morning such a licence of debate weighed upon him like a crime, and he would seek out his father, where he walked before breakfast on a terrace overlooking all the Vale of Thyme.

"I have to apologise, sir, for last night—" he would begin.

"Of course you have," the old gentleman would cut in cheerfully. "You spoke like a fool. Say no more about it."

"You do not understand me, sir. I refer to a particular point. I confess there is much force in your argument from the doctrine of possibilities."

"Of course there is," returned his father. "Come down and look at the stables. Only," he would add, "bear this in mind, and do remember that a man of my age and experience knows more about what he is saying than a raw boy."

He would utter the word 'boy' even more offensively than the average of fathers, and the light way in which he accepted these apologies cut Richard to the heart. The latter drew slighting comparisons, and remembered that he was the only one who ever apologised. This gave him a high station in his own esteem, and thus contributed indirectly to his better behaviour; for he was scrupulous as well as high-spirited, and prided himself on nothing more than on a just submission.

So things went on until the famous occasion when Mr Naseby, becoming engrossed in securing the election of a sound party candidate to Parliament, wrote a flaming letter to the papers. The letter had about every demerit of party letters in general; it was expressed with the energy of a believer; it was personal; it was a little more than half unfair, and about a quarter untrue. The old man did not mean to say what was untrue, you may be sure; but he had rashly picked up gossip, as his prejudice suggested, and now rashly launched it on the public with the sanction of his name.

"The Liberal candidate," he concluded, "is thus a public turncoat. Is that the sort of man we want? He has been given the lie, and has swallowed the insult. Is that the sort of man we want? I answer No! With all the force of my conviction, I answer, *No!*"

And then he signed and dated the letter with an amateur's pride, and looked to be famous by the morrow.

Dick, who had heard nothing of the matter, was up first on that inauspicious day, and took the journal to an arbour in the garden. He found his father's manifesto in one column; and in another a leading article. "No one that we are aware of," ran the article, "had consulted Mr Naseby on the subject, but if he had been appealed to by the whole body of electors, his letter would be none the less ungenerous and unjust to Mr Dalton. We do not choose to give the lie to Mr Naseby, for we are too well aware of the consequences; but we shall venture instead to print the facts of both cases referred to by this red-hot partisan in another portion of our issue. Mr Naseby is of course a large proprietor in our neighbourhood; but fidelity to facts, decent feeling, and English grammar, are all of them qualities more important than the possession of land. Mr— is doubtless a great man; in his large gardens and that half-mile of greenhouses, where he has probably ripened his intellect and temper, he may say what he will to his hired vassals, but (as the Scotch say)—

here

He mauna think to domineer.

"Liberalism," continued the anonymous journalist, "is of too free and sound a growth," etc.

Richard Naseby read the whole thing from beginning to end; and a crushing shame fell upon his spirit. His father had played the fool; he had gone out noisily to war, and come back with confusion. The moment that his trumpets sounded, he had been disgracefully unhorsed. There was no question as to the facts; they were one and all against the Squire. Richard would have given his ears to have suppressed the issue; but as that could not be done, he had his horse saddled, and furnishing himself with a convenient staff, rode off at once to Thymebury.

The editor was at breakfast in a large, sad apartment. The absence of furniture, the extreme meanness of the meal, and the haggard, bright-eyed, consumptive look of the culprit, unmanned our hero; but he clung to his stick, and was stout and warlike.

"You wrote the article in this morning's paper?" he demanded.

"You are young Mr Naseby? I *published* it," replied the editor, rising.

"My father is an old man," said Richard; and then with an outburst, "And a damned sight finer fellow than either you or Dalton!" He stopped and swallowed; he was determined that all should go with regularity. "I have but one question to put to you, sir," he resumed. "Granted that my father was misinformed, would it not have been more decent to withhold the letter and communicate with him in private?"

"Believe me," returned the editor, "that alternative was not open to me. Mr Naseby told me in a note that he had sent his letter to three other journals, and in fact threatened me with what he called exposure if I kept it back from mine. I am really concerned at what has happened; I sympathise and approve of your emotion, young gentleman; but the attack on Mr Dalton was gross, very gross, and I had no choice but to offer him my columns to reply. Party has its duties, sir," added the scribe, kindling, as one who should propose a sentiment; "and the attack was gross."

Richard stood for half a minute digesting the answer; and then the god of fair play came upper-most in his heart, and murmuring "Good morning," he made his escape into the street.

His horse was not hurried on the way home, and he was late for breakfast. The Squire was standing with his back to the fire in a state bordering on apoplexy, his fingers violently knitted under his coat tails. As Richard came in, he opened and shut his mouth like a cod-fish, and his eyes protruded.

"Have you seen that, sir?" he cried, nodding towards the paper.

"Yes, sir," said Richard.

"Oh, you've read it, have you?"

"Yes, I have read it," replied Richard, looking at his foot.

"Well," demanded the old gentleman, "and what have you to say to it, sir?"

"You seem to have been misinformed," said Dick.

"Well? What then? Is your mind so sterile, sir? Have you not a word of comment? no proposal?"

"I fear, sir, you must apologise to Mr Dalton. It would be more handsome, indeed it would be only just, and a free acknowledgment would go far—" Richard paused, no language appearing delicate enough to suit the case.

"That is a suggestion which should have come from me, sir," roared the father. "It is out of place upon your lips. It is not the thought of a loyal son. Why, sir, if my father had been plunged in such deplorable circumstances, I should have thrashed the editor of that vile sheet within an inch of his life. I should have thrashed the man, sir. It would have been the action of an ass; but it would have shown that I had the blood and the natural affections of a man. Son? You are no son, no son of mine, sir!"

"Sir!" said Dick.

"I'll tell you what you are, sir," pursued the Squire. "You're a Benthamite. I disown you. Your mother would have died for shame; there was no modern cant about your mother; she thought – she said to me, sir – I'm glad she's in her grave, Dick Naseby. Misinformed! Misinformed, sir? Have you no loyalty, no spring, no natural affections? Are you clockwork, hey? Away! This is no place for you. Away!" (waving his hands in the air). "Go away! Leave me!"

At this moment Dick beat a retreat in a disarray of nerves, a whistling and clamour of his own arteries, and in short in such a final bodily disorder as made him alike incapable of speech or hearing. And in the midst of all this turmoil, a sense of unpardonable injustice remained graven in his memory.

CHAPTER 3

In the Admiral's Name

There was no return to the subject. Dick and his father were henceforth on terms of coldness. The upright old gentleman grew more upright when he met his son, buckrammed with immortal anger; he asked after Dick's health, and discussed the weather and the crops with an appalling courtesy; his pronunciation was *point-de-vice*, his voice was distant, distinct, and sometimes almost trembling with suppressed indignation.

As for Dick, it seemed to him as if his life had come abruptly to an end. He came out of his theories and clevernesses; his premature man-of-the-worldness, on which he had prided himself on his travels, "shrank like a thing ashamed" before this real sorrow. Pride, wounded honour, pity and respect tussled together daily in his heart; and now he was within an ace of throwing himself upon his father's mercy, and now of slipping forth at night and coming back no more to Naseby House. He suffered from the sight of his father, nay, even from the neighbourhood of this familiar valley, where every corner had its legend, and he was besieged with memories of childhood. If he fled into a new land, and among none but strangers, he might escape his destiny, who knew? and begin again light-heartedly. From that chief peak of the hills, that now and then, like an uplifted finger, shone in an arrow of sunlight through the broken clouds, the shepherd in clear weather might perceive the shining of the sea. There, he thought, was hope. But his heart failed him when he saw the Squire; and he remained. His fate was not that of the voyager by sea and land; he was to travel in the spirit, and begin his journey sooner than he supposed.

For it chanced one day that his walk led him into a portion of the uplands which was almost unknown to him. Scrambling through some rough woods, he came out upon a moorland reaching towards the hills. A few lofty Scotch firs grew hard by upon a knoll; a clear fountain near the foot of the knoll sent up a miniature streamlet which meandered in the heather. A shower had just skimmed by, but now the sun shone brightly, and the air smelt of the pines and the grass. On a stone under the trees sat a young lady sketching. We have learned to think of women in a sort of symbolic transfiguration, based on clothes; and one of the readiest ways in which we conceive our mistress is as a composite thing, principally petticoats. But humanity has triumphed over clothes; the look, the touch of a dress has become alive; and the woman who stitched herself into these material integuments has now permeated right through and gone out to the tip of her skirt. It was only a black dress that caught Dick Naseby's eye; but it took possession of his mind, and all other thoughts departed. He drew near, and the girl turned round. Her face startled him; it was a face he wanted; and he took it in at once like breathing air.

"I beg your pardon," he said, taking off his hat, "you are sketching."

"Oh!" she exclaimed, "for my own amusement. I despise the thing."

"Ten to one, you do yourself injustice," returned Dick. "Besides, it's a freemasonry. I sketch myself, and you know what that implies."

"No. What?" she asked.

"Two things," he answered. "First, that I am no very difficult critic; and second, that I have a right to see your picture."

She covered the block with both her hands. "Oh no," she said; "I am ashamed."

"Indeed, I might give you a hint," said Dick. "Although no artist myself, I have known many; in Paris I had many for friends, and used to prowl among studios."

"In Paris?" she cried, with a leap of light into her eyes. "Did you ever meet Mr Van Tromp?"

"I? Yes. Why, you're not the Admiral's daughter, are you?"

"The Admiral? Do they call him that?" she cried. "Oh, how nice, how nice of them! It is the younger men who call him so, is it not?"

"Yes," said Dick, somewhat heavily.

"You can understand now," she said, with an unspeakable accent of contented noble-minded pride, "why it is I do not choose to show my sketch. Van Tromp's daughter! The Admiral's daughter! I delight in that name. The Admiral! And so you know my father?"

"Well," said Dick, "I met him often; we were even intimate. He may have mentioned my name – Naseby."

"He writes so little. He is so busy, so devoted to his art! I have had a half wish," she added laughing, "that my father was a plainer man, whom I could help – to whom I could be a credit; but only sometimes, you know, and with only half my heart. For a great painter! You have seen his works?"

"I have seen some of them," returned Dick; "they – they are very nice."

She laughed aloud. "Nice?" she repeated. "I see you don't care much for art."

"Not much," he admitted; "but I know that many people are glad to buy Mr Van Tromp's pictures."

"Call him the Admiral!" she cried. "It sounds kindly and familiar; and I like to think that he is appreciated and looked up to by young painters. He has not always been appreciated; he had a cruel life for many years; and when I think" – there were tears in her eyes – "when

I think of that, I feel incline to be a fool," she broke off. "And now I shall go home. You have filled me full of happiness; for think, Mr Naseby, I have not seen my father since I was six years old; and yet he is in my thoughts all day! You must come and call on me; my aunt will be delighted, I am sure; and then you will tell me all – all about my father, will you not?"

Dick helped her to get her sketching traps together; and when all was ready, she gave Dick her hand and a frank return of pressure.

"You are my father's friend," she said; "we shall be great friends too. You must come and see me soon."

Then she was gone down the hillside at a run; and Dick stood by himself in a state of some bewilderment and even distress. There were elements of laughter in the business; but the black dress, and the face that belonged to it, and the hand that he had held in his, inclined him to a serious view. What was he, under the circumstances, called upon to do? Perhaps to avoid the girl? Well, he would think about that. Perhaps to break the truth to her? Why, ten to one, such was her infatuation, he would fail. Perhaps to keep up the illusion, to colour the raw facts; to help her to false ideas, while yet not plainly stating falsehoods? Well, he would see about that; he would also see about avoiding the girl. He saw about this last so well, that the next afternoon beheld him on his way to visit her.

In the meantime the girl had gone straight home, light as a bird, tremulous with joy, to the little cottage where she lived alone with a maiden aunt; and to that lady, a grim, sixty years old Scotchwoman, with a nodding head, communicated news of her encounter and invitation.

"A friend of his?" cried the aunt. "What like is he? What did ye say was his name?"

She was dead silent, and stared at the old woman darkling. Then very slowly, "I said he was my father's friend; I have invited him to my house, and come he shall," she said; and with that she walked off to her room, where she sat staring at the wall all the evening. Miss M'Glashan, for that was the aunt's name, read a large bible in the kitchen with some of the joys of martyrdom.

It was perhaps half-past three when Dick presented himself, rather scrupulously dressed, before the cottage door; he knocked, and a voice bade him enter. The kitchen, which opened directly off the garden, was somewhat darkened by foliage; but he could see her as she approached from the far end to meet him. This second sight of her surprised him. Her strong black brows spoke of temper easily aroused and hard to quiet; her mouth was small, nervous and weak; there was something dangerous and sulky underlying, in her nature, much that was honest, compassionate, and even noble.

"My father's name," she said, "has made you very welcome."

And she gave him her hand, with a sort of curtsy. It was a pretty greeting, although somewhat mannered; and Dick felt himself among the gods. She led him through the kitchen to a parlour, and presented him to Miss M'Glashan.

"Esther," said the aunt, "see and make Mr Naseby his tea."

And as soon as the girl was gone upon this hospitable intent, the old woman crossed the room and came quite near to Dick as if in menace.

"Ye know that man?" she asked in an imperious whisper.

"Mr Van Tromp?" said Dick. "Yes, I know him."

"Well, and what brings ye here?" she said. "I couldn't save the mother – her that's dead – but the bairn!" She had a note in her voice that filled poor Dick with consternation. "Man," she went on, "what is it now? Is it money?"

"My dear lady," said Dick, "I think you misinterpret my position. I am young Mr Naseby of Naseby House. My acquaintance with Mr Van Tromp is really very slender; I am only afraid that Miss Van

Tromp has exaggerated our intimacy in her own imagination. I know positively nothing of his private affairs, and do not care to know. I met him casually in Paris – that is all."

Miss M'Glashan drew along breath. "In Paris?" she said. "Well, and what do you think of him? – what do ye think of him?" she repeated, with a different scansion, as Richard, who had not much taste for such a question, kept her waiting for an answer.

"I found him a very agreeable companion," he said.

"Ay," said she, "did ye! And how does he win his bread?"

"I fancy," he gasped, "that Mr Van Tromp has many generous friends."

"I'll warrant!" she sneered; and before Dick could find more to say, she was gone from the room.

Esther returned with the tea-things, and sat down.

"Now," she said cosily, "tell me all about my father."

"He" – stammered Dick, "he is a very agreeable companion."

"I shall begin to think it is more than you are, Mr Naseby," she said, with a laugh. "I am his daughter, you forget. Begin at the beginning, and tell me all you have seen of him, all he said and all you answered. You must have met somewhere; begin with that."

So with that he began: how he had found the Admiral painting in a café; how his art so possessed him that he could not wait till he got home to – well, to dash off his idea; how (this in reply to a question) his idea consisted of a cock crowing and two hens eating corn; how he was fond of cocks and hens; how this did not lead him to neglect more ambitious forms of art; how he had a picture in his studio of a Greek subject which was said to be remarkable from several points of view; how no one had seen it nor knew the precise site of the studio in which it was being vigorously though secretly confected; how (in answer to a suggestion) this shyness was common to the Admiral, Michelangelo, and others; how they (Dick and Van Tromp) had struck up an acquaintance at once, and dined together that same night; how he (the Admiral) had once given money to a beggar; how he spoke with effusion of his little daughter; how he had once borrowed money to send her a doll – a trait worthy of Newton, she being then in her nineteenth year at least; how, if the doll never arrived (which it appeared it never did), the trait was only more characteristic of the highest order of creative intellect; how he was – no, not beautiful – striking, yes, Dick would go so far, decidedly striking in appearance; how his boots were made to lace and his coat was black, not cut-away, a frock; and so on, and so on by the yard. It was astonishing how few lies were necessary. After all, people exaggerated the difficulty of life. A little steering, just a touch of the rudder now and then, and with a willing listener there is no limit to the domain of equivocal speech. Sometimes Miss M'Glashan made a freezing sojourn in the parlour; and then the task seemed unaccountably more difficult; but to Esther, who was all eyes and ears, her face alight with interest, his stream of language flowed without break or stumble, and his mind was ever fertile in ingenious evasions and—

What an afternoon it was for Esther!

"Ah!" she said at last, "it's good to hear all this! My aunt, you should know, is narrow and too religious; she cannot understand an artist's life. It does not frighten me," she added grandly; 'I am an artist's daughter.'

With that speech, Dick consoled himself for his imposture; she was not deceived so grossly after all; and then if a fraud, was not the fraud piety itself? – and what could be more obligatory than to keep alive in the heart of a daughter that filial trust and honour which, even although misplaced, became her like a jewel of the mind? There might be another thought, a shade of cowardice, a selfish desire to please; poor Dick was merely human; and what would you have had him do?

CHAPTER 4

Esther on the Filial Relation

A month later Dick and Esther met at the stile beside the cross roads; had there been any one to see them but the birds and summer insects, it would have been remarked that they met after a different fashion from the day before. Dick took her in his arms, and their lips were set together for a long while. Then he held her at arm's-length, and they looked straight into each other's eyes.

"Esther!" he said; you should have heard his voice!

"Dick!" said she.

"My darling!"

It was some time before they started for their walk; he kept an arm about her, and their sides were close together as they walked; the sun, the birds, the west wind running among the trees, a pressure, a look, the grasp tightening round a single finger, these things stood them in lieu of thought and filled their hearts with joy. The path they were following led them through a wood of pine-trees carpeted with heather and blue-berry, and upon this pleasant carpet, Dick, not without some seriousness, made her sit down.

"Esther!" he began, "there is something you ought to know. You know my father is a rich man, and you would think, now that we love each other, we might marry when we pleased. But

I fear, darling, we may have long to wait, and shall want all our courage."

"I have courage for anything," she said, "I have all I want; with you and my father, I am so well off, and waiting is made so happy, that I could wait a lifetime and not weary."

He had a sharp pang at the mention of the Admiral. "Hear me out," he continued. "I ought to have told you this before; but it is a thought I shrink from; if it were possible, I should not tell you even now. My poor father and I are scarce on speaking terms."

"Your father," she repeated, turning pale.

"It must sound strange to you; but yet I cannot think I am to blame," he said. "I will tell you how it happened."

"Oh Dick!" she said, when she had heard him to an end, "how brave you are, and how proud. Yet I would not be proud with a father. I would tell him all."

"What!" cried Dick, "go in months after, and brag that I had meant to thrash the man, and then didn't. And why? Because my father had made a bigger ass of himself than I supposed. My dear, that's nonsense."

She winced at his words and drew away. "But when that is all he asks," she pleaded. "If he only knew that you had felt that impulse, it would make him so proud and happy. He would see you were his own son after all, and had the same thoughts and the same chivalry of spirit. And then you did yourself injustice when you spoke just now. It was because the editor was weak and poor and excused himself, that you repented your first determination. Had he been a big red man, with whiskers, you would have beaten him – you know you would – if Mr Naseby had been ten times more committed. Do you think, if you can tell it to me, and I understand at once, that it would be more difficult to tell it to your own father, or that he would not be more ready to sympathise with you than I am? And I love you, Dick; but then he is your father."

"My dear," said Dick, desperately, "you do not understand; you do not know what it is to be treated with daily want of comprehension and daily small injustices, through childhood and boyhood and manhood, until you despair of a hearing, until the thing rides you like a nightmare, until you almost hate the sight of the man you love, and who's your father after all. In short, Esther, you don't know what it is to have a father, and that's what blinds you."

"I see," she said musingly, "you mean that I am fortunate in my father. But I am not so fortunate after all; you forget, I do not know him; it is you who know him; he is already more your father than mine." And here she took his hand. Dick's heart had grown as cold as ice. "But I am sorry for you, too," she continued, "it must be very sad and lonely."

"You misunderstand me," said Dick, chokingly. "My father is the best man I know in all this world; he is worth a hundred of me, only he doesn't understand me, and he can't be made to."

There was a silence for a while. "Dick," she began again, "I am going to ask a favour, it's the first since you said you loved me. May I see your father – see him pass, I mean, where he will not observe me?"

"Why?" asked Dick.

"It is a fancy; you forget, I am romantic about fathers."

The hint was enough for Dick; he consented with haste, and full of hang-dog penitence and disgust, took her down by a backway and planted her in the shrubbery, whence she might see the Squire ride by to dinner. There they both sat silent, but holding hands, for nearly half an hour. At last the trotting of a horse sounded in the distance, the park gates opened with a clang, and then Mr

Naseby appeared, with stooping shoulders and a heavy, bilious countenance, languidly rising to the trot. Esther recognized him at once; she had often seen him before, though with her huge indifference for all that lay outside the circle of her love, she had never so much as wondered who he was; but now she recognized him, and found him ten years older, leaden and springless, and stamped by an abiding sorrow.

"Oh Dick, Dick!" she said, and the tears began to shine upon her face as she hid it in his bosom; his own fell thickly too. They had a sad walk home, and that night, full of love and good counsel, Dick exerted every art to please his father, to convince him of his respect and affection, to heal up this breach of kindness, and reunite two hearts. But alas! the Squire was sick and peevish; he had been all day glooming over Dick's estrangement – for so he put it to himself, and now with growls, cold words, and the cold shoulder, he beat off all advances, and entrenched himself in a just resentment.

CHAPTER 5

The Prodigal Father Makes His Debut at Home

hat took place upon a Tuesday. On the Thursday following, as Dick was walking by appointment, earlier than usual, in the direction of the cottage, he was appalled to meet in the lane a fly from Thymebury, containing the human form of Miss M'Glashan. The lady did not deign to remark him in her passage; her face was suffused with tears, and expressed much concern for the packages by which she was surrounded. He stood still, and asked himself what this circumstance might portend. It was so beautiful a day that he was loth to forecast evil, yet something must perforce have happened at the cottage, and that of a decisive nature; for here was Miss M'Glashan on her travels, with a small patrimony in brown paper parcels, and the old lady's bearing implied hot battle and unqualified defeat. Was the house to be closed against him? Was Esther left alone, or had some new protector made his appearance from among the millions of Europe? It is the character of love to loathe the near relatives of the loved one; chapters in the history of the human race have justified this feeling, and the conduct of uncles, in particular, has frequently met with censure from the independent novelist. Miss M'Glashan was now seen in the rosy colours of regret; whoever succeeded her, Dick felt the change would be for the worse. He hurried forward in this spirit; his anxiety grew upon him with

THE STORY OF A LIE

every step; as he entered the garden a voice fell upon his ear, and he was once more arrested, not this time by doubt, but by indubitable certainty of ill.

The thunderbolt had fallen; the Admiral was here.

Dick would have retreated, in the panic terror of the moment; but Esther kept a bright look-out when her lover was expected. In a twinkling she was by his side, brimful of news and pleasure, too glad to notice his embarrassment, and in one of those golden transports of exultation which transcend not only words but caresses. She took him by the end of the fingers (reaching forward to take them, for her great preoccupation was to save time), she drew him towards her, pushed him past her in the door, and planted him face to face with Mr Van Tromp, in a suit of French country velveteens and with a remarkable carbuncle on his nose. Then, as though this was the end of what she could endure in the way of joy, Esther turned and ran out of the room.

The two men remained looking at each other with some confusion on both sides. Van Tromp was naturally the first to recover; he put out his hand with a fine gesture.

"And you know my little lass, my Esther?" he said. "This is pleasant; this is what I have conceived of home. A strange word for the old rover; but we all have a taste for home and the home-like, disguise it how we may. It has brought me here, Mr Naseby," he concluded, with an intonation that would have made his fortune on the stage, so just, so sad, so dignified, so like a man of the world and a philosopher, "and you see a man who is content."

"I see," said Dick.

"Sit down," continued the parasite, setting the example. "Fortune has gone against me. (I am just sirrupping a little brandy – after my journey.) I was going down, Mr Naseby; between you and me, I was *décavé*; I borrowed fifty francs, smuggled my valise past the concierge – a work of considerable tact – and here I am!"

"Yes," said Dick; "and here you are." He was quite idiotic.

Esther, at this moment, re-entered the room.

"Are you glad to see him?" she whispered in his ear, the pleasure in her voice almost bursting through the whisper into song.

"Oh yes," said Dick, "very."

"I knew you would be," she replied; "I told him how you loved him."

"Help yourself," said the Admiral, "help yourself; and let us drink to a new existence."

"To a new existence," repeated Dick; and he raised the tumbler to his lips, but set it down untasted. He had had enough of novelties for one day.

Esther was sitting on a stool beside her father's feet, holding her knees in her arms, and looking with pride from one to the other of her two visitors. Her eyes were so bright that you were never sure if there were tears in them or not; little voluptuous shivers ran about her body; sometimes she nestled her chin into her throat, sometimes threw back her head, with ecstasy; in a word, she was in that state when it is said of people that they cannot contain themselves for happiness. It would be hard to exaggerate the agony of Richard.

And, in the meantime, Van Tromp ran on interminably.

"I never forget a friend," said he, "nor yet an enemy: of the latter, I never had but two – myself and the public; and I fancy I have had my vengeance pretty freely out of both." He chuckled. "But those days are done. Van Tromp is no more. He was a man who had successes; I believe you knew I had successes – to which we shall refer no farther," pulling down his neckcloth with a smile. "That man exists no more: by an exercise of will I have destroyed him. There is something like it in the poets. First, a brilliant and conspicuous career – the observed,

I may say, of all observers, including the bum-bailie: and then, presto! a quiet, sly, old, rustic *bonhomme*, cultivating roses. In Paris, Mr Naseby—"

"Call him Richard, father," said Esther.

"Richard, if he will allow me. Indeed, we are old friends, and now near neighbours; and, *à propos*, how are we off for neighbours, Richard? The cottage stands, I think, upon your father's land – a family which I respect – and the wood, I understand, is Lord Trevanion's. Not that I care; I am an old Bohemian. I have cut society with a cut direct; I cut it when I was prosperous, and now I reap my reward, and can cut it with dignity in my declension. These are our little *amours propres*, my daughter: your father must respect himself. Thank you, yes; just a leetle, leetle, tiny – thanks, thanks; you spoil me. But, as I was saying, Richard, or was about to say, my daughter has been allowed to rust; her aunt was a mere duenna; hence, in parenthesis, Richard, her distrust of me; my nature and that of the duenna are poles asunder – poles! But, now that I am here, now that I have given up the fight, and live henceforth for one only of my works – I have the modesty to say it is my best – my daughter – well, we shall put all that to rights. The neighbours, Richard?"

Dick was understood to say that there were many good families in the Vale of Thyme.

"You shall introduce us," said the Admiral.

Dick's shirt was wet; he made a lumbering excuse to go; which Esther explained to herself by a fear of intrusion, and so set down to the merit side of Dick's account, while she proceeded to detain him.

"Before our walk?" she cried. "Never! I must have my walk."

"Let us all go," said the Admiral, rising.

"You do not know that you are wanted," she cried, leaning on his shoulder with a caress. "I might wish to speak to my old friend about my new father. But you shall come today, you shall do all you want; I have set my heart on spoiling you."

"I will just take *one* drop more," said the Admiral, stooping to help himself to brandy. "It is surprising how this journey has fatigued me. But I am growing old, I am growing old, I am growing old, and – I regret to add – bald."

He cocked a white wide-awake coquettishly upon his head – the habit of the lady-killer clung to him; and Esther had already thrown on her hat, and was ready, while he was still studying the result in a mirror: the carbuncle had somewhat painfully arrested his attention.

"We are papa now; we must be respectable," he said to Dick, in explanation of his dandyism: and then he went to a bundle and chose himself a staff. Where were the elegant canes of his Parisian epoch? This was a support for age, and designed for rustic scenes. Dick began to see and appreciate the man's enjoyment in a new part, when he saw how carefully he had 'made it up.' He had invented a gait for this first country stroll with his daughter, which was admirably in key. He walked with fatigue, he leaned upon the staff; he looked round him with a sad, smiling sympathy on all that he beheld; he even asked the name of a plant, and rallied himself gently for an old town bird, ignorant of nature. "This country life will make me young again," he sighed. They reached the top of the hill towards the first hour of evening; the sun was descending heaven, the colour had all drawn into the west; the hills were modelled in their least contour by the soft, slanting shine; and the wide moorlands, veined with glens and hazelwoods, ran west and north in a hazy glory of light. Then the painter wakened in Van Tromp.

"Gad, Dick," he cried, "what value!"

An ode in four hundred lines would not have seemed so touching to Esther; her eyes filled with happy tears; yes, here was the father of whom she had dreamed, whom Dick had described; simple, enthusiastic, unworldly, kind, a painter at heart and a fine gentleman in manner.

And just then the Admiral perceived a house by the wayside, and something depending over the house door which might be construed as a sign by the hopeful and thirsty.

"Is that," he asked, pointing with his stick, "an inn?"

There was a marked change in his voice, as though he attached importance to the inquiry: Esther listened, hoping she should hear wit or wisdom.

Dick said it was.

"You know it?" inquired the Admiral.

"I have passed it a hundred times, but that is all," replied Dick.

"Ah," said Van Tromp, with a smile, and shaking his head; "you are not an old campaigner; you have the world to learn. Now I, you see, find an inn so very near my own home, and my first thought is my neighbours. I shall go forward and make my neighbours' acquaintance; no, you needn't come; I shall not be a moment."

And he walked off briskly towards the inn, leaving Dick alone with Esther on the road.

"Dick," she exclaimed, "I am so glad to get a word with you; I am so happy, I have such a thousand things to say; and I want you to do me a favour. Imagine, he has come without a paint-box, without an easel; and I want him to have all. I want you to get them for me in Thymebury. You saw, this moment, how his heart turned to painting. They can't live without it," she added; meaning perhaps Van Tromp and Michelangelo.

Up to that moment, she had observed nothing amiss in Dick's behaviour. She was too happy to be curious; and his silence, in presence of the great and good being whom she called her father, had seemed both natural and praiseworthy. But now that they were alone, she became conscious of a barrier between her lover and herself, and alarm sprang up in her heart.

"Dick," she cried, "you don't love me."

"I do that," he said heartily.

"But you are unhappy; you are strange; you – you are not glad to see my father," she concluded, with a break in her voice.

"Esther," he said, "I tell you that I love you; if you love me, you know what that means, and that all I wish is to see you happy. Do you think I cannot enjoy your pleasures? Esther, I do. If I am uneasy, if I am alarmed, if – Oh, believe me, try and believe in me," he cried, giving up argument with perhaps a happy inspiration.

But the girl's suspicions were aroused; and though she pressed the matter no farther (indeed, her father was already seen returning), it by no means left her thoughts. At one moment she simply resented the selfishness of a man who had obtruded his dark looks and passionate language on her joy; for there is nothing that a woman can less easily forgive than the language of a passion which, even if only for the moment, she does not share. At another, she suspected him of jealousy against her father; and for that, although she could see excuses for it, she yet despised him. And at least, in one way or the other, here was the dangerous beginning of a separation between two hearts. Esther found herself at variance with her sweetest friend; she could no longer look into his heart and find it written with the same language as her own; she could no longer think of him as the sun which radiated happiness upon her life, for she had turned to him once, and he had breathed upon her black and chilly, radiated blackness and frost. To put the whole matter in a word, she was beginning, although ever so slightly, to fall out of love.

CHAPTER 6

The Prodigal Father Goes on From Strength to Strength

We will **not follow** all the steps of the Admiral's return and installation, but hurry forward towards the catastrophe, merely chronicling by the way a few salient incidents, wherein we must rely entirely upon the evidence of Richard, for Esther to this day has never opened her mouth upon this trying passage of her life, and as for the Admiral – well, that naval officer, although still alive, and now more suitably installed in a seaport town where he has a telescope and a flag in his front garden, is incapable of throwing the slightest gleam of light upon the affair. Often and often has he remarked to the present writer: "If I know what it was all about, sir, I'll be—" in short, be what I hope he will not. And then he will look across at his daughter's portrait, a photograph, shake his head with an amused appearance, and mix himself another grog by way of consolation. Once I heard him go farther, and express his feelings with regard to Esther in a single but eloquent word. "A minx, sir," he said, not in anger, rather in amusement: and he cordially drank her health upon the back of it. His worst enemy must admit him to be a man without malice; he never bore a grudge in his life, lacking the necessary taste and industry of attention.

Yet it was during this obscure period that the drama was really performed; and its scene was in the heart of Esther, shut away from all eyes. Had this warm, upright, sullen girl been differently used by destiny, had events come upon her even in a different succession, for some things lead easily to others, the whole course of this tale would have been changed, and Esther never would have run away. As it was, through a series of acts and words of which we know but few, and a series of thoughts which any one may imagine for himself, she was awakened in four days from the dream of a life.

The first tangible cause of disenchantment was when Dick brought home a painter's arsenal on Friday evening. The Admiral was in the chimney-corner, once more 'sirrupping' some brandy and water, and Esther sat at the table at work. They both came forward to greet the new arrival; and the girl, relieving him of his monstrous burthen, proceeded to display her offerings to her father. Van Tromp's countenance fell several degrees; he became quite querulous.

"God bless me," he said; and then, "I must really ask you not to interfere, child," in a tone of undisguised hostility.

"Father," she said, "forgive me; I knew you had given up your art—"

"Oh yes!" cried the Admiral; "I've done with it to the judgment-day!"

"Pardon me again," she said firmly, "but I do not, I cannot think that you are right in this. Suppose the world is unjust, suppose that no one understands you, you have still a duty to yourself. And, oh, don't spoil the pleasure of your coming home to me; show me that you can be my father and yet not neglect your destiny. I am not like some daughters; I will not be jealous of your art, and I will try to understand it."

The situation was odiously farcical. Richard groaned under it; he longed to leap forward and denounce the humbug. And the humbug himself? Do you fancy he was easier in his mind? I am

sure, on the other hand, that he was acutely miserable; and he
betrayed his sufferings by a perfectly silly and undignified access
of temper, during which he broke his pipe in several pieces, threw
his brandy and water in the fire, and employed words which were
very plain although the drift of them was somewhat vague. It was
of very brief duration. Van Tromp was himself again, and in a most
delightful humour within three minutes of the first explosion.

"I am an old fool," he said frankly. "I was spoiled when a
child. As for you, Esther, you take after your mother; you have
a morbid sense of duty, particularly for others; strive against it,
my dear – strive against it. And as for the pigments, well, I'll use
them, some of these days; and to show that I'm in earnest, I'll get
Dick here to prepare a canvas."

Dick was put to this menial task forthwith, the Admiral not
even watching how he did, but quite occupied with another grog
and a pleasant vein of talk.

A little after Esther arose, and making some pretext, good or
bad, went off to bed. Dick was left hobbled by the canvas, and was
subjected to Van Tromp for about an hour.

The next day, Saturday, it is believed that little intercourse took place
between Esther and her father; but towards the afternoon Dick met
the latter returning from the direction of the inn, where he had struck
up quite a friendship with the landlord. Dick wondered who paid for
these excursions, and at the thought that the reprobate must get his
pocket money where he got his board and lodging, from poor Esther's
generosity, he had it almost in his heart to knock the old gentleman
down. He, on his part, was full of airs and graces and geniality.

"Dear Dick," he said, taking his arm, "this is neighbourly of
you; it shows your tact to meet me when I had a wish for you. I am
in pleasant spirits; and it is then that I desire a friend."

"I am glad to hear you are so happy," retorted Dick bitterly. "There's certainly not much to trouble *you*."

"No," assented the Admiral, "not much. I got out of it in time; and here – well, here everything pleases me. I am plain in my tastes. "*A propos*, you have never asked me how I liked my daughter?"

"No," said Dick roundly; "I certainly have not."

"Meaning you will not. And why, Dick? She is my daughter, of course; but then I am a man of the world and a man of taste, and perfectly qualified to give an opinion with impartiality – yes, Dick, with impartiality. Frankly, I am not disappointed in her. She has good looks; she has them from her mother. So I may say I *chose* her looks. She is devoted, quite devoted to me—"

"She is the best woman in the world!" broke out Dick.

"Dick," cried the Admiral, stopping short; "I have been expecting this. Let us – let us go back to the 'Trevanion Arms' and talk this matter out over a bottle."

"Certainly not," went Dick. "You have had far too much already."

The parasite was on the point of resenting this; but a look at Dick's face, and some recollection of the terms on which they had stood in Paris, came to the aid of his wisdom and restrained him.

"As you please," he said; "although I don't know what you mean – nor care. But let us walk, if you prefer it. You are still a young man; when you are my age – But, however, to continue. You please me, Dick; you have pleased me from the first; and to say truth, Esther is a trifle fantastic, and will be better when she is married. She has means of her own, as of course you are aware. They come, like the looks, from her poor, dear, good creature of a mother. She was blessed in her mother. I mean she shall be blessed in her husband, and you are the man, Dick, you and not another. This very night I will sound her affections."

Dick stood aghast.

"Mr Van Tromp, I implore you," he said; "do what you please with yourself, but, for God's sake, let your daughter alone."

"It is my duty," replied the Admiral, "and between ourselves, you rogue, my inclination too. I am as matchmaking as a dowager. It will be more discreet for you to stay away tonight. Farewell. You leave your case in good hands; I have the tact of these little matters by heart; it is not my first attempt.'

All arguments were in vain; the old rascal stuck to his point; nor did Richard conceal from himself how seriously this might injure his prospects, and he fought hard. Once there came a glimmer of hope. The Admiral again proposed an adjournment to the 'Trevanion Arms,' and when Dick had once more refused, it hung for a moment in the balance whether or not the old toper would return there by himself. Had he done so, of course Dick could have taken to his heels, and warned Esther of what was coming, and of how it had begun. But the Admiral, after a pause, decided for the brandy at home, and made off in that direction.

We have no details of the sounding.

Next day the Admiral was observed in the parish church, very properly dressed. He found the places, and joined in response and hymn, as to the manner born; and his appearance, as he intended it should, attracted some attention among the worshippers. Old Naseby, for instance, had observed him.

"There was a drunken-looking blackguard opposite us in church," he said to his son as they drove home; "do you know who he was?"

"Some fellow – Van Tromp, I believe," said Dick.

"A foreigner, too!" observed the Squire.

Dick could not sufficiently congratulate himself on the escape he had effected. Had the Admiral met him with his father, what would have been the result? And could such a catastrophe be long postponed? It seemed to him as if the storm were nearly ripe; and it was so more nearly than he thought.

He did not go to the cottage in the afternoon, withheld by fear and shame; but when dinner was over at Naseby House, and the Squire had gone off into a comfortable doze, Dick slipped out of the room, and ran across country, in part to save time, in part to save his own courage from growing cold; for he now hated the notion of the cottage or the Admiral, and if he did not hate, at least feared to think of Esther. He had no clue to her reflections; but he could not conceal from his own heart that he must have sunk in her esteem, and the spectacle of her infatuation galled him like an insult.

He knocked and was admitted. The room looked very much as on his last visit, with Esther at the table and Van Tromp beside the fire; but the expression of the two faces told a very different story. The girl was paler than usual; her eyes were dark, the colour seemed to have faded from round about them, and her swiftest glance was as intent as a stare. The appearance of the Admiral, on the other hand, was rosy, and flabby and moist; his jowl hung over his shirt collar, his smile was loose and wandering, and he had so far relaxed the natural control of his eyes, that one of them was aimed inward, as if to watch the growth of the carbuncle. We are warned against bad judgments; but the Admiral was certainly not sober. He made no attempt to rise when Richard entered, but waved his pipe flightily in the air, and gave a leer of welcome. Esther took as little notice of him as might be.

"Aha! Dick!" cried the painter. "I've been to church; I have, upon my word. And I saw you there, though you didn't see me. And I saw a devilish pretty woman, by Gad. If it were not for this

baldness, and a kind of crapulous air I can't disguise from myself
– if it weren't for this and that and t'other thing – I – I've forgot
what I was saying. Not that that matters, I've heaps of things to
say. I'm in a communicative vein tonight. I'll let out all my cats,
even unto seventy times seven. I'm in what I call *the* stage, and
all I desire is a listener, although he were deaf, to be as happy
as Nebuchadnezzar.'

Of the two hours which followed upon this it is unnecessary
to give more than a sketch. The Admiral was extremely silly, now
and then amusing, and never really offensive. It was plain that
he kept in view the presence of his daughter, and chose subjects
and a character of language that should not offend a lady. On
almost any other occasion Dick would have enjoyed the scene.
Van Tromp's egotism, flown with drink, struck a pitch above
mere vanity. He became candid and explanatory; sought to take
his auditors entirely into his confidence, and tell them his inmost
conviction about himself. Between his self-knowledge, which was
considerable, and his vanity, which was immense, he had created
a strange hybrid animal, and called it by his own name. How he
would plume his feathers over virtues which would have gladdened
the heart of Cæsar or St Paul; and anon, complete his own portrait
with one of those touches of pitiless realism which the satirist so
often seeks in vain.

"Now, there's Dick," he said, "he's shrewd; he saw through me
the first time we met, and told me so – told me so to my face,
which I had the virtue to keep. I bear you no malice for it, Dick;
you were right; I am a humbug."

You may fancy how Esther quailed at this new feature of the
meeting between her two idols.

And then, again, in a parenthesis –

"That," said Van Tromp, "was when I had to paint those dirty daubs of mine."

And a little further on, laughingly said perhaps, but yet with an air of truth –

"I never had the slightest hesitation in sponging upon any human creature."

Thereupon Dick got up.

"I think perhaps," he said, "we had better all be thinking of going to bed." And he smiled with a feeble and deprecatory smile.

"Not at all," cried the Admiral, "I know a trick worth two of that. Puss here," indicating his daughter, "shall go to bed; and you and I will keep it up till all's blue."

Thereupon Esther arose in sullen glory. She had sat and listened for two mortal hours while her idol defiled himself and sneered away his godhead. One by one, her illusions had departed. And now he wished to order her to bed in her own house! now he called her Puss! now, even as he uttered the words, toppling on his chair, he broke the stem of his tobacco-pipe in three! Never did the sheep turn upon her shearer with a more commanding front. Her voice was calm, her enunciation a little slow, but perfectly distinct, and she stood before him as she spoke, in the simplest and most maidenly attitude.

"No," she said, "Mr Naseby will have the goodness to go home at once and you will go to bed."

The broken fragments of pipe fell from the Admiral's fingers; he seemed by his countenance to have lived too long in a world unworthy of him; but it is an odd circumstance, he attempted no reply, and sat thunderstruck, with open mouth.

Dick she motioned sharply towards the door, and he could only obey her. In the porch, finding she was close behind him, he ventured to pause and whisper, "You have done right."

"I have done as I pleased," she said. "Can he paint?"

"Many people like his paintings," returned Dick, in stifled tones; "I never did; I never said I did," he added, fiercely defending himself before he was attacked.

"I ask you if he can paint. I will not be put off. *Can* he paint?" she repeated.

"No," said Dick.

"Does he even like it?"

"Not now, I believe."

"And he is drunk?" – she leaned upon the word with hatred.

"He has been drinking."

"Go," she said, and was turning to re-enter the house when another thought arrested her. "Meet me tomorrow morning at the stile," she said.

"I will," replied Dick.

And then the door closed behind her, and Dick was alone in the darkness. There was still a chink of light above the sill, a warm, mild glow behind the window; the roof of the cottage and some of the banks and hazels were defined in denser darkness against the sky; but all else was formless, breathless and noiseless like the pit. Dick remained as she had left him, standing squarely upon one foot and resting only on the toe of the other, and as he stood he listened with his soul. The sound of a chair pushed sharply over the floor startled his heart into his mouth; but the silence which had thus been disturbed settled back again at once upon the cottage and its vicinity. What took place during this interval is a secret from the world of men; but when it was over the voice of Esther spoke evenly and without interruption for perhaps half a minute, and as soon as that ceased heavy and uncertain footfalls crossed the parlour and mounted lurching up the stairs. The girl had tamed her father, Van Tromp had gone obediently to bed: so much was obvious to the watcher in the road. And yet he still waited, straining his ears, and with terror and sickness at his heart; for if Esther had followed her father, if she had even made one movement in this great conspiracy of men and nature to be still, Dick must have had instant knowledge of it from his station before the door; and if she had not moved, must she not have fainted? or might she not be dead?

He could hear the cottage clock deliberately measure out the seconds; time stood still with him; an almost superstitious terror took command of his faculties; at last, he could bear no more, and, springing through the little garden in two bounds, he put his face against the window. The blind, which had not been drawn fully down, left an open chink about an inch in height along the bottom of the glass, and the whole parlour was thus exposed to Dick's investigation. Esther sat upright at the table, her head resting on her hand, her eyes fixed upon the candle. Her brows were slightly bent, her mouth slightly open; her whole attitude so still and settled that Dick could hardly fancy that she breathed. She had not stirred at the sound of Dick's arrival. Soon after, making a considerable disturbance amid the vast silence of the night, the clock lifted up its voice, whined for a while like a partridge, and then eleven times hooted like a cuckoo. Still Esther continued immovable and gazed upon the candle. Midnight followed, and then one of the morning; and still she had not stirred, nor had Richard Naseby dared to quit the window. And then, about half-past one, the candle she had been thus intently watching flared up into a last blaze of paper, and she leaped to her feet with an ejaculation, looked about her once, blew out the light, turned round, and was heard rapidly mounting the staircase in the dark.

Dick was left once more alone to darkness and to that dulled and dogged state of mind when a man thinks that misery must now have done her worst, and is almost glad to think so. He turned and walked slowly towards the stile; she had told him no hour, and he was determined, whenever she came, that she should find him waiting. As he got there the day began to dawn, and he leaned over a hurdle and beheld the shadows flee away. Up went the sun at last out of a bank of clouds that were already disbanding in the east; a herald wind had already sprung up to sweep the leafy earth and scatter the congregated dewdrops. "Alas!" thought Dick Naseby, "how can any other day come so distastefully to me?" He still wanted his experience of the morrow.

CHAPTER 7

The Elopement

It was probably on the stroke of ten, and Dick had been half asleep for some time against the bank, when Esther came up the road carrying a bundle. Some kind of instinct, or perhaps the distant light footfalls, recalled him, while she was still a good way off, to the possession of his faculties, and he half raised himself and blinked upon the world. It took him some time to recollect his thoughts. He had awakened with a certain blank and childish sense of pleasure, like a man who had received a legacy overnight; but this feeling gradually died away, and was then suddenly and stunningly succeeded by a conviction of the truth. The whole story of the past night sprang into his mind with every detail, as by an exercise of the direct and speedy sense of sight, and he arose from the ditch and, with rueful courage, went to meet his love.

She came up to him walking steady and fast, her face still pale, but to all appearance perfectly composed; and she showed neither surprise, relief, nor pleasure at finding her lover on the spot. Nor did she offer him her hand.

"Here I am," said he.

"Yes," she replied; and then, without a pause or any change of voice, "I want you to take me away," she added.

"Away?" he repeated. "How? Where?"

"Today," she said. "I do not care where it is, but I want you to take me away."

"For how long? I do not understand," gasped Dick.

"I shall never come back here any more," was all she answered.

Wild words uttered, as these were, with perfect quiet of manner and voice, exercise a double influence on the hearer's mind. Dick was confounded; he recovered from astonishment only to fall into doubt and alarm. He looked upon her frozen attitude, so discouraging for a lover to behold, and recoiled from the thoughts which it suggested.

"To me?" he asked. "Are you coming to me, Esther?"

"I want you to take me away," she repeated with weary impatience. "Take me away – take me away from here."

The situation was not sufficiently defined. Dick asked himself with concern whether she were altogether in her right wits. To take her away, to marry her, to work off his hands for her support, Dick was content to do all this; yet he required some show of love upon her part. He was not one of those tough-hided and small-hearted males who would marry their love at the point of the bayonet rather than not marry her at all. He desired that a woman should come to his arms with an attractive willingness, if not with ardour. And Esther's bearing was more that of despair than that of love. It chilled him and taught him wisdom.

"Dearest," he urged, "tell me what you wish, and you shall have it; tell me your thoughts, and then I can advise you. But to go from here without a plan, without forethought, in the heat of a moment, is madder than madness, and can help nothing. I am not speaking like a man, but I speak the truth; and I tell you again, the thing's absurd, and wrong, and hurtful."

She looked at him with a lowering, languid look of wrath.

"So you will not take me?" she said. "Well, I will go alone."

And she began to step forward on her way. But he threw himself before her.

"Esther, Esther!" he cried.

"Let me go – don't touch me – what right have you to interfere? Who are you, to touch me?" she flashed out, shrill with anger.

Then, being made bold by her violence, he took her firmly, almost roughly, by the arm, and held her while he spoke.

"You know well who I am, and what I am, and that I love you. You say I will not help you; but your heart knows the contrary. It is you who will not help me; for you will not tell me what you want. You see – or you could see, if you took the pains to look – how I have waited here all night to be ready at your service. I only asked information; I only urged you to consider; and I still urge and beg you to think better of your fancies. But if your mind is made up, so be it; I will beg no longer; I give you my orders; and I will not allow – not allow you to go hence alone."

She looked at him for awhile with cold, unkind scrutiny like one who tries the temper of a tool.

"Well, take me away, then," she said with a sigh.

"Good," said Dick. "Come with me to the stables; there we shall get the pony-trap and drive to the junction. Tonight you shall be in London. I am yours so wholly that no words can make me more so; and, besides, you know it, and the words are needless. May God help me to be good to you, Esther – may God help me! for I see that you will not."

So, without more speech, they set out together, and were already got some distance from the spot, ere he observed that she was still carrying the hand-bag. She gave it up to him, passively, but when he offered her his arm, merely shook her head and pursed up her lips. The sun shone clearly and pleasantly; the wind was fresh and brisk upon their faces, and smelt racily of woods and meadows. As they went down into the valley of the Thyme, the babble of the stream rose into the air like a perennial laughter. On the far-away hills, sunburst and shadow raced along the slopes and leaped from peak to peak. Earth, air and water, each seemed in better health and had more of the shrewd salt of life in them than upon ordinary mornings; and from east to west, from the lowest glen to the height of heaven, from every look and touch and scent, a human creature could gather the most encouraging intelligence as to the durability and spirit of the universe.

Through all this walked Esther, picking her small steps like a bird, but silent and with a cloud under her thick eyebrows. She seemed insensible, not only of nature, but of the presence of her companion. She was altogether engrossed in herself, and looked neither to right nor to left, but straight before her on the road. When they came to the bridge, however, she halted, leaned on the parapet, and stared for a moment at the clear, brown pool, and swift, transient snowdrift of the rapids.

"I am going to drink," she said; and descended the winding footpath to the margin.

There she drank greedily in her hands and washed her temples with water. The coolness seemed to break, for an instant, the spell that lay upon her; for, instead of hastening forward again in her dull, indefatigable tramp, she stood still where she was, for near a minute, looking straight before her. And Dick, from above on the bridge where he stood to watch her, saw a strange, equivocal smile dawn slowly on her face and pass away again at once and suddenly, leaving her as grave as ever; and the sense of distance, which it is so cruel for a lover to endure, pressed with every moment more heavily on her companion. Her thoughts were all secret; her heart was locked and bolted; and he stood without, vainly wooing her with his eyes.

"Do you feel better?" asked Dick, as she at last rejoined him; and after the constraint of so long a silence, his voice sounded foreign to his own ears.

She looked at him for an appreciable fraction of a minute ere she answered, and when she did, it was in the monosyllable – "Yes."

Dick's solicitude was nipped and frosted. His words died away on his tongue. Even his eyes, despairing of encouragement, ceased to attend on hers. And they went on in silence through Kirton hamlet, where an old man followed them with his eyes, and perhaps envied them their youth and love; and across the Ivy beck where the mill was splashing and grumbling low thunder to itself in the chequered shadow of the dell, and the miller before the door was beating flour from his hands as he whistled a modulation; and up by the high spinney, whence they saw the mountains upon either hand; and down the hill again to the back courts and offices of Naseby House. Esther had kept ahead all the way, and Dick plodded obediently in her wake; but as they neared the stables, he pushed on and took the lead. He would have preferred her to await him in the road while he went on and brought the carriage back, but after so many repulses and rebuffs he lacked courage to offer the suggestion. Perhaps, too, he felt it wiser to keep his convoy within sight. So they entered the yard in Indian file, like a tramp and his wife.

The grooms eyebrows rose as he received the order for the pony-phaeton, and kept rising during all his preparations. Esther stood bolt upright and looked steadily at some chickens in the corner of the yard. Master Richard himself, thought the groom, was not in his ordinary; for in truth, he carried the hand-bag like a talisman, and either stood listless, or set off suddenly walking in one direction after another with brisk, decisive footsteps. Moreover he had apparently neglected to wash his hands, and bore the air of one returning from a prolonged nutting ramble. Upon the groom's countenance there began to grow up an expression as of one about to whistle. And hardly had the carriage turned the corner and rattled into the high road with this inexplicable pair, than the whistle broke forth – prolonged, and low and tremulous; and the groom, already so far relieved, vented the rest of his surprise in one simple English word, friendly to the mouth of Jack-tar and the sooty pitman, and hurried to spread the news round the servants' hall of Naseby House. Luncheon would be on the table in little beyond an hour; and the Squire, on sitting down, would hardly fail to ask for Master Richard. Hence, as the intelligent reader can foresee, this groom has a part to play in the imbroglio.

Meantime, Dick had been thinking deeply and bitterly. It seemed to him as if his love had gone from him, indeed, yet gone but a little way; as if he needed but to find the right touch or intonation, and her heart would recognize him and be melted. Yet he durst not open his mouth, and drove in silence till they had passed the main park-gates and turned into the cross-cut lane along the wall. Then it seemed to him as if it must be now, or never.

"Can't you see you are killing me?" he cried. "Speak to me, look at me, treat me like a human man."

She turned slowly and looked him in the face with eyes that seemed kinder. He dropped the reins and caught her hand, and she made no resistance, although her touch was unresponsive. But when, throwing one arm round her waist, he sought to kiss her lips, not like a lover indeed, not because he wanted to do so, but as a desperate man who puts his fortunes to the touch, she drew away from him, with a knot in her forehead, backed and shied about fiercely with her head, and pushed him from her with her hand. Then there was no room left for doubt, and Dick saw, as clear as sunlight, that she had a distaste or nourished a grudge against him.

"Then you don't love me?" he said, drawing back from her, he also, as though her touch had burnt him; and then, as she made no answer, he repeated with another intonation, imperious and yet still pathetic, "You don't love me, *do* you, *do* you?"

"I don't know," she replied. "Why do you ask me? Oh, how should I know? It has all been lies together – lies, and lies, and lies!"

He cried her name sharply, like a man who has taken a physical hurt, and that was the last word that either of them spoke until they reached Thymebury Junction.

This was a station isolated in the midst of moorlands, yet lying on the great up line to London. The nearest town, Thymebury itself, was seven miles distant along the branch they call the Vale of Thyme Railway. It was now nearly half an hour past noon, the down train had just gone by, and there would be no more traffic at the junction until half-past three, when the local train comes in to meet the up express at a quarter before four. The stationmaster had already gone off to his garden, which was half a mile away in a hollow of the moor; a porter, who was just leaving, took charge of the phaeton, and promised to return it before night to Naseby House; only a deaf, snuffy, and stern old man remained to play propriety for Dick and Esther.

Before the phaeton had driven off, the girl had entered the station and seated herself upon a bench. The endless, empty moorlands stretched before her, entirely unenclosed, and with no boundary but the horizon. Two lines of rails, a waggon shed, and a few telegraph posts, alone diversified the outlook. As for sounds, the silence was unbroken save by the chant of the telegraph wires and the crying of the plovers on the waste. With the approach of midday the wind had more and more fallen, it was now sweltering hot and the air trembled in the sunshine.

Dick paused for an instant on the threshold of the platform. Then, in two steps, he was by her side and speaking almost with a sob.

"Esther," he said, "have pity on me. What have I done? Can you not forgive me? Esther, you loved me once – can you not love me still?"

"How can I tell you? How am I to know?" she answered. "You are all a lie to me – all a lie from first to last. You were laughing at my folly, playing with me like a child, at the very time when you declared you loved me. Which was true? was any of it true? or was it all, all a mockery? I am weary trying to find out. And you say I loved you; I loved my father's friend. I never loved, I never heard of, you, until that man came home and I began to find myself deceived. Give me back my father, be what you were before, and you may talk of love indeed!"

"Then you cannot forgive me – cannot?" he asked.

"I have nothing to forgive," she answered. "You do not understand."

"Is that your last word, Esther?" said he, very white, and biting his lip to keep it still.

"Yes, that is my last word," replied she.

"Then we are here on false pretences, and we stay here no longer," he said. "Had you still loved me, right or wrong, I should have taken you away, because then I could have made you happy. But as it is – I must speak plainly – what you propose is degrading to you, and an insult to me, and a rank unkindness to your father. Your father may be this or that, but you should use him like a fellow-creature."

"What do you mean?" she flashed. "I leave him my house and all my money; it is more than he deserves. I wonder you dare speak to me about that man. And besides, it is all he cares for; let him take it, and let me never hear from him again."

"I thought you romantic about fathers," he said.

"Is that a taunt?" she demanded.

"No," he replied, "it is an argument. No one can make you like him, but don't disgrace him in his own eyes. He is old, Esther, old and broken down. Even I am sorry for him, and he has been the loss of all I cared for. Write to your aunt; when I see her answer you can leave quietly and naturally, and I will take you to your aunt's door. But in the meantime you must go home. You have no money, and so you are helpless, and must do as I tell you; and believe me, Esther, I do all for your good, and your good only, so God help me."

She had put her hand into her pocket and withdrawn it empty.

"I counted upon you," she wailed.

"You counted rightly then," he retorted. "I will not, to please you for a moment, make both of us unhappy for our lives; and since I cannot marry you, we have only been too long away, and must go home at once."

"Dick," she cried suddenly, "perhaps I might – perhaps in time – perhaps—"

"There is no perhaps about the matter," interrupted Dick. "I must go and bring the phaeton." And with that he strode from the station, all in a glow of passion and virtue. Esther, whose eyes had come alive and her cheeks flushed during these last words, relapsed in a second into a state of petrifaction. She remained without motion during his absence, and when he returned suffered herself to be put back into the phaeton, and driven off on the return journey like an idiot or a tired child. Compared with what she was now, her condition of the morning seemed positively natural. She sat white and cold and silent, and there was no speculation in her eyes. Poor Dick flailed and flailed at the pony, and once tried to whistle, but his courage was going down; huge clouds of despair gathered together in his soul, and from time to time their darkness was divided by a piercing flash of longing and regret. He had lost his love – he had lost his love for good.

The pony was tired, and the hills very long and steep, and the air sultrier than ever, for now the breeze began to fail entirely. It seemed as if this miserable drive would never be done, as if poor Dick would never be able to go away and be comfortably wretched by himself; for all his desire was to escape from her presence and the reproach of her averted looks. He had lost his love, he thought – he had lost his love for good.

They were already not far from the cottage, when his heart again faltered and he appealed to her once more, speaking low and eagerly in broken phrases.

"I cannot live without your love," he concluded.

"I do not understand what you mean," she replied, and I believe with perfect truth.

"Then," said he, wounded to the quick, "your aunt might come and fetch you herself. Of course you can command me as you please. But I think it would be better so."

"Oh yes," she said wearily, "better so."

This was the only exchange of words between them till about four o'clock; the phaeton, mounting the lane, 'opened out' the cottage between the leafy banks. Thin smoke went straight up from the chimney; the flowers in the garden, the hawthorn in the lane, hung down their heads in the heat; the stillness was broken only by the sound of hoofs. For right before the gate a livery servant rode slowly up and down, leading a saddle horse. And in this last Dick shuddered to identify his father's chestnut.

Alas! poor Richard, what should this portend?

The servant, as in duty bound, dismounted and took the phaeton into his keeping; yet Dick thought he touched his hat to him with something of a grin. Esther, passive as ever, was helped out and crossed the garden with a slow and mechanical gait; and Dick, following close behind her, heard from within the cottage his father's voice upraised in an anathema, and the shriller tones of the Admiral responding in the key of war.

CHAPTER 8

Battle Royal

Squire Naseby, on sitting down to lunch, had inquired for Dick, whom he had not seen since the day before at dinner; and the servant answering awkwardly that Master Richard had come back but had gone out again with the pony phaeton, his suspicions became aroused, and he cross-questioned the man until the whole was out. It appeared from this report that Dick had been going about for nearly a month with a girl in the Vale – a Miss Van Tromp; that she lived near Lord Trevanion's upper wood; that recently Miss Van Tromp's papa had returned home from foreign parts after a prolonged absence; that this papa was an old gentleman, very chatty and free with his money in the public-house – whereupon Mr Naseby's face became encrimsoned; that the papa, furthermore, was said to be an admiral – whereupon Mr Naseby spat out a whistle brief and fierce as an oath; that Master Dick seemed very friendly with the papa – "God help him!" said Mr Naseby; that last night Master Dick had not come in, and today he had driven away in the phaeton with the young lady.

"Young woman," corrected Mr Naseby.

"Yes, sir," said the man, who had been unwilling enough to gossip from the first, and was now cowed by the effect of his communications on the master. "Young woman, sir!"

"Had they luggage?" demanded the Squire.

"Yes, sir."

Mr Naseby was silent for a moment, struggling to keep down his emotion, and he mastered it so far as to mount into the sarcastic vein, when he was in the nearest danger of melting into the sorrowful.

"And was this – this Van Dunk with them?" he asked, dwelling scornfully upon the name.

The servant believed not, and being eager to shift the responsibility of speech to other shoulders, suggested that perhaps the master had better inquire further from George the stableman in person.

"Tell him to saddle the chestnut and come with me. He can take the gray gelding; for we may ride fast. And then you can take away this trash," added Mr Naseby, pointing to the luncheon; and he arose, lordly in his anger, and marched forth upon the terrace to await his horse.

There Dick's old nurse shrunk up to him, for the news went like wildfire over Naseby House, and timidly expressed a hope that there was nothing much amiss with the young master.

"I'll pull him through," the Squire said grimly, as though he meant to pull him through a threshing-mill; "I'll save him from this gang; God help him with the next! He has a taste for low company, and no natural affections to steady him. His father was no society for him; he must go fuddling with a Dutchman, Nance, and now he's caught. Let us pray he'll take the lesson," he added more gravely, "but youth is here to make troubles, and age to pull them out again."

Nance whimpered and recalled several episodes of Dick's childhood, which moved Mr Naseby to blow his nose and shake her hard by the hand; and then, the horse arriving opportunely, to get himself without delay into the saddle and canter off.

He rode straight, hot spur, to Thymebury, where, as was to be expected, he could glean no tidings of the runaways. They had not been seen at the George; they had not been seen at the station. The shadow darkened on Mr Naseby's face; the junction did not occur to him; his last hope was for Van Tromp's cottage; thither he bade George guide him, and thither he followed, nursing grief, anxiety and indignation in his heart.

"Here it is, sir," said George stopping.

"What! on my own land!" he cried. "How's this? I let this place to somebody – M'Whirter or M'Glashan."

"Miss M'Glashan was the young lady's aunt, sir, I believe," returned George.

"Ay – dummies," said the Squire. "I shall whistle for my rent too. Here, take my horse."

The Admiral, this hot afternoon, was sitting by the window with a long glass. He already knew the Squire by sight, and now, seeing him dismount before the cottage and come striding through the garden, concluded without doubt he was there to ask for Esther's hand.

"This is why the girl is not yet home," he thought: "a very suitable delicacy on young Naseby's part."

And he composed himself with some pomp, answered the loud rattle of the riding-whip upon the door with a dulcet invitation to enter, and coming forward with a bow and a smile, "Mr Naseby, I believe," said he.

The Squire came armed for battle; took in his man from top to toe in one rapid and scornful glance, and decided on a course at once. He must let the fellow see that he understood him.

"You are Mr Van Tromp?" he returned roughly, and without taking any notice of the proffered hand.

"The same, sir," replied the Admiral. "Pray be seated."

"No sir," said the Squire, point-blank, "I will not be seated. I am told that you are an admiral," he added.

"No sir, I am not an admiral," returned Van Tromp, who now began to grow nettled and enter into the spirit of the interview.

"Then why do you call yourself one, sir?"

"I have to ask your pardon, I do not," says Van Tromp, as grand as the Pope.

But nothing was of avail against the Squire.

"You sail under false colours from beginning to end," he said. "Your very house was taken under a sham name."

"It is not my house. I am my daughter's guest," replied the Admiral. "If it *were* my house—"

"Well?" said the Squire, "what then? hey?"

The Admiral looked at him nobly, but was silent.

"Look here," said Mr Naseby, "this intimidation is a waste of time; it is thrown away on me, sir; it will not succeed with me. I will not permit you even to gain time by your fencing. Now, sir, I presume you understand what brings me here."

"I am entirely at a loss to account for your intrusion," bows and waves Van Tromp.

"I will try to tell you then. I come here as a father" – down came the riding-whip upon the table – "I have right and justice upon my side. I understand your calculations, but you calculated without me. I am a man of the world, and I see through you and your manoeuvres. I am dealing now with a conspiracy – I stigmatize it as such, and I will expose it and crush it. And now I order you to tell me how far things have gone, and whither you have smuggled my unhappy son."

"My God, sir!" Van Tromp broke out, "I have had about enough of this. Your son? God knows where he is for me! What the devil have I to do with your son? My daughter is out, for the matter of that; I might ask you where she was, and what would you say to that? But this is all midsummer madness. Name your business distinctly, and be off."

"How often am I to tell you?" cried the Squire. "Where did your daughter take my son today in that cursed pony carriage?"

"In a pony carriage?" repeated Van Tromp.

"Yes, sir – with luggage."

"Luggage?" – Van Tromp had turned a little pale.

"Luggage, I said – luggage!" shouted Naseby. "You may spare me this dissimulation. Where's my son. You are speaking to a father, sir, a father."

"But, sir, if this be true," out came Van Tromp in a new key, "it is I who have an explanation to demand?"

"Precisely. There is the conspiracy," retorted Naseby. "Oh!" he added, "I am a man of the world. I can see through and through you."

Van Tromp began to understand.

"You speak a great deal about being a father, Mr Naseby," said he; "I believe you forget that the appellation is common to both of us. I am at a loss to figure to myself, however dimly, how any man – I have not said any gentleman – could so brazenly insult another as you have been insulting me since you entered this house. For the first time I appreciate your base insinuations, and I despise them and you. You were, I am told, a manufacturer; I am an artist; I have seen better days; I have moved in societies where you would not be received, and dined where you would be glad to pay a pound to see me dining. The so-called aristocracy of wealth, sir, I despise. I refuse to help you; I refuse to be helped by you. There lies the door."

And the Admiral stood forth in a halo.

It was then that Dick entered. He had been waiting in the porch for some time back, and Esther had been listlessly standing by his side. He had put out his hand to bar her entrance, and she had submitted without surprise; and though she seemed to listen, she scarcely appeared to comprehend. Dick, on his part, was as white as a sheet; his eyes burned and his lips trembled with anger as he thrust the door suddenly open, introduced Esther with ceremonious gallantry, and stood forward and knocked his hat firmer on his head like a man about to leap.

"What is all this?" he demanded.

"Is this your father, Mr Naseby?" inquired the Admiral.

"It is," said the young man.

"I make you my compliments," returned Van Tromp.

"Dick!" cried his father, suddenly breaking forth, "it is not too late, is it? I have come here in time to save you. Come, come away with me – come away from this place."

And he fawned upon Dick with his hands.

"Keep your hands off me," cried Dick, not meaning unkindness, but because his nerves were shattered by so many successive miseries.

"No, no," said the old man, "don't repulse your father, Dick, when he has come here to save you. Don't repulse me, my boy. Perhaps I have not been kind to you, not quite considerate, too harsh; my boy, it was not for want of love. Think of old times. I was kind to you then, was I not? When you were a child, and your mother was with us." Mr Naseby was interrupted by a sort of sob. Dick stood looking at him in a maze. "Come away," pursued the father in a whisper; "you need not be afraid of any consequences. I am a man of the world, Dick; and she can have no claim on you – no claim, I tell you; and we'll be handsome too, Dick – we'll give them a good round figure, father and daughter, and there's an end."

He had been trying to get Dick towards the door, but the latter stood off.

"You had better take care, sir, how you insult that lady," said the son, as black as night.

"You would not choose between your father and your mistress?" said the father.

"What do you call her, sir?" cried Dick, high and clear.

Forbearance and patience were not among Mr Naseby's qualities.

"I called her your mistress," he shouted, "and I might have called her a—"

"That is an unmanly lie," replied Dick, slowly.

"Dick!" cried the father, "Dick!"

"I do not care," said the son, strengthening himself against his own heart; "I – I have said it, and it is the truth."

There was a pause.

"Dick," said the old man at last, in a voice that was shaken as by a gale of wind, "I am going. I leave you with your friends, sir – with your friends. I came to serve you, and now I go away a broken man. For years I have seen this coming, and now it has come. You never loved me. Now you have been the death of me. You may boast of that. Now I leave you. God pardon you."

With that he was gone; and the three who remained together heard his horse's hoofs descend the lane. Esther had not made a sign throughout the interview, and still kept silence now that it was over; but the Admiral, who had once or twice moved forward and drawn back again, now advanced for good.

"You are a man of spirit, sir," said he to Dick; "but though I am no friend to parental interference, I will say that you were heavy on the governor." Then he added with a chuckle: "You began, Richard, with a silver spoon, and here you are in the water like the rest. Work,

work, nothing like work. You have parts, you have manners; why, with application you may die a millionaire!" Dick shook himself. He took Esther by the hand, looking at her mournfully.

"Then this is farewell," he said.

"Yes," she answered. There was no tone in her voice, and she did not return his gaze.

"For ever," added Dick.

"For ever," she repeated mechanically.

"I have had hard measure," he continued. "In time I believe I could have shown you I was worthy, and there was no time long enough to show how much I loved you. But it was not to be. I have lost all."

He relinquished her hand, still looking at her, and she turned to leave the room.

"Why, what in fortune's name is the meaning of all this?" cried Van Tromp. "Esther come back!"

"Let her go," said Dick, and he watched her disappear with strangely mingled feelings. For he had fallen into that stage when men have the vertigo of misfortune, court the strokes of destiny, and rush towards anything decisive, that it may free them from suspense though at the cost of ruin. It is one of the many minor forms of suicide.

"She did not love me," he said, turning to her father.

"I feared as much," said he, "when I sounded her. Poor Dick, poor Dick. And yet I believe I am as much cut up as you are. I was born to see others happy."

"You forget," returned Dick, with something like a sneer, "that I am now a pauper."

Van Tromp snapped his fingers.

"Tut!" said he; "Esther has plenty for us all."

Dick looked at him with some wonder. It had never dawned upon him that this shiftless, thriftless, worthless, sponging parasite was yet, after and in spite of all, not mercenary in the issue of his thoughts; yet so it was.

"Now," said Dick, "I must go."

"Go?" cried Van Tromp. "Where? Not one foot, Mr Richard Naseby. Here you shall stay in the meantime! and – well, and do something practical – advertise for a situation as private secretary – and when you have it, go and welcome. But in the meantime, sir, no false pride; we must stay with our friends; we must sponge a while on Papa Van Tromp, who has sponged so often upon us."

"By God," cried Dick, "I believe you are the best of the lot."

"Dick, my boy," replied the Admiral, winking, "you mark me, I am not the worst."

"Then why," began Dick, and then paused. "But Esther," he began again, once more to interrupt himself. "The fact is, Admiral," he came out with it roundly now, "your daughter wished to run away from you today, and I only brought her back with difficulty."

"In the pony carriage?" asked the Admiral, with the silliness of extreme surprise.

"Yes," Dick answered.

"Why, what the devil was she running away from?"

Dick found the question unusually hard to answer.

"Why," said he, "you know, you're a bit of a rip."

"I behave to that girl, sir, like an archdeacon," replied Van Tromp warmly.

"Well – excuse me – but you know you drink," insisted Dick.

"I know that I was a sheet in the wind's eye, sir, once – once only, since I reached this place," retorted the Admiral. "And even then I was fit for any drawing-room. I should like you to tell me how many fathers, lay and clerical, go upstairs every day with a face like a lobster and cod's eyes – and are dull, upon the back of it – not even mirth for the money! No, if that's what she runs for, all I say is, let her run."

"You see," Dick tried it again, "she has fancies—"

"Confound her fancies!" cried Van Tromp. "I used her kindly; she had her own way; I was her father. Besides I had taken quite a liking to the girl, and meant to stay with her for good. But I tell you what it is, Dick, since she has trifled with you – Oh, yes, she did though! – and since her old papa's not good enough for her – the devil take her, say I."

"You will be kind to her at least?" said Dick.

"I never was unkind to a living soul," replied the Admiral. "Firm I can be, but not unkind."

"Well," said Dick, offering his hand, "God bless you, and farewell."

The Admiral swore by all his gods he should not go. "Dick," he said, "You are a selfish dog; you forget your old Admiral. You wouldn't leave him alone, would you?"

It was useless to remind him that the house was not his to dispose of, that being a class of considerations to which his intelligence was closed; so Dick tore himself off by force, and, shouting a good-bye, made off along the lane to Thymebury.

CHAPTER 9

In Which the Liberal Editor Re-Appears
As 'Deus Ex Machina'

It was perhaps a week later, as old Mr Naseby sat brooding in his study, that there was shown in upon him, on urgent business, a little hectic gentleman shabbily attired.

"I have to ask pardon for this intrusion, Mr Naseby," he said; "but I come here to perform a duty. My card has been sent in, but perhaps you may not know, what it does not tell you, that I am the editor of the *Thymebury Star*."

Mr Naseby looked up, indignant.

"I cannot fancy," he said, "that we have much in common to discuss."

"I have only a word to say - one piece of information to communicate. Some months ago, we had - you will pardon my referring to it, it is absolutely necessary - but we had an unfortunate difference as to facts."

"Have you come to apologise?" asked the Squire, sternly.

"No, sir; to mention a circumstance. On the morning in question, your son, Mr Richard Naseby—"

"I do not permit his name to be mentioned."

"You will, however, permit me," replied the Editor.

"You are cruel," said the Squire. He was right, he was a broken man.

Then the Editor described Dick's warning visit; and how he had seen in the lad's eye that there was a thrashing in the wind, and had escaped through pity only – so the Editor put it – "through pity only sir. And oh, sir," he went on, "if you had seen him speaking up for you, I am sure you would have been proud of your son. I know I admired the lad myself, and indeed that's what brings me here."

"I have misjudged him," said the Squire. "Do you know where he is?"

"Yes, sir, he lies sick at Thymebury."

"You can take me to him?"

"I can."

"I pray God he may forgive me," said the father.

And he and the Editor made post-haste for the country town.

Next day the report went abroad that Mr Richard was reconciled to his father and had been taken home to Naseby House. He was still ailing, it was said, and the Squire nursed him like the proverbial woman. Rumour, in this instance, did no more than justice to the truth; and over the sickbed many confidences were exchanged, and clouds that had been growing for years passed away in a few hours, and as fond mankind loves to hope, for ever. Many long talks had been fruitless in external action, though fruitful for the understanding of the pair; but at last, one showery Tuesday, the Squire might have been observed upon his way to the cottage in the lane.

The old gentleman had arranged his features with a view to self-command, rather than external cheerfulness; and he entered the cottage on his visit of conciliation with the bearing of a clergyman come to announce a death.

The Admiral and his daughter were both within, and both looked upon their visitor with more surprise than favour.

"Sir," said he to Van Tromp, "I am told I have done you much injustice."

There came a little sound in Esther's throat, and she put her hand suddenly to her heart.

"You have, sir; and the acknowledgment suffices," replied the Admiral. "I am prepared, sir, to be easy with you, since I hear you have made it up with my friend Dick. But let me remind you that you owe some apologies to this young lady also."

"I shall have the temerity to ask for more than her forgiveness," said the Squire. "Miss Van Tromp," he continued, "once I was in great distress, and knew nothing of you or your character; but I believe you will pardon a few rough words to an old man who asks forgiveness from his heart. I have heard much of you since then; for you have a fervent advocate in my house. I believe you will understand that I speak of my son. He is, I regret to say, very far from well; he does not pick up as the doctors had expected; he has a great deal upon his mind and, to tell you the truth, my girl, if you won't help us, I am afraid I shall lose him. Come now, forgive him! I was angry with him once myself, and I found I was in the wrong. This is only a misunderstanding, like the other, believe me; and with one kind movement, you may give happiness to him, and to me, and to yourself."

Esther made a movement towards the door, but long before she reached it she had broken forth sobbing.

"It is all right," said the Admiral; "I understand the sex. Let me make you my compliments, Mr Naseby."

The Squire was too much relieved to be angry.

"My dear," said he to Esther, "you must not agitate yourself."

"She had better go up and see him right away," suggested Van Tromp.

"I had not ventured to propose it," replied the Squire. "*Les convenances*, I believe—"

"*Je m'en fiche*," cried the Admiral, snapping his fingers. "She shall go and see my friend Dick. Run and get ready, Esther."

Esther obeyed.

"She has not – has not run away again?" inquired Mr Naseby, as soon as she was gone.

"No," said Van Tromp, "not again. She is a devilish odd girl though, mind you that."

"But I cannot stomach the man with the carbuncles," thought the Squire.

And this is why there is a new household and a brand-new baby in Naseby Dower House; and why the great Van Tromp lives in pleasant style upon the shores of England; and why twenty-six individual copies of the *Thymebury Star* are received daily at the door of Naseby House.

ROBERT LOUIS STEVENSON
MARKHEIM

Yes," said the dealer, "our windfalls are of various kinds. Some customers are ignorant, and then I touch a dividend on my superior knowledge. Some are dishonest," and here he held up the candle, so that the light fell strongly on his visitor, "and in that case," he continued, "I profit by my virtue."

Markheim had but just entered from the daylight streets, and his eyes had not yet grown familiar with the mingled shine and darkness in the shop. At these pointed words, and before the near presence of the flame, he blinked painfully and looked aside.

The dealer chuckled. "You come to me on Christmas Day," he resumed, "when you know that I am alone in my house, put up my shutters, and make a point of refusing business. Well, you will have to pay for that; you will have to pay for my loss of time, when I should be balancing my books; you will have to pay, besides, for a kind of manner that I remark in you today very strongly. I am the essence of discretion, and ask no awkward questions; but when a customer cannot look me in the eye, he has to pay for it." The dealer once more chuckled; and then, changing to his usual business voice, though still with a note of irony, "You can give, as usual, a clear account of how you came into the possession of the object?" he continued. "Still your uncle's cabinet? A remarkable collector, sir!"

And the little pale, round-shouldered dealer stood almost on tip-toe, looking over the top of his gold spectacles, and nodding his head with every mark of disbelief. Markheim returned his gaze with one of infinite pity, and a touch of horror.

"This time," said he, "you are in error. I have not come to sell, but to buy. I have no curios to dispose of; my uncle's cabinet is bare to the wainscot; even were it still intact, I have done well on the Stock Exchange, and should more likely add to it than otherwise, and my errand today is simplicity itself. I seek a Christmas present for a lady," he continued, waxing more fluent as he struck into the speech he had prepared; "and certainly I owe you every excuse for thus disturbing you upon so small a matter. But the thing was neglected yesterday; I must produce my little compliment at dinner; and, as you very well know, a rich marriage is not a thing to be neglected."

There followed a pause, during which the dealer seemed to weigh this statement incredulously. The ticking of many clocks among the curious lumber of the shop, and the faint rushing of the cabs in a near thoroughfare, filled up the interval of silence.

"Well, sir," said the dealer, "be it so. You are an old customer after all; and if, as you say, you have the chance of a good marriage, far be it from me to be an obstacle. Here is a nice thing for a lady now," he went on, "this hand glass – fifteenth century, warranted; comes from a good collection, too; but I reserve the name, in the interests of my customer, who was just like yourself, my dear sir, the nephew and sole heir of a remarkable collector."

The dealer, while he thus ran on in his dry and biting voice, had stooped to take the object from its place; and, as he had done so, a shock had passed through Markheim, a start both of hand and foot, a sudden leap of many tumultuous passions to the face. It passed as swiftly as it came, and left no trace beyond a certain trembling of the hand that now received the glass.

"A glass," he said hoarsely, and then paused, and repeated it more clearly. "A glass? For Christmas? Surely not?"

"And why not?" cried the dealer. "Why not a glass?"

Markheim was looking upon him with an indefinable expression. "You ask me why not?" he said. "Why, look here – look in it – look at yourself! Do you like to see it? No! nor – nor any man."

The little man had jumped back when Markheim had so suddenly confronted him with the mirror; but now, perceiving there was nothing worse on hand, he chuckled. "Your future lady, sir, must be pretty hard favoured," said he.

"I ask you," said Markheim, "for a Christmas present, and you give me this – this damned reminder of years, and sins and follies – this hand-conscience! Did you mean it? Had you a thought in your mind? Tell me. It will be better for you if you do. Come, tell me about yourself. I hazard a guess now, that you are in secret a very charitable man?"

The dealer looked closely at his companion. It was very odd, Markheim did not appear to be laughing; there was something in his face like an eager sparkle of hope, but nothing of mirth.

"What are you driving at?" the dealer asked.

"Not charitable?" returned the other gloomily. "Not charitable; not pious; not scrupulous; unloving, unbeloved; a hand to get money, a safe to keep it. Is that all? Dear God, man, is that all?"

"I will tell you what it is," began the dealer, with some sharpness, and then broke off again into a chuckle. "But I see this is a love match of yours, and you have been drinking the lady's health."

"Ah!" cried Markheim, with a strange curiosity. "Ah, have you been in love? Tell me about that."

"I," cried the dealer. "I in love! I never had the time, nor have I the time today for all this nonsense. Will you take the glass?"

"Where is the hurry?" returned Markheim. "It is very pleasant to stand here talking; and life is so short and insecure that I would not hurry away from any pleasure – no, not even from so mild a one as this. We should rather cling, cling to what little we can get, like a man at a cliff's edge. Every second is a cliff, if you think upon it – a cliff a mile high – high enough, if we fall, to dash us out of every feature of humanity. Hence it is best to talk pleasantly. Let us talk of each other: why should we wear this mask? Let us be confidential. Who knows, we might become friends?"

"I have just one word to say to you," said the dealer. "Either make your purchase, or walk out of my shop!"

"True, true," said Markheim. "Enough fooling. To business. Show me something else."

The dealer stooped once more, this time to replace the glass upon the shelf, his thin blond hair falling over his eyes as he did so. Markheim moved a little nearer, with one hand in the pocket of his greatcoat; he drew himself up and filled his lungs; at the same time many different emotions were depicted together on his face – terror, horror, and resolve, fascination and a physical repulsion; and through a haggard lift of his upper lip, his teeth looked out.

"This, perhaps, may suit," observed the dealer: and then, as he began to re-arise, Markheim bounded from behind upon his victim. The long, skewerlike dagger flashed and fell. The dealer struggled like a hen, striking his temple on the shelf, and then tumbled on the floor in a heap.

Time had some score of small voices in that shop, some stately and slow as was becoming to their great age; others garrulous and hurried. All these told out the seconds in an intricate chorus of tickings. Then the passage of a lad's feet, heavily running on the pavement, broke in upon these smaller voices and startled Markheim into the consciousness of his surroundings. He looked about him awfully. The candle stood on the counter, its flame solemnly wagging in a draught; and by that inconsiderable movement, the whole room was filled with noiseless bustle and kept heaving like a sea: the tall shadows nodding, the gross blots of darkness swelling and dwindling as with respiration, the faces of the portraits and the china gods changing and wavering like images in water. The inner door stood ajar, and peered into that leaguer of shadows with a long slit of daylight like a pointing finger.

From these fear-stricken rovings, Markheim's eyes returned to the body of his victim, where it lay both humped and sprawling, incredibly small and strangely meaner than in life. In these poor, miserly clothes, in that ungainly attitude, the dealer lay like so much sawdust. Markheim had feared to see it, and, lo! it was nothing. And yet, as he gazed, this bundle of old clothes and pool of blood began to find eloquent voices. There it must lie; there was none to work the cunning hinges or direct the miracle of locomotion – there it must lie till it was found. Found! ay, and then? Then would this dead flesh lift up a cry that would ring over England, and fill the world with the echoes of pursuit. Ay, dead or not, this was still the enemy. "Time was that when the brains were out," he thought; and the first word struck into his mind. Time, now that the deed was accomplished – time, which had closed for the victim, had become instant and momentous for the slayer.

The thought was yet in his mind, when, first one and then another, with every variety of pace and voice – one deep as the bell from a cathedral turret, another ringing on its treble notes the prelude of a waltz – the clocks began to strike the hour of three in the afternoon.

The sudden outbreak of so many tongues in that dumb chamber staggered him. He began to bestir himself, going to and fro with the candle, beleaguered by moving shadows, and startled to the soul by chance reflections. In many rich mirrors, some of home designs, some from Venice or Amsterdam, he saw his face repeated and repeated, as it were an army of spies; his own eyes met and detected him; and the sound of his own steps, lightly as they fell, vexed the surrounding quiet. And still, as he continued to fill his pockets, his mind accused him with a sickening iteration, of the thousand faults of his design. He should have chosen a more quiet hour; he should have prepared an alibi; he should not have used a knife; he should have been more cautious, and only bound and gagged the dealer, and not killed him; he should have been more bold, and killed the servant also; he should have done all things otherwise: poignant regrets, weary, incessant toiling of the mind to change what was unchangeable, to plan what was now useless, to be the architect of the irrevocable past. Meanwhile, and behind all this activity, brute terrors, like the scurrying of rats in a deserted attic, filled the more remote chambers of his brain with riot; the hand of the constable would fall heavy on his shoulder, and his nerves would jerk like a hooked fish; or he beheld, in galloping defile, the dock, the prison, the gallows, and the black coffin.

Terror of the people in the street sat down before his mind like a besieging army. It was impossible, he thought, but that some rumour of the struggle must have reached their ears and set on edge their curiosity; and now, in all the neighbouring houses, he divined them sitting motionless and with uplifted ear - solitary people, condemned to spend Christmas dwelling alone on memories of the past, and now startingly recalled from that tender exercise; happy family parties, struck into silence round the table, the mother still with raised finger: every degree and age and humour, but all, by their own hearths, prying and hearkening and weaving the rope that was to hang him. Sometimes it seemed to him he could not move too softly; the clink of the tall Bohemian goblets rang out loudly like a bell; and alarmed by the bigness of the ticking, he was tempted to stop the clocks. And then, again, with a swift transition of his terrors, the very silence of the place appeared a source of peril, and a thing to strike and freeze the passer-by; and he would step more boldly, and bustle aloud among the contents of the shop, and imitate, with elaborate bravado, the movements of a busy man at ease in his own house.

But he was now so pulled about by different alarms that, while one portion of his mind was still alert and cunning, another trembled on the brink of lunacy. One hallucination in particular took a strong hold on his credulity. The neighbour hearkening with white face beside his window, the passer-by arrested by a horrible surmise on the pavement – these could at worst suspect, they could not know; through the brick walls and shuttered windows only sounds could penetrate. But here, within the house, was he alone? He knew he was; he had watched the servant set forth sweethearting, in her poor best, "out for the day" written in every ribbon and smile. Yes, he was alone, of course; and yet, in the bulk of empty house above him, he could surely hear a stir of delicate footing – he was surely conscious, inexplicably conscious of some presence. Ay, surely; to every room and corner of the house his imagination followed it; and now it was a faceless thing, and yet had eyes to see with; and again it was a shadow of himself; and yet again behold the image of the dead dealer, reinspired with cunning and hatred.

At times, with a strong effort, he would glance at the open door which still seemed to repel his eyes. The house was tall, the skylight small and dirty, the day blind with fog; and the light that filtered down to the ground story was exceedingly faint, and showed dimly on the threshold of the shop. And yet, in that strip of doubtful brightness, did there not hang wavering a shadow?

Suddenly, from the street outside, a very jovial gentleman began to beat with a staff on the shop-door, accompanying his blows with shouts and railleries in which the dealer was continually called upon by name. Markheim, smitten into ice, glanced at the dead man. But no! he lay quite still; he was fled away far beyond earshot of these blows and shoutings; he was sunk beneath seas of silence; and his name, which would once have caught his notice above the howling of a storm, had become an empty sound. And presently the jovial gentleman desisted from his knocking and departed.

Here was a broad hint to hurry what remained to be done, to get forth from this accusing neighbourhood, to plunge into a bath of London multitudes, and to reach, on the other side of day, that haven of safety and apparent innocence – his bed. One visitor had come: at any moment another might follow and be more obstinate. To have done the deed, and yet not to reap the profit, would be too abhorrent a failure. The money, that was now Markheim's concern; and as a means to that, the keys.

He glanced over his shoulder at the open door, where the shadow was still lingering and shivering; and with no conscious repugnance of the mind, yet with a tremor of the belly, he drew near the body of his victim. The human character had quite departed. Like a suit half-stuffed with bran, the limbs lay scattered, the trunk doubled, on the floor; and yet the thing repelled him. Although so dingy and inconsiderable to the eye, he feared it might have more significance to the touch. He took the body by the shoulders, and turned it on its back. It was strangely light and supple, and the limbs, as if they had been broken, fell into the oddest postures. The face was robbed of all expression; but it was as pale as wax, and shockingly smeared with blood about one temple. That was, for Markheim, the one displeasing circumstance. It carried him back, upon the instant, to a certain fair day in a fishers' village: a gray day, a piping wind, a crowd upon the street, the blare of the brasses, the booming of drums, the nasal voice of a ballad singer; and a boy going to and fro, buried over head in the crowd and divided between interest and fear, until, coming out upon the chief place of concourse, he beheld a booth and a great screen with pictures, dismally designed, garishly coloured: Brownrigg with her apprentice; the Mannings with their murdered guest; Weare in the death-grip of Thurtell; and a score besides of famous crimes. The thing was as clear as an illusion; he was once again that little boy; he was looking once again, and with the same sense of physical revolt, at these vile pictures; he was still stunned by the thumping of the drums. A bar of that day's music returned upon his memory; and at that, for the first time, a qualm came over him, a breath of nausea, a sudden weakness of the joints, which he must instantly resist and conquer.

He judged it more prudent to confront than to flee from these considerations; looking the more hardily in the dead face, bending his mind to realise the nature and greatness of his crime. So little a while ago that face had moved with every change of sentiment, that pale mouth had spoken, that body had been all on fire with governable energies; and now, and by his act, that piece of life had been arrested as the horologist, with interjected finger, arrests the beating of the clock. So he reasoned in vain; he could rise to no more remorseful consciousness; the same heart which had shuddered before the painted effigies of crime, looked on its reality unmoved. At best, he felt a gleam of pity for one who had been endowed in vain with all those faculties that can make the world a garden of enchantment, one who had never lived and who was now dead. But of penitence, no, not a tremor.

With that, shaking himself clear of these considerations, he found the keys and advanced towards the open door of the shop. Outside, it had begun to rain smartly; and the sound of the shower upon the roof had banished silence. Like some dripping cavern, the chambers of the house were haunted by an incessant echoing, which filled the ear and mingled with the ticking of the clocks. And, as Markheim approached the door, he seemed to hear, in answer to his own cautious tread, the steps of another foot withdrawing up the stair. The shadow still palpitated loosely on the threshold. He threw a ton's weight of resolve upon his muscles, and drew back the door.

The faint, foggy daylight glimmered dimly on the bare floor and stairs; on the bright suit of armour posted, halbert in hand, upon the landing; and on the dark wood-carvings, and framed pictures that hung against the yellow panels of the wainscot. So loud was the beating of the rain through all the house that, in Markheim's ears, it began to be distinguished into many different sounds. Footsteps and sighs, the tread of regiments marching in the distance, the chink of money in the counting, and the creaking of doors held stealthily ajar, appeared to mingle with the patter of the drops upon the cupola and the gushing of the water in the pipes. The sense that he was not alone grew upon him to the verge of madness. On every side he was haunted and begirt by presences. He heard them moving in the upper chambers; from the shop, he heard the dead man getting to his legs; and as he began with a great effort to mount the stairs, feet fled quietly before him and followed stealthily behind. If he were but deaf, he thought, how tranquilly he would posses his soul! And then again, and hearkening with ever fresh attention, he blessed himself for that unresting sense which held the outposts and stood a trusty sentinel upon his life. His head turned continually on his neck; his eyes, which seemed starting from their orbits, scouted on every side, and on every side were half-rewarded as with the tail of something nameless vanishing. The four-and-twenty steps to the first floor were four-and-twenty agonies.

On that first story, the doors stood ajar, three of them like three ambushes, shaking his nerves like the throats of cannon. He could never again, he felt, be sufficiently immured and fortified from men's observing eyes; he longed to be home, girt in by walls, buried among bedclothes, and invisible to all but God. And at that

thought he wondered a little, recollecting tales of other murderers
and the fear they were said to entertain of heavenly avengers. It
was not so, at least, with him. He feared the laws of nature, lest, in
their callous and immutable procedure, they should preserve some
damning evidence of his crime. He feared tenfold more, with a
slavish, superstitious terror, some scission in the continuity of man's
experience, some wilful illegality of nature. He played a game of
skill, depending on the rules, calculating consequence from cause;
and what if nature, as the defeated tyrant overthrew the chessboard,
should break the mould of their succession? The like had befallen
Napoleon (so writers said) when the winter changed the time of its
appearance. The like might befall Markheim: the solid walls might
become transparent and reveal his doings like those of bees in a glass
hive; the stout planks might yield under his foot like quicksands
and detain him in their clutch; ay, and there were soberer accidents
that might destroy him: if, for instance, the house should fall and
imprison him beside the body of his victim; or the house next door
should fly on fire, and the firemen invade him from all sides. These
things he feared; and, in a sense, these things might be called the
hands of God reached forth against sin. But about God Himself
he was at ease; his act was doubtless exceptional, but so were his
excuses, which God knew; it was there, and not among men, that
he felt sure of justice.

When he had got safe into the drawing-room, and shut the
door behind him, he was aware of a respite from alarms. The
room was quite dismantled, uncarpeted besides, and strewn
with packing cases and incongruous furniture; several great
pier-glasses, in which he beheld himself at various angles, like an
actor on a stage; many pictures, framed and unframed, standing,
with their faces to the wall; a fine Sheraton sideboard, a cabinet

of marquetry, and a great old bed, with tapestry hangings. The windows opened to the floor; but by great good fortune the lower part of the shutters had been closed, and this concealed him from the neighbours. Here, then, Markheim drew in a packing case before the cabinet, and began to search among the keys. It was a long business, for there were many; and it was irksome, besides; for, after all, there might be nothing in the cabinet, and time was on the wing. But the closeness of the occupation sobered him. With the tail of his eye he saw the door – even glanced at it from time to time directly, like a besieged commander pleased to verify the good estate of his defences. But in truth he was at peace. The rain falling in the street sounded natural and pleasant. Presently, on the other side, the notes of a piano were wakened to the music of a hymn, and the voices of many children took up the air and words. How stately, how comfortable was the melody! How fresh the youthful voices! Markheim gave ear to it smilingly, as he sorted out the keys; and his mind was thronged with answerable ideas and images; church-going children and the pealing of the high organ; children afield, bathers by the brookside, ramblers on the brambly common, kite-flyers in the windy and cloud-navigated sky; and then, at another cadence of the hymn, back again to church, and the somnolence of summer Sundays, and the high genteel voice of the parson (which he smiled a little to recall) and the painted Jacobean tombs, and the dim lettering of the Ten Commandments in the chancel.

And as he sat thus, at once busy and absent, he was startled to his feet. A flash of ice, a flash of fire, a bursting gush of blood, went over him, and then he stood transfixed and thrilling. A step mounted the stair slowly and steadily, and presently a hand was laid upon the knob, and the lock clicked and the door opened.

Fear held Markheim in a vice. What to expect he knew not, whether the dead man walking, or the official ministers of human justice, or some chance witness blindly stumbling in to consign him to the gallows. But when a face was thrust into the aperture, glanced round the room, looked at him, nodded and smiled as if in friendly recognition, and then withdrew again, and the door closed behind it, his fear broke loose from his control in a hoarse cry. At the sound of this the visitant returned.

"Did you call me?" he asked pleasantly, and with that he entered the room and closed the door behind him.

Markheim stood and gazed at him with all his eyes. Perhaps there was a film upon his sight, but the outlines of the newcomer seemed to change and waver like those of the idols in the wavering candlelight of the shop; and at times he thought he knew him; and at times he thought he bore a likeness to himself; and always, like a lump of living terror, there lay in his bosom the conviction that this thing was not of the earth and not of God.

And yet the creature had a strange air of the commonplace, as he stood looking on Markheim with a smile; and when he added: "You are looking for the money, I believe?" it was in the tones of everyday politeness.

Markheim made no answer.

"I should warn you," resumed the other, "that the maid has left her sweetheart earlier than usual and will soon be here. If Mr Markheim be found in this house, I need not describe to him the consequences."

"You know me?" cried the murderer.

The visitor smiled. "You have long been a favourite of mine," he said; "and I have long observed and often sought to help you."

"What are you?" cried Markheim: "the devil?"

"What I may be," returned the other, "cannot affect the service I propose to render you."

"It can," cried Markheim; "it does! Be helped by you? No, never; not by you! You do not know me yet; thank God, you do not know me!"

"I know you," replied the visitant, with a sort of kind severity or rather firmness. "I know you to the soul."

"Know me!" cried Markheim. "Who can do so? My life is but a travesty and slander on myself. I have lived to belie my nature. All men do; all men are better than this disguise that grows about and stifles them. You see each dragged away by life, like one whom bravos have seized and muffled in a cloak. If they had their own control – if you could see their faces, they would be altogether different, they would shine out for heroes and saints! I am worse than most; myself is more overlaid; my excuse is known to men and God. But, had I the time, I could disclose myself."

"To me?" inquired the visitant.

"To you before all," returned the murderer. "I supposed you were intelligent. I thought – since you exist – you could prove a reader of the heart. And yet you would propose to judge me by my acts! Think of it; my acts! I was born and I have lived in a land of giants; giants have dragged me by the wrists since I was born out of my mother – the giants of circumstance. And you would judge me by my acts! But can you not look within? Can you not understand that evil is hateful to me? Can you not see within me the clear writing of conscience, never blurred by any wilful sophistry, although too often disregarded? Can you not read me for a thing that surely must be common as humanity – the unwilling sinner?"

"All this is very feelingly expressed," was the reply, "but it regards me not. These points of consistency are beyond my province, and I care not in the least by what compulsion you may have been dragged away, so as you are but carried in the right direction. But time flies; the servant delays, looking in the faces of the crowd and at the pictures on the hoardings, but still she keeps moving nearer; and remember, it is as if the gallows itself was striding towards you through the Christmas streets! Shall I help you; I, who know all? Shall I tell you where to find the money?"

"For what price?" asked Markheim.

"I offer you the service for a Christmas gift," returned the other.

Markheim could not refrain from smiling with a kind of bitter triumph. "No," said he, "I will take nothing at your hands; if I were dying of thirst, and it was your hand that put the pitcher to my lips, I should find the courage to refuse. It may be credulous, but I will do nothing to commit myself to evil."

"I have no objection to a deathbed repentance," observed the visitant.

"Because you disbelieve their efficacy!" Markheim cried.

"I do not say so," returned the other; "but I look on these things from a different side, and when the life is done my interest falls. The man has lived to serve me, to spread black looks under colour of religion, or to sow tares in the wheatfield, as you do, in a course of weak compliance with desire. Now that he draws so near to his deliverance, he can add but one act of service – to repent, to die smiling, and thus to build up in confidence and hope the more timorous of my surviving followers. I am not so hard a master. Try me. Accept my help. Please yourself in life as you have done hitherto; please yourself more amply, spread your elbows at the board; and when the night begins to fall and the curtains to be drawn, I tell you, for your greater comfort, that you will find it even easy to compound your quarrel with your conscience, and to make a truckling peace with God. I came but now from such a deathbed, and the room was full of sincere mourners, listening to the man's last words: and when I looked into that face, which had been set as a flint against mercy, I found it smiling with hope."

"And do you, then, suppose me such a creature?" asked Markheim. "Do you think I have no more generous aspirations than to sin, and sin, and sin, and, at the last, sneak into heaven? My heart rises at the thought. Is this, then, your experience of mankind? or is it because you find me with red hands that you presume such baseness? and is this crime of murder indeed so impious as to dry up the very springs of good?"

"Murder is to me no special category," replied the other.

"All sins are murder, even as all life is war. I behold your race, like starving mariners on a raft, plucking crusts out of the hands of famine and feeding on each other's lives. I follow sins beyond the moment of their acting; I find in all that the last consequence is death; and to my eyes, the pretty maid who thwarts her mother with such taking graces on a question of a ball, drips no less visibly with human gore than such a murderer as yourself. Do I say that I follow sins? I follow virtues also; they differ not by the thickness of a nail, they are both scythes for the reaping angel of Death. Evil, for which I live, consists not in action but in character. The bad man is dear to me; not the bad act, whose fruits, if we could follow them far enough down the hurtling cataract of the ages, might yet be found more blessed than those of the rarest virtues. And it is not because you have killed a dealer, but because you are Markheim, that I offer to forward your escape."

"I will lay my heart open to you," answered Markheim. "This crime on which you find me is my last. On my way to it I have learned many lessons; itself is a lesson, a momentous lesson. Hitherto I have been driven with revolt to what I would not; I was a bond-slave to poverty, driven and scourged. There are robust virtues that can stand in these temptations; mine are not so: I had a thirst of pleasure. But today, and out of this deed, I pluck both warning and riches – both the power and a fresh resolve to be myself. I become in all things a free actor in the world; I begin to see myself all changed, these hands the agents of good, this heart at peace. Something comes over me out of the past; something of what I have dreamed on Sabbath evenings to the sound of the church organ, of what I forecast when I shed tears over noble books, or talked, an innocent child, with my mother. There lies my life; I have wandered a few years, but now I see once more my city of destination."

"You are to use this money on the Stock Exchange, I think?" remarked the visitor; "and there, if I mistake not, you have already lost some thousands?"

"Ah," said Markheim, "but this time I have a sure thing."

"This time, again, you will lose," replied the visitor quietly.

"Ah, but I keep back the half!" cried Markheim.

"That also you will lose," said the other.

The sweat started upon Markheim's brow. "Well, then, what matter?" he exclaimed. "Say it be lost, say I am plunged again in poverty, shall one part of me, and that the worse, continue until the end to override the better? Evil and good run strong in me, haling me both ways. I do not love the one thing, I love all. I can conceive great deeds, renunciations, martyrdoms; and though I be fallen to such a crime as murder, pity is no stranger to my thoughts. I pity the poor; who knows their trials better than myself? I pity and help them; I prize love, I love honest laughter; there is no good thing nor true thing on earth but I love it from my heart. And are my vices only to direct my life, and my virtues without effect, like some passive lumber of the mind? Not so; good, also, is a spring of acts."

But the visitant raised his finger. "For six-and-thirty years that you have been in this world," said he, "through many changes of fortune and varieties of humour, I have watched you steadily fall. Fifteen years ago you would have started at a theft. Three years back you would have blenched at the name of murder. Is there any crime, is there any cruelty or meanness, from which you still recoil? – five years from now I shall detect you in the fact! Downward, downward, lies your way; nor can anything but death avail to stop you."

"It is true," Markheim said huskily, "I have in some degree complied with evil. But it is so with all: the very saints, in the mere exercise of living, grow less dainty, and take on the tone of their surroundings."

"I will propound to you one simple question," said the other; "and as you answer, I shall read to you your moral horoscope. You have grown in many things more lax; possibly you do right to be so; and at any account, it is the same with all men. But granting that, are you in any one particular, however trifling, more difficult to please with your own conduct, or do you go in all things with a looser rein?"

"In any one?" repeated Markheim, with an anguish of consideration. "No," he added, with despair, "in none! I have gone down in all."

"Then," said the visitor, "content yourself with what you are, for you will never change; and the words of your part on this stage are irrevocably written down."

Markheim stood for a long while silent, and indeed it was the visitor who first broke the silence. "That being so," he said, "shall I show you the money?"

"And grace?" cried Markheim.

"Have you not tried it?" returned the other. "Two or three years ago. Did I not see you on the platform of revival meetings, and was not your voice the loudest in the hymn?"

"It is true," said Markheim; "and I see clearly what remains for me by way of duty. I thank you for these lessons from my soul; my eyes are opened, and I behold myself at last for what I am."

At this moment, the sharp note of the door-bell rang through the house; and the visitant, as though this were some concerted signal for which he had been waiting, changed at once in his demeanour.

"The maid!" he cried. "She has returned, as I forewarned you, and there is now before you one more difficult passage. Her master, you must say, is ill; you must let her in, with an assured but rather serious countenance – no smiles, no overacting, and I promise you success! Once the girl within, and the door closed, the same dexterity that has already rid you of the dealer will relieve you of this last danger in your path. Thenceforward you have the whole evening – the whole night, if needful – to ransack the treasures of the house and to make good your safety. This is help that comes to you with the mask of danger. Up!" he cried; "up, friend; your life hangs trembling in the scales: up, and act!"

Markheim steadily regarded his counsellor. "If I be condemned to evil acts," he said, "there is still one door of freedom open – I can cease from action. If my life be an ill thing, I can lay it down. Though I be, as you say truly, at the beck of every small temptation, I can yet, by one decisive gesture, place myself beyond the reach of all. My love of good is damned to barrenness; it may, and let it be! But I have still my hatred of evil; and from that, to your galling disappointment, you shall see that I can draw both energy and courage."

The features of the visitor began to undergo a wonderful and lovely change: they brightened and softened with a tender triumph, and, even as they brightened, faded and dislimned. But Markheim did not pause to watch or understand the transformation. He opened the door and went downstairs very slowly, thinking to himself. His past went soberly before him; he beheld it as it was, ugly and strenuous like a dream, random as chance-medley – a scene of defeat. Life, as he thus reviewed it, tempted him no longer; but on the farther side he perceived a quiet haven for his bark. He paused in the passage, and looked into the shop, where the candle still burned by the dead body. It was strangely silent. Thoughts of the dealer swarmed into his mind, as he stood gazing. And then the bell once more broke out into impatient clamour.

He confronted the maid upon the threshold with something like a smile.

"You had better go for the police," said he: "I have killed your master."

ROBERT LOUIS STEVENSON
THE BOTTLE IMP

There **was** a man of the Island of Hawaii, whom I shall call Keawe; for the truth is, he still lives, and his name must be kept secret; but the place of his birth was not far from Honaunau, where the bones of Keawe the Great lie hidden in a cave. This man was poor, brave, and active; he could read and write like a schoolmaster; he was a first-rate mariner besides, sailed for some time in the island steamers, and steered a whaleboat on the Hamakua coast. At length it came in Keawe's mind to have a sight of the great world and foreign cities, and he shipped on a vessel bound to San Francisco.

This is a fine town, with a fine harbour, and rich people uncountable; and in particular, there is one hill which is covered with palaces. Upon this hill Keawe was one day taking a walk with his pocket full of money, viewing the great houses upon either hand with pleasure. "What fine houses these are!" he was thinking, "and how happy must those people be who dwell in them, and take no care for the morrow!" The thought was in his mind when he came abreast of a house that was smaller than some others, but all finished and beautified like a toy; the steps of that house shone like silver, and the borders of the garden bloomed like garlands, and the windows were bright like diamonds; and Keawe stopped and wondered at the excellence of all he saw. So stopping, he was aware of a man that looked forth upon him through a window so clear that Keawe could see him as you see a fish in a pool upon the reef. The man was elderly, with a bald head and a black beard; and his face was heavy with sorrow, and he bitterly sighed. And the truth of it is, that as Keawe looked in upon the man, and the man looked out upon Keawe, each envied the other.

All of a sudden, the man smiled and nodded, and beckoned Keawe to enter, and met him at the door of the house.

"This is a fine house of mine," said the man, and bitterly sighed. "Would you not care to view the chambers?"

So he led Keawe all over it, from the cellar to the roof, and there was nothing there that was not perfect of its kind, and Keawe was astonished.

"Truly," said Keawe, "this is a beautiful house; if I lived in the like of it I should be laughing all day long. How comes it, then, that you should be sighing?"

"There is no reason," said the man, "why you should not have a house in all points similar to this, and finer, if you wish. You have some money, I suppose?"

"I have fifty dollars," said Keawe; "but a house like this will cost more than fifty dollars."

The man made a computation. "I am sorry you have no more," said he, "for it may raise you trouble in the future; but it shall be yours at fifty dollars."

"The house?" asked Keawe.

"No, not the house," replied the man; "but the bottle. For, I must tell you, although I appear to you so rich and fortunate, all my fortune, and this house itself and its garden, came out of a bottle not much bigger than a pint. This is it."

And he opened a lockfast place, and took out a round-bellied bottle with a long neck; the glass of it was white like milk, with changing rainbow colours in the grain. Withinsides something obscurely moved, like a shadow and a fire.

"This is the bottle," said the man; and, when Keawe laughed, "You do not believe me?" he added. "Try, then, for yourself. See if you can break it."

So Keawe took the bottle up and dashed it on the floor till he was weary; but it jumped on the floor like a child's ball, and was not injured.

"This is a strange thing," said Keawe. "For by the touch of it, as well as by the look, the bottle should be of glass."

"Of glass it is," replied the man, sighing more heavily than ever; "but the glass of it was tempered in the flames of hell. An imp lives in it, and that is the shadow we behold there moving; or so I suppose. If any man buy this bottle the imp is at his command; all that he desires – love, fame, money, houses like this house, ay, or a city like this city – all are his at the word uttered. Napoleon had this bottle, and by it he grew to be the king of the world; but he sold it at the last, and fell. Captain Cook had this bottle, and by it he found his way to so many islands; but he, too sold it, and was slain upon Hawaii. For, once it is sold, the power goes and the protection; and unless a man remain content with what he has, ill will befall him."

"And yet you talk of selling it yourself?" Keawe said.

"I have all I wish, and I am growing elderly," replied the man. "There is one thing the imp cannot do – he cannot prolong life; and, it would not be fair to conceal from you, there is a drawback to the bottle; for if a man die before he sells it, he must burn in hell for ever."

"To be sure, that is a drawback and no mistake," cried Keawe. "I would not meddle with the thing. I can do without a house, thank God; but there is on thing I could not be doing with one particle, and that is to be damned."

"Dear me, you must not run away with things, " returned the man. "All you have to do is to use the power of the imp in moderation, and then sell it to someone else, as I do to you, and finish your life in comfort."

"Well, I observe two things," said Keawe. "All the time you keep sighing like a maid in love, that is one; and, for the other, you sell this bottle very cheap."

"I have told you already why I sigh," said the man. "It is because I fear my health is breaking up; and, as you said yourself, to die and go to the devil is a pity for anyone. As for why I sell so cheap, I must explain to you there is a peculiarity about the bottle. Long ago, when the devil brought it first upon earth, it was extremely expensive, and was sold first of all to Prester John for many millions of dollars; but it cannot be sold at all, unless sold at a loss. If you sell it for as much as you paid for it, back it comes to you again like a homing pigeon. It follows that the price has kept falling in these centuries, and the bottle is now remarkably cheap. I bought it myself from one of my great neighbours on this hill, and the price I paid was only ninety dollars. I could sell it for as high as eighty-nine dollars and ninety-nine cents, but not a penny dearer, or back the thing must come to me. Now, about this there are two bothers. First, when you offer a bottle so singular for eighty odd dollars, people suppose you to be jesting. And second – but there is no hurry about that – and I need not go into it. Only remember it must be coined money that you sell it for."

"How am I to know that this is all true?" asked Keawe.

"Some of it you can try at once," replied the man. "Give me your fifty dollars, take the bottle, and wish your fifty dollars back into your pocket. If that does not happen, I pledge you my honour I will cry off the bargain and restore your money."

"You are not deceiving me?" said Keawe.

The man bound himself with a great oath.

"Well, I will risk that much," said Keawe, "for that can do no harm." And he paid over his money to the man, and the man handed him the bottle.

"Imp of the bottle," said Keawe, "I want my fifty dollars back." And sure enough he had scarce said the word before his pocket was as heavy as ever.

"To be sure this is a wonderful bottle," said Keawe.

"And now, good morning to you, my fine fellow, and the devil go with you for me!" said the man.

"Hold on," said Keawe, "I don't want any more of this fun. Here, take your bottle back."

"You have bought it for less than I paid for it," replied the man, rubbing his hands. "It is yours now; and, for my part, I am only concerned to see the back of you." And with that he rang for his Chinese servant, and had Keawe shown out of the house.

Now, when Keawe was in the street, with the bottle under his arm, he began to think. "If all is true about this bottle, I may have made a losing bargain," thinks he. "But perhaps the man was only fooling me." The first thing he did was to count his money; the sum was exact – forty-nine dollars American money, and one Chili piece. "That looks like the truth," said Keawe. "Now I will try another part."

The streets in that part of the city were as clean as a ship's decks, and though it was noon, there were no passengers. Keawe set the bottle in the gutter and walked away. Twice he looked back, and there was the milky, round-bellied bottle where he left it. A third time he looked back, and turned a corner; but he had scarce done so, when something knocked upon his elbow, and behold! it was the long neck sticking up; and as for the round belly, it was jammed into the pocket of his pilot-coat.

"And that looks like the truth," said Keawe.

The next thing he did was to buy a cork-screw in a shop, and go apart into a secret place in the fields. And there he tried to draw the cork, but as often as he put the screw in, out it came again, and the cork as whole as ever.

"This is some new sort of cork," said Keawe, and all at once he began to shake and sweat, for he was afraid of that bottle.

On his way back to the port-side, he saw a shop where a man sold shells and clubs from the wild islands, old heathen deities, old coined money, pictures from China and Japan, and all manner of things that sailors bring in their sea-chests. And here he had an idea. So he went in and offered the bottle for a hundred dollars. The man of the shop laughed at him at the first, and offered him five; but indeed, it was a curious bottle – such glass was never blown in any human glass-works, so prettily the colours shown under the milky white, and so strangely the shadow hovered in the midst; so, after he had disputed awhile after the manner of his kind, the shopman gave Keawe sixty silver dollars for the thing, and set it on a shelf in the midst of his window.

"Now," said Keawe, "I have sold that for sixty which I bought for fifty – so, to say truth, a little less, because one of my dollars was from Chili. Now I shall know the truth upon another point."

So he went back on board his ship, and, when he opened his chest, there was the bottle, and had come more quickly than himself. Now Keawe had a mate on board whose name was Lopaka.

"What ails you?" said Lopaka, "that you stare in your chest?"

They were alone in the ship's forecastle, and Keawe bound him to secrecy, and told all.

"This is a very strange affair," said Lopaka; "and I fear you will be in trouble about this bottle. But there is one point very clear – that you are sure of the trouble, and you had better have the profit in the bargain. Make up your mind what you want with it; give the order, and if it is done as you desire, I will buy the bottle myself; for I have an idea of my own to get a schooner, and go trading through the islands."

"That is not my idea," said Keawe; "but to have a beautiful house and garden on the Kona Coast, where I was born, the sun shining in at the door, flowers in the garden, glass in the windows, pictures on the walls, and toys and fine carpets on the tables, for all the world like the house I was in this day – only a storey higher, and with balconies all about like the king's palace; and to live there without care and make merry with my friends and relatives."

"Well," said Lopaka, "let us carry it back with us to Hawaii, and if all comes true, as you suppose, I will buy the bottle, as I said, and ask a schooner."

Upon that they were agreed, and it was not long before the ship returned to Honolulu, carrying Keawe and Lopaka, and the bottle. They were scarce come ashore when they met a friend upon the beach, who began at once to condole with Keawe.

"I do not know what I am to be condoled about," said Keawe.

"Is it possible you have not heard," said the friend, "your uncle – that good old man – is dead, and your cousin – that beautiful boy – was drowned at sea?"

Keawe was filled with sorrow, and, beginning to weep and to lament he forgot about the bottle. But Lopaka was thinking to himself, and presently, when Keawe's grief was a little abated, "I have been thinking," said Lopaka. "Had not your uncle lands in Hawaii, in the district of Kau?"

"No," said Keawe, "not in Kau; they are on the mountain-side – a little way south of Hookena."

"These lands will now be yours?" asked Lopaka.

"And so they will," says Keawe, and began again to lament for his relatives.

"No," said Lopaka, "do not lament at present. I have a thought in my mind. How if this should be the doing of the bottle? For here is the place ready for your house."

"If this be so," cried Keawe, "it is a very ill way to serve me by killing my relatives. But it may be, indeed; for it was in just such a station that I saw the house with my mind's eye."

"The house, however, is not yet built," said Lopaka.

"No, nor like to be!" said Keawe, "for though my uncle has some coffee and ava and bananas, it will not be more than will keep me in comfort; and the rest of that land is the black lava."

"Let us go to the lawyer," said Lopaka; "I have still this idea in my mind."

Now, when they came to the lawyer's, it appeared Keawe's uncle had grown monstrous rich in the last days, and there was a fund of money.

"And here is the money for the house!" cried Lopaka.

"If you are thinking of a new house," said the lawyer, "here is the card of a new architect, of whom they tell me great things."

"Better and better!" cried Lopaka. "Here is all made plain for us. Let us continue to obey orders."

So they went to the architect, and he had drawings of houses on his table.

"You want something out of the way," said the architect. "How do you like this?" and he handed a drawing to Keawe.

Now, when Keawe set eyes on the drawing, he cried out aloud, for it was the picture of his thought exactly drawn.

"I am in for this house," thought he. "Little as I like the way it comes to me, I am in for it now, and I may as well take the good along with the evil."

So he told the architect all that he wished, and how he would have that house furnished, and about the pictures on the wall and the knick-knacks on the tables; and he asked the man plainly for how much he would undertake the whole affair.

The architect put many questions, and took his pen and made a computation; and when he had done he named the very sum that Keawe had inherited.

Lopaka and Keawe looked at one another and nodded.

"It is quite clear," thought Keawe, "that I am to have this house, whether or no. It comes from the devil, and I fear I will get little good by that; and of one thing I am sure, I will make no more wishes as long as I have this bottle. But with the house I am saddled, and I may as well take the good along with the evil."

So he made his terms with the architect, and they signed a paper; and Keawe and Lopaka took ship again and sailed to Australia; for it was concluded between them they should not interfere at all, but leave the architect and the bottle imp to build and to adorn that house at their own pleasure.

The voyage was a good voyage, only all the time Keawe was holding in his breath, for he had sworn he would utter no more wishes, and take no more favours from the devil. The time was up when they got back. The architect told them that the house was ready, and Keawe and Lopaka took a passage in the *Hall*, and went down Kona way to view the house, and see if all had been done fitly according to the thought that was in Keawe's mind.

Now, the house stood on the mountain-side, visible to ships. Above, the forest ran up into the clouds of rain; below, the black lava fell in cliffs, where the kings of old lay buried. A garden bloomed about that house with every hue of flowers; and there was an orchard of papaia on the one hand and an orchard of breadfruit on the other, and right in front, toward the sea, a ship's mast had been rigged up and bore a flag. As for the house, it was three storeys high, with great chambers and broad balconies on each. The windows were of glass, so excellent that it was as clear as water and as bright as day. All manner of furniture adorned the chambers. Pictures hung upon the wall in golden frames: pictures of ships, and men fighting, and of the most beautiful women, and of singular places; nowhere in the world are there pictures of so bright a colour as those Keawe found hanging in his house. As for the knick-knacks, they were extraordinary fine; chiming clocks and musical boxes, little men with nodding heads, books filled with pictures, weapons of price from all quarters of the world, and the most elegant puzzles to entertain the leisure of a solitary man. And as no one would care to live in such chambers, only to walk through and view them, the balconies were made so broad that a whole town might have lived upon them in delight; and Keawe knew not which to prefer, whether the back porch, where you got the land breeze, and looked upon the orchards and the flowers, or the front balcony, where you could drink the wind of the sea, and look down the steep wall of the mountain and see the *Hall* going by once a week or so between Hookena and the hills of Pele, or the schooners plying up the coast for wood and ava and bananas.

When they had viewed all, Keawe and Lopaka sat on the porch.

"Well," asked Lopaka, "is it all as you designed?"

"Words cannot utter it," said Keawe. "It is better than I dreamed, and I am sick with satisfaction."

"There is but one thing to consider," said Lopaka; "all this may be quite natural, and the bottle imp have nothing whatever to say to it. If I were to buy the bottle, and got no schooner after all, I should have put my hand in the fire for nothing. I gave you my word, I know; but yet I think you would not grudge me one more proof."

"I have sworn I would take no more favours," said Keawe. "I have gone already deep enough."

"This is no favour I am thinking of," replied Lopaka. "It is only to see the imp himself. There is nothing to be gained by that, and so nothing to be ashamed of; and yet, if I once saw him, I should be sure of the whole matter. So indulge me so far, and let me see the imp; and, after that, here is the money in my hand, and I will buy it."

"There is only one thing I am afraid of," said Keawe. "The imp may be very ugly to view; and if you once set eyes upon him you might be very undesirous of the bottle."

"I am a man of my word," said Lopaka. "And here is the money betwixt us."

"Very well," replied Keawe. "I have a curiosity myself. So come, let us have one look at you, Mr Imp."

Now as soon as that was said, the imp looked out of the bottle, and in again, swift as a lizard; and there sat Keawe and Lopaka turned to stone. The night had quite come, before either found a thought to say or voice to say it with; and then Lopaka pushed the money over and took the bottle.

"I am a man of my word," said he, "and had need to be so, or I would not touch this bottle with my foot. Well, I shall get my schooner and a dollar or two for my pocket; and then I will be rid of this devil as fast as I can. For to tell you the plain truth, the look of him has cast me down."

"Lopaka," said Keawe, "do not you think any worse of me than you can help; I know it is night, and the roads bad, and the pass by the tombs an ill place to go by so late, but I declare since I have seen that little face, I cannot eat or sleep or pray till it is gone from me. I will give you a lantern, and a basket to put the bottle in, and any picture or fine thing in all my house that takes your fancy; and be gone at once, and go sleep at Hookena with Nahinu."

"Keawe," said Lopaka, "many a man would take this ill; above all, when I am doing you a turn so friendly, as to keep my word and buy the bottle; and for that matter, the night and the dark, and the way by the tombs, must be all tenfold more dangerous to a man with such a sin upon his conscience, and such a bottle under his arm. But for my part, I am so extremely terrified myself, I have not the heart to blame you. Here I go then; and I pray God you may be happy in your house, and I fortunate with my schooner, and both get to heaven in the end in spite of the devil and his bottle."

So Lopaka went down the mountain; and Keawe stood in his front balcony, and listened to the clink of the horse's shoes, and watched the lantern go shining down the path, and along the cliff of caves where the old dead are buried; and all the time he trembled and clasped his hands, and prayed for his friend, and gave glory to God that he himself had escaped out of that trouble.

But the next day came very brightly, and that new house of his was so delightful to behold that he forgot his terrors. One day followed another, and Keawe dwelt there in perpetual joy. He had his place on the back porch; it was there he ate and lived, and read the stories in the Honolulu newspapers; but when anyone came by they would go in and view the chambers and the pictures. And the fame of the house went far and wide; it was called *Ka-Hale Nui* – the Great House – in all Kona; and sometimes the Bright House, for Keawe kept a Chinaman, who was all day dusting and furbishing; and the glass and the gilt, and the fine stuffs, and the pictures, shown as bright as the morning. As for Keawe himself, he could not walk in the chambers without singing, his heart was so enlarged; and when ships sailed by upon the sea, he would fly his colours on the mast.

So time went by, until one day Keawe went upon a visit as far as Kailua to certain of his friends. There he was well feasted; and left as soon as he could the next morning, and rode hard, for he was impatient to behold his beautiful house; and, besides, the night then coming on was the night in which the dead of old days go abroad in the sides of Kona; and having already meddled with the devil, he was the more chary of meeting with the dead. A little beyond Honaunau, looking far ahead, he was aware of a woman bathing in the edge of the sea; and she seemed a well grown girl, but he thought no more of it. Then he saw her white shift flutter as she put it on, and then her red holoku; and by the time he came abreast of her she was done with her toilet, and had come up from the sea, and stood by the track-side in her red holoku, and she was all freshened with the bath, and her eyes shone and were kind. Now Keawe no sooner beheld her than he drew rein.

"I thought I knew everyone in this country," said he. "How comes it that I do not know you?"

"I am Kokua, daughter of Kiano," said the girl, "and I have just returned from Oahu. Who are you?"

"I will tell you who I am in a little," said Keawe, dismounting from his horse, "but not now. For I have a thought in my mind, and if you knew who I was, you might have heard of me, and would not give me a true answer. But tell me, first of all, one thing: Are you married?"

At this Kokua laughed out aloud. "It is you who ask questions," said she. "Are you married yourself?"

"Indeed, Kokua, I am not," repled Keawe, "and never thought to be until this hour. But here is the plain truth. I have met you here at the roadside, and I saw your eyes, which are like the stars, and my heart went to you as swift as a bird. And so now, if you want none of me, say so, and I will go on to my own place; but if you think me no worse than any other young man, say so, too, and I will turn aside to your father's for the night, and tomorrow I will talk with the good man."

Kokua said never a word, but she looked at the sea and laughed.

"Kokua," said Keawe, "if you say nothing, I will take that for the good answer; so let us be stepping to your father's door."

She went on ahead of him, still without speech; only sometimes she glanced back and glanced away again, and she kept the string of her hat in her mouth.

Now, when they had come to the door, Kiano came out on his verandah, and cried out and welcomed Keawe by name. At that the girl looked over, for the fame of the great house had come to her ears; and, to be sure, it was a great temptation. All that evening they were very merry together; and the girl was as bold as brass under the eyes of her parents, and made a mock of Keawe, for she had a quick wit. The next day he had a word with Kiano, and found the girl alone.

"Kokua," said he, "you made a mock of me all the evening; and it is still time to bid me go. I would not tell you who I was, because I have so fine a house, and I feared you would think too much of that house and too little of the man that loves you. Now you know all, and if you wish to have seen the last of me, say so at once."

"No," said Kokua; but this time she did not laugh, nor did Keawe ask for more.

This was the wooing of Keawe; things had gone quickly; but so an arrow goes, and the ball of a rifle swifter still, and yet both may strike the target. Things had gone fast, but they had gone far also, and the thought of Keawe rang in the maiden's head; she heard his voice in the breach of the surf upon the lava, and for this young man that she had seen but twice she would have left father and mother and her native islands. As for Keawe himself, his horse flew up the path of the mountain under the cliff of tombs, and the sound of the hoofs, and the sound of Keawe singing to himself for pleasure echoed in the caverns of the dead. He came to the Bright House, and still he was singing. He sat and ate in the broad balcony, and the Chinaman wondered at his master, to hear how he sang between the mouthfuls. The sun went down into the sea, and the night came; and Keawe walked the balconies by lamplight, high on the mountains, and the voice of his singing startled men on ships.

"Here am I now upon my high place," he said to himself. "Life may be no better; this is the mountain top; and all shelves about me towards the worse. For the first time I will light up the chambers, and bathe in my fine bath with the hot water and the cold, and sleep alone in the bed of my bridal chamber."

So the Chinaman had word, and he must rise from sleep and light the furnaces; and as he wrought below, beside the boilers, he heard his master singing and rejoicing above him in the lighted chambers. When the water began to be hot the Chinaman cried to his master; and Keawe went into the bathroom; and the Chinaman heard him sing as he filled the marble basin; and heard him sing, and the singing broken, as he undressed; until of a sudden, the song ceased. The Chinaman listened, and listened; he called up the house to Keawe to ask if all were well, and Keawe answered him "Yes," and bade him go to bed; but there was no more singing in the Bright House; and all night long, the Chinaman heard his master's feet go round and round the balconies without repose.

Now the truth of it was this: as Keawe undressed for his bath, he spied upon his flesh a patch like a patch of lichen on a rock, and it was then that he stopped singing. For he knew the likeness of that patch, and knew that he was fallen in the Chinese Evil [Leprosy].

Now, it is a sad thing for any man to fall into this sickness. And it would be a sad thing for anyone to leave a house so beautiful and so commodious, and depart from all his friends to the north coast of Molokai between the mighty cliff and the sea-breakers. But what was that to the case of the man Keawe, he who had met his love but yesterday, and won her but that morning, and now saw all his hopes break, in a moment, like a piece of glass?

Awhile he sat upon the edge of the bath; then sprang, with a cry and ran outside; and to and fro, to and fro, along the balcony, like one despairing.

"Very willingly could I leave Hawaii, the home of my fathers," Keawe was thinking. "Very lightly could I leave my house, the high-placed, the many-windowed, here upon the mountains. Very bravely could I go to Molokai, to Kalaupapa by the cliffs, to live with the smitten and to sleep there, far from my fathers. But what wrong have I done, what sin lies upon my soul, that I should have encountered Kokua coming cool from the sea-water in the evening? Kokua, the soul ensnarer! Kokua, the light of my life! Her may I never wed, her may I look upon no longer, her may I no more handle with my living hand; and it is for this, it is for you, O Kokua! that I pour my lamentations!"

Now you are to observe what sort of a man Keawe was, for he might have dwelt there in the Bright House for years, and no one been the wiser of his sickness; but he reckoned nothing of that, if he must lose Kokua. And again, he might have wed Kokua even as he was; and so many would have done, because they have the souls of pigs; but Keawe loved the maid manfully, and he would do her no hurt and bring her in no danger.

A little beyond the midst of the night, there came in his mind the recollection of that bottle. He went round to the back porch, and called to memory the day when the devil had looked forth; and at the thought ice ran in his veins.

"A dreadful thing is the bottle," thought Keawe, "and dreadful is the imp, and it is a dreadful thing to risk the flames of hell. But what other hope have I to cure the sickness or to wed Kokua? What!" he thought, "would I beard the devil once, only to get me a house, and not face him again to win Kokua?"

Thereupon he called to mind it was the next day the *Hall* went by on her return to Honolulu. "There must I go first," he thought, "and see Lopaka. For the best hope that I have now is to find that same bottle I was so pleased to be rid of."

Never a wink could he sleep; the food stuck in his throat; but he sent a letter to Kiano, and about the time when the steamer would be coming, rode down beside the cliff of the tombs. It rained; his horse went heavily; he looked up at the black mouths of the caves, and he envied the dead that slept there and were done with trouble; and called to mind how he had galloped by the day before, and was astonished. So he came down to Hookena, and there was all the country gathered for the steamer as usual. In the shed before the store they sat and jested and passed the news; but there was no matter of speech in Keawe's bosom, and he sat in their midst and looked without on the rain falling on the houses, and the surf beating among the rocks, and the sighs arose in his throat.

"Keawe of the Bright House is out of spirits," said one to another. Indeed, and so he was, and little wonder.

Then the *Hall* came, and the whaleboat carried him on board. The after-part of the ship was full of Haoles [whites] who had been to visit the volcano, as their custom is; and the midst was crowded with Kanakas, and the forepart with wild bulls from Hilo and horses from Kau; but Keawe sat apart from all in his sorrow, and watched for the house of Kiano. There is sat, low upon the shore in the black rocks and shaded by the cocoa palms, and there by the door was a red holoku, no greater than a fly, and going to and fro with a fly's busyness.

"Ah, queen of my heart," he cried, "I'll venture my dear soul to win you!"

Soon after, darkness fell, and the cabins were lit up, and the Haoles sat and played at the cards and drank whisky as their custom is; but Keawe walked the deck all night; and all the next day, as they steamed under the lee of Maui or of Molokai, he was still pacing to and from like a wild animal in a menagerie.

Towards evening they passed Diamond Head, and came to the pier of Honolulu. Keawe stepped out among the crowd and began to ask for Lopaka. It seemed he had become the owner of a schooner – none better in the islands – and was gone upon an adventure as far as Pola-Pola or Kahiki; so there was no help to be looked for from Lopaka. Keawe called to mind a friend of his, a lawyer in the town (I must not tell his name), and inquired of him. They said he was grown suddenly rich, and had a fine new house upon Waikiki shore; and this put a thought in Keawe's head, and he called a hack and drove to the lawyer's house.

The house was all brand new, and the trees in the garden no greater than walking-sticks, and the lawyer, when he came, had the air of a man well pleased.

"What can I do to serve you?" said the lawyer.

"You are a friend of Lopaka's," replied Keawe, "and Lopaka purchased from me a certain piece of goods that I thought you might enable me to trace."

The lawyer's face became very dark. "I do not profess to misunderstand you, Mr Keawe," said he, "though this is an ugly business to be stirring in. You may be sure I know nothing, but yet I have a guess, and if you would apply in a certain quarter I think you might have news."

And he named the name of a man, which, again, I had better not repeat. So it was for days, and Keawe went from one to another, finding everywhere new clothes and carriages, and fine new houses and men everywhere in great contentment, although, to be sure, when he hinted at his business their faces would cloud over.

"No doubt I am upon the track," thought Keawe. "These new clothes and carriages are all the gifts of the little imp, and these glad faces are the faces of men who have taken their profit and got rid of the accursed thing in safety. When I see pale cheeks and hear sighing, I shall know that I am near the bottle."

So it befell at last that he was recommended to a Haole in Beritania Street. When he came to the door, about the hour of the evening meal, there were the usual marks of the new house, and the young garden, and the electric light shining in the windows; but when the owner came, a shock of hope and fear ran through Keawe; for here was a young man, white as a corpse, and black about the eyes, the hair shedding from his head, and such a look in his countenance as a man may have when he is waiting for the gallows.

"Here it is, to be sure," thought Keawe, and so with this man he noways veiled his errand. "I am come to buy the bottle," said he.

At the word, the young Haole of Beritania Street reeled against the wall.

"The bottle!" he gasped. "To buy the bottle!" Then he seemed to choke, and seizing Keawe by the arm carried him into a room and poured out wine in two glasses.

"Here is my respects," said Keawe, who had been much about with Haoles in his time. "Yes," he added, "I am come to buy the bottle. What is the price by now?"

At that word the young man let his glass slip through his fingers, and looked upon Keawe like a ghost.

"The price," says he; "the price! you do not know the price?"

"It is for that I am asking you," returned Keawe. "But why are you so much concerned? Is there anything wrong about the price?"

"It has dropped a great deal in value since your time, Mr Keawe," said the young man, stammering.

"Well, well, I shall have the less to pay for it," said Keawe. "How much did it cost you?"

The young man was as white as a sheet. "Two cents," said he.

"What?" cried Keawe, "two cents? Why, then, you can only sell it for one. And he who buys it–" The words died upon Keawe's tongue; he who bought it could never sell it again, the bottle and the bottle imp must abide with him until he died, and when he died must carry him to the red end of hell.

The young man of Beritania Street fell upon his knees. "For God's sake buy it!" he cried. "You can have all my fortune in the bargain. I was mad when I bought it at that price. I had embezzled money at my store; I was lost else; I must have gone to jail."

"Poor creature," said Keawe, "you would risk your soul upon so desperate an adventure, and to avoid the proper punishment of your own disgrace; and you think I could hesitate with love in front of me. Give me the bottle, and the change which I make sure you have all ready. Here is a five-cent piece."

It was as Keawe supposed; the young man had the change ready in a drawer; the bottle changed hands, and Keawe's fingers were no sooner clasped upon the stalk than he had breathed his wish to be a clean man. And, sure enough, when he got home to his room and stripped himself before a glass, his flesh was whole like an infant's. And here was the strange thing: he had no sooner seen this miracle, than his mind was changed within him, and he cared naught for the Chinese Evil, and little enough for Kokua; and had but the one thought, that here he was bound to the bottle imp for time and for eternity, and had no better hope but to be a cinder for ever in the flames of hell. Away ahead of him he saw them blaze with his mind's eye, and his soul shrank, and darkness fell upon the light.

When Keawe came to himself a little, he was aware it was the night when the band played at the hotel. Thither he went, because he feared to be alone; and there, among happy faces, walked to and fro, and heard the tunes go up and down, and saw Berger beat the measure, and all the while he heard the flames crackle, and saw the red fire burning in the bottomless pit. Of a sudden the band played *Hiki-ao-ao*; that was a song that he had sung with Kokua, and at the strain courage returned to him.

"It is done now," he thought, "and once more let me take the good along with the evil."

So it befell that he returned to Hawaii by the first steamer, and as soon as it could be managed he was wedded to Kokua, and carried her up the mountain side to the Bright House.

Now it was so with these two, that when they were together, Keawe's heart was stilled; but so soon has he was alone he fell into a brooding horror, and heard the flames crackle, and saw the red fire burn in the bottomless pit. The girl, indeed, had come to him wholly; her heart leapt in her side at sight of him, her hand clung to his; and she was so fashioned from the hair upon her head to the nails upon her toes that none could see her without joy. She was pleasant in her nature. She had the good word always. Full of song she was, and went to and fro in the Bright House, the brightest thing in its three storeys, carolling like the birds. And Keawe beheld and heard her with delight, and then must shrink upon one side, and weep and groan to think upon the price that he had paid for her; and then he must dry his eyes, and wash his face, and go and sit with her on the broad balconies joining in her songs, and, with a sick spirit, answering her smiles.

There came a day when her feet began to be heavy and her songs more rare; and now it was not Keawe only that would weep apart, but each would sunder from the other and sit in opposite balconies with the whole width of the Bright House betwixt. Keawe was so sunk in his despair, he scarce observed the change, and was only glad he had more hours to sit alone and brood upon his destiny and was not so frequently condemned to pull a smiling face on a sick heart. But one day, coming softly through the house, he heard the sound of a child sobbing, and there was Kokua rolling her face upon the balcony floor, and weeping like the lost.

"You do well to weep in this house, Kokua," he said. "And yet I would give the head off my body that you (at least) might have been happy."

"Happy!" she cried. "Keawe, when you lived alone in your Bright House, you were the word of the island for a happy man; laughter and song were in your mouth, and your face was as bright as the sunrise. Then you wedded pour Kokua; and the good God knows what is amiss in her – but from that day you have not smiled. Ah!" she cried, "what ails me? I thought I was pretty, and I knew I loved him. What ails me that I throw this cloud upon my husband?"

"Poor Kokua," said Keawe. He sat down by her side, and sought to take her hand; but that she plucked away. "Poor Kokua," he said, again. "My poor child – my pretty. And I thought all this while to spare you! Well, you shall know all. Then, at least, you will pity poor Keawe; then you will understand how much he loved you in the past – that he dared hell for your possession – and how much he loves you still (the poor condemned one), that he can yet call up a smile when he beholds you."

With that, he told her all, even from the beginning.

"You have done this for me?" she cried. "Ah, well then what do I care!" – and she clasped and wept upon him.

"Ah, child!" said Keawe, "and yet, when I consider of the fire of hell, I care a good deal!"

"Never tell me," said she; "no man can be lost because he loved Kokua, and no other fault. I tell you, Keawe, I shall save you with these hands, or perish in your company. What! you loved me, and gave your soul, and you think I will not die to save you in return?"

"Ah, my dear! you might die a hundred times, and what difference would that make?" he cried, "except to leave me lonely till the time comes of my damnation?"

"You know nothing," said she. "I was educated in a school in Honolulu; I am no common girl. And I tell you, I shall save my lover. What is this you say about a cent? But all the world is not American. In England they have a piece they call a farthing, which is about half a cent. Ah! sorrow!" she cried, "that makes it scarcely better, for the buyer must be lost, and we shall find none so brave as my Keawe! But, then, there is France; they have a small coin there which they call a centime, and these go five to the cent or thereabout. We could not do better. Come, Keawe, let us go to the French islands; let us go to Tahiti, as fast as ships can bear us. There we have four centimes, three centimes, two centimes one centime; four possible sales to come and go on; and two of us to push the bargain. Come, my Keawe! Kiss me, and banish care. Kokua will defend you."

"Gift of God!" he cried. "I cannot think that God will punish me for desiring aught so good! Be it as you will, then; take me where you please: I put my life and my salvation in your hands."

Early the next day Kokua was about her preparations. She took Keawe's chest that he went with sailoring; and first she put the bottle in a corner; and then packed it with the richest of the clothes and the bravest of the knick-knacks in the house. "For," said she, "we must seem to be rich folks, or who will believe in the bottle?" All the time of her preparation she was as gay as a bird; only when she looked upon Keawe, the tears would spring in her eye, and she must run and kiss him. As for Keawe, a weight was off his soul; now that he had his secret shared, and some hope in front of him, he seemed like a new man, his feet went lightly on the earth, and his breath was good to him again. Yet was terror still at his elbow; and ever and again, as the wind blows out a taper, hope died in him, and he saw the flames toss and the red fire burn in hell.

It was given out in the country they were gone pleasuring to the States, which was thought a strange thing, and yet not so strange as the truth, if any could have guessed it. So they went to Honolulu in the *Hall*, and thence in the *Umatilla* to San Francisco with a crowd of Haoles, and at San Francisco took their passage by the mail brigantine, the *Tropic Bird* for Papeete, the chief place of the French in the south islands. Thither they came, after a pleasant voyage, on a fair day of the Trade Wind, and saw the reef with the surf breaking, and Motuiti with its palms, and the schooner riding within-side, and the white houses of the town low down along the shore among green trees, and overhead the mountains and the clouds of Tahiti, the wise island.

It was judged the most wise to hire a house, which they did accordingly, opposite the British Consul's, to make a great parade of money, and themselves conspicuous with carriages and horses. This it was very easy to do, so long as they had the bottle in their possession; for Kokua was more bold than Keawe, and whenever she had a mind, called on the imp for twenty or a hundred dollars. At this rate they soon grew to be remarked in the town; and the strangers from Hawaii, their riding and their driving, the fine holokus and the rich lace of Kokua, became the matter of much talk.

They got on well after the first with the Tahitian language, which is indeed like to the Hawaiian, with a change of certain letters; and as soon as they had any freedom of speech, began to push the bottle. You are to consider it was not an easy subject to introduce; it was not easy to persuade people you were in earnest, when you offered to sell them for four centimes the spring of health and riches inexhaustible. It was necessary besides to explain the dangers of the bottle; and either people disbelieved the whole thing and laughed or they thought the more of the darker part, became overcast with gravity, and drew away from Keawe and Kokua, as from persons who had dealings with the devil. So far from gaining ground, these two began to find they were avoided in the town; the children ran away from them screaming, a thing intolerable to Kokua; Catholics crossed themselves as they went by; and all persons began with one accord to disengage themselves from their advances.

Depression fell upon their spirits. They would sit at night in their new house, after a day's weariness, and not exchange one word, or the silence would be broken by Kokua bursting suddenly into sobs. Sometimes they would pray together; sometimes they would have the bottle out upon the floor, and sit all evening watching how the shadow hovered in the midst. At such times they would be afraid to go to rest. It was long ere slumber came to them, and if either dozed off, it would be to wake and find the other silently weeping in the dark, or perhaps, to wake alone, the other having fled from the house and the neighbourhood of that bottle, to pace under the bananas in the little garden, or to wander on the beach by moonlight.

One night it was so when Kokua awoke. Keawe was gone. She felt in the bed and his place was cold. Then fear fell upon her, and she sat up in bed. A little moonshine filtered through the shutters. The room was bright, and she could spy the bottle on the floor. Outside it blew high, the great trees of the avenue cried aloud, and the fallen leaves rattled in the verandah. In the midst of this Kokua was aware of another sound; whether of a beast or of a man she could scarce tell, but it was as sad as death, and cut her to the soul. Softly she arose, set the door ajar, and looked forth in the moonlit yard. There, under the bananas, lay Keawe, his mouth in the dust, and as he lay he moaned.

It was Kokua's first thought to run forward and console him; her second potently withheld her. Keawe had borne himself before his wife like a brave man; it became her little in the hour of weakness to intrude upon his shame. With the thought she drew back into the house.

"Heavens!" she thought, "how careless have I been – how weak! It is he, not I that stands in this eternal peril; it was he, not I, that took the curse upon his soul. It is for my sake, and for the love of a creature of so little worth and such poor help, that he now beholds so close to him the flames of hell – ay, and smells the smoke of it, lying without there in the wind and moonlight. Am I so dull of spirit that never till now I have surmised my duty, or have I seen it before and turned aside? But now, at least, I take upon my soul in both the hands of my affection; now I say farewell to the white steps of heaven and the waiting faces of my friends. A love for a love, and let mine be equalled with Keawe's! A soul for a soul, and be it mine to perish!"

She was a deft woman with her hands, and was soon apparelled. She took in her hands the change – the precious centimes they kept ever at their side; for this coin is little used, and they had made provision at a Government office. When she was forth in the avenue clouds came on the wind, and the moon was blackened. The town slept, and she knew not whither to turn till she heard one coughing in the shadow of the trees.

"Old man," said Kokua, "what do you here abroad in the cold night?"

The old man could scarce express himself for coughing, but she made out that he was old and poor, and a stranger in the island.

"Will you do me a service?" said Kokua. "As one stranger to another, and as an old man to a young woman, will you help a daughter of Hawaii?"

"Ah," said the old man. "So you are the witch from the eight islands, and even my old soul you seek to entangle. But I have heard of you, and defy your wickedness."

"Sit down here," said Kokua, "and let me tell you a tale." And she told him the story of Keawe from the beginning to the end.

"And now," said she, "I am his wife, whom he bought with his soul's welfare. And what should I do? If I went to him myself and offered to buy it, he would refuse. But if you go, he will sell it eagerly; I will await you here; you will buy it for four centimes, and I will buy it again for three. And the Lord strengthen a poor girl!"

"If you meant falsely," said the old man, "I think God would strike you dead."

"He would!" cried Kokua. "Be sure he would. I could not be so treacherous – God would not suffer it."

"Give me the four centimes and await me here," said the old man.

Now, when Kokua stood alone in the street, her spirit died. The wind roared in the trees, and it seemed to her the rushing of the flames of hell; the shadows tossed in the light of the street lamp, and they seemed to her the snatching hands of evil ones. If she had had the strength, she must have run away, and if she had had the breath she must have screamed aloud; but, in truth, she could do neither, and stood trembled in the avenue, like an affrighted child.

Then she saw the old man returning, and he had the bottle in his hand.

"I have done your bidding," said he. "I left your husband weeping like a child; tonight he will sleep easy." And he held the bottle forth.

"Before you give it me," Kokua panted, "take the good with the evil – ask to be delivered from your cough."

"I am an old man," replied the other, "and too near the gate of the grave to take a favour from the devil. But what is this? Why do you not take the bottle? Do you hesitate?"

"Not hesitate!" cried Kokua. "I am only weak. Give me a moment. It is my hand resists, my flesh shrinks back from the accursed thing. One moment only!"

The old man looked upon Kokua kindly. "Poor child!" said he, "you fear; your soul misgives you. Well, let me keep it. I am old and can never more be happy in this world, and as for the next—"

"Give it me!" gasped Kokua. "There is your money. Do you think I am so base as that? Give me the bottle."

"God bless you, child," said the old man.

Kokua concealed the bottle under her holoku, said farewell to the old man, and walked off along the avenue, she cared not whither. For all roads were not the same to her, and led equally to hell. Sometimes she walked, and sometimes ran; sometimes she screamed out loud in the night, and sometimes lay by the wayside in the dust and wept. All that she had heard of hell came back to her; she saw the flames blaze, and she smelt the smoke, and her flesh withered on the coals.

Near the day she came to her mind again, and returned to the house. It was even as the old man said – Keawe slumbered like a child. Kokua stood and gazed upon his face.

"Now, my husband," said she, "it is your turn to sleep. When you wake it will be your turn to sing and laugh. But for poor Kokua, alas! That meant no evil – for poor Kokua no more sleep, no more singing, no more delight, whether in earth or heaven."

With that she lay down in the bed by his side, and her misery was so extreme that she fell in a deep slumber instantly.

Late in the morning her husband woke her and gave her the good news. It seemed he was silly with delight, for he paid no heed to her distress, ill though she dissembled it. The words stuck in her mouth, it mattered not; Keawe did the speaking. She ate not a bite, but who was to observe it? for Keawe cleared the dish. Kokua saw and heard him, like some strange thing in a dream; there were times when she forgot or doubted, and put her hands to her brow; to know herself doomed and hear her husband babble, seemed so monstrous.

All the while Keawe was eating and talking, and planning the time of their return, and thanking her for saving him, and fondling her, and calling her the true helper after all. He laughed at the old man that was fool enough to buy that bottle.

"A worthy old man he seemed," Keawe said. "But no one can judge by appearances. For why did the old reprobate require the bottle?"

"My husband," said Kokua, humbly, "his purpose may have been good."

Keawe laughed like an angry man.

"Fiddle-de-dee!" cried Keawe. "An old rogue, I tell you; and an old ass to boot. For the bottle was hard enough to sell at four centimes; and at three it will be quite impossible. The margin is not broad enough, the thing begins to smell of scorching – brrr!" said he, and shuddered. "It is true I bought it myself at a cent, when I knew not there were smaller coins. I was a fool for my pains; there will never be found another: and whoever has that bottle now will carry it to the pit."

"O my husband!" said Kokua. "It is not a terrible thing to save oneself by the eternal ruin of another? It seems to me I could not laugh. I would be humbled. I would be filled with melancholy. I would pray for the poor holder."

Then Keawe, because he felt the truth of what she said, grew the more angry. "Heighty-teighty!" cried he. "You may be filled with melancholy if you please. It is not the mind of a good wife. If you thought at all of me, you would sit shamed."

Thereupon he went out, and Kokua was alone.

What chance had she to sell that bottle at two centimes? None, she perceived. And if she had any, here was her husband hurrying her away to a country where there was nothing lower than a cent. And here – on the morrow of her sacrifice – was her husband leaving her and blaming her.

She would not even try to profit by what time she had, but sat in the house, and now had the bottle out and viewed it with unutterable fear, and now, with loathing, hid it out of sight.

By-and-by, Keawe came back, and would have her take a drive.

"My husband, I am ill," she said. "I am out of heart. Excuse me, I can take no pleasure."

Then was Keawe more wroth than ever. With her, because he thought she was brooding over the case of the old man; and with himself, because thought she was right, and was ashamed to be so happy.

"This is your truth," cried he, "and this your affection! Your husband is just saved from eternal ruin, which he encountered for the love of you – and you take no pleasure! Kokua, you have a disloyal heart."

He went forth again furious, and wandered in the town all day. He met friends, and drank with them; they hired a carriage and drove into the country, and there drank again. All the time Keawe was ill at ease, because he was taking this pastime while his wife was sad, and because he knew in his heart that she was more right than he; and the knowledge made him drink the deeper.

Now there was an old brutal Haole drinking with him, one that had been a boatswain of a whaler, a runaway, a digger in gold mines, a convict in prisons. He had a low mind and a foul mouth; he loved to drink and to see other drunken; and he pressed the glass upon Keawe. Soon there was no more money in the company.

"Here, you!" says the boatswain, "you are rich, you have been always saying. You have a bottle or some foolishness."

"Yes," says Keawe, "I am rich; I will go back and get some money from my wife, who keeps it."

"That's a bad idea, mate," said the boatswain. "Never you trust a petticoat with dollars. They're all as false as water; you keep an eye on her."

Now, this word struck in Keawe's mind; for he was muddled with what he had been drinking.

"I should not wonder but she was false, indeed," thought he. "Why else should she be so cast down at my release? But I will show her I am not the man to be fooled, I will catch her in the act."

Accordingly, when they were back in town, Keawe bade the boatswain wait for him at the corner, by the old calaboose, and went forward up the avenue alone to the door of his house. The night had come again; there was a light within, but never a sound; and Keawe crept about the corner, opened the back door softly, and looked in.

There was Kokua on the floor, the lamp at her side, before her was a milk-white bottle, with a round belly and a long neck; and as she viewed it, Kokua wrung her hands.

A long time Keawe stood and looked in the doorway. At first he was struck stupid; and then fear fell upon him that the bargain had been made amiss, and the bottle had come back to him as it came at San Francisco; and at that his knees were loosened, and the fumes of the wine departed from his head like mists off a river in the morning. And then he had another thought; and it was a strange one, that made his cheeks to burn.

"I must make sure of this," thought he.

So he closed the door, and went softly round the corner again, and then came noisily in, as though he were but now returned. And, lo! by the time he opened the front door no bottle was to be seen; and Kokua sat in a chair and started up like one awakened out of sleep.

"I have been drinking all day and making merry," said Keawe. "I have been with good companions, and now I only come back for money, and return to drink and carouse with them again."

Both his face and voice were as stern as judgment, but Kokua was too troubled to observe.

"You do well to use your own, my husband," said she, and her words trembled.

"O, I do well in all things," said Keawe, and he went straight to the chest and took out money. But he looked besides in the corner where they kept the bottle, and there was no bottle there.

At that the chest heaved upon the floor like a sea-billow, and the house span about him like a wreath of smoke, for he saw he was lost now, and there was no escape. "It is what I feared," he thought. "It is she who bought it."

And then he came to himself a little and rose up; but the sweat streamed on his face as thick as the rain and as cold as the well-water.

"Kokua," said he, "I said to you today what ill became me. Now I return to carouse with my jolly companions," and at that he laughed a little quietly. "I will take more pleasure in the cup if you forgive me."

She clasped his knees in a moment; she kissed his knees with flowing tears.

"O," she cried, "I asked but a kind word!"

"Let us never one think hardly of the other," said Keawe, and was gone out of the house.

Now, the money that Keawe had taken was only some of that store of centime piece they had laid in at their arrival. It was very sure he had no mind to be drinking. His wife had given her soul for him, now he must give his for hers; no other thought was in the world with him.

At the corner, by the old calaboose, there was the boatswain waiting.

"My wife has the bottle," said Keawe, "and, unless you help me to recover it, there can be no more money and no more liquor tonight."

"You do not mean to say you are serious about that bottle?" cried the boatswain.

"There is the lamp," said Keawe. "Do I look as if I was jesting?"

"That is so," said the boatswain. "You look as serious as a ghost."

"Well, then," said Keawe, "here are two centimes; you must go to my wife in the house, and offer her these for the bottle, which (if I am not much mistaken) she will give you instantly. Bring it to me here, and I will buy it back from you for one; for that is the law with this bottle, that it still must be sold for a less sum. But whatever you do, never breathe a word to her that you have come from me."

"Mate, I wonder are you making a fool of me?" asked the boatswain.

"It will do you no harm if I am," returned Keawe.

"That is so, mate," said the boatswain.

"And if you doubt me," added Keawe, "you can try. As soon as you are clear of the house, wish to have your pocket full of money, or a bottle of the best rum, or what you please, and you will see the virtue of the thing."

"Very well, Kanaka," says the boatswain. "I will try; but if you are having your fun out of me, I will take my fun out of you with a belaying pin."

So the whaler-man went off upon the avenue; and Keawe stood and waited. It was near the same spot where Kokua had waited the night before; but Keawe was more resolved, and never faltered in his purpose; only his soul was bitter with despair.

It seemed a long time he had to wait before he heard a voice singing in the darkness of the avenue. He knew the voice to be the boatswain's; but it was strange how drunken it appeared upon a sudden.

Next, the man himself came stumbling into the light of the lamp. He had the devil's bottle buttoned in his coat; another bottle was in his hand; and even as he came in view he raised it to his mouth and drank.

"You have it," said Keawe. "I see that."

"Hands off!" cried the boatswain, jumping back. "Take a step near me, and I'll smash your mouth. You thought you could make a cat's-paw of me, did you?"

"What do you mean?" cried Keawe.

"Mean?" cried the boatswain. "This is a pretty good bottle, this is; that's what I mean. How I got it for two centimes I can't make out; but I'm sure you shan't have it for one."

"You mean you won't sell?" gasped Keawe.

"No, sir!" cried the boatswain. "But I'll give you a drink of the rum, if you like."

"I tell you," said Keawe, "the man who has that bottle goes to hell."

"I reckon I'm going anyway," returned the sailor; "and this bottle's the best thing to go with I've struck yet. No, sir!" he cried again, "this is my bottle now, and you can go and fish for another."

"Can this be true?" Keawe cried. "For your own sake, I beseech you, sell it me!"

"I don't value any of your talk," replied the boatswain. "You thought I was a flat; now you see I'm not; and there's an end. If you won't have a swallow of the rum, I'll have one myself. Here's your health, and goodnight to you!"

So off he went down the avenue toward town, and there goes the bottle out of the story.

But Keawe ran to Kokua light as the wind; and great was their joy that night; and great, since then has been the peace of all their days in the Bright House.

ROBERT LOUIS STEVENSON
THE PAVILION ON THE LINKS

CHAPTER 1

was a great solitary when I was young. I made it my pride to keep aloof and suffice for my own entertainment; and I may say that I had neither friends nor acquaintances until I met that friend who became my wife and the mother of my children. With one man only was I on private terms; this was R. Northmour, Esquire, of Graden Easter, in Scotland. We had met at college; and though there was not much liking between us, nor even much intimacy, we were so nearly of a humour that we could associate with ease to both. Misanthropes, we believed ourselves to be; but I have thought since that we were only sulky fellows. It was scarcely a companionship, but a co-existence in unsociability. Northmour's exceptional violence of temper made it no easy affair for him to keep the peace with anyone but me; and as he respected my silent ways, and let me come and go as I pleased, I could tolerate his presence without concern. I think we called each other friends.

When Northmour took his degree and I decided to leave the university without one, he invited me on a long visit to Graden Easter; and it was thus that I first became acquainted with the scene of my adventures. The mansion house of Graden stood in a bleak stretch of country some three miles from the shore of the German Ocean. It was as large as a barrack; and as it had been built of a soft stone, liable to consume in the eager air of the seaside, it was damp and draughty within and half ruinous without. It was impossible for two young men to lodge with comfort in such a dwelling. But there stood in the northern part of the estate, in a wilderness of links and blowing sand hills, and between a plantation and the sea, a small pavilion or belvedere, of modern design, which was exactly suited to our wants; and in this hermitage, speaking little, reading much, and rarely associating except at meals, Northmour and I spent four tempestuous winter months. I might have stayed longer; but one March night there sprung up between us a dispute, which rendered my departure necessary. Northmour spoke hotly, I remember, and I suppose I must have made some tart rejoinder. He leaped from his chair and grappled me; I had to fight, without exaggeration, for my life; and it was only with a great effort that I mastered him, for he was near as strong in body as myself, and seemed filled with the devil. The next morning, we met on our usual terms; but I judged it more delicate to withdraw; nor did he attempt to dissuade me.

It was nine years before I revisited the neighbourhood. I travelled at that time with a tilt-cart, a tent and a cooking stove, tramping all day beside the wagon, and at night, whenever it was possible, gypsying in a cove of the hills, or by the side of a wood. I believe I visited in this manner most of the wild and desolate regions both in England and Scotland; and, as I had neither friends nor relations, I was troubled with no correspondence, and had nothing in the nature of headquarters, unless it was the office of my solicitors, from whom I drew my income twice a year. It was a life in which I delighted; and I fully thought to have grown old upon the march, and at last died in a ditch.

It was my whole business to find desolate corners, where I could camp without the fear of interruption; and hence, being in another part of the same shire, I bethought me suddenly of the Pavilion on the Links. No thoroughfare passed within three miles of it. The nearest town, and that was but a fisher village, was at a distance of six or seven. For ten miles of length, and from a depth varying from three miles to half a mile, this belt of barren country lay along the sea. The beach, which was the natural approach, was full of quicksands. Indeed I may say there is hardly a better place of concealment in the United Kingdom. I determined to pass a week in the Sea-Wood of Graden-Easter, and making a long stage, reached it about sundown on a wild September day.

The country, I have said, was mixed sand hill and links; *links* being a Scottish name for sand which has ceased drifting and become more or less solidly covered with turf. The pavilion stood on an even space: a little behind it, the wood began in a hedge of elders huddled together by the wind; in front, a few tumbled sand hills stood between it and the sea. An outcropping of rock had formed a bastion for the sand, so that there was here a promontory in the coast line between two shallow bays; and just beyond the tides, the rock again cropped out and formed an islet of small dimensions but strikingly designed. The quicksands were of great extent at low water, and had an infamous reputation in the country. Close in shore, between the islet and the promontory, it was said they would swallow a man in four minutes and a half; but there may have been little ground for this precision. The district was alive with rabbits, and haunted by gulls which made a continual piping about the pavilion. On summer days the outlook was bright and even gladsome; but at sundown in September, with a high wind, and a heavy surf rolling in close along the links, the place told of nothing but dead mariners and sea disaster. A ship beating to windward on the horizon, and a huge truncheon of wreck half buried in the sands at my feet, completed the innuendo of the scene.

The pavilion – it had been built by the last proprietor, Northmour's uncle, a silly and prodigal virtuoso – presented little signs of age. It was two stories in height, Italian in design, surrounded by a patch of garden in which nothing had prospered but a few coarse flowers; and looked, with its shuttered windows, not like a house that had been deserted, but like one that had never been tenanted by man. Northmour was plainly from home; whether, as usual, sulking in the cabin of his yacht, or in one of his fitful and extravagant appearances in the world of society, I had, of course, no means of guessing. The place had an air of solitude that daunted even a solitary like myself; the wind cried in the chimneys with a strange and wailing note; and it was with a sense of escape, as if I were going indoors, that I turned away and, driving my cart before me, entered the skirts of the wood.

The Sea-Wood of Graden had been planted to shelter the cultivated fields behind, and check the encroachments of the blowing sand. As you advanced into it from coastward, elders were succeeded by other hardy shrubs; but the timber was all stunted and bushy; it led a life of conflict; the trees were accustomed to swing there all night long in fierce winter tempests; and even in early spring, the leaves were already flying, and autumn was beginning, in this exposed plantation. Inland the ground rose into a little hill, which, along with the islet, served as a sailing mark for seamen. When the hill was open of the islet to the north, vessels must bear well to the eastward to clear Graden Ness and the Graden Bullers. In the lower ground, a streamlet ran among the trees, and, being dammed with dead leaves and clay of its own carrying, spread out every here and there, and lay in stagnant pools. One or two ruined cottages were dotted about the wood; and, according to Northmour, these were ecclesiastical foundations, and in their time had sheltered pious hermits.

I found a den, or small hollow, where there was a spring of pure water; and there, clearing away the brambles, I pitched the tent, and made a fire to cook my supper. My horse I picketed farther in the wood where there was a patch of sward. The banks of the den not only concealed the light of my fire, but sheltered me from the wind, which was cold as well as high.

The life I was leading made me both hardy and frugal. I never drank but water, and rarely eat anything more costly than oatmeal; and I required so little sleep, that, although I rose with the peep of day, I would often lie long awake in the dark or starry watches of the night. Thus in Graden Sea-Wood, although I fell thankfully asleep by eight in the evening I was awake again before eleven with a full possession of my faculties, and no sense of drowsiness or fatigue. I rose and sat by the fire, watching the trees and clouds tumultuously tossing and fleeing overhead, and hearkening to the wind and the rollers along the shore; till at length, growing weary of inaction, I quitted the den, and strolled toward the borders of the wood. A young moon, buried in mist, gave a faint illumination to my steps; and the light grew brighter as I walked forth into the links. At the same moment, the wind, smelling salt of the open ocean and carrying particles of sand, struck me with its full force, so that I had to bow my head.

When I raised it again to look about me, I was aware of a light in the pavilion. It was not stationary; but passed from one window to another, as though some one were reviewing the different apartments with a lamp or candle. I watched it for some seconds in great surprise. When I had arrived in the afternoon the house had been plainly deserted; now it was as plainly occupied. It was my first idea that a gang of thieves might have broken in and be now ransacking Northmour's cupboards, which were many and not ill supplied. But what should bring thieves at Graden Easter? And, again, all the shutters had been thrown open, and it would have been more in the character of such gentry to close them. I dismissed the notion, and fell back upon another. Northmour himself must have arrived, and was now airing and inspecting the pavilion.

I have said that there was no real affection between this man and me; but, had I loved him like a brother, I was then so much more in love with solitude that I should none the less have shunned his company. As it was, I turned and ran for it; and it was with genuine satisfaction that I found myself safely back beside the fire. I had escaped an acquaintance; I should have one more night in comfort. In the morning, I might either slip away before Northmour was abroad, or pay him as short a visit as I chose.

But when morning came, I thought the situation so diverting that I forgot my shyness. Northmour was at my mercy; I arranged a good practical jest, though I knew well that my neighbour was not the man to jest with in security; and, chuckling beforehand over its success, took my place among the elders at the edge of the wood, whence I could command the door of the pavilion. The shutters were all once more closed, which I remember thinking odd; and the house, with its white walls and green venetians, looked spruce and habitable in the morning light. Hour after hour passed, and still no sign of Northmour. I knew him for a sluggard in the morning; but, as it drew on toward noon, I lost my patience. To say the truth, I had promised myself to break my fast in the pavilion, and hunger began to prick me sharply. It was a pity to let the opportunity go by without some cause for mirth; but the grosser appetite prevailed, and I relinquished my jest with regret, and sallied from the wood.

The appearance of the house affected me, as I drew near, with disquietude. It seemed unchanged since last evening; and I had expected it, I scarce knew why, to wear some external signs of habitation. But no: the windows were all closely shuttered, the chimneys breathed no smoke, and the front door itself was closely padlocked. Northmour, therefore, had entered by the back; this was the natural, and indeed, the necessary conclusion; and you may judge of my surprise when, on turning the house, I found the back door similarly secured.

My mind at once reverted to the original theory of thieves; and I blamed myself sharply for my last night's inaction. I examined all the windows on the lower story, but none of them had been tampered with; I tried the padlocks, but they were both secure. It thus became a problem how the thieves, if thieves they were, had managed to enter the house. They must have got, I reasoned, upon the roof of the outhouse where Northmour used to keep his photographic battery; and from thence, either by the window of the study or that of my old bedroom, completed their burglarious entry.

I followed what I supposed was their example; and, getting on the roof, tried the shutters of each room. Both were secure; but I was not to be beaten; and, with a little force, one of them flew open, grazing, as it did so, the back of my hand. I remember, I put the wound to my mouth, and stood for perhaps half a minute licking it like a dog, and mechanically gazing behind me over the waste links and the sea; and, in that space of time, my eye made note of a large schooner yacht some miles to the northeast. Then I threw up the window and climbed in.

I went over the house, and nothing can express my mystification. There was no sign of disorder, but, on the contrary, the rooms were unusually clean and pleasant. I found fires laid, ready for lighting; three bedrooms prepared with a luxury quite foreign to Northmour's habits, and with water in the ewers and the beds turned down; a table set for three in the dining-room; and an ample supply of cold meats, game and vegetables on the pantry shelves. There were guests expected, that was plain; but why guests, when Northmour hated society? And, above all, why was the house thus stealthily prepared at dead of night? and why were the shutters closed and the doors padlocked?

I effaced all traces of my visit, and came forth from the window feeling sobered and concerned.

The schooner yacht was still in the same place; and it flashed for a moment through my mind that this might be the *Red Earl* bringing the owner of the pavilion and his guests. But the vessel's head was set the other way.

CHAPTER 2

I returned to the den to cook myself a meal, of which I stood in great need, as well as to care for my horse, whom I had somewhat neglected in the morning. From time to time I went down to the edge of the wood; but there was no change in the pavilion, and not a human creature was seen all day upon the links. The schooner in the offing was the one touch of life within my range of vision. She, apparently with no set object, stood off and on or lay to, hour after hour; but as the evening deepened, she drew steadily nearer. I became more convinced that she carried Northmour and his friends, and that they would probably come ashore after dark; not only because that was of a piece with the secrecy of the preparations, but because the tide would not have flowed sufficiently before eleven to cover Graden Floe and the other sea quags that fortified the shore against invaders.

All day the wind had been going down, and the sea along with it; but there was a return toward sunset of the heavy weather of the day before. The night set in pitch dark. The wind came off the sea in squalls, like the firing of a battery of cannon; now and then there was a flaw of rain, and the surf rolled heavier with the rising tide. I was down at my observatory among the elders, when a light was run up to the masthead of the schooner, and showed she was closer in than when I had last seen her by the dying daylight. I concluded that this must be a signal to Northmour's associates on shore; and, stepping forth into the links, looked around me for something in response.

A small footpath ran along the margin of the wood, and formed the most direct communication between the pavilion and the mansion house; and, as I cast my eyes to that side, I saw a spark of light, not a quarter of a mile away, and rapidly approaching. From its uneven course it appeared to be the light of a lantern carried by a person who followed the windings of the path, and was often staggered, and taken aback by the more violent squalls. I concealed myself once more among the elders, and waited eagerly for the newcomer's advance. It proved to be a woman; and, as she passed within half a rod of my ambush, I was able to recognize the features. The deaf and silent old dame, who had nursed Northmour in his childhood, was his associate in this underhand affair.

I followed her at a little distance, taking advantage of the innumerable heights and hollows, concealed by the darkness, and favoured not only by the nurse's deafness, but by the uproar of the wind and surf. She entered the pavilion, and, going at once to the upper story, opened and set a light in one of the windows that looked toward the sea. Immediately afterwards the light at the schooner's masthead was run down and extinguished. Its purpose had been attained, and those on board were sure that they were expected. The old woman resumed her preparations; although the other shutters remained closed, I could see a glimmer going to and fro about the house; and a gush of sparks from one chimney after another soon told me that the fires were being kindled.

Northmour and his guests, I was now persuaded, would come ashore as soon as there was water on the floe. It was a wild night for boat service; and I felt some alarm mingle with my curiosity as I reflected on the danger of the landing. My old acquaintance, it was true, was the most eccentric of men; but the present eccentricity was both disquieting and lugubrious to consider. A variety of feelings thus led me toward the beach, where I lay flat on my face in a hollow within six feet of the track that led to the pavilion. Thence, I should have the satisfaction of recognizing the arrivals, and, if they should prove to be acquaintances, greeting them as soon as they landed.

Some time before eleven, while the tide was still dangerously low, a boat's lantern appeared close in shore; and, my attention being thus awakened, I could perceive another still far to seaward, violently tossed, and sometimes hidden by the billows. The weather, which was getting dirtier as the night went on, and the perilous situation of the yacht upon a lee shore, had probably driven them to attempt a landing at the earliest possible moment.

A little afterwards, four yachtsmen carrying a very heavy chest, and guided by a fifth with a lantern, passed close in front of me as I lay, and were admitted to the pavilion by the nurse. They returned to the beach, and passed me a third time with another chest, larger but apparently not so heavy as the first. A third time they made the transit; and on this occasion one of the yachtsmen carried a leather portmanteau, and the others a lady's trunk and carriage bag. My curiosity was sharply excited. If a woman were among the guests of Northmour, it would show a change in his habits, and an apostasy from his pet theories of life, well calculated to fill me with surprise. When he and I dwelt there together, the pavilion had been a temple of misogyny. And now, one of the detested sex was to be installed under its roof. I remembered one or two particulars, a few notes of daintiness and almost of coquetry which had struck me the day before as I surveyed the preparations in the house; their purpose was now clear, and I thought myself dull not to have perceived it from the first.

While I was thus reflecting, a second lantern drew near me from the beach. It was carried by a yachtsman whom I had not yet seen, and who was conducting two other persons to the pavilion. These two persons were unquestionably the guests for whom the house was made ready; and, straining eye and ear, I set myself to watch them as they passed. One was an unusually tall man, in a travelling hat slouched over his eyes, and a highland cape closely buttoned and turned up so as to conceal his face. You could make out no more of him than that he was, as I have said, unusually tall, and walked feebly with a heavy stoop. By his side, and either clinging to him or giving him support – I could not make out which – was a young, tall, and slender figure of a woman. She was extremely pale; but in the light of the lantern her face was so marred by strong and changing shadows, that she might equally well have been as ugly as sin or as beautiful as I afterwards found her to be.

When they were just abreast of me, the girl made some remark which was drowned by the noise of the wind.

"Hush!" said her companion; and there was something in the tone with which the word was uttered that thrilled and rather shook my spirits. It seemed to breathe from a bosom labouring under the deadliest terror; I have never heard another syllable so expressive; and I still hear it again when I am feverish at night, and my mind runs upon old times. The man turned toward the girl as he spoke; I had a glimpse of much red beard and a nose which seemed to have been broken in youth; and his light eyes seemed shining in his face with some strong and unpleasant emotion.

But these two passed on and were admitted in their turn to the pavilion.

One by one, or in groups, the seamen returned to the beach. The wind brought me the sound of a rough voice crying, "Shove off!" Then, after a pause, another lantern drew near. It was Northmour alone.

My wife and I, a man and a woman, have often agreed to wonder how a person could be, at the same time, so handsome and so repulsive as Northmour. He had the appearance of a finished gentleman; his face bore every mark of intelligence and courage; but you had only to look at him, even in his most amiable moment, to see that he had the temper of a slaver captain. I never knew a character that was both explosive and revengeful to the same degree; he combined the vivacity of the south with the sustained and deadly hatreds of the north; and both traits were plainly written on his face, which was a sort of danger signal. In person, he was tall, strong, and active; his hair and complexion very dark; his features handsomely designed, but spoiled by a menacing expression.

At that moment he was somewhat paler than by nature; he wore a heavy frown; and his lips worked, and he looked sharply round him as he walked, like a man besieged with apprehensions. And yet I thought he had a look of triumph underlying all, as though he had already done much, and was near the end of an achievement.

Partly from a scruple of delicacy – which I dare say came too late – partly from the pleasure of startling an acquaintance, I desired to make my presence known to him without delay.

I got suddenly to my feet, and stepped forward.

"Northmour!" said I.

I have never had so shocking a surprise in all my days. He leaped on me without a word; something shone in his hand; and he struck for my heart with a dagger. At the same moment I knocked him head over heels. Whether it was my quickness, or his own uncertainty, I know not; but the blade only grazed my shoulder, while the hilt and his fist struck me violently on the mouth.

I fled, but not far. I had often and often observed the capabilities of the sand hills for protracted ambush or stealthy advances and retreats; and, not ten yards from the scene of the scuffle, plumped down again upon the grass. The lantern had fallen and gone out. But what was my astonishment to see Northmour slip at a bound into the pavilion, and hear him bar the door behind him with a clang of iron!

He had not pursued me. He had run away. Northmour, whom I knew for the most implacable and daring of men, had run away! I could scarce believe my reason; and yet in this strange business, where all was incredible, there was nothing to make a work about in an incredibility more or less. For why was the pavilion secretly prepared? Why had Northmour landed with his guests at dead of night, in half a gale of wind, and with the floe scarce covered? Why had he sought to kill me? Had he not recognized my voice? I wondered. And, above all, how had he come to have a dagger ready in his hand? A dagger, or even a sharp knife, seemed out of keeping with the age in which we lived; and a gentleman landing from his yacht on the shore of his own estate, even although it was at night and with some mysterious circumstances, does not usually, as a matter of fact, walk thus prepared for deadly onslaught. The more I reflected, the further I felt at sea. I recapitulated the elements of mystery, counting them on my fingers: the pavilion secretly prepared for guests; the guests landed at the risk of their lives and to the imminent peril of the yacht; the guests, or at least one of them, in undisguised and seemingly causeless terror; Northmour with a naked weapon; Northmour stabbing his most intimate acquaintance at a word; last, and not least strange, Northmour fleeing from the man whom he had sought to murder, and barricading himself, like a hunted creature, behind the door of the pavilion. Here were at least six separate causes for extreme surprise; each part and parcel with the others, and forming all together one consistent story. I felt almost ashamed to believe my own senses.

As I thus stood, transfixed with wonder, I began to grow painfully conscious of the injuries I had received in the scuffle; skulked round among the sand hills; and, by a devious path, regained the shelter of the wood. On the way, the old nurse passed again within several yards of me, still carrying her lantern, on the return journey to the mansion house of Graden. This made a seventh suspicious feature in the case. Northmour and his guests, it appeared, were to cook and do the cleaning for themselves, while the old woman continued to inhabit the big empty barrack among the policies. There must surely be great cause for secrecy, when so many inconveniences were confronted to preserve it.

So thinking, I made my way to the den. For greater security, I trod out the embers of the fire, and lighted my lantern to examine the wound upon my shoulder. It was a trifling hurt, although it bled somewhat freely, and I dressed it as well as I could (for its position made it difficult to reach) with some rag and cold water from the spring. While I was thus busied, I mentally declared war against Northmour and his mystery. I am not an angry man by nature, and I believe there was more curiosity than resentment in my heart. But war I certainly declared; and, by way of preparation, I got out my revolver, and, having drawn the charges, cleaned and reloaded it with scrupulous care. Next I became preoccupied about my horse. It might break loose, or fall to neighing, and so betray my camp in the Sea-Wood. I determined to rid myself of its neighbourhood; and long before dawn I was leading it over the links in the direction of the fisher village.

CHAPTER 3

For two days I skulked round the pavilion, profiting by the uneven surface of the links. I became an adept in the necessary tactics. These low hillocks and shallow dells, running one into another, became a kind of cloak of darkness for my enthralling, but perhaps dishonourable, pursuit.

Yet, in spite of this advantage, I could learn but little of Northmour or his guests.

Fresh provisions were brought under cover of darkness by the old woman from the mansion house. Northmour, and the young lady, sometimes together, but more often singly, would walk for an hour or two at a time on the beach beside the quicksand. I could not but conclude that this promenade was chosen with an eye to secrecy; for the spot was open only to seaward. But it suited me not less excellently; the highest and most accidented of the sand hills immediately adjoined; and from these, lying flat in a hollow, I could overlook Northmour or the young lady as they walked.

The tall man seemed to have disappeared. Not only did he never cross the threshold, but he never so much as showed face at a window; or, at least, not so far as I could see; for I dared not creep forward beyond a certain distance in the day, since the upper floors commanded the bottoms of the links; and at night, when I could venture further, the lower windows were barricaded as if to stand a siege. Sometimes I thought the tall man must be confined to bed, for I remembered the feebleness of his gait; and sometimes I thought he must have gone clear away, and that Northmour and the young lady remained alone together in the pavilion. The idea, even then, displeased me.

Whether or not this pair were man and wife, I had seen abundant reason to doubt the friendliness of their relation. Although I could hear nothing of what they said, and rarely so much as glean a decided expression on the face of either, there was a distance, almost a stiffness, in their bearing which showed them to be either unfamiliar or at enmity. The girl walked faster when she was with Northmour than when she was alone; and I conceived that any inclination between a man and a woman would rather delay than accelerate the step. Moreover, she kept a good yard free of him, and trailed her umbrella, as if it were a barrier, on the side between them. Northmour kept sidling closer; and, as the girl retired from his advance, their course lay at a sort of diagonal across the beach, and would have landed them in the surf had it been long enough continued. But, when this was imminent, the girl would unostentatiously change sides and put Northmour between her and the sea. I watched these manoeuvres, for my part, with high enjoyment and approval, and chuckled to myself at every move.

On the morning of the third day, she walked alone for some time, and I perceived, to my great concern, that she was more than once in tears. You will see that my heart was already interested more than I supposed. She had a firm yet airy motion of the body, and carried her head with unimaginable grace; every step was a thing to look at, and she seemed in my eyes to breathe sweetness and distinction.

The day was so agreeable, being calm and sunshiny, with a tranquil sea, and yet with a healthful piquancy and vigour in the air, that, contrary to custom, she was tempted forth a second time to walk. On this occasion she was accompanied by Northmour, and they had been but a short while on the beach, when I saw him take forcible possession of her hand. She struggled, and uttered a cry that was almost a scream. I sprung to my feet, unmindful of my strange position; but, ere I had taken a step, I saw Northmour bareheaded and bowing very low, as if to apologize; and dropped again at once into my ambush. A few words were interchanged; and then, with another bow, he left the beach to return to the pavilion. He passed not far from me, and I could see him, flushed and lowering, and cutting savagely with his cane among the grass. It was not without satisfaction that I recognized my own handiwork in a great cut under his right eye, and a considerable discoloration round the socket.

For some time the girl remained where he had left her, looking out past the islet and over the bright sea. Then with a start, as one who throws off preoccupation and puts energy again upon its mettle, she broke into a rapid and decisive walk. She also was much incensed by what had passed. She had forgotten where she was. And I beheld her walk straight into the borders of the quicksand where it is most abrupt and dangerous. Two or three steps farther and her life would have been in serious jeopardy, when I slid down the face of the sand hill, which is there precipitous, and, running halfway forward, called to her to stop.

She did so, and turned round. There was not a tremor of fear in her behaviour, and she marched directly up to me like a queen. I was barefoot, and clad like a common sailor, save for an Egyptian scarf round my waist; and she probably took me at first for some one from the fisher village, straying after bait. As for her, when I thus saw her face to face, her eyes set steadily and imperiously upon mine, I was filled with admiration and astonishment, and thought her even more beautiful than I had looked to find her. Nor could I think enough of one who, acting with so much boldness, yet preserved a maidenly air that was both quaint and engaging; for my wife kept an old-fashioned precision of manner through all her admirable life – an excellent thing in woman, since it sets another value on her sweet familiarities.

"What does this mean?" she asked.

"You were walking," I told her, "directly into Graden Floe."

"You do not belong to these parts," she said again. "You speak like an educated man."

"I believe I have a right to that name," said I, "although in this disguise."

But her woman's eye had already detected the sash.

"Oh!" she said; "your sash betrays you."

"You have said the word *betray*," I resumed. "May I ask you not to betray me? I was obliged to disclose myself in your interest; but if Northmour learned my presence it might be worse than disagreeable for me."

"Do you know," she asked, "to whom you are speaking?"

"Not to Mr Northmour's wife?" I asked, by way of answer.

She shook her head. All this while she was studying my face with an embarrassing intentness. Then she broke out—

"You have an honest face. Be honest like your face, sir, and tell me what you want and what you are afraid of. Do you think I could hurt you? I believe you have far more power to injure me! And yet you do not look unkind. What do you mean – you, a gentleman – by skulking like a spy about this desolate place? Tell me," she said, "who is it you hate?"

"I hate no one," I answered; "and I fear no one face to face. My name is Cassilis – Frank Cassilis. I lead the life of a vagabond for my own good pleasure. I am one of Northmour's oldest friends; and three nights ago, when I addressed him on these links, he stabbed me in the shoulder with a knife."

"It was you!" she said.

"Why he did so," I continued, disregarding the interruption, "is more than I can guess, and more than I care to know. I have not many friends, nor am I very susceptible to friendship; but no man shall drive me from a place by terror. I had camped in the Graden Sea-Wood ere he came; I camp in it still. If you think I mean harm to you or yours, madame, the remedy is in your hand. Tell him that my camp is in the Hemlock Den, and tonight he can stab me in safety while I sleep."

With this I doffed my cap to her, and scrambled up once more among the sand hills. I do not know why, but I felt a prodigious sense of injustice, and felt like a hero and a martyr; while as a matter of fact, I had not a word to say in my defense, nor so much as one plausible reason to offer for my conduct. I had stayed at Graden out of a curiosity natural enough, but undignified; and though there was another motive growing in along with the first, it was not one which, at that period, I could have properly explained to the lady of my heart.

Certainly, that night, I thought of no one else; and, though her whole conduct and position seemed suspicious, I could not find it in my heart to entertain a doubt of her integrity. I could have staked my life that she was clear of blame, and, though all was dark at the present, that the explanation of the mystery would show her part in these events to be both right and needful. It was true, let me cudgel my imagination as I pleased, that I could invent no theory of her relations to Northmour; but I felt none the less sure of my conclusion because it was founded on instinct in place of reason, and, as I may say, went to sleep that night with the thought of her under my pillow.

Next day she came out about the same hour alone, and, as soon as the sand hills concealed her from the pavilion, drew nearer to the edge, and called me by name in guarded tones. I was astonished to observe that she was deadly pale, and seemingly under the influence of strong emotion.

"Mr Cassilis!" she cried; "Mr Cassilis!"

I appeared at once, and leaped down upon the beach. A remarkable air of relief overspread her countenance as soon as she saw me.

"Oh!" she cried, with a hoarse sound, like one whose bosom had been lightened of a weight. And then, "Thank God you are still safe!" she added; "I knew, if you were, you would be here." (Was not this strange? So swiftly and wisely does Nature prepare our hearts for these great lifelong intimacies, that both my wife and I had been given a presentiment on this the second day of our acquaintance. I had even then hoped that she would seek me; she had felt sure that she would find me.) "Do not," she went on swiftly, "do not stay in this place. Promise me that you sleep no longer in that wood. You do not know how I suffer; all last night I could not sleep for thinking of your peril."

"Peril!" I repeated. "Peril from whom? From Northmour?"

"Not so," she said. "Did you think I would tell him after what you said?"

"Not from Northmour?" I repeated. "Then how? From whom? I see none to be afraid of."

"You must not ask me," was her reply, "for I am not free to tell you. Only believe me, and go hence – believe me, and go away quickly, quickly, for your life!"

An appeal to his alarm is never a good plan to rid oneself of a spirited young man. My obstinacy was but increased by what she said, and I made it a point of honour to remain. And her solicitude for my safety still more confirmed me in the resolve.

"You must not think me inquisitive, madame," I replied, "but, if Graden is so dangerous a place, you yourself perhaps remain here at some risk."

She only looked at me reproachfully.

"You and your father—" I resumed; but she interrupted me almost with a gasp.

"My father! How do you know that?" she cried.

"I saw you together when you landed," was my answer; and I do not know why, but it seemed satisfactory to both of us, as indeed it was truth. "But," I continued, "you need have no fear from me. I see you have some reason to be secret, and, you may believe me, your secret is as safe with me as if I were in Graden Floe. I have scarce spoken to anyone for years; my horse is my only companion, and even he, poor beast, is not beside me. You see, then, you may count on me for silence. So tell me the truth, my dear young lady, are you not in danger?"

"Mr Northmour says you are an honourable man," she returned, "and I believe it when I see you. I will tell you so much; you are right: we are in dreadful, dreadful danger, and you share it by remaining where you are."

"Ah!" said I; "you have heard of me from Northmour? And he gives me a good character?"

"I asked him about you last night," was her reply. "I pretended," she hesitated, "I pretended to have met you long ago, and spoken to you of him. It was not true; but I could not help myself without betraying you, and you had put me in a difficulty. He praised you highly."

"And – you may permit me one question – does this danger come from Northmour?" I asked.

"From Mr Northmour?" she cried. "Oh, no, he stays with us to share it."

"While you propose that I should run away?" I said. "You do not rate me very high."

"Why should you stay?" she asked. "You are no friend of ours."

I know not what came over me, for I had not been conscious of a similar weakness since I was a child, but I was so mortified by this retort that my eyes pricked and filled with tears, as I continued to gaze upon her face.

"No, no," she said, in a changed voice; "I did not mean the words unkindly."

"It was I who offended," I said; and I held out my hand with a look of appeal that somehow touched her, for she gave me hers at once, and even eagerly. I held it for awhile in mine, and gazed into her eyes. It was she who first tore her hand away, and, forgetting all about her request and the promise she had sought to extort, ran at the top of her speed, and without turning, till she was out of sight. And then I knew that I loved her, and thought in my glad heart that she – she herself – was not indifferent to my suit. Many a time she has denied it in after days, but it was with a smiling and not a serious denial. For my part, I am sure our hands would not have lain so closely in each other if she had not begun to melt to me already. And, when all is said, it is no great contention, since, by her own avowal, she began to love me on the morrow.

And yet on the morrow very little took place. She came and called me down as on the day before, upbraided me for lingering at Graden, and, when she found I was still obdurate, began to ask me more particularly as to my arrival. I told her by what series of accidents I had come to witness their disembarkation, and how I had determined to remain, partly from the interest which had been awakened in me by Northmour's guests, and partly because of his own murderous attack. As to the former, I fear I was disingenuous, and led her to regard herself as having been an attraction to me from the first moment that I saw her on the links. It relieves my heart to make this confession even now, when my wife is with God, and already knows all things, and the honesty of my purpose even in this; for while she lived, although it often pricked my conscience,

I had never the hardihood to undeceive her. Even a little secret, in such a married life as ours, is like the rose leaf which kept the princess from her sleep.

From this the talk branched into other subjects, and I told her much about my lonely and wandering existence; she, for her part, giving ear, and saying little. Although we spoke very naturally, and latterly on topics that might seem indifferent, we were both sweetly agitated. Too soon it was time for her to go; and we separated, as if by mutual consent, without shaking hands, for both knew that, between us, it was no idle ceremony.

The next, and that was the fourth day of our acquaintance, we met in the same spot, but early in the morning, with much familiarity and yet much timidity on either side. While she had once more spoken about my danger – and that, I understood, was her excuse for coming – I, who had prepared a great deal of talk during the night, began to tell her how highly I valued her kind interest, and how no one had ever cared to hear about my life, nor had I ever cared to relate it, before yesterday. Suddenly she interrupted me, saying with vehemence—

"And yet, if you knew who I was, you would not so much as speak to me!"

I told her such a thought was madness, and, little as we had met, I counted her already a dear friend; but my protestations seemed only to make her more desperate.

"My father is in hiding!" she cried.

"My dear," I said, forgetting for the first time to add "young lady," "what do I care? If I were in hiding twenty times over, would it make one thought of change in you?"

"Ah, but the cause!" she cried, "the cause! It is" – she faltered for a second – "it is disgraceful to us!"

CHAPTER 4

This **was** my wife's story, as I drew it from her among tears and sobs. Her name was Clara Huddlestone: it sounded very beautiful in my ears; but not so beautiful as that other name of Clara Cassilis, which she wore during the longer and, I thank God, the happier portion of her life. Her father, Bernard Huddlestone, had been a private banker in a very large way of business. Many years before, his affairs becoming disordered, he had been led to try dangerous, and at last criminal, expedients to retrieve himself from ruin. All was in vain; he became more and more cruelly involved, and found his honour lost at the same moment with his fortune. About this period, Northmour had been courting his daughter with great assiduity, though with small encouragement; and to him, knowing him thus disposed in his favour, Bernard Huddlestone turned for help in his extremity. It was not merely ruin and dishonour, nor merely a legal condemnation, that the unhappy man had brought upon his head. It seems he could have gone to prison with a light heart. What he feared, what kept him awake at night or recalled him from slumber into frenzy, was some secret, sudden, and unlawful attempt upon his life. Hence, he desired to bury his existence and escape to one of the islands in the South Pacific, and it was in Northmour's yacht, the *Red Earl*, that he designed to go. The yacht picked them up clandestinely upon the coast of Wales, and had once more deposited them at Graden, till she could be refitted and provisioned for the longer voyage. Nor could Clara doubt that her hand had been stipulated as the price of passage. For, although Northmour was neither unkind, nor even discourteous, he had shown himself in several instances somewhat overbold in speech and manner.

I listened, I need not say, with fixed attention, and put many questions as to the more mysterious part. It was in vain. She had no clear idea of what the blow was, nor of how it was expected to fall. Her father's alarm was unfeigned and physically prostrating, and he had thought more than once of making an unconditional surrender to the police. But the scheme was finally abandoned, for he was convinced that not even the strength of our English prisons could shelter him from his pursuers. He had had many affairs in Italy, and with Italians resident in London, in the latter years of his business; and these last, as Clara fancied, were somehow connected with the doom that threatened him. He had shown great terror at the presence of an Italian seaman on board the *Red Earl*, and had bitterly and repeatedly accused Northmour in consequence. The latter had protested that Beppo (that was the seaman's name) was a capital fellow, and could be trusted to the death; but Mr Huddlestone had continued ever since to declare that all was lost, that it was only a question of days, and that Beppo would be the ruin of him yet.

I regarded the whole story as the hallucination of a mind shaken by calamity. He had suffered heavy loss by his Italian transactions; and hence the sight of an Italian was hateful to him, and the principal part in his nightmare would naturally enough be played by one of that nation.

"What your father wants," I said, "is a good doctor and some calming medicine."

"But Mr Northmour?" objected Clara. "He is untroubled by losses, and yet he shares in this terror."

I could not help laughing at what I considered her simplicity.

"My dear," said I, "you have told me yourself what reward he has to look for. All is fair in love, you must remember; and if Northmour foments your father's terrors, it is not at all because he is afraid of any Italian man, but simply because he is infatuated with a charming English woman."

She reminded me of his attack upon myself on the night of the disembarkation, and this I was unable to explain. In short, and from one thing to another, it was agreed between us that I should set out at once for the fisher village, Graden Wester, as it was called, look up all the newspapers I could find, and see for myself if there seemed any basis of fact for these continued alarms. The next morning, at the same hour and place, I was to make my report to Clara. She said no more on that occasion about my departure; nor, indeed, did she make it a secret that she clung to the thought of my proximity as something helpful and pleasant; and, for my part, I could not have left her, if she had gone upon her knees to ask it.

I reached Graden Wester before ten in the forenoon; for in those days I was an excellent pedestrian, and the distance, as I think I have said, was little over seven miles; fine walking all the way upon the springy turf. The village is one of the bleakest on that coast, which is saying much: there is a church in the hollow; a miserable haven in the rocks, where many boats have been lost as they returned from fishing; two or three score of stone houses arranged along the beach and in two streets, one leading from the harbour, and another striking out from it at right angles; and, at the corner of these two, a very dark and cheerless tavern, by way of principal hotel.

I had dressed myself somewhat more suitably to my station in life, and at once called upon the minister in his little manse beside the graveyard. He knew me, although it was more than nine years since we had met; and when I told him that I had been long upon a walking tour, and was behind with the news, readily lent me an armful of newspapers, dating from a month back to the day before. With these I sought the tavern, and, ordering some breakfast, sat down to study the "Huddlestone Failure."

It had been, it appeared, a very flagrant case. Thousands of persons were reduced to poverty; and one in particular had blown out his brains as soon as payment was suspended. It was strange to myself that, while I read these details, I continued rather to sympathize with Mr Huddlestone than with his victims; so complete already was the empire of my love for my wife. A price was naturally set upon the banker's head; and, as the case was inexcusable and the public indignation thoroughly aroused, the unusual figure of £750 was offered for his capture. He was reported to have large sums of money in his possession. One day, he had been heard of in Spain; the next, there was sure intelligence that he was still lurking between Manchester and Liverpool, or along the border of Wales; and the day after, a telegram would announce his arrival in Cuba or Yucatan. But in all this there was no word of an Italian, nor any sign of mystery.

In the very last paper, however, there was one item not so clear. The accountants who were charged to verify the failure had, it seemed, come upon the traces of a very large number of thousands, which figured for some time in the transactions of the house of Huddlestone; but which came from nowhere, and disappeared in the same mysterious fashion. It was only once referred to by name, and then under the initials "X.X."; but it had plainly been floated for the first time into the business at a period of great depression some six years ago. The name of a distinguished royal personage had been mentioned by rumour in connection with this sum. "The cowardly desperado" – such, I remember, was the editorial expression – was supposed to have escaped with a large part of this mysterious fund still in his possession.

I was still brooding over the fact, and trying to torture it into some connection with Mr Huddlestone's danger, when a man entered the tavern and asked for some bread and cheese with a decided foreign accent.

"*Siete Italiano?*" said I.

"*Si, Signor,*" was his reply.

I said it was unusually far north to find one of his compatriots; at which he shrugged his shoulders, and replied that a man would go anywhere to find work. What work he could hope to find at Graden Wester, I was totally unable to conceive; and the incident struck so unpleasantly upon my mind, that I asked the landlord, while he was counting me some change, whether he had ever before seen an Italian in the village. He said he had once seen some Norwegians, who had been shipwrecked on the other side of Graden Ness and rescued by the lifeboat from Cauldhaven.

"No!" said I; "but an Italian, like the man who has just had bread and cheese."

"What?" cried he, "yon black-avised fellow wi' the teeth? Was he an I-talian? Weel, yon's the first that ever I saw, an' I dare say he's like to be the last."

Even as he was speaking, I raised my eyes, and, casting a glance into the street, beheld three men in earnest conversation together, and not thirty yards away. One of them was my recent companion in the tavern parlor; the other two, by their handsome sallow features and soft hats, should evidently belong to the same race. A crowd of village children stood around them, gesticulating and talking gibberish in imitation. The trio looked singularly foreign to the bleak dirty street in which they were standing and the dark gray heaven that overspread them; and I confess my incredulity received at that moment a shock from which it never recovered. I might reason with myself as I pleased, but I could not argue down the effect of what I had seen, and I began to share in the Italian terror.

It was already drawing toward the close of the day before I had returned the newspapers to the manse, and got well forward on to the links on my way home. I shall never forget that walk. It grew very cold and boisterous; the wind sung in the short grass about my feet; thin rain showers came running on the gusts; and an immense mountain range of clouds began to arise out of the bosom of the sea. It would be hard to imagine a more dismal evening; and whether it was from these external influences, or because my nerves were already affected by what I had heard and seen, my thoughts were as gloomy as the weather.

The upper windows of the pavilion commanded a considerable spread of links in the direction of Graden Wester. To avoid observation, it was necessary to hug the beach until I had gained cover from the higher sand hills on the little headland, when I might strike across, through the hollows, for the margin of the wood. The sun was about setting; the tide was low, and all the quicksands uncovered; and I was moving along, lost in unpleasant thought, when I was suddenly thunderstruck to perceive the prints of human feet. They ran parallel to my own course, but low down upon the beach, instead of along the border of the turf; and, when I examined them, I saw at once, by the size and coarseness of the impression, that it was a stranger to me and to those of the pavilion who had recently passed that way. Not only so; but from the recklessness of the course which he had followed, steering near to the most formidable portions of the sand, he was evidently a stranger to the country and to the ill-repute of Graden beach.

Step by step I followed the prints; until, a quarter of a mile farther, I beheld them die away into the southeastern boundary of Graden Floe. There, whoever he was, the miserable man had perished. One or two gulls, who had, perhaps, seen him disappear, wheeled over his sepulchre with their usual melancholy piping. The sun had broken through the clouds by a last effort, and coloured the wide level of quicksands with a dusky purple. I stood for some time gazing at the spot, chilled and disheartened by my own reflections, and with a strong and commanding consciousness of death. I remember wondering how long the tragedy had taken, and whether his screams had been audible at the pavilion. And then, making a strong resolution, I was about to tear myself away, when a gust fiercer than usual fell upon this quarter of the beach, and I saw, now whirling high in air, now skimming lightly across the surface of the sands, a soft, black, felt hat, somewhat conical in shape, such as I had remarked already on the heads of the Italians.

I believe, but I am not sure, that I uttered a cry. The wind was driving the hat shoreward, and I ran round the border of the floe to be ready against its arrival. The gust fell, dropping the hat for awhile upon the quicksand, and then, once more freshening, landed it a few yards from where I stood. I seized it with the interest you may imagine. It had seen some service; indeed, it was rustier than either of those I had seen that day upon the street. The lining was red, stamped with the name of the maker, which I have forgotten, and that of the place of manufacture, *Venedig*. This (it is not yet forgotten) was the name given by the Austrians to the beautiful city of Venice, then, and for long after, a part of their dominions.

The shock was complete. I saw imaginary Italians upon every side; and for the first, and, I may say, for the last time in my experience, became overpowered by what is called a panic terror. I knew nothing, that is, to be afraid of, and yet I admit that I was heartily afraid; and it was with sensible reluctance that I returned to my exposed and solitary camp in the Sea-Wood.

There I eat some cold porridge which had been left over from the night before, for I was disinclined to make a fire; and, feeling strengthened and reassured, dismissed all these fanciful terrors from my mind, and lay down to sleep with composure.

How long I may have slept it is impossible for me to guess; but I was awakened at last by a sudden, blinding flash of light into my face. It woke me like a blow. In an instant I was upon my knees. But the light had gone as suddenly as it came. The darkness was intense. And, as it was blowing great guns from the sea, and pouring with rain, the noises of the storm effectually concealed all others.

It was, I dare say, half a minute before I regained my self-possession. But for two circumstances, I should have thought I had been awakened by some new and vivid form of nightmare. First, the flap of my tent, which I had shut carefully when I retired, was now unfastened; and, second, I could still perceive, with a sharpness that excluded any theory of hallucination, the smell of hot metal and of burning oil. The conclusion was obvious. I had been awakened by some one flashing a bull's-eye lantern in my face. It had been but a flash, and away. He had seen my face, and then gone. I asked myself the object of so strange a proceeding, and the answer came pat. The man, whoever he was, had thought to recognize me, and he had not. There was another question unresolved; and to this, I may say, I feared to give an answer; if he had recognized me, what would he have done?

My fears were immediately diverted from myself, for I saw that I had been visited in a mistake; and I became persuaded that some dreadful danger threatened the pavilion. It required some nerve to issue forth into the black and intricate thicket which surrounded and overhung the den; but I groped my way to the links, drenched with rain, beaten upon and deafened by the gusts, and fearing at every step to lay my hand upon some lurking adversary. The darkness was so complete that I might have been surrounded by an army and yet none the wiser, and the uproar of the gale so loud that my hearing was as useless as my sight.

For the rest of that night, which seemed interminably long, I patrolled the vicinity of the pavilion, without seeing a living creature or hearing any noise but the concert of the wind, the sea, and the rain. A light in the upper story filtered through a cranny of the shutter, and kept me company till the approach of dawn.

CHAPTER 5

With the first peep of day, I retired from the open to my old lair among the sand hills, there to await the coming of my wife. The morning was gray, wild, and melancholy; the wind moderated before sunrise, and then went about, and blew in puffs from the shore; the sea began to go down, but the rain still fell without mercy. Over all the wilderness of links there was not a creature to be seen. Yet I felt sure the neighbourhood was alive with skulking foes. The light that had been so suddenly and surprisingly flashed upon my face as I lay sleeping, and the hat that had been blown ashore by the wind from over Graden Floe, were two speaking signals of the peril that environed Clara and the party in the pavilion.

It was, perhaps, half-past seven, or nearer eight, before I saw the door open, and that dear figure come toward me in the rain. I was waiting for her on the beach before she had crossed the sand hills.

"I have had such trouble to come!" she cried. "They did not wish me to go walking in the rain."

"Clara," I said, "you are not frightened!"

"No," said she, with a simplicity that filled my heart with confidence. For my wife was the bravest as well as the best of women; in my experience, I have not found the two go always together, but with her they did; and she combined the extreme of fortitude with the most endearing and beautiful virtues.

I told her what had happened; and, though her cheek grew visibly paler, she retained perfect control over her senses.

"You see now that I am safe," said I, in conclusion. "They do not mean to harm me; for, had they chosen, I was a dead man last night."

She laid her hand upon my arm.

"And I had no presentiment!" she cried.

Her accent thrilled me with delight. I put my arm about her, and strained her to my side; and, before either of us was aware, her hands were on my shoulders and my lips upon her mouth. Yet up to that moment no word of love had passed between us. To this day I remember the touch of her cheek, which was wet and cold with the rain; and many a time since, when she has been washing her face, I have kissed it again for the sake of that morning on the beach. Now that she is taken from me, and I finish my pilgrimage alone, I recall our old loving kindnesses and the deep honesty and affection which united us, and my present loss seems but a trifle in comparison.

We may have thus stood for some seconds – for time passes quickly with lovers – before we were startled by a peal of laughter close at hand. It was not natural mirth, but seemed to be affected in order to conceal an angrier feeling. We both turned, though I still kept my left arm about Clara's waist; nor did she seek to withdraw herself; and there, a few paces off upon the beach, stood Northmour, his head lowered, his hands behind his back, his nostrils white with passion.

"Ah! Cassilis!" he said, as I disclosed my face.

"That same," said I; for I was not at all put about.

"And so, Miss Huddlestone," he continued slowly, but savagely, "this is how you keep your faith to your father and to me? This is the value you set upon your father's life? And you are so infatuated with this young gentleman that you must brave ruin, and decency, and common human caution—"

"Miss Huddlestone—" I was beginning to interrupt him, when he, in his turn, cut in brutally—

"You hold your tongue," said he; "I am speaking to that girl."

"That girl, as you call her, is my wife," said I; and my wife only leaned a little nearer, so that I knew she had affirmed my words.

"Your what?" he cried. "You lie!"

"Northmour," I said, "we all know you have a bad temper, and I am the last man to be irritated by words. For all that, I propose that you speak lower, for I am convinced that we are not alone."

He looked round him, and it was plain my remark had in some degree sobered his passion. "What do you mean?" he asked.

I only said one word: "Italians."

He swore a round oath, and looked at us, from one to the other.

"Mr Cassilis knows all that I know," said my wife.

"What I want to know," he broke out, "is where the devil Mr Cassilis comes from, and what the devil Mr Cassilis is doing here. You say you are married; that I do not believe. If you were, Graden Floe would soon divorce you; four minutes and a half, Cassilis. I keep my private cemetery for my friends."

"It took somewhat longer," said I, "for that Italian."

He looked at me for a moment half daunted, and then, almost civilly, asked me to tell my story. "You have too much the advantage of me, Cassilis," he added. I complied of course; and he listened, with several ejaculations, while I told him how I had come to Graden: that it was I whom he had tried to murder on the night of landing; and what I had subsequently seen and heard of the Italians.

"Well," said he, when I had done, "it is here at last; there is no mistake about that. And what, may I ask, do you propose to do?"

"I propose to stay with you and lend a hand," said I.

"You are a brave man," he returned, with a peculiar intonation.

"I am not afraid," said I.

"And so," he continued, "I am to understand that you two are married? And you stand up to it before my face, Miss Huddlestone?"

"We are not yet married," said Clara; "but we shall be as soon as we can."

"Bravo!" cried Northmour. "And the bargain? D——n it, you're not a fool, young woman; I may call a spade a spade with you. How about the bargain? You know as well as I do what your father's life depends upon. I have only to put my hands under my coat tails and walk away, and his throat would be cut before the evening."

"Yes, Mr Northmour," returned Clara, with great spirit; "but that is what you will never do. You made a bargain that was unworthy of a gentleman; but you are a gentleman for all that, and you will never desert a man whom you have begun to help."

"Aha!" said he. "You think I will give my yacht for nothing? You think I will risk my life and liberty for love of the old gentleman; and then, I suppose, be best man at the wedding, to wind up? Well," he added, with an odd smile, "perhaps you are not altogether wrong. But ask Cassilis here. *He* knows me. Am I a man to trust? Am I safe and scrupulous? Am I kind?"

"I know you talk a great deal, and sometimes, I think, very foolishly," replied Clara, "but I know you are a gentleman, and I am not the least afraid."

He looked at her with a peculiar approval and admiration; then, turning to me, "Do you think I would give her up without a struggle, Frank?" said he. "I tell you plainly, you look out. The next time we come to blows—"

"Will make the third," I interrupted, smiling.

"Aye, true; so it will," he said. "I had forgotten. Well, the third time's lucky."

"The third time, you mean, you will have the crew of the *Red Earl* to help," I said.

"Do you hear him?" he asked, turning to my wife.

"I hear two men speaking like cowards," said she. "I should despise myself either to think or speak like that. And neither of you believe one word that you are saying, which makes it the more wicked and silly."

"She's a trump!" cried Northmour. "But she's not yet Mrs Cassilis. I say no more. The present is not for me."

Then my wife surprised me.

"I leave you here," she said suddenly. "My father has been too long alone. But remember this: you are to be friends, for you are both good friends to me."

She has since told me her reason for this step. As long as she remained, she declares that we two would have continued to quarrel; and I suppose that she was right, for when she was gone we fell at once into a sort of confidentiality.

Northmour stared after her as she went away over the sand hill.

"She is the only woman in the world!" he exclaimed with an oath. "Look at her action."

I, for my part, leaped at this opportunity for a little further light.

"See here, Northmour," said I; "we are all in a tight place, are we not?"

"I believe you, my boy," he answered, looking me in the eyes, and with great emphasis. "We have all hell upon us, that's the truth. You may believe me or not, but I'm afraid of my life."

"Tell me one thing," said I. "What are they after, these Italians? What do they want with Mr Huddlestone?"

"Don't you know?" he cried. "The black old scamp had *carbonari* funds on a deposit – two hundred and eighty thousand; and of course he gambled it away on stocks. There was to have been a revolution in the Tridentino, or Parma; but the revolution is off, and the whole wasp's nest is after Huddlestone. We shall all be lucky if we can save our skins.»

"The *carbonari*!" I exclaimed; "God help him indeed!"

"Amen!" said Northmour. "And now, look here: I have said that we are in a fix; and, frankly, I shall be glad of your help. If I can't save Huddlestone, I want at least to save the girl. Come and stay in the pavilion; and, there's my hand on it, I shall act as your friend until the old man is either clear or dead. But," he added, "once that is settled, you become my rival once again, and I warn you – mind yourself."

"Done!" said I; and we shook hands.

"And now let us go directly to the fort," said Northmour; and he began to lead the way through the rain.

CHAPTER 6

We **were** admitted to the pavilion by Clara, and I was surprised by the completeness and security of the defenses. A barricade of great strength, and yet easy to displace, supported the door against any violence from without; and the shutters of the dining-room, into which I was led directly, and which was feebly illuminated by a lamp, were even more elaborately fortified. The panels were strengthened by bars and crossbars; and these, in their turn, were kept in position by a system of braces and struts, some abutting on the floor, some on the roof, and others, in fine, against the opposite wall of the apartment. It was at once a solid and well-designed piece of carpentry; and I did not seek to conceal my admiration.

"I am the engineer," said Northmour. "You remember the planks in the garden? Behold them?"

"I did not know you had so many talents," said I.

"Are you armed?" he continued, pointing to an array of guns and pistols, all in admirable order, which stood in line against the wall or were displayed upon the sideboard.

"Thank you," I returned; "I have gone armed since our last encounter. But, to tell you the truth, I have had nothing to eat since early yesterday evening."

Northmour produced some cold meat, to which I eagerly set myself, and a bottle of good Burgundy, by which, wet as I was, I did not scruple to profit. I have always been an extreme temperance man on principle; but it is useless to push principle to excess, and on this occasion I believe that I finished three quarters of the bottle. As I eat, I still continued to admire the preparations for defense.

"We could stand a siege," I said at length.

"Ye—es," drawled Northmour; "a very little one, per—haps. It is not so much the strength of the pavilion I misdoubt; it is the double danger that kills me. If we get to shooting, wild as the country is, some one is sure to hear it, and then – why then it's the same thing, only different, as they say: caged by law, or killed by *carbonari*. There's the choice. It is a devilish bad thing to have the law against you in this world, and so I tell the old gentleman upstairs. He is quite of my way of thinking."

"Speaking of that," said I, "what kind of person is he?"

"Oh, he!" cried the other; "he's a rancid fellow, as far as he goes. I should like to have his neck wrung tomorrow by all the devils in Italy. I am not in this affair for him. You take me? I made a bargain for missy's hand, and I mean to have it too."

"That, by the way," said I. "I understand. But how will Mr Huddlestone take my intrusion?"

"Leave that to Clara," returned Northmour.

I could have struck him in the face for his coarse familiarity; but I respected the truce, as, I am bound to say, did Northmour, and so long as the danger continued not a cloud arose in our relation. I bear him this testimony with the most unfeigned satisfaction; nor am I without pride when I look back upon my own behaviour. For surely no two men were ever left in a position so invidious and irritating.

As soon as I had done eating, we proceeded to inspect the lower floor. Window by window we tried the different supports, now and then making an inconsiderable change; and the strokes of the hammer sounded with startling loudness through the house. I proposed, I remember, to make loop-holes; but he told me they were already made in the windows of the upper story. It was an anxious business, this inspection, and left me down-hearted. There were two doors and five windows to protect, and, counting Clara, only four of us to defend them against an unknown number of foes. I communicated my doubts to Northmour, who assured me, with unmoved composure, that he entirely shared them.

"Before morning," said he, "we shall all be butchered and buried in Graden Floe. For me, that is written."

I could not help shuddering at the mention of the quicksand, but reminded Northmour that our enemies had spared me in the wood.

"Do not flatter yourself," said he. "Then you were not in the same boat with the old gentleman; now you are. It's the floe for all of us, mark my words."

I trembled for Clara; and just then her dear voice was heard calling us to come upstairs. Northmour showed me the way, and, when he had reached the landing, knocked at the door of what used to be called *My Uncle's Bedroom*, as the founder of the pavilion had designed it especially for himself.

"Come in, Northmour; come in, dear Mr Cassilis," said a voice from within.

Pushing open the door, Northmour admitted me before him into the apartment. As I came in I could see the daughter slipping out by the side door into the study, which had been prepared as her bedroom. In the bed, which was drawn back against the wall, instead of standing, as I had last seen it, boldly across the window, sat Bernard Huddlestone, the defaulting banker. Little as I had seen of him by the shifting light of the lantern on the links, I had no difficulty in recognizing him for the same. He had a long and sallow countenance, surrounded by a long red beard and side-whiskers. His broken nose and high cheek-bones gave him somewhat the air of a Kalmuck, and his light eyes shone with the excitement of a high fever. He wore a skull-cap of black silk; a huge Bible lay open before him on the bed, with a pair of gold spectacles in the place, and a pile of other books lay on the stand by his side. The green curtains lent a cadaverous shade to his cheek; and, as he sat propped on pillows, his great stature was painfully hunched, and his head protruded till it overhung his knees. I believe if he had not died otherwise, he must have fallen a victim to consumption in the course of but a very few weeks.

He held out to me a hand, long, thin, and disagreeably hairy.

"Come in, come in, Mr Cassilis," said he. "Another protector – ahem! – another protector. Always welcome as a friend of my daughter's, Mr Cassilis. How they have rallied about me, my daughter's friends! May God in heaven bless and reward them for it!"

I gave him my hand, of course, because I could not help it; but the sympathy I had been prepared to feel for Clara's father was immediately soured by his appearance, and the wheedling, unreal tones in which he spoke.

"Cassilis is a good man," said Northmour; "worth ten."

"So I hear," cried Mr Huddlestone eagerly; "so my girl tells me. Ah, Mr Cassilis, my sin has found me out, you see! I am very low, very low; but I hope equally penitent. We must all come to the throne of grace at last, Mr Cassilis. For my part, I come late indeed; but with unfeigned humility, I trust."

"Fiddle-de-dee!" said Northmour roughly.

"No, no, dear Northmour!" cried the banker. "You must not say that; you must not try to shake me. You forget, my dear, good boy, you forget I may be called this very night before my Maker."

His excitement was pitiful to behold; and I felt myself grow indignant with Northmour, whose infidel opinions I well knew, and heartily despised, as he continued to taunt the poor sinner out of his humour of repentance.

"Pooh, my dear Huddlestone!" said he. "You do yourself injustice. You are a man of the world inside and out, and were up to all kinds of mischief before I was born. Your conscience is tanned like South American leather – only you forgot to tan your liver, and that, if you will believe me, is the seat of the annoyance."

"Rogue, rogue! bad boy!" said Mr Huddlestone, shaking his finger. "I am no precisian, if you come to that; I always hated a precisian; but I never lost hold of something better through it all. I have been a bad boy, Mr Cassilis; I do not seek to deny that; but it was after my wife's death, and you know, with a widower, it's a different thing: sinful – I won't say no; but there is a gradation, we shall hope. And talking of that – Hark!" he broke out suddenly, his hand raised, his fingers spread, his face racked with interest and terror. "Only the rain, bless God!" he added, after a pause, and with indescribable relief.

For some seconds he lay back among the pillows like a man near to fainting; then he gathered himself together, and, in somewhat tremulous tones, began once more to thank me for the share I was prepared to take in his defense.

"One question, sir," said I, when he had paused. "Is it true that you have money with you?"

He seemed annoyed by the question, but admitted with reluctance that he had a little.

"Well," I continued, "it is their money they are after, is it not? Why not give it up to them?"

"Ah!" replied he, shaking his head, "I have tried that already, Mr Cassilis; and alas! that it should be so, but it is blood they want."

"Huddlestone, that's a little less than fair," said Northmour. "You should mention that what you offered them was upward of two hundred thousand short. The deficit is worth a reference; it is for what they call a cool sum, Frank. Then, you see, the fellows reason in their clear Italian way; and it seems to them, as indeed it seems to me, that they may just as well have both while they're about it – money and blood together, by George, and no more trouble for the extra pleasure."

"Is it in the pavilion?" I asked.

"It is; and I wish it were in the bottom of the sea instead," said Northmour; and then suddenly – "What are you making faces at me for?" he cried to Mr Huddlestone, on whom I had unconsciously turned my back. "Do you think Cassilis would sell you?"

Mr Huddlestone protested that nothing had been further from his mind.

"It is a good thing," retorted Northmour in his ugliest manner. "You might end by wearying us. What were you going to say?" he added, turning to me.

"I was going to propose an occupation for the afternoon," said I. "Let us carry that money out, piece by piece, and lay it down before the pavilion door. If the *carbonari* come, why, it's theirs at any rate.»

"No, no," cried Mr Huddlestone; "it does not, it cannot, belong to them! It should be distributed *pro rata* among all my creditors.»

"Come now, Huddlestone," said Northmour, "none of that."

"Well, but my daughter," moaned the wretched man.

"Your daughter will do well enough. Here are two suitors, Cassilis and I, neither of us beggars, between whom she has to choose. And as for yourself, to make an end of arguments, you have no right to a farthing, and, unless I'm much mistaken, you are going to die."

It was certainly very cruelly said; but Mr Huddlestone was a man who attracted little sympathy; and, although I saw him wince and shudder, I mentally indorsed the rebuke; nay, I added a contribution of my own.

"Northmour and I," I said, "are willing enough to help you to save your life, but not to escape with stolen property."

He struggled for awhile with himself, as though he were on the point of giving way to anger, but prudence had the best of the controversy.

"My dear boys," he said, "do with me or my money what you will. I leave all in your hands. Let me compose myself."

And so we left him, gladly enough I am sure.

The last that I saw, he had once more taken up his great Bible, and with tremulous hands was adjusting his spectacles to read.

CHAPTER 7

The recollection of that afternoon will always be graven on my mind. Northmour and I were persuaded that an attack was imminent; and if it had been in our power to alter in any way the order of events, that power would have been used to precipitate rather than delay the critical moment. The worst was to be anticipated; yet we could conceive no extremity so miserable as the suspense we were now suffering. I have never been an eager, though always a great, reader; but I never knew books so insipid as those which I took up and cast aside that afternoon in the pavilion. Even talk became impossible, as the hours went on. One or other was always listening for some sound, or peering from an upstairs window over the links. And yet not a sign indicated the presence of our foes.

We debated over and over again my proposal with regard to the money; and had we been in complete possession of our faculties, I am sure we should have condemned it as unwise; but we were flustered with alarm, grasped at a straw, and determined, although it was as much as advertising Mr Huddlestone's presence in the pavilion, to carry my proposal into effect.

The sum was part in specie, part in bank paper, and part in circular notes payable to the name of James Gregory. We took it out, counted it, enclosed it once more in a dispatch box belonging to Northmour, and prepared a letter in Italian which he tied to the handle. It was signed by both of us under oath, and declared that this was all the money which had escaped the failure of the house of Huddlestone. This was, perhaps, the maddest action ever perpetrated by two persons professing to be sane. Had the dispatch box fallen into other hands than those for which it was intended, we stood criminally convicted on our own written testimony; but, as I have said, we were neither of us in a condition to judge soberly, and had a thirst for action that drove us to do something, right or wrong, rather than endure the agony of waiting. Moreover, as we were both convinced that the hollows of the links were alive with hidden spies upon our movements, we hoped that our appearance with the box might lead to a parley, and, perhaps, a compromise.

It was nearly three when we issued from the pavilion. The rain had taken off; the sun shone quite cheerfully. I had never seen the gulls fly so close about the house or approach so fearlessly to human beings. On the very doorstep one flapped heavily past our heads, and uttered its wild cry in my very ear.

"There is an omen for you," said Northmour, who like all freethinkers was much under the influence of superstition. "They think we are already dead."

I made some light rejoinder, but it was with half my heart; for the circumstance had impressed me.

A yard or two before the gate, on a patch of smooth turf, we set down the dispatch box; and Northmour waved a white handkerchief over his head. Nothing replied. We raised our voices, and cried aloud in Italian that we were there as ambassadors to arrange the quarrel, but the stillness remained unbroken save by the seagulls and the surf. I had a weight at my heart when we desisted; and I saw that even Northmour was unusually pale. He looked over his shoulder nervously, as though he feared that some one had crept between him and the pavilion door.

"By God," he said in a whisper, "this is too much for me!"

I replied in the same key: "Suppose there should be none, after all!"

"Look there," he returned, nodding with his head, as though he had been afraid to point.

I glanced in the direction indicated; and there, from the northern quarter of the Sea-Wood, beheld a thin column of smoke rising steadily against the now cloudless sky.

"Northmour," I said (we still continued to talk in whispers), "it is not possible to endure this suspense. I prefer death fifty times over. Stay you here to watch the pavilion; I will go forward and make sure, if I have to walk right into their camp."

He looked once again all round him with puckered eyes, and then nodded assentingly to my proposal.

My heart beat like a sledge-hammer as I set out walking rapidly in the direction of the smoke; and, though up to that moment I had felt chill and shivering, I was suddenly conscious of a glow of heat all over my body. The ground in this direction was very uneven; a hundred men might have lain hidden in as many square yards about my path. But I who had not practiced the business in vain, chose such routes as cut at the very root of concealment, and, by keeping along the most convenient ridges, commanded several hollows at a time. It was not long before I was rewarded for my caution. Coming suddenly on to a mound somewhat more elevated than the surrounding hummocks, I saw, not thirty yards away, a man bent almost double, and running as fast as his attitude permitted, along the bottom of a gully. I had dislodged one of the spies from his ambush. As soon as I sighted him, I called loudly both in English and Italian; and he, seeing concealment was no longer possible, straightened himself out, leaped from the gully, and made off as straight as an arrow for the borders of the wood. It was none of my business to pursue; I had learned what I wanted – that we were beleaguered and watched in the pavilion; and I returned at once, and walked as nearly as possible in my old footsteps, to where Northmour awaited me beside the dispatch box. He was even paler than when I had left him, and his voice shook a little.

"Could you see what he was like?" he asked.

"He kept his back turned," I replied.

"Let us get into the house, Frank. I don't think I'm a coward, but I can stand no more of this," he whispered.

All was still and sunshiny about the pavilion, as we turned to re-enter it; even the gulls had flown in a wider circuit, and were seen flickering along the beach and sand hills; and this loneliness terrified me more than a regiment under arms. It was not until the door was barricaded that I could draw a full inspiration and relieve the weight that lay upon my bosom. Northmour and I exchanged a steady glance; and I suppose each made his own reflections on the white and startled aspect of the other.

"You were right," I said. "All is over. Shake hands, old man, for the last time."

"Yes," replied he, "I will shake hands; for, as sure as I am here, I bear no malice. But, remember, if, by some impossible accident, we should give the slip to these blackguards, I'll take the upper hand of you by fair or foul."

"Oh," said I, "you weary me!"

He seemed hurt, and walked away in silence to the foot of the stairs, where he paused.

"You do not understand," said he. "I am not a swindler, and I guard myself; that is all. I may weary you or not, Mr Cassilis, I do not care a rush; I speak for my own satisfaction, and not for your amusement. You had better go upstairs and court the girl; for my part, I stay here."

"And I stay with you," I returned. "Do you think I would steal a march, even with your permission?"

"Frank," he said, smiling, "it's a pity you are an ass, for you have the makings of a man. I think I must be fey today; you cannot irritate me even when you try. Do you know," he continued softly, "I think we are the two most miserable men in England, you and I? we have got on to thirty without wife or child, or so much as a shop to look after – poor, pitiful, lost devils, both! And now we clash about a girl! As if there were not several millions in the United Kingdom! Ah, Frank, Frank, the one who loses his throw, be it you or me, he has my pity! It were better for him – how does the Bible say? – that a millstone were hanged about his neck and he were cast into the depth of the sea. Let us take a drink," he concluded suddenly, but without any levity of tone.

I was touched by his words, and consented. He sat down on the table in the dining-room, and held up the glass of sherry to his eye.

"If you beat me, Frank," he said, "I shall take to drink. What will you do, if it goes the other way?"

"God knows," I returned.

"Well," said he, "here is a toast in the meantime: '*Italia irredenta!*'"

The remainder of the day was passed in the same dreadful tedium and suspense. I laid the table for dinner, while Northmour and Clara prepared the meal together in the kitchen. I could hear their talk as I went to and fro, and was surprised to find it ran all the time upon myself. Northmour again bracketed us together, and rallied Clara on a choice of husbands; but he continued to speak of me with some feeling, and uttered nothing to my prejudice unless he included himself in the condemnation. This awakened a sense of gratitude in my heart, which combined with the immediateness of our peril to fill my eyes with tears. After all, I thought – and perhaps the thought was laughably vain – we were here three very noble human beings to perish in defense of a thieving banker.

Before we sat down to table, I looked forth from an upstairs window. The day was beginning to decline; the links were utterly deserted; the dispatch box still lay untouched where we had left it hours before.

Mr Huddlestone, in a long yellow dressing gown, took one end of the table, Clara the other; while Northmour and I faced each other from the sides. The lamp was brightly trimmed; the wine was good; the viands, although mostly cold, excellent of their sort. We seemed to have agreed tacitly; all reference to the impending catastrophe was carefully avoided; and, considering our tragic circumstances, we made a merrier party than could have been expected. From time to time, it is true, Northmour or I would rise from the table and make a round of the defenses; and, on each of these occasions, Mr Huddlestone was recalled to a sense of his tragic predicament, glanced up with ghastly eyes, and bore for an instant on his countenance the stamp of terror. But he hastened to empty his glass, wiped his forehead with his handkerchief, and joined again in the conversation.

I was astonished at the wit and information he displayed. Mr Huddlestone's was certainly no ordinary character; he had read and observed for himself; his gifts were sound; and, though I could never have learned to love the man, I began to understand his success in business, and the great respect in which he had been held before his failure. He had, above all, the talent of society; and though I never heard him speak but on this one and most unfavourable occasion, I set him down among the most brilliant conversationalists I ever met.

He was relating with great gusto, and seemingly no feeling of shame, the manoeuvres of a scoundrelly commission merchant whom he had known and studied in his youth, and we were all listening with an odd mixture of mirth and embarrassment, when our little party was brought abruptly to an end in the most startling manner.

A noise like that of a wet finger on the window pane interrupted Mr Huddlestone's tale; and in an instant we were all four as white as paper, and sat tongue-tied and motionless round the table.

"A snail," I said at last; for I had heard that these animals make a noise somewhat similar in character.

"Snail be d——d!" said Northmour. "Hush!"

The same sound was repeated twice at regular intervals; and then a formidable voice shouted through the shutters the Italian word, "*Traditore!*"

Mr Huddlestone threw his head in the air; his eyelids quivered; next moment he fell insensible below the table. Northmour and I had each run to the armory and seized a gun. Clara was on her feet with her hand at her throat.

So we stood waiting, for we thought the hour of attack was certainly come; but second passed after second, and all but the surf remained silent in the neighbourhood of the pavilion.

"Quick," said Northmour; "upstairs with him before they come."

CHAPTER 8

Somehow or other, by hook and crook, and between the three of us, we got Bernard Huddlestone bundled upstairs and laid upon the bed in *My Uncle's Room*. During the whole process, which was rough enough, he gave no sign of consciousness, and he remained, as we had thrown him, without changing the position of a finger. His daughter opened his shirt and began to wet his head and bosom; while Northmour and I ran to the window. The weather continued clear; the moon, which was now about full, had risen and shed a very clear light upon the links; yet, strain our eyes as we might, we could distinguish nothing moving. A few dark spots, more or less, on the uneven expanse were not to be identified; they might be crouching men, they might be shadows; it was impossible to be sure.

"Thank God," said Northmour, "Aggie is not coming tonight."

Aggie was the name of the old nurse; he had not thought of her until now; but that he should think of her at all was a trait that surprised me in the man.

We were again reduced to waiting. Northmour went to the fireplace and spread his hands before the red embers, as if he were cold. I followed him mechanically with my eyes, and in so doing turned my back upon the window. At that moment a very faint report was audible from without, and a ball shivered a pane of glass, and buried itself in the shutter two inches from my head. I heard Clara scream; and though I whipped instantly out of range and into a corner, she was there, so to speak, before me, beseeching to know if I were hurt. I felt that I could stand to be shot at every day and all day long, with such remarks of solicitude for a reward; and I continued to reassure her, with, the tenderest caresses and in complete forgetfulness of our situation, till the voice of Northmour recalled me to myself.

"An air gun," he said. "They wish to make no noise."

I put Clara aside, and looked at him. He was standing with his back to the fire and his hands clasped behind him; and I knew by the black look on his face, that passion was boiling within. I had seen just such a look before he attacked me, that March night, in the adjoining chamber; and, though I could make every allowance for his anger, I confess I trembled for the consequences. He gazed straight before him; but he could see us with the tail of his eye, and his temper kept rising like a gale of wind. With regular battle awaiting us outside, this prospect of an internecine strife within the walls began to daunt me.

Suddenly, as I was thus closely watching his expression and prepared against the worst, I saw a change, a flash, a look of relief, upon his face. He took up the lamp which stood beside him on the table, and turned to us with an air of some excitement.

"There is one point that we must know," said he. "Are they going to butcher the lot of us, or only Huddlestone? Did they take you for him, or fire at you for your own *beaux yeux*?"

"They took me for him, for certain," I replied. "I am near as tall, and my head is fair."

"I am going to make sure," returned Northmour; and he stepped up to the window, holding the lamp above his head, and stood there, quietly affronting death, for half a minute.

Clara sought to rush forward and pull him from the place of danger; but I had the pardonable selfishness to hold her back by force.

"Yes," said Northmour, turning coolly from the window, "it's only Huddlestone they want."

"Oh, Mr Northmour!" cried Clara; but found no more to add; the temerity she had just witnessed seeming beyond, the reach of words.

He, on his part, looked at me, cocking his head, with a fire of triumph in his eyes; and I understood at once that he had thus hazarded his life, merely to attract Clara's notice, and depose me from my position as the hero of the hour. He snapped his fingers.

"The fire is only beginning," said he. "When they warm up to their work, they won't be so particular."

A voice was now heard hailing us from the entrance. From the window we could see the figure of a man in the moonlight; he stood motionless, his face uplifted to ours, and a rag of something white on his extended arm; and as we looked right down upon him, though he was a good many yards distant on the links, we could see the moonlight glitter on his eyes.

He opened his lips again, and spoke for some minutes on end, in a key so loud that he might have been heard in every corner of the pavilion, and as far away as the borders of the wood. It was the same voice that had already shouted, "*Traditore!*" through the shutters of the dining-room; this time it made a complete and clear statement. If the traitor "Oddlestone" were given up, all others should be spared; if not, no one should escape to tell the tale.

"Well, Huddlestone, what do you say to that?" asked Northmour, turning to the bed.

Up to that moment the banker had given no sign of life, and I, at least, had supposed him to be still lying in a faint; but he replied at once, and in such tones as I have never heard elsewhere, save from a delirious patient, adjured and besought us not to desert him. It was the most hideous and abject performance that my imagination can conceive.

"Enough," cried Northmour; and then he threw open the window, leaned out into the night, and in a tone of exultation, and with a total forgetfulness of what was due to the presence of a lady, poured out upon the ambassador a string of the most abominable raillery both in English and Italian, and bade him be gone where he had come from. I believe that nothing so delighted Northmour at that moment as the thought that we must all infallibly perish before the night was out.

Meantime, the Italian put his flag of truce into his pocket, and disappeared, at a leisurely pace, among the sand hills.

"They make honourable war," said Northmour. "They are all gentlemen and soldiers. For the credit of the thing, I wish we could change sides – you and I, Frank, and you, too, missy, my darling – and leave that being on the bed to some one else. Tut! Don't look shocked! We are all going post to what they call eternity, and may as well be above board while there's time. As far as I am concerned, if I could first strangle Huddlestone and then get Clara in my arms, I could die with some pride and satisfaction. And as it is, by God, I'll have a kiss!"

Before I could do anything to interfere, he had rudely embraced and repeatedly kissed the resisting girl. Next moment I had pulled him away with fury, and flung him heavily against the wall. He laughed loud and long, and I feared his wits had given way under the strain; for even in the best of days he had been a sparing and a quiet laugher.

"Now, Frank," said he, when his mirth was somewhat appeased, "it's your turn. Here's my hand. Good-bye, farewell!" Then, seeing me stand rigid and indignant, and holding Clara to my side – "Man!" he broke out, "are you angry? Did you think we were going to die with all the airs and graces of society? I took a kiss; I'm glad I did it; and now you can take another if you like, and square accounts."

I turned from him with a feeling of contempt which I did not seek to dissemble.

"As you please," said he. "You've been a prig in life; a prig you'll die."

And with that he sat down in a chair, a rifle over his knee, and amused himself with snapping the lock; but I could see that his ebullition of light spirits (the only one I ever knew him to display) had already come to an end, and was succeeded by a sullen, scowling humour.

All this time our assailants might have been entering the house, and we been none the wiser; we had in truth almost forgotten the danger that so imminently overhung our days. But just then Mr Huddlestone uttered a cry, and leaped from the bed.

I asked him what was wrong.

"Fire!" he cried. "They have set the house on fire!"

Northmour was on his feet in an instant, and he and I ran through the door of communication with the study. The room was illuminated by a red and angry light. Almost at the moment of our entrance, a tower of flame arose in front of the window, and, with a tingling report, a pane fell inward on the carpet. They had set fire to the lean-to outhouse, where Northmour used to nurse his negatives.

"Hot work," said Northmour. "Let us try in your old room."

We ran thither in a breath, threw up the casement, and looked forth. Along the whole back wall of the pavilion piles of fuel had been arranged and kindled; and it is probable they had been drenched with mineral oil, for, in spite of the morning's rain, they all burned bravely. The fire had taken a firm hold already on the outhouse, which blazed higher and higher every moment; the back door was in the centre of a red-hot bonfire; the eaves we could see, as we looked upward, were already smoldering, for the roof overhung, and was supported by considerable beams of wood. At the same time, hot, pungent and choking volumes of smoke began to fill the house. There was not a human being to be seen to right or left.

"Ah, well!" said Northmour, "here's the end, thank God!"

And we returned to *My Uncle's Room.* Mr Huddlestone was putting on his boots, still violently trembling, but with an air of determination such as I had not hitherto observed. Clara stood close by him, with her cloak in both hands ready to throw about her shoulders, and a strange look in her eyes, as if she were half hopeful, half doubtful of her father.

"Well, boys and girls," said Northmour, "how about a sally? The oven is heating; it is not good to stay here and be baked; and, for my part, I want to come to my hands with them, and be done."

"There's nothing else left," I replied.

And both Clara and Mr Huddlestone, though with a very different intonation, added, "Nothing."

As we went downstairs the heat was excessive, and the roaring of the fire filled our ears; and we had scarce reached the passage before the stairs window fell in, a branch of flame shot brandishing through the aperture, and the interior of the pavilion became lighted up with that dreadful and fluctuating glare. At the same moment we heard the fall of something heavy and inelastic in the upper story. The whole pavilion, it was plain, had gone alight like a box of matches, and now not only flamed sky high to land and sea, but threatened with every moment to crumble and fall in about our ears.

Northmour and I cocked our revolvers. Mr Huddlestone, who had already refused a firearm, put us behind him with a manner of command.

"Let Clara open the door," said he. "So, if they fire a volley, she will be protected. And in the meantime stand behind me. I am the scapegoat; my sins have found me out."

I heard him, as I stood breathless by his shoulder, with my pistol ready, pattering off prayers in a tremulous, rapid whisper; and, I confess, horrid as the thought may seem, I despised him for thinking of supplications in a moment so critical and thrilling. In the meantime, Clara, who was dead white but still possessed her faculties, had displaced the barricade from the front door. Another moment, and she had pulled it open. Firelight and moonlight illuminated the links with confused and changeful luster, and far away against the sky we could see a long trail of glowing smoke.

Mr Huddlestone, filled for the moment with a strength greater than his own, struck Northmour and myself a back-hander in the chest; and while we were thus for the moment incapacitated from action, lifting his arms above his head like one about to dive, he ran straight forward out of the pavilion.

"Here am I!" he cried – "Huddlestone! Kill me, and spare the others!"

His sudden appearance daunted, I suppose, our hidden enemies; for Northmour and I had time to recover, to seize Clara between us, one by each arm, and to rush forth to his assistance, ere anything further had taken place. But scarce had we passed the threshold when there came near a dozen reports and flashes from every direction among the hollows of the links. Mr Huddlestone staggered, uttered a weird and freezing cry, threw up his arms over his head, and fell backward on the turf.

"*Traditore! Traditore!*" cried the invisible avengers.

And just then a part of the roof of the pavilion fell in, so rapid was the progress of the fire. A loud, vague, and horrible noise accompanied the collapse, and a vast volume of flame went soaring up to heaven. It must have been visible at that moment from twenty miles out at sea, from the shore at Graden Wester, and far inland from the peak of Graystiel, the most eastern summit of the Caulder Hills. Bernard Huddlestone, although God knows what were his obsequies, had a fine pyre at the moment of his death.

CHAPTER 9

should have the greatest difficulty to tell you what followed next after this tragic circumstance. It is all to me, as I look back upon it, mixed, strenuous, and ineffectual, like the struggles of a sleeper in a nightmare. Clara, I remember, uttered a broken sigh and would have fallen forward to earth, had not Northmour and I supported her insensible body. I do not think we were attacked: I do not remember even to have seen an assailant; and I believe we deserted Mr Huddlestone without a glance. I only remember running like a man in a panic, now carrying Clara altogether in my own arms, now sharing her weight with Northmour, now scuffling confusedly for the possession of that dear burden. Why we should have made for my camp in the Hemlock Den, or how we reached it, are points lost forever to my recollection. The first moment at which I became definitely sure, Clara had been suffered to fall against the outside of my little tent, Northmour and I were tumbling together on the ground, and he, with contained ferocity, was striking for my head with the butt of his revolver. He had already twice wounded me on the scalp; and it is to the consequent loss of blood that I am tempted to attribute the sudden clearness of my mind.

I caught him by the wrist.

"Northmour," I remember saying, "you can kill me afterwards. Let us first attend to Clara."

He was at that moment uppermost. Scarcely had the words passed my lips, when he had leaped to his feet and ran toward the tent; and the next moment, he was straining Clara to his heart and covering her unconscious hands and face with his caresses.

"Shame!" I cried. "Shame to you, Northmour!"

And, giddy though I still was, I struck him repeatedly upon the head and shoulders.

He relinquished his grasp, and faced me in the broken moonlight.

"I had you under, and I let you go," said he; "and now you strike me! Coward!"

"You are the coward," I retorted. "Did she wish your kisses while she was still sensible of what you wanted? Not she! And now she may be dying; and you waste this precious time, and abuse her helplessness. Stand aside, and let me help her."

He confronted me for a moment, white and menacing; then suddenly he stepped aside.

"Help her then," said he.

I threw myself on my knees beside her, and loosened, as well as I was able, her dress and corset; but while I was thus engaged, a grasp descended on my shoulder.

"Keep your hands off her," said Northmour, fiercely. "Do you think I have no blood in my veins?"

"Northmour," I cried, "if you will neither help her yourself, nor let me do so, do you know that I shall have to kill you?"

"That is better!" he cried. "Let her die also, where's the harm? Step aside from that girl! and stand up to fight."

"You will observe," said I, half rising, "that I have not kissed her yet."

"I dare you to," he cried.

I do not know what possessed me; it was one of the things I am most ashamed of in my life, though, as my wife used to say, I knew that my kisses would be always welcome were she dead or living; down I fell again upon my knees, parted the hair from her forehead, and, with the dearest respect, laid my lips for a moment on that cold brow. It was such a caress as a father might have given; it was such a one as was not unbecoming from a man soon to die to a woman already dead.

"And now," said I, "I am at your service, Mr Northmour."

But I saw, to my surprise, that he had turned his back upon me.

"Do you hear?" I asked.

"Yes," said he, "I do. If you wish to fight, I am ready. If not, go on and save Clara. All is one to me."

I did not wait to be twice bidden; but, stooping again over Clara, continued my efforts to revive her. She still lay white and lifeless; I began to fear that her sweet spirit had indeed fled beyond recall, and horror and a sense of utter desolation seized upon my heart. I called her by name with the most endearing inflections; I chafed and beat her hands; now I laid her head low, now supported it against my knee; but all seemed to be in vain, and the lids still lay heavy on her eyes.

"Northmour," I said, "there is my hat. For God's sake bring some water from the spring."

Almost in a moment he was by my side with the water.

"I have brought it in my own," he said. "You do not grudge me the privilege?"

"Northmour," I was beginning to say, as I laved her head and breast; but he interrupted me savagely.

"Oh, you hush up!" he said. "The best thing you can do is to say nothing."

I had certainly no desire to talk, my mind being swallowed up in concern for my dear love and her condition; so I continued in silence to do my best toward her recovery, and, when the hat was empty, returned it to him, with one word – "More." He had, perhaps, gone several times upon this errand, when Clara reopened her eyes.

"Now," said he, "since she is better, you can spare me, can you not? I wish you a good night, Mr Cassilis."

And with that he was gone among the thicket. I made a fire, for I had now no fear of the Italians, who had even spared all the little possessions left in my encampment; and, broken as she was by the excitement and the hideous catastrophe of the evening, I managed, in one way or another – by persuasion, encouragement, warmth, and such simple remedies as I could lay my hand on – to bring her back to some composure of mind and strength of body.

Day had already come, when a sharp "Hist!" sounded from the thicket. I started from the ground; but the voice of Northmour was heard adding, in the most tranquil tones: "Come here, Cassilis, and alone; I want to show you something."

I consulted Clara with my eyes, and, receiving her tacit permission, left her alone, and clambered out of the den. At some distance off I saw Northmour leaning against an elder; and, as soon as he perceived me, he began walking seaward. I had almost overtaken him as he reached the outskirts of the wood.

"Look," said he, pausing.

A couple of steps more brought me out of the foliage. The light of the morning lay cold and clear over that well-known scene. The pavilion was but a blackened wreck; the roof had fallen in, one of the gables had fallen out; and, far and near, the face of the links was cicatrized with little patches of burned furze. Thick smoke still went straight upward in the windless air of the morning, and a great pile of ardent cinders filled the bare walls of the house, like coals in an open grate. Close by the islet a schooner yacht lay to, and a well-manned boat was pulling vigorously for the shore.

"The *Red Earl*!" I cried. "The *Red Earl* twelve hours too late!"

"Feel in your pocket, Frank. Are you armed?" asked Northmour.

I obeyed him, and I think I must have become deadly pale. My revolver had been taken from me.

"You see, I have you in my power," he continued. "I disarmed you last night while you were nursing Clara; but this morning – here – take your pistol. No thanks!" he cried, holding up his hand. "I do not like them; that is the only way you can annoy me now."

He began to walk forward across the links to meet the boat, and I followed a step or two behind. In front of the pavilion I paused to see where Mr Huddlestone had fallen; but there was no sign of him, nor so much as a trace of blood.

"Graden Floe," said Northmour.

He continued to advance till we had come to the head of the beach.

"No farther, please," said he. "Would you like to take her to Graden House?"

"Thank you," replied I; "I shall try to get her to the minister at Graden Wester."

The prow of the boat here grated on the beach, and a sailor jumped ashore with a line in his hand.

"Wait a minute, lads!" cried Northmour; and then lower and to my private ear, "You had better say nothing of all this to her," he added.

"On the contrary!" I broke out, "she shall know everything that I can tell."

"You do not understand," he returned, with an air of great dignity. "It will be nothing to her; she expects it of me. Good-bye!" he added, with a nod.

I offered him my hand.

"Excuse me," said he. "It's small, I know; but I can't push things quite so far as that. I don't wish any sentimental business, to sit by your hearth a white-haired wanderer, and all that. Quite the contrary: I hope to God I shall never again clap eyes on either one of you."

"Well, God bless you, Northmour!" I said heartily.

"Oh, yes," he returned.

He walked down the beach; and the man who was ashore gave him an arm on board, and then shoved off and leaped into the bows himself. Northmour took the tiller; the boat rose to the waves, and the oars between the thole-pins sounded crisp and measured in the morning air.

They were not yet half way to the *Red Earl*, and I was still watching their progress, when the sun rose out of the sea.

One word more, and my story is done. Years after, Northmour was killed fighting under the colours of Garibaldi for the liberation of the Tyrol.

LIFE & WORKS
ROBERT LOUIS STEVENSON

Robert Louis Balfour Stevenson (1850-94) was born in oft dank and cold Edinburgh, but travelled greatly in search of less brutal weather, finally to pass away in the temperate climes of Samoa. For today's reader his reputation as a writer of adventure fiction is well established but as a poet, essayist, travel writer and masterful short story writer his range was great and varied. In his time, he was a popular author and associated with many of the most notable writers of the late Victorian period, although the elitism of some contemporary literary critics sought to bury him with the Romantics until his reputation was rescued in the twentieth century, as a skillfull storyteller of the gothic and fantastic.

EARLY YEARS

Born to respectable parents at the height of the British Empire, Stevenson's ill health led him to spend much of his time reading, or being read to, frequently unable to join his peers at school. His grandfather was Professor of Moral Philosophy at Edinburgh University, his father a civil engineer of over 40 prestigious lighthouses, so there were great expectations for the young Stevenson. However his mind was saturated by the works of Shakespeare, Sir Walter Scott, John Bunyan, *The Arabian Nights* and the elaborate, moralising fairy tales of Grimm and Hans Christian Andersen. His early instincts for storytelling were clear, in spite of the best attempts of his family who expected him to pursue a career in science.

Initially he consented to the study of engineering at the University of Edinbugh from 1867, but soon found the pull of literature to be too seductive. His parents were horrified at the prospect of their son relying on the unstable, and distasteful, pursuit of writing as career, so collectively they managed a compromise: Stevenson would study law instead. He was called to the bar in 1875, although never practised.

As he grew into adulthood Stevenson's conflicts with his parents – his father in particular, and all he stood for – intensified. In common with many artists, writers and musicians of the era Stevenson's behaviour and interests were thought to be dangerously Bohemian, and in his case led to a scandalous outcome: he fell in love with Fanny Van De Grift Osbourne. Fanny rendered four terrible sins for the young Scot, any one of which would have secured his social damnation: she was American, married, had borne two children, and was 10 years his senior. However, determined to follow his own path in life, eventually he travelled, at great cost to his health, to San Francisco, in 1880 and shortly after, married the then divorced Fanny Osbourne.

WORK, WRITINGS AND THEMES

The lifelong tension with his father provided much for Stevenson to explore in his writing, extending beyond the natural rebellion of youth, to deeper examinations of the conflict between the past and the present, and the superficiality of society undermined by the inherent ugliness of humankind.

Stevenson's single-minded dislike of authoritarianism provided the background to much of his writing. As with many late Victorian writers, from Arthur Machen to Oscar Wilde, the mood of hedonism and liberalism – the mode of the literate avant garde – had become attractive to those exposed to the diverse ideas of others. Stevenson's poor health released him to think, create and write in a way that might otherwise have been denied. (This experience would be echoed only a few decades later by H.P. Lovecraft.)

Although a monumental letter writer and poet (*A Child's Garden of Verses* in 1885), he is best known for his series of successful novels and short stories, *Treasure Island* (1883), *Kidnapped* (1886), *The Strange Case of Dr Jekyll and Mr Hyde* (1886), and *The Master of Ballantrae* (1889). As was the tradition in the Victorian era Stevenson's early work was initially serialized in magazines (as, of course, was that of Dickens, H.G. Wells and many others), building his readership and tuning his methods: in 1881 *Treasure Island* was serialized before publication as a book and allowed Stevenson to forge one of his key techniques, of page-turning suspense: 'No need for psychology or fine writing' he would later say.

HYPOCRISY AND DUALITY

The Strange Case of Jekyll and Hyde is an altogether darker story than most of his other novels, but an adventure springing from everyday life, it dwells on many of the same themes. Based on a story about the double life of Deacon William Brodie – cabinet maker by day, but dissolute and thief by night – it scrutinizes puritanism, secrecy and hypocrisy, hinting at dark affronts to the public consciousness of proud Victorians, suggesting murder and egregious sexual acts, which some modern critics imbue with undercurrents of homosexuality; Oscar Wilde's fate only a few years after Stevenson's death show the perils of this latter imputation in the Victorian age.

Stevenson was preoccupied with duality, the twin forces that wrestle for the mind and fortune of humankind, as he said in his posthumously published letter to his cousin Bob Stevenson:

'the prim, obliterated polite face of life, and the broad, bawdy and orgiastic'. Even *Kidnapped* uncoils alternative, dark futures for us, if we fall unexpectedly from our comfortable lives, into a grim world that runs in parallel to our own.

It's worth remembering that Edinburgh, the city of Stevenson's birth, exemplified these twin forces: the ambitious, striving energies of empire, underneath which lurked the secret city of despair and criminality, with its dark corridors and passages, hidden worlds beneath the bridges, the undulating streets with rooms carved into arches that reeked of poverty and disease. The grand streets above sought to flatten the landscape for their carriages and parties, with the great bridges of the industrial revolution, the pride of Scottish engineering. Stevenson, son of a celebrated civil engineer, seemed naturally attuned to, and repulsed by, this contrast.

CULTURAL LANDSCAPE

Often regarded as a children's writer, this highlights a significant misunderstanding of the literature of the Victorian period. This was the era of gothic exhortation, of intense recountings of grim fairy tales, full of bile and vitriol, the age of vivid storytelling. While the striving middle classes read great literature to their children, education had begun to snake its way through the working classes; the British Empire, with the Scots at its core, paraded itself as a moral and educating force to the world, exporting great industrial achievements in the form of the railway, the telegraph, and the mighty civil engineering projects – the ships, aqueducts and bridges.

But it was also the era of Jack the Ripper, of Bram Stoker's *Dracula*, springing from the unearthly flesh of *Frankenstein*, the era of accelerated scientific progress, as the trading prowess of the Victorian Era brought new ideas from around the world, in art, religion, science and philosophy, so that the question of an individual's place in the headlong charge of advancement lay suppressed, and unexamined. But the gothic literature, from Dickens' *Bleak House* to Oscar Wilde's tale of excess and greed, *The Portrait of Dorian Gray*, explored the tension at the heart of Empire, of the conflict between the beast and the man within.

Mary Shelley's masterpiece *Frankenstein* had raised questions about superficiality, the role of humankind in creating the world around it, of responsibility and desire, but in Stevenson's Jekyll was an everyday protagonist. A doctor by day, he was someone who could be understood by all of his readers, someone they, and we still, could all meet. Stevenson reveals the beast within, insinuating the fear of the civilized man, that the inner neanderthal might rise and overcome this new found sophistication, and drag down the advancement of science and nationhood.

Stevenson has been much criticised for his taste for the fantastic. His short novels, his racy plots, his emphasis on storytelling rather than the reflection of a supposed real life was out of step with the elite literary mood of the late Victorian, and early twentieth century. Indeed the writers who could share his inclinations were relatively unknown to him: Arthur Machen, Algernon Blackwood, H.P. Lovecraft, unaware – as is often the case – that he was writing in an emerging tradition.

CONNECTIONS, LEGACY AND LATER YEARS

Stevenson admired the economy of Henry James and Guy de Maupassant, reveled in the forboding gloom of Edgar Allan Poe, and Nathaniel Hawthorne's critique of religion and the dark moments of the soul. He was widely read, and respected for the eloquence of his writing by many fellow writers: he corresponded with J.M. Barrie, Arthur Conan Doyle and Thomas Hardy, and was lauded by Edith Wharton, and later by Jorge Luis Borges, Graham Greene, and John Buchan who brought Stevenson's page-turning adventures into the middle of the twentieth century, bridging the gap between the great nineteenth century novel and the shorter, more fragmented forms of modernism.

Stevenson's place is secure in the Gothic Tradition but his impact was wider, both during his life and after. His last 14 years, spent with his wife Fanny, were marked by ill health, bed rest and travel, but he wrote his most celebrated books during that period. He became a celebrated, successful writer and finished his years in the Islands of Samoa, his life extinguished by a heart attack, at the relatively young age of 46.

A GLOSSARY
OF GOTHIC, VICTORIAN & LITERARY TERMS

A

abbess: nun in charge of a convent; female brothel keeper, a madame

abhorrence: feeling of loathing or revulsion

abode: place where people live; period of living somewhere

abominable: causing revulsion or disgust

air-blebs: air heads, empty-headed people

afterlife: existence after death; eternal life

alchemy: mythical practice of turning base metals into gold, prolonging life or finding a universal remedy for disease

alderman: term for a half-Crown; senior local government official

ale: alcoholic drink made from hops and fermented malt, stronger and heavier than beer

almanac: annual calendar which contains information on important dates, tides, astronomical data, etc.

almshouse: lodgings for the poor, privately funded (often by the church), as opposed to the workhouse, which was publicly funded

anatomical: relating to the structure of the body

antagonist: enemy or adversary

apoplexy: a crippling cerebral stroke, sometimes fatal; a fit of anger

apothecary: pharmacist; one who prepares drugs and medicines and gives medical advice; lowest order of medical man

apprentice: someone who works under a skilled professional for a specific amount of time (usually seven years) in order to learn a trade. When one finished his apprenticeship, he became a journeyman and would get paid for work himself

Armageddon: the final battle between good and evil

asylum: institution for people with mental health problems, often referred to as lunatic asylums

automaton: someone who resembles a machine by going through motions repetitively, but without feeling or emotion

B

Babylonian finger: that which spells out the writing on the wall; delivering a judgment

balderdash: nonsense, senseless or exaggerated speech or writing

banns: announcement or notice of a forthcoming marriage in a parish church, proclaimed on three consecutive Sundays

beak: magistrate

bearer up: thief with a female accomplice who would distract the victim so the crime could be performed

beating: repeatedly hitting someone; scaring birds from bushes out into the open for shooting parties

Bedlam: nickname for the Hospital of St Mary of Bethlehem, a London psychiatric hospital; place or situation full of noise, frenzy and confusion

beg to: wish to

berserker: traditionally an ancient and ferocious Norse warrior known for savagery

Black Smoke: poisonous gas used by the Martians in *The War of the Worlds* to kill humans

blackleg: someone who works during a strike, often criticised by those who obey the strike (also known as a 'scab')

blag: to steal something, often by smash-and-grab; to trick or con someone

blasphemy: sacrilegious talk concerning God or religion

bloodletting: reducing the volume of blood in the body by either opening a vein or applying leeches as a way of restoring health, used from ancient times up to the nineteenth century

bloofer: vampire, usually female; term possibly comes from the mispronunciation of 'beautiful'

bludger: violent criminal who often used a bludgeon or heavy, stout weapon

blue bottle: policeman

boarder: person paying rent for a bed, a room and usually meals in a private home or boarding house

bob: cockney slang for a shilling or five-pence piece

body-snatching: the act of stealing corpses from graves, tombs or morgues, usually for dissection or scientific study

borough: town that had been given the right to self-govern by royal charter; in Victorian London, Southwark was referred to as 'the borough'

Bow Street Runners: detective force in London who pre-dated the police, organized by novelist Henry Fielding and his brother John in 1750 up to 1829, when Robert Peel founded London's first police force

buck cabbie: dishonest cab driver

bug hunting: stealing from or cheating drunks, especially at night in drinking dens

bull: cockney slang for five shillings

C

calamity: accident or distressing event

cant: a free meal; language or vocabulary spoken by thieves or groups of people perceived to be common

caper: criminal act; dangerous activity

cash carrier: pimp or whore's minder, who would literally hold the money earned by soliciting

census: official list of the British population, including address and details of age, gender, occupation and birthplace, carried out every ten years since 1841

charnel-house: vault containing the remains of dead bodies or skeletons

chilblains: red, itchy swelling to parts of face, fingers and toes caused by exposure to cold and damp

chimera: something wished for but impossible; a fire-breathing monster from Greek mythology

chink: money (from the noise coins make when they knock against each other)

chiv/shiv: knife, razor or sharpened stick used as a weapon

choker: clergyman, referring to the clerical collar worn around the neck

cholera: disease of the small intestine, often fatal, marked by symptoms of thirst, cramps, vomiting and diarrhoea, caused by drinking water tainted with human waste. Victorians were hit with several cholera epidemics before sanitation conditions were improved

choused: to have been cheated

christen: to remove identifying marks from; to use for the first time; to make something like new again

chronometer: tool for measuring accurate time

claustrophobia: abnormal dread of being imprisoned or confined in a close or narrow space

cly faking: to pick someone's pocket

coal scuttle: metal pail for carrying and pouring coal

commencement: the beginning or start of something

contagion: spread of disease caused by close contact

cop/copper: policeman

costermonger: street peddler, usually selling fruits or vegetables

cracksman: safecracker, someone who cracks or breaks locks

cravat: scarf or band of fabric worn around the neck and tied in a bow

creator: someone who makes something come alive

crib: building, house or lodging; location of a gaol

crow: lookout during criminal activities; doctor

crusher: policeman

cudgel: heavy stick used as a weapon

cursory: quick, superficial and not very thorough

D

daresay: venture to say; think probable

day boarder: someone who spends the day at school but lives at home, as opposed to someone who boards at the school

deadlurk: empty premises

deaner: shilling

deformity: disfigurement or malformation, often of a body part but can also refer to morals or the mind

deity: god or goddess; supreme being

deputation: group of people charged with a mission or to represent other people

despatch: send something; to send someone to carry out a task

deuce hog: two shillings

device: tuppence; an emblem or motto

Devil: the Devil, as depicted in Christianity and some other religions, stands as the enemy or opposite to God and tempts people to sin so that they go to Hell; the actual term 'Devil' comes from the Latin *diabolus*, meaning slanderous. Gothic characters are often tempted by agents of the Devil

dewskitch: a beating (bodily assault)

diligence: public stagecoach; taking care or attention over something

ding: to throw something away; to take something that has been thrown away

diphtheria: infectious disease caused by germs in the throat, causing difficulty in breathing, fever and damage to the heart and nervous system

dirge: funeral hymn, mournful lament for the dead

dispatches: loaded dice; sends someone to carry out a task

do down: to beat someone with fists, especially as a punishment

dogmatism: emphatic belief presented as fact without consideration of truth or others' opinions

dollyshop: unlicensed, often cheap, loan or pawn shop

don: eminent, professional or clever person; leader or head of a group

Doppelgänger: literally translated from German as 'doublegoer'; the ghostly apparition of another, living person; double or alter ego

double-knock: applied to the door by a confident visitor, one who was known to the family and comfortable with the purpose of his visit (a single-knock signified a more timid caller, often of an inferior class)

dowager: widow with an inherited title or property from her deceased husband; distinguished, respected older woman

down: cause suspicion or doubt; to inform on a person, when used in the expression 'to put down on someone'

dragsman: someone who steals from carriages or coaches

draught: cheque or bill of exchange; a small quantity of liquid drunk in one mouthful

duckett: street dealer or vendor's licence

duffer: someone who sells allegedly stolen or worthless goods, also known as a 'hawker'

E

ecod: mild curse, most likely derived from 'My God'

economy: cheapness; giving better value

employ: to hire someone to work for you; if you were in the employ of or employed by someone, you worked for them

entrapment: imprisoning someone; incarcerating or trapping someone, often in dark, strange or claustrophobic surroundings

epidemic: illness that spreads rapidly and extensively, affecting most of the people who come in contact with it

epoch: period of time marked by particular events

erethism: extreme excitement or stimulation

escop/eslop: policeman

establishment: shop, place of business

exorcism: act of forcing the Devil, a demon or evil spirits from the body of someone who is possessed, done through religious prayer or rituals

expectations: chance of coming into an inheritance, property or money

extermination: destruction of an entire group or civilization

extra-terrestrial: existing outside of the earth's atmosphere

F

fadge: slang term for farthing

fakement: sham or trick, often used when begging

fan: to feel surreptitiously under someone's clothing while they are wearing it, searching for objects to steal

farthing: monetary unit worth a quarter of a penny; something almost worthless or of the lowest value

fawney-dropping: trick where a criminal pretends to find a ring (which has no actual value) and sells it as an item of possible worth

fiend: evil demon; evil or wicked person

finny: slang term for five-pound note

flam: lie or deception

flash: to show off or try to impress; something special or expensive-looking

flash house: public house with criminals as clientele

flimp: snatch stealing or pickpocketing from a crowd

flue faker: chimney sweep, usually young boys

footman: servant in livery, usually in a mansion or palace; a servant who serves at table, tends the door or carriage, runs errands

forebodings: feelings of apprehension or anxiety

forfeits: parlour games where each player needs to supply a correct answer and has a forfeit if the answer is not given

foundling: orphan or abandoned child raised by someone else

furlong: unit of measurement equal to 201 m (660 ft), the length of the traditional furrow or plough trench on a farm

furtherance: helping or advancing the progress of something

fusillade: volleys of shots fired simultaneously or in rapid succession

G

gaff: show or exhibition; cheap, smutty theatre; hoax or trick

galvanize: to shock someone or something into action

gammon: misleading comment, meant to deceive

gammy: someone false who is not to be trusted

gaol: jail

garret: fob pocket in a waistcoat; room at the top of the house

gattering: public house

general post: mail that was sent from the London Post Office to the rest of England

ghost: phantom or spirit of somebody who has died and who has possibly not gone on to the afterlife, which often inspires fear or terror

gibbet: post with a projecting beam for hanging executed criminals, often done publicly as a warning to the public

gig: light, open, two-wheeled carriage drawn by a single horse

gill: unit of liquid equalling a quarter of a pint

glock: slow, half-witted person

gonoph: petty, small-time criminal

Gorgon: female monster from Greek mythology with snakes for hair

gothic: style of architecture, music, art or fiction generally associated with strange, frightening occurrences and mysterious or supernatural plots, characters or locations

gout: disease mainly affecting men, causing inflammation and swelling of the hands and feet, arthritis and deformity; caused by excess uric acid production

governess: woman employed to teach and care for children in a school or home

greatcoat: long, heavy overcoat worn outdoors, often with a short cape worn over the shoulders

grog: mixture of alcohol, often rum, and water, named after an English admiral who diluted sailors' rum

grotesque: misshapen or mutated character; something or someone unexpected, monstrous or bizarre

gruel: watery, unappetizing porridge, popular with the owners of the workhouse or orphanage due to its cheapness

guinea: gold coin, monetary value of twenty-one shillings or one pound and one shilling

gulpy: someone gullible or easy to fool

H

haberdasher: someone who sells personal items, often accessories such as thread or ribbons

hackney coach: carriage for hire

hansom cab: two-wheeled, horse-drawn carriage where the driver sat on a high seat at the back so that the passengers had a clear view of the road

haunted: visited by a ghost or supernatural being

haybag: derogatory term for a woman

Heat-Ray: infrared ray, used by the Martians in *The War of the Worlds*

heliograph: signalling device that works by moving a mirror to reflect sunlight

heresy: belief that contradicts generally accepted or official religious teaching

hob: metal shelf or rack over a fireplace where the pans or kettle could be warmed

hoisting: shoplifting; to lift something up

hopping: picking hops, used for making beer

humbug: something insincere or nonsensical, meant to deceive or cheat people; used to express disbelief or disgust; a hoax or fraud

hykey: pride, arrogance

I

incubus: name for a male demon, thought to be a fallen angel, who forces himself sexually upon sleeping women, which often resulted in the birth of a demon or deformed, half-human child

infusoria: single-celled organisms

indefatigable: tirelessly persistent; not giving in to fatigue

influenza/flu: viral illness causing aching joints, fever, headaches, sore throat, cough and sneezing, even followed by death in Victorian times

inmate: someone confined to an institution such as a lunatic asylum or prison

Inquisition: organization founded by the Catholic Church charged with the eradication of heresy or acting against God, by which those found guilty were often put to death

insensate: lacking understanding, sense or reason; without sensitivity or feeling

insurrection: uprising in revolt or rebellion, usually against an established government or authority

integument: tough, protective outer layer

interred: buried

ironclad: armoured warship

ironmonger: someone who sells metal goods, tools and hardware

irons: guns, usually pistols or revolvers

J

jolly: disturbance or brawl; to be cheerful or happy

journeyman: skilled worker who has finished an apprenticeship and is qualified to hire himself out for work

Judgment Day: the end of the world when God judges humanity and the dead come back to life; also known as doomsday

Judy: term for a woman, usually a prostitute

juggernaut: massive and destructive force that is almost impossible to stop

jump: ground-floor window, or a burglary committed by entering through the window

K

kecks: slang term for trousers

ken: house, lodging or public house

kidsman: organizer of child thieves

kith: someone's friends, neighbours or relatives

knaves: jacks in a deck of cards

knee breeches: trousers that reach the knee

knock up: to bang loudly on someone's door to wake them up

know life, to: to be familiar with criminal ways; to be street-wise

kopjes: small hill, South African term meaning 'little head'

L

lag: convict; someone sentenced to transportation or gaol

lassitude: feeling of weariness, lack of energy

laudanum: solution of opium and alcohol used as pain relief or to aid sleep, highly addictive

lavender, in: to hide from the police; to pawn something for money; to be dead

leg: dishonest person, cheat

leviathan: sea monster; large and powerful object or thing

liberal: generous; tolerant or open-minded

link boy: boy who carries a torch to light a person's way through the dark streets

lodger: person paying rent to stay in a room (or bed) in somebody else's house

logbook: book in which a teacher would comment on pupils' attendance, behaviour, learning progress, etc.

lumber: wood used for building or woodworking, often second-hand furniture; to pawn something; to go to gaol

lurker: criminal; beggar or someone who dresses as a beggar for money

lush: alcoholic drink; someone who drinks too much alcohol; luxurious

M

macer: cheat

mag: slang term for a ha'pence piece

magistrate: judge over trials of misdemeanours; civil officer who upholds the law

maid-of-all-work: usually a young girl, hired as the only servant in the house and required to do any job asked of her

mail coach: carrier of the mail and a limited number of passengers, replaced in the mid-nineteenth century by the railroad

malefactor: someone who commits a crime or wrongdoing

malignity: malevolence, bad feeling towards someone

malt: grain, such as barley, that has been allowed to ferment, used for brewing beer and sometimes whisky

mandrake: homosexual; type of plant

mania: mental obsession or abnormality which can cause mood swings

mark: the victim of a crime

market day: the regular day each week when country people would bring their livestock and goods to sell in town

market town: town that regularly held a market, usually the largest town of a farming area

masochism: psychosexual perversion where someone gains erotic pleasure by having pain, abuse or humiliation inflicted on them

materially reduced: having your circumstances and/or finances reduced or lessened

maxim: statement or saying

mead: fermented alcoholic drink made of water, honey, malt, yeast and sometimes spices

mecks: alcohol, usually wine or spirits

Messrs: plural of Mr., used when referring to more than one man

metamorphosis: change or complete transformation in physical form, shape or structure, thought to be caused by supernatural powers

miasma: unpleasant smell or vapour, often related to disease or death

Michaelmas: Christian festival celebrating the archangel Michael, celebrated on 29 September, one of the four quarters of the year

middle class: people who earn enough money to live comfortably, often in a skilled profession, such as doctors and lawyers

mist: cloud of water particles that condense in the atmosphere, often used in Gothic literature to obscure objects or to prelude something or someone terrifying

mizzle: steal or disappear; fine rain

moniker/monniker: signature; first name

mortality: death rate; the number of deaths in a given time or given group

moucher/moocher: rural vagrant or beggar, someone who lives on the road

mourning clothes: black garments worn after a relative dies, the length of which depended on your relationship to the deceased

muck snipe: someone down on their luck

muffler: scarf

mug-hunter: street thief or pickpocket, from which the modern term 'mugger' comes

mutcher: pickpocket who usually steals from drunks

N

nail: steal; to catch someone who is guilty of a crime

natural philosophy: the science of nature

necromancy: black art of conversing with the spirits of the dead, usually done to predict or influence the future, also for making the dead perform tasks for you; witchcraft or sorcery

nethers: charges or rent for lodgings

netherskens: cheap, unsavoury lodging houses, flophouses

new-fangled: new or original, not necessarily an improvement over a previous version

nib: point of a pen, often a fountain pen

nibbed: arrested

nickey: slow or simple-minded

nightmare: frightening or unsettling dream, often used in Gothic literature to heighten drama or fear; a malign spirit thought to haunt or suffocate people during sleep

nobble: to inflict severe pain or bodily harm

nose: informant or spy; to try to find something out

O

occult: relating to the supernatural, witchcraft or magic; something not capable of being understood by ordinary people, but known only by the initiated

occupation: job, means of earning a living

odour: smell

omnibus: single or double-decker bus which was pulled by horses, capable of carrying lots of people

omnipotent: having unlimited power, god-like, infinite

on the fly: while in motion, moving quickly; something done quickly or spontaneously

opium: drug extracted from the dried juice and seeds of the opium poppy which is highly addictive

orthodox: following established rules of religion or society; proper way of behaving

outdoor relief: charity for the poor which did not require them to enter the workhouse, eliminated in 1834 by the New Poor Law to stop people playing the system

outsider: instrument used for opening a lock from the wrong side; stranger or interloper

P

page: boy or young man working as a servant or running errands

pall: detect; become dull or fade; gloomy atmosphere or mood

palmer: shoplifter; someone who 'palms' items to steal them

palsy: medical condition producing uncontrollable shaking of the muscles

pandemonium: wild disorder, chaos

panegyric: impassioned speech or text praising something or someone

parlour: living room, usually for guests

patterer: someone who earns a living by recitation or hawker's sales talk, convincing people to buy goods

peach: inform against someone or give information against someone, often leading to imprisonment

pea-coat: short, heavy, double-breasted overcoat worn by seamen, usually dark blue or black

peelers: nickname for the new London police force, organized by Sir Robert Peel in 1829

pertaining to: concerning or to do with

phantasm: ghost or apparition

phenomenon: fact or occurrence that is out of the ordinary or hard to believe, even though it can be seen, felt, heard, etc.

phonograph: gramophone, machine for recording or playing sound

picnic: any informal social gathering for which each guest provided a share of the food; informal meal eaten outside

pidgeon: victim; also known as a plant

pig: policeman, usually a detective

pig in a poke: something for sale at more than its true value

pleurisy: inflammation of the lungs producing a fever, hacking cough, sharp chest pain and difficulty in breathing

polyglot: someone who can speak or understand several languages

poorhouse: place where poor, old or sick people lived, where anyone able was put to work; also known as the workhouse

portrait: likeness of an individual or group created through photography or in paintings

possession: being controlled by an evil, demonic, supernatural force

post chaise: enclosed, four-wheeled, horse-drawn carriage, used to transport mail and passengers

premonitory: premonition or warning

prig: self-righteous or superior person

proctor: court officer who manages the affairs of others, answering to an attorney or solicitor

prodigious: great in amount or size; a lot

profane: disrespectful of religious beliefs

Prometheus: a Titan who stole fire from the Greek god, Zeus, in order to give it to humankind

proprietor: owner of a commercial or business enterprise

puckering: jabbering; speaking in an incomprehensible manner

pugilistic: relating to the practice of boxing or fist fighting

punishers: men hired to give beatings or 'nobblings'

pursuit: the act of chasing after someone, usually to attack or catch them, often inspiring fear

push: slang term for money

putrefactive: causing decay or putrefaction

Q

quadrille: card game for four players using forty cards; dance

quarter days: four days of the year when quarterly payments were made: Lady Day (25 March), Midsummer (24 June), Michaelmas (29 September) and Christmas (25 December)

quay: wharf or platform in a port or harbour where ships are loaded or unloaded

quick-lime: white, corrosive, alkaline substance consisting of calcium oxide, acquired by heating limestone

quid: slang term for pound

R

racket: illicit or dishonest occupation or activity

ream: someone superior, real or genuine

red planet: name for the planet Mars, given due to its red colour

red weed: fictional plant found in *The War of the Worlds*, which gives the planet Mars its red colour

remembrance: memory

repeater: pocket watch that chimed on the hour or quarter past the hour, making it easier to tell the time in the dark

reservist: reserve member of the military

resurrectionist: body snatcher; someone who steals corpses from graves, usually to sell to medical students. Legally, only the bodies of criminals could be used, but demand for corpses was so high that resurrectionists dug up the graves of the recently dead

revenant: dead person who has returned to terrorize or to avenge a score with someone living

revenge: act of avenging or repaying someone for a harm that the person has caused; to punish someone in retaliation for something done to them or to a loved one, carried out by humans or by spirits; a popular theme in Gothic literature

ribald: description for vulgar, lewd humour, often involving jokes about sex

roller: thief who robs drunks; prostitute who steals from her (usually drunk) customers

Romanticism: arts and literature of the Romantic movement, characterized by the passion, emotion and often danger of love and associated feelings

Romany: gypsy or traveller; language spoken by gypsies

rookery: urban slum or ghetto; nesting place for rooks

rozzers: policemen

ruffles: slang term for handcuffs

ruin: to go out of business; lose all your money or possessions

S

saddle: loaf; cut of meat

sadism: perversion where one person gains sexual gratification by causing others physical or mental pain, first coined to describe the writings of the Marquis de Sade; delight in torment or excessive cruelty

salubrity: health or well-being

Salvation Army: worldwide religious organization founded by William Booth in 1865; it provided aid to the poor, helped those in need and sought to bring people back to God

sapper: military engineer

sawbones: physician or surgeon

scarlet fever: infection usually suffered by children, causing a red rash and high fever; also called Scarlatina

screever: forger; writer of fake documents

sealing wax: wax that is soft when heated, used to seal letters – red for business letters, black for mourning and other colours for general correspondence

sentinel: guard or soldier who keeps watch

servant's lurk: public house used primarily by crooked or dismissed servants

sharp: conman, card swindler

shilling: unit of money equal to five pence in today's money

shirkster: layabout, work-shy

shofulman: someone who makes or passes bad money

silicious: consisting of silica, a crystalline compound

slap-bang job: public house frequented by thieves, where no credit is given

slate: used to teach children to write; they would write on black slates with white chalk, instead of the paper used today

slum: ghetto; false or faked document; to cheat someone or pass money you know to be bad or false

smasher: someone who passes bad or false money

snakesman: small boy used for housebreaking, as they could enter a house through a small gap

snoozer: someone who steals from sleeping guests in hotels

snowing: stealing clothes that have been hung out on a washing line to dry

somnambulism: sleepwalking, a dissociated mental state that occurs during deep sleep during which, in Gothic literature, people would do things they would not normally do

spectroscope: tool for recording and measuring spectra of light or radiation

spike: slang term for the workhouse

sponging-house: temporary prison for those who cannot pay their debts, prior to them being sent to a prison such as Marshalsea in London

srew: skeleton key, for use in burglaries

stricken: affected by; suffering or struck by

sublime: the concept of being awed, moved or transported by something, such as religion, beauty or emotions; used in Gothic literature for the thrill of being terrified, because fear inspires such strong emotions

substratum: underlying layer

succubus: female demon, counterpart of the incubus (*q.v.*)

supernatural: used to describe phenomena or events that seem unbelievable or cannot be explained by natural laws or occurrences relating to magic or the occult

superstition: deep-seated but often irrational belief in something, such as an action or ritual, that is thought to bring good or bad luck

sweetmeat: sweet treat, such as candy or candied fruit, often served at the end of a meal

swell: elegantly or stylishly dressed gentleman; expensive dress

T

tallow: hard, fatty substance from sheep or oxen, used to make candles or soap

taper: small, slim wax candle, narrower at the top than at the bottom

taproom: bar room in a public house where working-class people ate and drank, as opposed to the parlour, used by the middle classes

terrestrial: an inhabitant of, or relating to, the earth

thick 'un: slang term for sovereign

thicker: slang for sovereign or pound

Thing, the: name given to the Martian spacecraft in *The War of the Worlds*

thriving: to be profitable or successful; flourishing

thwart: to prevent someone from doing something

timorous: timid or nervous

Titan: name for the giants from Greek mythology; one of Saturn's moons

tocsin: warning signal or bell

toff: elegant or stylish gentleman; someone rich or upper-class

toffken: house in which well-to-do, upper-class people lived

topped: to be hung

tradesman: man in a skilled trade, such as a carpenter or plumber; shopkeeper; someone who buys and sells goods

transfigure: to transform

transportation: when exiled British criminals were sent to the colonies, usually Australia, as punishment

trephining: surgery on the skull to remove sections of bone, sometimes used to treat mental illness

troglodytic: to describe a cave-dweller; bestial or brutal of character

turnkey: jailor; keeper of keys

typhoid: serious, often fatal, illness caused by drinking polluted water (contaminated by sewage)

U

ululation: howling or crying out, often from pain

unanimity: consensus or agreement

uncanny: something or someone too strange, weird or eerie to be natural or human; supernatural

unclean: dirty, impure

union workhouse: workhouse for the poor, which parishes were obligated to provide after the 1834 New Poor Law

unhallowed: unholy or not consecrated ground

unprovided for: left with no money or security

upper class: people from rich, moneyed families, such as landowners or aristocracy

V

vamp: to steal; to pawn something; to seduce or manipulate someone

vampire: supernatural being of a malignant nature, believed to leave its coffin at night to suck the blood of the living for sustenance, from European folklore

vapour: steam

venal: corrupt, capable of being bribed

vespers: evening church service, prayers

vintner: wine maker or merchant

vivisection: surgery performed upon living organisms for scientific research or investigation

W

watch: men chosen to guard the streets at night, periodically calling out the time and ensuring that no crimes were being committed

werewolf: someone who is human by day and turns into a wolf at night, living off humans, animals or even corpses, from European folklore

whist: popular card game, now known as bridge

witchcraft: spells and magic performed by a witch; in Gothic fiction the witch is usually depicted as an old, hag-like crone or a beautiful, seductive young woman

without: outside, usually referring to outside the house in which someone is

woe-begone: sad or miserable in appearance

work capitol: crime punishable by death

workhouse: place where the sick, poor, old and those in debt went or were sent for food and shelter. The New Poor Law (1834) made the workhouse almost a prison for the poor, who had to work hard in miserable conditions, often fed on gruel only and separated from their families

working class: those in heavy manual labour, usually for low, hourly wages, such as farm labourers, factory workers and builders

worrit: worry; worry-wort

wretch: miserable or unhappy person

Y

yack: slang term for a watch

Z

zoophagous: carnivorous, feeding on animal flesh

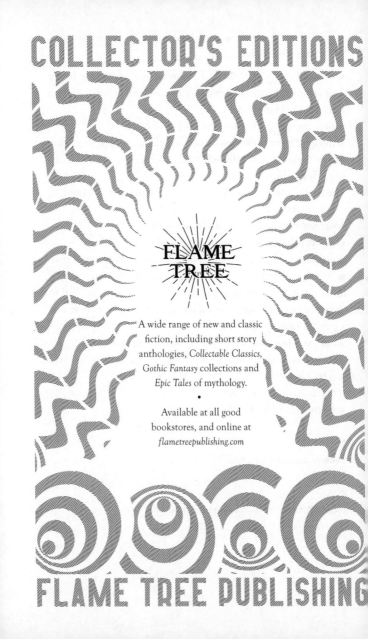

COLLECTOR'S EDITIONS

FLAME TREE

A wide range of new and classic
fiction, including short story
anthologies, *Collectable Classics*,
Gothic Fantasy collections and
Epic Tales of mythology.

•

Available at all good
bookstores, and online at
flametreepublishing.com

FLAME TREE PUBLISHING